DEATH IN THE DRIVER'S SEAT

Gallagher floored the accelerator. The *quattro* launched itself forward, gathered speed and hurtled away. It cleared the nose of the first truck just as the driver woke up to what had happened. The truck tried to swing in, but it was already much too late. The eighteen-wheeled monster began to jackknife.

The one behind, having had no warning of the car's braking, was much closer than he wanted to be. He had no room to maneuver. He jammed on his brakes, but on the soaked road, his momentum became his enemy. His truck plowed into the one that was now directly across his path. Both vehicles, like great dinosaurs, began to twist about each other, sliding with horrendous metallic noises that sounded like roars of combat. Then a huge explosion shook the night.

Also by Julian Jay Savarin

Trophy
Target Down!
Wolf Run
Windshear
Naja
Villiger*
Water Hole*

*Coming soon

Available from
HarperPaperbacks

ATTENTION: ORGANIZATIONS AND CORPORATIONS

Most HarperPaperbacks are available at special quantity discounts for bulk purchases for sales promotions, premiums, or fund-raising. For information, please call or write:
Special Markets Department, HarperCollins*Publishers*,
10 East 53rd Street, New York, N.Y. 10022.
Telephone: (212) 207-7528. Fax: (212) 207-7222.

THE QUIRAING LIST

JULIAN JAY SAVARIN

HarperPaperbacks
A Division of HarperCollinsPublishers

If you purchased this book without a cover, you should be aware that this book is stolen property. It was reported as "unsold and destroyed" to the publisher and neither the author nor the publisher has received any payment for this "stripped book."

This is a work of fiction. The characters, incidents, and dialogues are products of the author's imagination and are not to be construed as real. Any resemblance to actual events or persons, living or dead, is entirely coincidental.

HarperPaperbacks *A Division of* HarperCollins*Publishers*
10 East 53rd Street, New York, N.Y. 10022

Copyright © 1988 by Julian Savarin
All rights reserved. No part of this book may be used or reproduced in any manner whatsoever without written permission of the publisher, except in the case of brief quotations embodied in critical articles and reviews. For information address HarperCollins*Publishers*,
10 East 53rd Street, New York, N.Y. 10022.

An edition of this book was published in 1988 by W. H. Allen & Co. Plc.

Cover photograph by Herman Estevez

First HarperPaperbacks printing: June 1993

Printed in the United States of America

HarperPaperbacks and colophon are trademarks of HarperCollins*Publishers*

10 9 8 7 6 5 4 3 2 1

PROLOGUE

"Mayday! Mayday! Mayday!" Narenko began to broadcast in English. "This is a Soviet aircraft and we are falling! We have a weapon on board! I repeat. We have a weapon on board! Mayday. . . ."

Fighters that had been scrambled as soon as the bomber had appeared on the screens of NATO's Greenland-Iceland-UK air defense net were immediately ordered to hold off. Alert warnings were given. Communications links hummed with traffic. Surface and submarine fleets of both the major power blocs headed for the general area of predicted impact. The world braced itself.

The Tu-22P plunged into the freezing waters, taking its crew, and its weapon, with it.

Moscow.

Skoryatin looked out at the fresh fall of snow. It was December the first. A few days had passed since the aircraft had gone in. He smiled fleetingly. There was satisfaction in the smile, but a touch of sadness too.

He looked down at the glass in his hand, with the generous helping of vodka in it, moved closer to the window, and again stared down at the snow. He raised the glass to his lips and drank a silent toast to one of the dead crew, and to a young woman who had also perished far from her homeland.

An aide entered the room. "The Secretary will see you now, Comrade Colonel-General, to discuss your ideas for the salvage."

Skoryatin put down his glass, and smoothed down the jacket of his new uniform. He had recently been promoted.

"Thank you, Comrade."

The aide stood aside to let him pass.

Nine months later, despite all efforts, the aircraft would still be at the bottom of the sea, and constant naval and air patrols of both East and West would circle about each other, wary packs of dogs after the same long missing bone.

A wet July day in London.

Fowler entered Winterbourne's office, looking like a man prepared to do battle. Winterbourne sat behind a huge desk, his petulant face eager for confrontation. He did not speak until Fowler had walked across the long, red-carpeted room and had reached the desk.

"Must you always keep me waiting, Fowler?" Winterbourne said.

"I was busy, Sir John." Fowler's calm response served to madden Winterbourne. It worked every time. Fowler did not smile.

"What's all this I hear about a list?" Winterbourne demanded.

"Rumors, Sir John."

"Rumors, Fowler? I know your idea of a rumour. It usually means you're almost certain."

"One can never be certain about the other side's motives."

"It may have escaped your notice," Winterbourne began with heavy sarcasm, "that *I* am Head of Department. *Everything* is cleared through me!"

"As your Deputy, Sir John, it's my job to make certain only facts claim your attention. I am just as certain you would not want the Minister to be fed duff information. He would look quite stupid in Cabinet and would certainly not thank us for putting him into such a position. Given the state of things, we would become vulnerable to a subsequent budget cut. At the very least."

Winterbourne knew he had yet again lost the skirmish. It did not improve his temper.

"Well? What are your plans for that list?"

"We're first going to verify. . . ."

"Put Gallagher on it," Winterbourne interrupted rudely.

"Gallagher," Fowler said patiently, "is no longer on Department strength, and hasn't been for some time . . . as you well know, Sir John."

Winterbourne glared balefully at Fowler. "I'm not in the mood for one of your semantic contests. I know Gallagher is not on Department strength," he went on testily. "I am fully aware of that arrogant insubordinate's history. But I am also well aware that you're quite capable of pressing him into service when you appear to feel like it. . . ."

"Only when it involves him. . . ."

"This involves him! He was up to his neck in

that business on Skye, against my own wishes, I might add." Winterbourne paused, savoring a point he believed he had scored. "So use him. And if he proves reluctant, as he's bound to," he continued with relish, "lean on him. Make his life a misery." He stared at the silent Fowler. "What's the matter? Squeamish?"

Fowler did not show the distaste he felt. He felt that Winterbourne hated the Department, and saw it only as a stepping stone to greater things that would eventually lead to a peerage. But there was more than this, there was also the bitterness in Winterbourne's mind, because everyone in the Department, down to the lowest employee, considered Winterbourne to be incompetent. They were right.

Fowler said: "Gallagher is no pushover."

"We need that list," Winterbourne said, as if Fowler had not spoken.

"So will the Russians . . . if it exists."

"That's for you, or rather Gallagher, to find out."

"He'll be caught in the middle."

"Oh what a shame," Winterbourne said with undisguised malice. "If he upsets them, they might even kill him. I do hope, Fowler, you're not going to jeopardize what could be a massive intelligence coup for this Department, simply because you've . . . er . . . gone soft."

Winterbourne's eyes glittered with pleasure, certain he'd at last nailed Fowler.

Late August

1

The beach at Pampelonne in the south of France was pleasantly free of crowds, and the day was hot. The waters of the bay glistened and sparkled beneath a dark blue sky. Out to sea, a motor yacht that could pass as a liner lay dead in the water. Every now and then, snatches of music from the yacht reached the shore. It sounded like a party.

Gallagher had been at the Plage de Pampelonne since eight o'clock. It was now eleven. At the water's edge, two rake-thin models in minute bikinis were cavorting with a fat man in bermuda shorts.

"Don't you find that obscene?" Fowler said with faint distaste, pointing at the three figures.

"Go away, Fowler."

"That's not very welcoming of you, Gordon."

"You noticed."

Gallagher had been looking at the figures through his tripod-mounted Nikon. The 300mm zoom lens he had fitted for the shot brought the images up sharp and close, with the sea turning into a blurred white background of fire. It was the shot he had waited three hours to take. The sun was at the perfect angle. If only the fat idiot would get out of the way.

Fowler said: "I didn't think you took those sort of pictures."

Gallagher sighed, and said without looking round: "Still here, Fowler? Can her Majesty's Government afford to send you on day trips to the south of France? Or is harrassment considered a legitimate excuse to give to those misers in Accounts?"

Fowler chose to ignore what had been said. Instead, he gave a brief smile.

Gallagher was sitting at one of those shaded tables constructed to look as if it was really on some south sea island. The tripod was planted in the sand to one side. He'd had his swim and was dressed in white jeans and a white short-sleeved shirt that hung unbuttoned upon him. His feet were bare, but on the sandy ground close by was a pair of white rope-soled casuals. Next to those were Rhiannon's sandals. Her dress, a lightweight and sleeveless lemon-colored affair with a row of buttons at the front, was slung across the back of one of the five chairs. Other items of clothing, belonging to the models and their self-appointed guardian, were scattered among the remaining three.

Gallagher was an inch over six feet. Just past his thirty-fifth birthday, his body was still lean and muscled. His was not a physique that would run to fat easily. He was therefore one of those lucky people who could get by with the barest minimum of exercise, which suited him perfectly. He'd had enough of the punishing routines he had suffered during his term of service, especially after he'd gone to work for the Department. Grudgingly, he sometimes admitted to himself that the training was in large measure responsible for his continuing fitness.

His complexion, a light bronze, did not owe itself to the ministrations of the Côte d'Azur sunshine, but had been inherited from his mother, herself a descendant of Scottish estate owners and honey-skinned Jamaicans. His hair, a cap of soft brown curls, grew down to the back of his neck. His nose was sharp, but a slight flare to the nostrils bespoke of his mixed heritage. Women found him attractive, although he did not think this of himself. There were times when he wished his chin were more pronounced.

"I don't take 'those sort of pictures,' as you call it."

"Oh?" Fowler was skepticism itself.

Gallagher still did not look round. "For your information, those animated broomsticks out there are secondary elements in this little exercise. They're here because those little triangles they're wearing are the stars of the show. Next summer's collection for your neighborhood high street store. *Get out of the bloody way!*" he yelled suddenly at the fat man, and sighed again.

"You sound as if you're really enjoying yourself," Fowler commented with barely concealed glee.

"It pays very well."

"Oh how are the mighty fallen."

Gallagher looked round. The hazel eyes stared emotionlessly at Fowler. "You're not going to needle me, Fowler. I won't let you. I happen to make a very nice living, thank you very much."

Fowler smiled thinly as Gallagher turned once more to look through the lens. "For God's sake, get out of it!" he yelled again at the fat man in the water. To Fowler, he went on: "Production Manager, he calls himself. I think he came along for the free ride on exorbitant expenses, and the hope of getting into their knickers."

"As I said. Obscene."

The large man reluctantly left the two women alone and Gallagher triggered off a series of shots.

"I didn't think they allowed such poses in family catalogs," Fowler said. He sounded amused.

"I've seen more daring stuff in art galleries." Gallagher took another series of shots.

"Aren't you finished yet?" came a hopeful cry from the water's edge.

"Can't wait to get his paws on them again," Gallagher said with distaste.

"Why do they let him?"

"His company's paying them a fat fee."

"Money can buy anything."

"You weren't born yesterday, Fowler."

A new sound had faintly intruded upon the hot day. Gallagher recognized the thrumming noise of a helicopter. He paid it little attention. After the recent devastation of the brush fires in the arid hills of Provence, the air patrols were almost constantly aloft in an attempt to spot them early. There were a lot of idiots around who were careless with matches.

He glanced at Fowler. "Aren't you hot?"

Fowler did not look hot. But he looked out of place on the beach. Tall, slim and in his fifties, he wore a pale gray lightweight suit, a spotless white shirt, and an RAF tie. His shoes gleamed. His hair, just beginning to gray at the temples, was neatly cut and groomed. Steely eyes gazed out upon the world from behind scrupulously polished spectacles.

Gallagher had frequently wondered whether those glasses were for show; a smokescreen that was an effective weapon in Fowler's line of work. Fowler did not look like someone with weak eyesight.

Fowler said: "Borodin."

"What's this? A music lesson? History, perhaps. In which case it should be Borodino. . . ."

"He wants to see you. He wants a meet."

The sound of the helicopter had grown louder.

Another plaintive cry came from the water's edge. "Gordon! Come on!"

"Control your lust!" Gallagher shouted back. The young women giggled loudly enough to be heard. To Fowler, he added: "I don't know anyone called Borodin."

"Not a real name, of course. He knows you."

Fowler's sudden appearance had already cast a pall on the day, but his words now sent alarm bells ringing within Gallagher.

"Well I don't know him. You'll make me very happy indeed if you'll just go away and leave me alone to get on with my work. In case you've forgotten, I stopped working for the Department a long time ago. . . ."

"Three years, wasn't it? Or is it four?"

"Don't play the absent-minded professor with me. It's all in my file. You'll know to the day, if not the hour."

Fowler ignored the remark. "Borodin," he repeated.

"I've just told you," Gallagher said with a patience he did not feel. "I don't know anyone called. . . ."

"Yes, yes. I heard the first time. But we do have a problem."

"We?"

"Gordon!" came from the beach.

"Oh shit," Gallagher said, exasperated. "This is bloody hopeless. You've just ruined my shot, Fowler."

"Sorry."

"You sound it," Gallagher said sarcastically.

Out to sea, someone was swimming strongly toward the shore. The swimmer had been doing a series of fast crawls, out of camera shot. Gallagher focussed the camera on the churning water.

"Good swimming," Fowler commented with genuine admiration.

"That's Rhiannon Jameson," Gallagher told him in a voice tinged with a sharp edge of hostility. "Remember? She's the one who was nearly killed the last time you dragged me into one of your cockups. Her brother, and a close friend of hers, were not so lucky."

"Ah yes. Miss Jameson. I haven't forgotten . . . or about her friend, and her brother."

"Oh how nice. I'll give her your regards and tell her you couldn't wait."

The sound of the helicopter was much closer now but as yet there was no sign of it. Unaccountably, Gallagher felt a sense of foreboding. He told himself it was because of Fowler's presence. Fowler in a suit on a beach in the south of France was a harbinger of ill tidings. Yet oddly, the focus of his fear was not directed at himself. He continued to point the lens at Rhiannon.

What did he expect to see? A shark chasing her? Come on, Gallagher. You've been watching too many movies.

Nothing was chasing Rhiannon. She was still swimming strongly, in no apparent difficulty. The music from the large yacht continued uninterruptedly. The sound of the helicopter continued to swell. All was apparently normal.

But Gallagher knew it wasn't. The instincts that had kept him alive when flying Phantoms for the RAF and subsequently, when doing dangerous work for the Department, were sending out early warning signals.

Something was wrong. But what?

"Gordon!" came an irritable yell from the water's edge.

"That's it!" Gallagher shouted back. "Session's over."

"But you said we'd use the afternoon!"

"I've got all I want!" Gallagher continued to Fowler: "I couldn't work any more today. You've seen to that."

"You make me sound important."

"Don't play games with me, Fowler. You're not. But you're an itch and I've got to scratch. How the hell did you find me? The advertising agency doesn't know where I am, except that it's somewhere in France; and Fat Jack over there is keeping it all secret until he returns to the UK in case they realize what fun he's having and call him back."

"And the two Aphrodites? I use the term cautiously. Aphrodite was more voluptuous."

"He booked them. I suspect he's kept their whereabouts equally secret."

There was a smile in Fowler's voice as he said: "We can find you anywhere, Gordon. Besides, there's that car of yours. Not totally unnoticeable, is it?"

Fowler was talking about the Audi *quattro,* a car that was almost a companion to Gallagher. It had undergone many updates and had now been replaced by a newer, much modified version. The job had been done for him by his garage; but in his mind, it was still the same car. The first time he'd bought it, it had been silver metallic. After the woman he'd been about to marry had been killed, he'd had it repainted black and had given it her name. In his moments of despair, he used to talk to it, addressing it as if *she* were still alive.

Then had come Rhiannon. The car was still black, but he no longer called it Lauren. Rhiannon had come close to being killed. He didn't want her to suffer Lauren's fate. Fowler's presence was definitely not helping. He kept the lens on Rhiannon. She was still safe. He wished, however, he did not feel the familiar tightening in his guts. There was danger somewhere out there.

Come on, Rhiannon. Get out of the water.

He said with a calm he did not feel: "You're very bad at taking hints, Fowler."

"On the contrary. I'm very good at it. But we've still got the problem of Borodin to resolve."

"The royal 'we' again."

"I'm afraid so. You've got the problem too.

You don't know who he is. Neither do we. The message came, asking for you. Specifically."

"And it was so urgent, you had to come to me personally."

"I could have sent someone, of course; but we know from experience, don't we, how messy that can sometimes get? You don't appear to get on too well with our emissaries. They also tend to suffer broken bones, poor chaps. Plays hell with their temper. Some of them don't like you at all."

"Some of them should take a course on how to win friends and influence people." Gallagher still kept the lens focussed on Rhiannon.

Fowler's eyes had zeroed in on the lens's target. "She'll be alright," he said.

"Got your word on that, have I?"

"Of course."

"Now where have I heard that before?"

"Borodin," Fowler went on, ignoring the sarcasm, "is a high-ranking man in Windshear."

Gallagher turned away from the camera to stare at Fowler.

"Ah!" Fowler said mildly. "Interest at last."

Gallagher knew more about Windshear than he cared to. The name had been given by the Department to a group of supposed dissidents within both the KGB *and* the GRU—Soviet Army Intelligence—deadly rivals normally, working for the same cause: maintenance of the status quo between East and West, to nullify the influence of the hawks in both power blocs. They did not want trigger-happy morons from either side turning the world into nuclear crisp.

One of their number, Irina Alieva, who'd been

in deep cover as Lucinda MacAusland, had died on Skye in the Hebrides, working with Gallagher.

Gallagher said: "Lucinda told me she never passed my name on, or my description. I believed her." She would always be remembered as Lucinda. That was how he had known her.

"She kept her word. The message was for a meet with the person who had looked after her. No name, no description."

"How do you know Borodin is who he says he is? This might be a snatch attempt. Although I can't see what value I could have. . . .'

'Don't be so modest, Gordon. Windshear opponents would love to have you. They seem to think you've got a list of Windshear personnel. . . ."

"What?" Gallagher said. "Are you out of your mind?"

"Did you say something?" came from the water.

Gallagher was not aware he had shouted. He stared balefully in the direction of the three splashing figures. "No!" he snarled. To Fowler, he went on tightly: "What bloody list? What are you talking about?"

"I thought you might be able to tell me."

"You are out of your mind."

"I'm afraid not," Fowler said in his mildest of voices, as if being sane was something to be regretted. "Borodin appears to think he's doing you a favor. He wants the list, so as to take the hounds off the scent, so to speak. He has his methods of letting them know the list no longer exists, when he's managed to dispose of it. And here we come to the nub of the whole affair. *We* would like that list."

Gallagher felt the nightmare descend upon him. "And where am I supposed to be keeping this non-existent list?"

"*You* say it's non-existent. . . ."

"Because as far as I'm concerned, it bloody well is."

"You'll have a lot of convincing to do. According to Borodin. . . ."

"Sod Borodin!"

"According to Borodin, Major Alieva of the GRU—Lucinda to you—handed it to you for safekeeping, after first having taken it from Dalgleish, who should not have brought it out in the first place. We would have liked it. And we hope to put that right very soon. You do remember Dalgleish."

Gallagher remembered well enough. Dalgleish. University friend, Air Force colleague, Department colleague. Taken by the other side, terrified into turning. Dalgleish had died on Skye too. Gallagher had shot him. The KGB, the GRU, the nebulous Windshear, and the Department, all had wanted Dalgleish dead: and Gallagher had been neatly manoeuvred into carrying out their combined wish.

"I know nothing about any list," Gallagher said, emphasizing each word.

"Perhaps," Fowler said, unexpectedly turning down the heat a little. "Perhaps you *think* you don't know. Perhaps it's still up there on Skye: in the Quiraing, where Dalgleish hid it."

"Then go and look for it yourself. Send one of your many minions."

"But we do still have a problem, Gordon. Only Alieva and yourself managed to see Dalgleish. We wouldn't know where to begin. It would be an awful lot of ground to cover, dangerously precipitous in places. And what about the list itself? It would hardly be a slip of paper. What kind of document are we looking for?"

"Why ask me? All this happened last year. I never saw any list. I'm not going to repeat myself further. If you think there's a list, then go and look for it. And you can tell Borodin thanks, but no bloody thanks. Keep me out of your soup this time. *Please.*"

The helicopter had at last put in an appearance. Gallagher recognized it as an Aerospatiale Écureuil, in civilian colors. It cruised slowly across the bay from the direction of Cap Camarat, heading toward Cap du Pinet and the Plage de Tahiti. Gallagher's own position was roughly midway between the two, near the narrow road that led up to the village of Pampelonne itself. The *quattro* was parked just off the road.

"Sorry, Gordon," Fowler said. "Borodin wants you to meet. I think you should."

"Then we'll just have to agree to differ."

"Pity."

"What do you mean?"

"I had hoped we'd have been able to reach an agreement of some kind, other than the one you've just mentioned."

"Something tells me I'm not going to like what I'm about to hear. I wondered when the strong arm stuff would come."

"I did try the nice way."

"There's never a nice way, Fowler. There never was, and there never will be."

"The last time you were in France...."

"Lauren Tanner got killed. Don't remind me."

"I was going to remind you of something else entirely, or to be more precise, some*one* else."

Gallagher waited for the axe to fall.

"I have in mind," Fowler went on, "a certain counter-intelligence colonel. A man of small stature, but with a massive ego and a long memory. You made a fool of him, but we got you out of that. You also managed to ... er ... terminate a French national. ..."

"For which you were all grateful."

"Of course. But Galbin's pride is still wounded. He was sacked not long after that, for something quite unconnected: the overenthusiastic interrogation of a couple of gentlemen from the Middle East. While this had absolutely nothing to do with your little *contretemps,* his subsequently nurtured sense of injustice would find you a convenient target upon which to take some form of revenge. He has, I'm afraid, been reinstated. Things have changed a little since you were last in France. His new masters do not appear to find his methods as ... er ... abhorrent as their predecessors clearly did."

"What are you trying to tell me, Fowler?" Gallagher demanded in a flat voice. He knew exactly what Fowler was leading up to.

"Galbin does not know you are here and the Department sees no reason why he should be informed."

Fowler did not add the "yet" but it was implicit in his tone.

"Killing French nationals," Fowler went on blithely, "is frowned upon, particularly when the foul deed has been committed upon the soil of *La Belle France*."

"Diderot was responsible for Lauren Tanner's death," Gallagher said coldly, no remorse in his own voice. "The Department was also well aware of what he was about; as was Galbin's mob, *and* the Americans. All of you were very happy for me to do your dirty work for you." The hazel eyes had again turned from the lens to fix a hard stare upon Fowler. Gallagher touched his temple briefly. "I've still got a tiny idea in here that you all knew she would be killed, and let it happen so that I would go on the rampage. I haven't forgotten. I might take my own revenge one day, if I ever get solid proof. You wouldn't believe what I could get up to."

He returned his attention to the lens before Fowler could say anything.

He had chosen the twilight of August to come here, because he knew that most of the crowds would have headed back to the north for another year of unpleasantness toward each other, leaving the four-kilometer curve of the beach practically deserted. Fowler's presence had changed all that. The place felt crowded once more. It was time to leave.

He had taken the photo assignment because it had coincided with his own plans to spend some time with Rhiannon, away from the terrible August weather back home. She had also needed the break: time to try and forget what had taken place during June, to try and forget that Fowler and the Department existed.

Some hope.

Rhiannon was much closer to the shore now

and Gallagher felt a sense of relief. Soon, it would be too shallow for her to swim. She was in no danger, after all.

Fowler has made me jumpy, he thought wryly.

"How about one more, Gordon?" someone was shouting.

Fat man on the beach. Gallagher ignored him.

Fowler said: "There you are. What did I say? She's quite alright."

Rhiannon had stood up in the water and was wading toward the beach. Gallagher focussed on her, deriving great pleasure from the image of her body in the lens.

The water streamed off her, glistening down her magnificent form. He studied her lovingly through the lens as she shook her hair, normally a pale brown with lighter streaks, now made dark by its wetness. She paused suddenly, looking up the beach toward him. Though the distance and the camera prevented her from noting his expression clearly, she smiled for the lens, pleased that it was focussed upon her.

A gently curved five foot eight, her body gave the impression that it brimmed with a barely contained energy that would escape at any moment, even when she was standing still. Her figure was much fuller than those of the minikini ladies, but there was no fat upon her.

As he allowed the lens to caress her, Gallagher let himself relish the excitement that this quality of hers gave to him. Just being with her set him tingling; but the energy found its true explosiveness each time they made love. And each time felt like a new experience.

If Fowler thought he would do anything to

jeopardize this stroke of fortune that Fate had dealt him, then Fowler was in for disappointment.

Ah Rhiannon, Gallagher said in his mind as he continued to watch her. *My lady of mists and legend. Hurry up and let's get to bed.*

Had her cheekbones not possessed their prominence, her face would have been too round. Her mouth was redeemed by the suffused redness of full lips. Her chin rescued itself by being on the safe side of too sharp a point, and her nose just managed to escape being too small and too pointed. All in all, her design had been pushed to the very limit, and then halted. The result made many a male envious of Gallagher.

He saw her frown, and realized she had seen Fowler. That did not please him. He had hoped that Fowler would have had the decency to leave before she'd come out of the water. It would have saved the awkward explanations that would now be inevitable.

She began walking toward them slowly, with a grace that despite Fowler's presence, had its usual effect of sending a warm glow through Gallagher. Her bikini set off the honeyed tan of her body perfectly, and the subtle movements of the muscles beneath the smooth curves of her thighs and legs struck at the very core of his being; as they always did.

He triggered off a few shots of her. She was a far better subject than the emaciated broomsticks. He was unashamedly biased and quite unrepentant.

"There's an Aphrodite," Gallagher said to Fowler. "A true one."

As she drew closer he zoomed right in until

only her eyes filled his vision. They were of the palest brown and at times, seemed to be a luminous gold. They had taken on that aspect now and he took a shot of them.

She knew what he had done for the eyes crinkled suddenly at the corners as she smiled again at him, through the lens.

Fowler said: "You'll only be away from her for a few days at the most. Perhaps three."

"No," Gallagher said. He'd made up his mind. Let Fowler do the worst. He began to dismantle his equipment, in preparation for departure.

The sound of the helicopter had increased once more. Gallagher took a fleeting glance upwards. The aircraft was returning, on a reciprocal heading. It had lost some height too and was down to about 500 feet, he judged.

Probably a chopper jock earning his crust giving holiday-makers a quick thrill. It was the same at most resorts throughout the world: flights round the bay, trips through spectacular canyons, flits through high mountains. He had picked up his own taste for flying through one such trip on the Isle of Wight when his father had bundled him into a light plane flown by an ex-World War II pilot. That one flight had culminated in his becoming a Phantom jock which in turn, had eventually led him to the Department. If he could have looked into the future, he would have run away from that seminal little aircraft.

As he began to put his gear into the camera case, he thought of his father, a don at Oxford who had been blown up in his own car in St. Aldate's. Perhaps if he'd never been involved with the Department, Gallagher felt, Liam Gallagher would now be alive.

Whether this had any basis or not, he still experienced a continuing sense of guilt about his father's death. The list kept growing: Lauren, Liam, Dalgleish, Diderot, Lucinda, O'Keefe.... All people who had, in one way or another, been close to him. That thought gave him nightmares sometimes when he looked at Rhiannon.

His uneasiness returned abruptly. The air of danger was still around. But from which quarter?

Don't waste the energy looking for trouble, sir. It will find you in its own time. Use the energy to prepare.

O'Keefe.

O'Keefe had died on a mission when Gallagher's gun had jammed, robbing him of covering fire. In times of stress, Gallagher tended to imagine he could hear the Belfast accent that had patiently schooled him through the rigorous training and those early operations, when he was still a green novice in the game.

Now, he thought grimly, *I've seen too much, and done too much.*

"You're suddenly quiet, Fowler," he said. He had finished his packing, had put on his shoes, and was about to turn round.

Rhiannon was quite close now.

But he did not complete the turn. The helicopter had claimed his attention. Something was happening to it.

And Rhiannon had stopped to look up.

The aircraft was swooping low, heading directly for Rhiannon, it seemed. Gallagher felt a new tightening in his stomach. *She was going to be killed.*

"Rhiannon!" he shouted. "Get out of there!"

She turned to look at him, startled.

"Come on!" he yelled. *"Move!"*

"What . . . ?" she began, confused.

He ran forward and grabbed her by the arm. "Come on," he repeated urgently.

The helicopter was screaming earthward now. Then it was swooping past to clatter low above the beach. Just a pilot doing a certainly illegal beat up. No threat. No threat at all.

Gallagher suddenly felt drained.

"Fowler," he began, looking round, "if you. . . ."

But Fowler had disappeared.

Rhiannon said: "What was all that about? You look . . . well . . . sort of strange."

Gallagher said nothing for a while as he stared at the receding aircraft. He turned his head slowly, as if searching for something in a beachscape that had in an instant become hostile. His scrutiny took in the yacht. It was not hostile. He continued to look about him. Nothing on the beach was.

But he still felt the unease. The sense of impending danger had not faded. It was definitely time to leave. He didn't trust Fowler.

He looked at the helicopter once more. It was now a speck in the distance.

"What's wrong?" Rhiannon was asking. "What's so special about the helicopter?"

"I thought . . ." he began, after a pause, "I thought it was going to kill you. I'm obviously a little jumpy today."

He watched as her face paled with shock. She made no comment and slowly picked up her dress, sandals, and the towels.

This is just bloody great, Gallagher thought grimly, cursing Fowler in his mind.

Rhiannon had taken leave from her job at an art gallery in London's Bond Street to be with him, after turning down a lucrative offer to spend a few months with the gallery's American branch. Now Fowler had managed to ruin it all.

Bloody great, Gallagher thought once more, wishing all sorts of hell down upon Fowler and the Department.

He grabbed the camera case, and they hurried to where he'd left the *quattro*.

2

When they were still fifty meters or so from the car, Gallagher took the multi-function remote from his pocket and squeezed briefly at its surface. The car lights flashed once, telling him that the doors were now unlocked and had been sprung open by six inches. There were no locks and no handles to mar the smoothness of their surfaces.

The remote was roughly the size of a credit card, but slightly thicker. It was all black, with no indentations. Only careful scrutiny would reveal the faint quarterings that betrayed the presence of push-buttons. The remote's functions included an alarm system that would warn him if anyone tried to break in, or attempted to plant anything beneath the car. It could not be stolen either. Enforced entry would simply immobilize the *quattro* totally.

There had been no warning bleeps, which meant that Fowler's people, whom Gallagher was sure were around somewhere, had not yet tried to put a tracer on the car.

Even so.

They got in, and he started it up. The engine burst into menacing life, rumbling with the five-cylinder off-beat he liked so much. It was a non-standard engine: the twenty-valver taken from the Sport version of the *quattro,* breathed on by Treser, and slotted into place by his garage in Cobham. The result was 325bhp and a top speed that left everything else in the cold. To Gallagher, the car was a substitute for his Phantom.

As he slotted it into gear, he thought it was not beyond Fowler to have organized the little stunt with the helicopter. A timely warning, to demonstrate just how vulnerable Rhiannon made him. But perhaps Fowler had nothing to do with it. Perhaps it had just been a show-off pilot out to impress a girlfriend.

Perhaps.

Gallagher decided he was not going to give Fowler the benefit of the doubt. Experience had taught him otherwise; and Fowler would not have come alone.

The beach road to the D93 was a straight of just under a kilometer, but no car had sneaked up in his mirrors.

"Who was that man?" Rhiannon asked suddenly. "Is he the reason we're leaving?" She'd never actually met Fowler.

He'd been expecting the question. She was staring at him, waiting for his reply. He knew she was remembering what had occurred the last time the Department had come into her life.

"Let's say it's a good time for a change of scenery."

"I'm not a child, Gordon. Don't treat me like one." She leaned across to kiss him briefly on the cheek. "I'm sorry. I didn't mean to sound so cross. He's one of your people, isn't he?"

"Not *my* people," he replied grimly.

"He didn't seem to think so."

"That's his problem."

"What did he want?"

"Something I haven't got."

"Did he believe you?"

"No."

They came to the junction, and Gallagher turned left for Ramatuelle. The other way was to St. Tropez, where he hoped Fowler's people would expect him to be heading. They wouldn't do anything as crude as waiting in a chase car by the side of the road. The worrying thing was, they had felt secure enough not to put a tracer on the *quattro*: for the time being.

She said: "So what do we do?"

"We continue our holiday. We'll leave France earlier than we'd planned."

"When?"

"As fast as we can pack. Let's see what Bavaria has in store."

"What if they follow us?"

He patted the steering wheel. "Let's see them try and keep up."

A tiny, hesitant smile played on her lips. "You really do love this car, don't you."

"So do you. You enjoy being driven in it as much as I like driving it."

"It's that nice fat gear lever," she said, and gave him a wicked smile.

"That's much better," he said. "More like the Rhiannon I know and love."

"And ravish from time to time. Alright. Let's head for Germany. Drive me fast."

Gallagher gave a mental sigh of relief. It had been a lot easier than he'd dared hope.

The house in the old Saracen village belonged to a friend in advertising who had preserved its exterior, while refurbishing it with the materials of modern living. It had its own little vineyard, enclosed within high walls. From the top floor, the windows of its two bedrooms looked out upon a fine view of the winegrowing plains of Pampelonne, and the bay beyond.

"What about the girls?" Rhiannon asked as they hurried with their packing.

"My job with them is finished. I'm certain they'd like to sample more of the delights of St. Tropez. They're very welcome to them. Besides, they'll be in good hands."

"You can say that again. Ugh!"

"Tried it on with you, did he?"

The golden eyes seemed to blaze. "Not unless he wanted his balls kicked in."

"Rhiannon!" Gallagher exclaimed, feigning shock. "Such language." He smiled at the vision of a well-aimed foot striking home.

She zipped shut two red bags of soft leather, roughly the size of the kind of luggage airlines allowed in the cabin.

"I'm ready," she said. She had changed into jeans and a loose blouse.

"So am I." Gallagher secured the lightweight traveling wardrobe and picked it up. The camera case was his only other item of luggage, and that was already in the boot of the car. The remote had given no warning. Fowler's men must still be waiting in St. Tropez. He hoped they would remain there long enough.

"We'll leave the windows. The Bourjacs will attend to that. Besides, closing them now would create interest. The wrong kind."

The Bourjacs, husband and wife, were the friendly caretakers of the property.

"Fit?"

Rhiannon nodded.

"Let's go then."

The remote had still not sounded its warning.

In the courtyard, they met Solange Bourjac. Well into her fifties, large and still handsome, she beamed when she saw them. She doted on Rhiannon. Then she saw the luggage.

"You are leaving?"

"We are, Madame," Gallagher said regretfully. "A magazine wants me to do some work in Marseille. . . ."

"Magazine?" She frowned, clearly thinking of a store, believing Gallagher to have used the wrong word, or pronounced it wrongly.

"Journal," he suggested.

"Ah!" she said. "Magazine!"

"Yes," Gallagher agreed, giving up.

"You are coming back?"

"Perhaps. If the work does not take too long. I'll telephone Mr. Nellis in London. He'll let you know."

"Bon," she said, nodding. "We will take good care of your little house." She smiled at them, as if they were a honeymoon couple. "And drive well

in that car of yours. You must look after Madame." She insisted on addressing Rhiannon in that manner.

"I will," Gallagher assured her.

Rhiannon kissed her on the cheek, receiving another beam of pleasure.

Gallagher kissed her other cheek. "Thank you for looking after us so well. We'll be back."

"A promise?"

"A promise."

Madame Bourjac shouted "Au 'voir" at them as they drove away.

Rhiannon said: "We're not going to Marseille, I take it."

"You take it correctly."

"So you expect someone to come asking for us."

"I most certainly do."

Gallagher headed for the notorious Col de Collebasse road, a winding, precipitous route that would eventually take them to la Croix-Valmer. From there, he intended to turn right onto the N559 then cut across country four kilometers or so later, for Cogolin. This would by-pass St. Tropez completely. After Cogolin, the situation would dictate the next move.

At least, there were no tracers on the *quattro*. The big exhausts echoed along the Col.

Fowler sat at a waterfront table drinking iced Perrier.

The man with him stared at a gleaming white three-masted schooner and said: "Must be nice owning something like that."

"All you need is a couple of million quid,

George," Fowler said mildly, descending for a rare moment into slang.

"Oh good," George Haslam said. "I'll ask Her Majesty's government to beef up my pension so that I can buy one—not to sail it, mind you—but to keep permanently moored in a place like this so that all these young women can troop aboard, the way they're doing right now. Some people have got it made."

"Shame on you, George. You're old enough to be their grandfather."

"Too old to be here on this jaunt of yours, too."

"If only this were a jaunt," Fowler said.

From somewhere beyond the cluster of buildings behind them, came the *hee-haw* of a siren.

Haslam was a big man, early sixties. Tiny globules of moisture had formed an intricate pattern at the very top of his balding head. Where Fowler seemed impeccably controlled, Haslam, also dressed in a lightweight suit, appeared to be feeling the heat. He looked like an aging but still reasonably fit businessman out for some distraction.

This facade was precisely what Fowler wanted. He had plans for Haslam.

In his younger years, Haslam had been a field operative with other sections, before eventually coming to the then newly activated Department. Legend had it that only Gallagher could possibly have given him a close match during those days of his youth. To see him now, sprawling in his chair, it was something that was difficult to believe. But those who really knew would say there was still plenty that was dangerous about him. Though he now worked mainly as a liaison man for the Department, there were times when Fowler chose to use him in the field.

Haslam said: "Do you think Gallagher will have left the beach by now?"

"I'd be surprised if he hasn't. In fact, he should be well on his way out of the area completely and we . . . or rather you, George . . . will be trailing him."

"Without a tracer?"

"Even if it had been possible to put one on that car of his, I wouldn't have trusted Prinknash with the job. As it is, Gallagher has had the car wired up. There are no handles on the doors, or even locks. That means infra-red remote, or possibly radio. Personally, I favor infra-red as his choice. Gallagher would not risk radio interference, or possible jamming. I suspect he has sensors beneath the vehicle, just in case someone has the bright idea of planting something there.

"As for the interior of the car itself, I noted four tiny red lights, one set into each door capping, and one each into the cappings at the fixed rear quarterlights. Comprehensive alarm system, if I'm any judge. Careful man, our Gordon."

"He didn't survive with the Department by being careless."

Fowler gave a strangely secretive smile. "He would not agree with you, George. He considers he's made too many mistakes. One of the reasons he resigned."

"Ah yes. That problem he has with O'Keefe's death. O'Keefe would not have blamed him."

"I'm sure you're right; but that only makes it worse."

"Yet for all that, he's still the best since my

day." Haslam gave his own knowing smile. "Which of course explains why you're always hauling him in like a fish whenever you feel like it."

"Not guilty this time, George. Someone else wants him. That's really why we're here. To find out."

"And the rest," Haslam said. He'd been in the game too long.

"Mistrust in your old age?"

"I've always been old. Was it necessary for you to come?" Haslam went on. "I could have done whatever was needed."

"I cannot tell you more at this stage, George, but yes, it was necessary."

"And how do I follow Gallagher, without a tracer? He could be anywhere by now and besides, he'd spot me a mile off and in that car, would lose me in no time."

"That he most certainly would."

"Well then."

"How well do you know Provence?"

"Not quite my stamping ground," Haslam replied, gazing about him meaningfully. "My style's really the Cornish coast on a wild day. . . ."

"You were here during the war. . . ."

"A nineteen year old dodging the *Milice*. A few things have changed."

"Not the landscape," Fowler said mildly. "The landscape will tell us where Gallagher's gone . . . for the time being. We know he's staying in Ramatuelle, or rather *was* staying. As he's hardly likely to come into St. Tropez on his way out, this leaves him a limited number of choices. We can ignore the D61, and the D93. Both come too close. This leaves the Col road to la Croix, or across country to Gassin. That's a very narrow road. It would slow him down.

"My guess is he'll make for la Croix, then on to Cogolin. He'll not take the Corniche to le Lavandou, although he could do that and then leave it to cut across the mountains. But somehow, I doubt it."

"How can you be sure?"

"I'm not. It's a gamble, but we do have unwitting help." Fowler smiled, and would say no more.

Prinknash left the new white 3.6 Jaguar XJ6 and walked the few yards to the front door of the house where Gallagher had been staying. He bounced as he walked, cropped head jerking back and forth like an inquisitive bird, shoulders swinging aggressively. An observer would have been reminded of a bantam looking for a fight.

Prinknash was one of those who, two hundred years before, would have been a foot soldier of the Empire. At the bottom of the heap himself, finding others whom he could look upon as being beneath him would have enormously increased his self-esteem. Anyone therefore unable to speak English was naturally beneath contempt. It never occurred to him that he should learn another language. That would have been tantamount to treason. As for *French*. Napoleon's lingo. Look what happened to *him*.

It also never occurred to Prinknash to consider that there would be many French citizens who felt exactly the same way about their own language. Solange Bourjac was not one of those. Having met many nationals through many years of looking after rented property, she could also speak German and Italian fluently. Her English was itself not as bad as she sometimes made it sound.

Prinknash, dressed like both Fowler and Haslam in a summer suit, stood before the door to the courtyard and stuck his hands in his pockets. It was unfortunate that the person who came to inspect the visitor was Maurice Bourjac. Bourjac was even more of a chauvinist than Prinknash.

He stared at Prinknash unhelpfully.

"Er . . . excuse me," Prinknash began. "I wonder if you can help. I'm looking for a man called Gallagher. . . ." He paused.

Bourjac was still looking at him unhelpfully. "Monsieur?" Bourjac at last said.

"Gallagher," Prinknash repeated. "I am looking for Gallagher."

"Monsieur?" Bourjac said again.

Prinknash tightened his lips, his impatience with stupid people who did not understand English beginning to show signs of betraying itself.

"A man called Gallagher is staying here. Is he in?"

Bourjac continued to regard him stonily.

Prinknash glanced imploringly up at the sky, shook his head, and sighed. "God save me from bloody Frogs who can't speak English."

Bourjac, who could understand English perfectly well, felt his earlier dislike for Prinknash turn to hostility. He remained stubbornly silent.

Prinknash tried once more. "Gallagher is staying here with a young woman. . . ." He described Rhiannon's shape graphically with his hands. "Have you seen them?" He spoke loudly, as if to the deaf.

Bourjac's eyes appeared to gleam. "Ah!" Then they became contemptuous. *"Non, monsieur! Pas des femmes ici!"*

"What? Famm? Oh. Oh, I see. No, you bloody idiot. I'm not after that sort of woman. Oh Christ. . . . Hello the house!" Prinknash yelled suddenly. "Anybody home?"

After a short wait, Solange Bourjac appeared. She glanced questioningly at her husband who fired off a burst of rapid French at her.

"My husband says you are asking him for a woman," she said to Prinknash. "We have no such women here."

Prinknash brightened. "Oh thank God. You speak English." Then he realized what she had said. "No, no. I don't want a bloody . . . um sorry. No. I didn't ask for a woman. I'm looking for a friend. Gallagher. I believe he's staying here with his girlfriend. We arranged back in London, to meet here. Is he in?"

"Aah. Monsieur Gallagher and Madame. Yes, yes. They are here. But *quel domage,* you have missed them."

"Missed them? Where have they gone?"

"St. Tropez, monsieur. They will soon be back." Neither Bourjac was a fool. It had long occurred to them that Gallagher would not have such an unpleasant person for a friend. Experiences of their earlier years had also taught them to spot a security man at a hundred paces.

"Can I come in and wait?" Prinknash was nothing if not game. He wanted to check for himself.

"Monsieur!" Solange Bourjac was outrage itself. "I do not know you are Monsieur's friend because you have said so. I cannot let you come in. It would be very bad for me if Monsieur complains to the managers that I am not good at my work. Please return a little later, when they are back again. Oui?"

Prinknash tried to stare them out, but reluctantly had to admit defeat. They watched him return to the Jaguar.

"Stupid bastard," Maurice Bourjac said with contempt. He'd learnt his English during the war.

"Maurice!" his wife said admonishingly.

But she smiled.

The D93 went into the first of its tight hairpin bends just after Roumegou. The fat wheels of the *quattro* clung to the road surface with leech-like tenacity as Gallagher powered the car through. Then he began to slow down.

Rhiannon stared at him. "Why are we stopping?"

The car had come to a halt near a junction with a narrow road that went off to the right. Seconds later, Gallagher turned into it.

"Change of plan," he said.

He had thought of Fowler, somewhere in St. Tropez, working out the options, evaluating possible routes and eliminating them one by one. This narrow road eventually led to Gassin from where he could still cross over the N559 and make it to Cogolin. The route via la Croix was roughly two sides of a triangle while going through Gassin would be traveling along the base; much shorter and quicker, even allowing for the width of the road. The *quattro* could handle it.

The journey to the Moorish village afforded

spectacular views which Rhiannon enjoyed while Gallagher got on with the business of keeping the car on the road at as fast a speed as was possible. Every now and then, he needed to stamp on the brakes as suicidal *deux chevaux* and little Peugeots came haring toward him. The anti-lock braking system kept the car fully under control, while the other cars performed impossible feats to get out of the way. Sometimes, furious blares of their horns signaled their outrage.

"Sorry," Gallagher would mutter at them. "I'm in a hurry."

And the black car would hurl itself roaring, into another bend.

Haslam said: "I wonder how Prinknash got on."

Fowler glanced at his watch. "He ought to be back soon. I told him not to hang about. Time for you two to get going; and I've got a plane to catch."

"You don't like him, do you?"

"I don't like seconded coppers. They tend to get in the way. I know it's now your job to liaise with them, George, which is perfectly alright. But we don't need them *in* the Department."

"Winterbourne likes the idea."

"He would."

Rear-Admiral Sir John Winterbourne, appointed over Fowler when the post of Head of Department had become suddenly vacant due to the suicide of the previous incumbent, had not gone down well with Department personnel. Staffed mainly by serving and ex-members of the RAF, the appointment of a senior Navy man had particularly rankled. Many suspected foul play. It did not help that Winterbourne was a bit of a disaster and, as a result, was frequently at loggerheads with Fowler.

But Fowler played Winterbourne at his own game, while getting on with the job. It was commonly accepted that it was Fowler who really controlled the Department; a fact that did not make for harmonious relationship between them.

"And here comes Prinknash," Fowler continued, "looking rather down in the mouth." He sounded pleased.

Prinknash bounced up to them. "Jag's parked just up the road, Mr. Fowler."

"Don't bother to sit down," Fowler said. "You'll be on your way soon with Mr. Haslam. How did you get on in Ramatuelle?"

Prinknash's face clouded briefly. It was a toss up whether this was because he'd been told to remain standing, or because of the memory of his futile conversation with the Bourjacs. He reported what had occurred.

"They were lying, of course," he finished.

"I'm certain they were," Fowler agreed mildly. He did not seem particularly worried. "Gallagher tends to command loyalty. Makes life difficult sometimes, Prinknash, but not to worry. A policeman's lot has never been a happy one."

Prinknash's eyes danced with a brief spark of suspicion, not sure whether Fowler was laughing at him.

To Haslam, Fowler said: "Cogolin, George. That's where you'll pick the tail up."

"Tail?"

"The people who'll be following Gallagher. They are the ones I don't want you to lose."

Haslam gave Fowler a sideways look. "I wish I knew what game you're playing."

"All in due course, George." Fowler stood up. "I'll be leaving you two to it. I've got that plane to catch in Nice. See you in London, George." His expression gave nothing away. "Prinknash." He left them to go to a waiting taxi.

"He's not really one of us, Mr. Haslam, is he? Gallagher, I mean." The emphasis Prinknash had put on the "us" told Haslam exactly what was meant.

"Prinknash."

"Yes, Mr. Haslam."

"Shut up."

"Mr. Haslam. . . ."

"The last time you tangled with Gallagher, he tapped you and you thought your arm had been broken. Keep up these stupid remarks and I'll let him really take you apart. We've got a job to do, and you're supposed to have attended the advanced police driving school. Let's see if you're up to it."

"Mr. Haslam I. . . ."

"Just shut your face, Prinknash, and we'll get on like a house on fire."

3

Gallagher stopped in Cogolin for petrol. They had made good time and he reasoned it would be the best opportunity to fill up. Besides, they were low on fuel and as yet there appeared to be no pursuers.

Twin flushes of excitement were on Rhiannon's cheeks. The drive had sent the adrenaline pumping through her. Gallagher's previous car had been left-hand-drive, but this had the wheel on the right. As a result, she was sitting on the "wrong" side for continental traffic and on some of the tight bends, as the *quattro* had powered through them, she had raised both her hands at startled drivers going past. The horror on their faces had been something to see.

"No more of that no hands stuff," he warned her with a smile.

"Yes, oh Master," she now said.

"As long as you know."

For reply, she pinched him where it hurt.

"You'll pay for that."

"Promises, promises."

His intended retort was stopped by the arrival of a dirty blue Citroen BX. It stopped on the other side of the road, pointing in the opposite direction. There were three men in it. They stared at the *quattro* expressionlessly.

Rhiannon had noticed them too. "Those men . . ." she began as Gallagher climbed out unhurriedly.

"I know. Could be nothing. There must be a lot of dirty blue Citroens around."

"I don't like the way they're looking at us."

"Don't look at them."

She obeyed, and pretended to search for something in the footwell.

As Gallagher went round the car to open up the filler cap, the petrol attendant came up, an admiring grin on his face. He was a man in his thirties in overalls and a few days growth of beard. His clothes were stained with several applications of oil. Probably owned the place, Gallagher thought. It looked like that sort of establishment.

"C'est à la coque, cette voiture!" he said enthusiastically.

"Merci," Gallagher said.

"You want full?" the man asked, trying out his English.

"Yes please."

"Okay. I do for you."

Gallagher left him to it, did a walk-round of the car, then reached in to pull at the bonnet release. This was on Rhiannon's side.

"What did he say?" she inquired.

"He likes the car. Said it was fantastic."

"Didn't sound like my schoolgirl French to me."

"It wasn't. It was slang."

"What about those men?"

"I've been watching them. They don't seem particularly interested in us."

"But you don't believe that."

"No."

Had Fowler really betrayed him to Galbin? he now wondered. So soon? It seemed unlikely: but it never paid to make quick assumptions.

Never, never assume, sir. Assumptions kill.
O'Keefe.

Gallagher went to open the bonnet, taking his time about it. The *quattro's* fuel capacity, at nearly 20 gallons, would take a little while to be replenished: enough time to enable him to surreptitiously survey the men in the Citroen, from the cover of the raised bonnet.

The powerful engine, with its massive turbocharger, gleamed up at him, its pipework glinting in the bright sun. He checked the oil, though there was no need to do so. The men in the Citroen were now pretending they had not seen him; but their faces were etched upon his mind, for future reference.

Presently, he heard the garage man replace the pump nozzle. The man came round to the front to stare at the engine.

"Ai-yi," he exclaimed softly, an engineer's admiration all over his face.

Gallagher smiled briefly at him and said: *"Combien?"*

"Quatres-vingt liters . . . trois cents cinquante francs, Monsieur."

Gallagher paid up and the man went away wishing him well, after another longing glance at the engine. Gallagher closed the bonnet unhurriedly, then went round to take his place behind the wheel. He turned the key and the blank face of the instrument panel glowed with a pale green display of numerals.

He started the engine and it growled into life. He left the garage, accelerating slowly, keeping a watchful check in the mirrors.

When the Citroen eventually disappeared from view, it had still not moved.

Just outside Cogolin, the road forked. The D48 went left, and the D558 went on toward Grimaud. Both roads would merge once more, some seven kilometers later.

Gallagher took the D48 and gave the car its head. The fat tires gave the briefest of shrill squawks as the *quattro* gave its impression of being launched off the deck of a carrier and hurled itself forward.

The Citroen remained where it was.

Haslam and Prinknash arrived at the fork in the white Jaguar, ten minutes after Gallagher's departure from Cogolin. They had observed but not fully registered the presence of the blue Citroen as they had driven through. It was just another car.

"Pull up over there," Haslam commanded.

Prinknash pulled into the side of the road and stopped. From that position, they had a clear view of the fork. There was no other way north, out of the little town. If Gallagher came through, they would see him.

"Think we've beaten him to it?" Prinknash asked.

From the front passenger seat on the left hand side of the car, Haslam said: "Who knows? You've showed me how fast they taught you to drive at that school; but Gallagher's car is a flyer and he doesn't hang about when he's behind that wheel. It's anybody's guess. We'll just stay here for a bit and see what turns up."

Five minutes passed, with most of the traffic going to and from Grimaud.

"It's bloody hot in here," Prinknash said. "Why buy a car like this and leave out the air conditioning?"

They had removed their jackets and slung them on the back seat. All four windows were down.

"What do you think you are, Sergeant? A pools winner? This car belongs to HM Government. You don't rate air conditioning."

Prinknash said: "He could be up ahead."

"We wait," Haslam told him flatly.

The tension between them rose perceptibly. Haslam made a mental note to tell Fowler he'd had it with Prinknash. The man was wrong for the job and to hell with Winterbourne.

They both heard the sound well before the car arrived on the scene. It was the noise of a very powerful engine being wound up through the gears.

The dark blue metallic Brabus Mercedes 190E hurtled past on fat wheels, within a thin veil of dust. Its slipstream rocked the waiting Jaguar. There were three men in it.

"What the hell was that?" Prinknash queried, startled.

"That, Sergeant, we follow."

"But how...." Despite his uncertainty, Prinknash had started the engine.

"Just take my word for it. Get moving."

The Jaguar shot onto the road, rear wheels spinning and squealing, scorching the rubber in a cloud of blue-black smoke. The AJ6 engine built its power smoothly with a subdued roar as Prinknash shifted the gears upward. He handled the big car like a sportscar and it seemed to respond eagerly.

"Notice anything about that car?" Haslam asked, pressing all the window buttons. The gale-like bellow of the rushing air died as if switched off.

"Some sort of Mercedes," came the uncertain reply.

"It was a Mercedes, certainly: a special one. But there was something else."

"I'm not sure what you mean."

"The license plate, Sergeant," Haslam said patiently. "It was German. The first letters were MZ. That's Mainz."

"Is that a reason to follow them? Germans always drive fast."

Haslam did not sigh, but his voice betrayed his desire to do so. "A car like that tearing up this back road seems normal to you?"

"He may be in a hurry to get back home."

"He would have done better on the autoroutes, despite their speed limits. I think Gallagher's up ahead and they're following him. We waited long enough at that fork and nothing came through. I don't believe he would have taken so long. He must have left immediately after seeing Fowler. That would put him well ahead."

"So who are those people in the Mercedes?"

"That's what we're here to find out."

"It might take some time to catch up."

"Then you'll just have to make up in skill what we may lack in power. This car is supposed to be nimble. So come on, Jack. Be nimble."

"My name's not Jack, Mr. Haslam," Prinknash said.

"I know."

The white Jaguar swooped along the short straight toward Grimaud.

Gallagher swung the *quattro* into the tight right-hander just after la Tourre, revelled in its surefootedness as the 'G' forces held them briefly; then it was into the left-hander for the gentle curve that would rejoin the D558.

Glances in his mirrors had still showed no pursuit.

Rhiannon said: "No one following?"

"No one. But that doesn't mean there's not someone out there, waiting."

They came to the junction which was mercifully clear of traffic and Gallagher came straight out, turning left toward la Garde Freinet with a bare reduction in speed. The road twisted its way through a forested landscape that became denser the further north it went.

Their route took them around the base of the 1500 foot peak upon which perched Notre Dame de Miramar. Every now and then, as he guided the car through the bends, Gallagher would catch glimpses of the church. Remembering another time, he briefly wondered if a man with a rifle could take them out at that distance, given their speed and constant changes of direction.

He allowed the thought to die. No one could have known they would be coming this way. He glanced at Rhiannon. She seemed relaxed, a tiny smile on the corners of her mouth, taking as much pleasure out of the fast driving as he was. He promised himself he would let nothing happen to her.

He dared not think of this vow for too long, lest it prove unlucky. He had seen enough movies where right in the last reel a character would say "we've made it" or some such line and bang, a shot would ring out and the character would fall dead.

So it would be no thinking about how safe Rhiannon was going to be. He's simply have to ensure she was kept well out of danger.

"What are you thinking?" she asked suddenly.

The question startled him and he had to pause to marshal his thoughts. "Oh . . . this and that."

A hand wandered toward his inner thigh and stroked gently. "This? Or that?"

"Hey," he said. "I've got to concentrate on these bends."

She let her hand remain for a few moments longer before removing it, her smile suggestive.

"You pick the craziest of places sometimes," he said.

"I've told you. It's the gear lever."

"Oh shit!" Gallagher exclaimed, feeling a wave of despair.

"What is it?" Rhiannon had been looking at him. Now she turned to look ahead of the car. "Oh no!"

Directly across their path, a lorry had stopped.

It had shed its load of sawn logs. There were no side turnings.

"We're stuck," Gallagher said grimly.

Even as he'd seen the danger, he had begun to slow down. Now he brought the *quattro* to a gentle halt, a good hundred meters from the lorry. The logs were all over the place.

As he surveyed the scene, Gallagher was weighing up the chances of a possible ambush. Already, he had shifted into neutral, hand poised for a fast snick into reverse and a quick turnaround. As yet, no other car had appeared in the mirrors. Ahead, two men were seemingly desperate to roll the logs off the road.

"Shouldn't we help?" Rhiannon asked.

"Absolutely not."

Her eyes widened briefly at him. "You can't believe they're. . . ."

"When in doubt, don't . . . and I'm very much in doubt." Gallagher watched the men, senses on full alert. It seemed a bad place for an ambush: no cover to speak of, no back-up vehicle to complete the sandwich.

But you never could tell. The blow could come from the sky.

He listened, tuning his ears for a tell-tale sound above the rumble of the idling engine. Nothing.

One of the men had looked toward the car and had held up a hand, asking them to wait, and had promptly gone back to his task.

Gallagher kept up his scrutiny of the mirrors. Still nothing. Perhaps. . . .

"They're going to be here for ages," Rhiannon began. "Maybe we should. . . ."

"No. We'll stay right here. Besides, we couldn't use our bare hands. They're having to shift the logs with those bloody great hooks."

And I don't want to get near them, he didn't say, *just in case.*

"Where would they be taking logs like that, anyway?"

"Perhaps to Port Grimaud for boat-building, or to St. Tropez to build more of those genuine south sea island huts. Who knows?"

"I can tell by your voice you don't think it's anything like that."

"Maybe. Maybe," he said softly.

He kept his attention on both the working men and the mirrors. An ambush, he decided, should have been sprung by now. The longer they remained, the greater the chance of other traffic arriving to upset the plan. Then Gallagher remembered how in England, an armed robbery had once been successfully carried out in the middle of a motorway.

He decided not to give the men the benefit of the doubt.

Even if they were guilty of nothing more than spilling their load, it still meant that the time and distance put between the *quattro* and possible pursuers were inexorably narrowing.

Not a comfortable thought.

The man at the garage spat on the dusty ground. After the black car had gone, a shiny blue Mercedes had paused briefly next to the Citroen, before setting off again at high speed.

He was not sure, but he fancied he'd seen a

package of some kind being passed from the Citroen to the Mercedes.

He spat once more. It was none of his business.

Gallagher said: "I can see a gap. I'm going to take it."

Some of the logs had been cleared from the crown of the road, but there were still plenty of them about. Gallagher thought he could see a narrow slalom path through the logs and just past the nose of the lorry. It would be a close thing and one error would mean slamming into the logs, doing God knew what kind of horrific damage to the car, not to mention themselves.

Even so.

"Are you sure?" Rhiannon queried uncertainly.

"I'm sure of one thing . . . we can't wait here for traffic to build up. If that happens, eventually the police will arrive. That will mean even more chaos. I'd rather be out of it by then. Those two up front are going to be here all day. You were right."

From time to time, one of the men had raised a delaying hand. His partner had also run round the lorry, presumably to halt traffic coming the other way. As yet, no impatient horns had been sounded; unusual in France, if any sizeable tailback had formed. Perhaps it was still clear. The lorry blocked the view beyond completely. Gallagher decided he would have to go for it blind in the initial stages, and trust his reactions when the time came.

"I can't see a route," Rhiannon said.

"There's one just beyond those logs. You probably can't see it from where you're sitting. It's there."

"What about behind the lorry? Could be other cars."

"I know, but if there's going to be an almighty traffic jam around here, I'd like us to be well away from it."

"And anyone who may be following us...."

"Caught in it. At least, that's the idea."

"If you make a mistake, you could damage the car."

"Don't remind me. Here we go."

Gallagher selected second gear, and floored the accelerator. Second would give him the necessary acceleration, but with a flexible powerband to allow him to complete the maneuver. First would have been too fierce and too short-winded for the purpose.

The *quattro* seemed to leap off the mark with a howl, the turbo cut in and the surge forward pinned them to their seats. Then things began to happen very quickly.

One of the men heard the sudden roar of the engine, looked up startled then *ran into the road* to try and stop the car. Gallagher saw an opened disbelieving mouth, then the man was leaping for his life.

Gallagher had no time to think about him. The logs and the narrow passage were coming up. He went through, committed now, speed approaching 90 kph, the digits glowing ominously.

Let the next passage be there. Let it be there!

Gallagher felt the desperate words in his mind. If he'd made a mistake....

Don't think about it. Keep going.

Rhiannon staring at him. Ignore. Keep *going*.

The logs, the *logs!* Sod the logs. *Keep* going. There's the passage. There, there, right in front of your nose. Tiny turn to the right. Hold it. Correct it. *Now*. Speed dropping. Not too much. Good. Tap the brakes. ABS. No skid. No worry. Fat wheels holding. Splinters and bark on the road surface. *Skid pan*. No skid. Good. Nose of lorry inches away. Watch it! Other side. No traffic, no logs. *Wrong!* Car coming up. Don't swerve! Hold the line. You're on right side of road, the *correct* side. Other car swerving away. Jesus he left it late. Horn blowing. Other car hitting the brakes. You made it. You made it!

"Oh my God," Rhiannon was saying. "I can't believe we made it." She broke into a fit of giggles that was very close to hysteria.

Gallagher felt his left knee tremble slightly. "You and me both," he said. "For a second, I thought I'd been wrong about that route through the logs."

"For a second I thought we were going straight into the front of that lorry. I don't know how you did it, and I don't want to know. I still think there was no route."

"Well," Gallagher said. "It was close. Very close."

The man by the logs heard the howl of the powerful engine echoing back at him as the car went on its way.

Mad, he thought. English tourists in fancy cars bringing their dangerous driving to Provence. Almost as bad as the Germans.

"Edouard!" his partner called. "Another one

is coming. Stop him this time before we have an accident."

"With what shall I stop him? My body? That black bastard of a car nearly got me."

"You shouldn't have forgotten the warning triangle."

"What's that got to do with it?"

Muttering obscenities about crazy foreign drivers, the man went forward with raised hands. The car was a meek little Citroen 2CV which stopped obediently: but storming up the road behind it, was the Brabus Mercedes. It tried to pass the Citroen, but the man was jumping up and down and waving furiously at it.

The Mercedes stopped. The man ran up to it, face suffused with anger.

"Are you stupid?" he yelled at them in French. "Can you not see the logs on the road?"

The three large men in the car, in business suits and with faces as hard as granite, stared up at him. They did not even lower their windows.

Irresolutely, he stared right back at them. At last, a window slid down.

"What has happened?" the one in the front passenger seat asked in French that was perfect, but without the inflections that would be expected of someone at ease with the language.

"As you can see, the logs fell off the lorry." The man called Edouard was a respector of no one in flashy cars, especially after what had just happened.

The man in the car stared at him with cold eyes. "Yes. I can see. When are you going to clear it up?"

"And what do you think we are doing?"

The cold-eyed man surveyed the road ahead briefly. The eyes swiveled back to Edouard. "Wasting my time," the man said in a chill voice. "Have you seen a black car come this way?"

Edouard became animated. "Yes. I've seen the bastard. He nearly ran me down."

The cold eyes showed an animation of their own. "Before, or after, the logs came off?"

Edouard pointed to the strewn logs. "Not five minutes ago, he went through there. If he's a friend of yours, you tell him I think he's a crazy son of a . . . a. . . ."

The cold-eyed man smiled. He looked even less friendly. "We'll tell him."

The window slid shut. The Brabus-modified V8 engine began to build the revs in preparation for departure.

Edouard banged on the roof. *"Hey!* You can't go through there. There's no room!"

The Mercedes did not move. The revs died. The window slid down for a second time. The cold-eyed man looked up.

"If you want to keep your hand, don't do that again."

The window slid home once more and again, the revs began to build. This time, the Mercedes shot past the 2CV and streaked toward the logs. Edouard stared disbelievingly. Where did the idiot think he was going?

"Espèce d'enviandé!" he yelled.

The driver of the 2CV, a middle-aged woman, looked shocked.

Then the brake lights on the Mercedes were suddenly flaring as its driver stamped on the pedal.

A puff of smoke came from the rear wheels. The car halted with a savage jerk.

As Edouard ran forward, he saw what had happened. His colleague had somehow managed to block the exit with a log. He slowed to a walk, a smug look on his face. Good old Gaspard. That will show them.

The brake lights on the Brabus died and the front passenger door opened. The cold-eyed man got out, turned to face Edouard, who came to an uncertain halt.

"Tell him," the man began in his lifeless French, "to move it. You, go over there and help him."

But Gaspard had joined them. A man with a creased face and built like a weightlifter, his manner showed clearly that he had no intention of being ordered around by anyone.

"You want it moved?" Gaspard said. "Move it yourself! It's either that, or you wait until we have finished. There are other cars on the other side. If you want an accident, you can have one with pleasure, but not with our help."

Gaspard and the cold-eyed man stared at each other for long moments, neither seemingly intent on backing down. Edouard thought that if eyes were weapons, Gaspard would now be a dead man.

Then without warning, the cold-eyed man opened the door of the Mercedes and climbed in without a word. The door shut with a menacing clunk.

"Come on," Gaspard said to Edouard. "The traffic is building." He glanced about him. "There's never a policeman around when you want one."

A kilometer away, two motorcycle police on routine patrol, were approaching the jam.

Prinknash slowed down when he saw the winking blue lights.

"Shit," he said. He slowed to a crawl, and stopped behind a rickety-looking van. "I'll bet Gallagher's missed this."

"I agree," Haslam said calmly. He unclipped his belt and opened his door. "I'll just take a little walk to see what's going on. Shan't be long."

He climbed out and walked along the line of cars, now twenty deep. One of the policemen, astride his machine, was close by. The other, dismounted, was up by the lorry that Haslam could now see.

The policeman on the motorcycle raised a hand at Haslam. "It is better to wait in your car, Monsieur."

"Just stretching my legs," Haslam said in impeccable French. Even the accent, which was Provençal, was phonetically correct.

The policeman had raised his amber goggles. His eyes surveyed Haslam quizzically. "You are French, Monsieur? Your car is English."

"I was here during the war," Haslam replied, then added a lie for good measure. "I married a Provençal lady."

The policeman smiled. "Not as good as being French, but almost."

They both laughed.

"What's going on?" Haslam asked.

"Some idiot of a lorry driver spilled his load. He didn't even have his triangle to warn oncoming traffic. One car has already gone through, missing the logs by millimeters. So the driver and his mate says. I think we'll throw the book at them. They should have fixed their load better than this."

Haslam nodded his agreement. "People do not take much care these days."

"You are so correct, Monsieur. Of course, it makes our job much harder."

"I'm sure it does," Haslam said sympathetically.

He glanced casually up the line of cars, noting without apparent interest the blue Brabus Mercedes at its head. None of its occupants had climbed out. Fully airconditioned no doubt, Haslam thought drily.

"How much longer do you think they'll be?" he asked the patrolman.

"Another half hour, I think. Then we must sort this mess out. Thankfully, no one was hurt." The policeman started his machine. "And now, Monsieur, if you will excuse me. I must go down the line to warn other cars that may be coming. Please return to your car."

The patrolman wheeled the motorcycle round and roared off.

Haslam returned to the Jaguar.

"Load fell off a lorry," he said to Prinknash. "The blue Merc's up ahead, at the front of the queue. Probably tried to follow Gallagher and couldn't make it."

"How long are we going to be here for? What did the bike boy say?"

"Half an hour."

"Shit."

"Exactly."

4

Moscow, the same day, 1600 hours.

Colonel-General Vladimir Mikhailovich Skoryatin of Army Intelligence, the GRU, looked up from his desk as a woman aide entered, a sheaf of papers in her hand. Natalia Kamapova, GRU Captain, with the grace and taut body of a ballet dancer, was a classic beauty. Her blonde hair, so fine it looked like spun gold, was primly done up in a bun. She was 24.

Skoryatin did not trust her. He was almost certain she was a KGB plant.

If the KGB and the GRU had been the intelligence services of separate countries, they could not have been more antagonistic toward each other, nor more suspicious of each other's motives. It was common knowledge in their shadowy world—though never admitted—that each continuingly tried to infiltrate the other. There was jealousy too, with the KGB, the greater organization in size and autonomy, constantly trying to wrongfoot it's smaller sister organization. It hated being left out of GRU special operations and frequently resented being forced to cooperate on terms it did not like: either through sheer necessity, or by specific orders from the Party Secretariat. At such times, it was obvious that its substantial lobby in the highest of places had been outmanoeuvred. It did not help that many GRU looked upon the KGB with contempt, seeing themselves as a tactical force whose activities, covert or otherwise, were carried out in defense of the homeland. The KGB they saw as a vast network of informers whose tentacles enfolded the state itself. The essential truth in this hurt deeply.

Skoryatin fully realized it and his present high rank was as much evidence of his capabilities as a soldier and intelligence man as it was of his ability to survive the sometimes quite murderous infighting between the two services.

Skoryatin, as many a thwarted KGB operative would admit if such an admission were ever to be recorded, was extremely slippery indeed. Many an attempt to snare him had resulted in unfortunate consequences for those trying it; some of which had proved fatal. But he knew they would not stop trying. Kamapova was only the latest in a long series of attempts.

She smiled winningly at him. "I have prepared your itinerary for the visit to the Far East units, Comrade Colonel-General."

He took the papers from her and placed them upon the almost bare top of his large, polished desk. The office would have surprised anyone expecting something gray and gloomy, to fit the much stereotyped image of a Russian general. It was a room that any western corporate chairman would have been pleased to be seen in.

"Kamapova," Skoryatin said, "how long have you been with me?"

"Three months, Comrade. . . ."

"Kamapova, what have I said to you about calling me Comrade every time you address me?"

Her smiled was now confused, almost shy. "That it is not necessary, Comrade. . . . I . . . I'm sorry, Colonel-Gen. . . ."

"Not even that. Plain General will do."

"I . . . I understand . . . General, but at my last unit. . . ."

"Yes, yes. I know all about that. But you are here now, and I'm not one of those pompous idiots who require obeisance at every turn. Do I make myself clear?" His eyes were benign as they looked at her. He might have been a father talking to a favorite daughter.

"Yes, General."

"Good. Now that's settled, let's look at the itinerary."

Skoryatin picked up the schedule, glanced through it quickly, almost perfunctorily. He put the papers down once more, looked up at Kamapova standing respectfully before him.

Skoryatin said: "They've been out of the world news over there since that little blunder in 1983. A surprise visit might put them on their toes."

"Is the General planning a surprise operation?"

Skoryatin gave her a quick smile. "For a surprise to work, it must be total."

"The General is not suggesting. . . ."

"Come, come, my child. I suggest nothing. It is

my way of working. The rest of my staff are accustomed to my little eccentricities. You are still new; but I have great hopes. So far, you have proved to be most excellent. My interim report will say so." He smiled conspiratorially at her.

"Oh, Comrade. . . ." she began, flushed with pleasure.

"Ah-ah!"

"General," she amended. "Oh thank you!" Clearly feeling the time was propitious for a request, she went on: "I would like to accompany the General, if the General would wish it."

"Would you indeed," Sokrayatin said, his expression giving nothing away. "I will have to think about it. You do realize that as you are relatively new here, there are others whom I should first select."

"I fully understand, General."

"However, I shall see what can be done. I shall also take note of your enthusiasm to serve the State."

"Thank you, General! Thank you!"

Skoryatin nodded. "Very well, Kamapova. You may go."

She walked out, a dancer crossing the stage, the cut of her uniform accentuating the sensuality of the curve of her back and the high prominence of her bottom.

Skoryatin watched her keenly as she left, but there was no lust in his gaze. He returned his attention to the itinerary. This time, he studied it much more closely. He smiled.

The Kuril Islands. As good a place as any.

* * *

Camp Militaire de Canjuers, Haute Provence, France.

The cursor danced along the inner rim of the tachometer quadrant display as Gallagher changed gear. At its radial center, the timer glowed 1400. Just under two hours since they'd left Ramatuelle. There was still no pursuer in the mirrors.

Rhiannon said: "Perhaps there's no one after us."

"Don't you believe it. The lorry and the logs gave us the breathing space. With luck, there might still be a real tailback down there, in both directions. Meanwhile, we'll keep increasing our distance."

They had made very good time, despite the stop for petrol and the delay with the logs, and had managed to put 100 kilometers between themselves and their point of departure.

The narrow, winding road took them upward, toward the Col du Bel Homme at nearly 3300 feet; where they met their next major obstacle. A sign had been planted at the side of the road.

INTERDIT, it said.

What gave added weight to the sign's command was the jeep-like Peugeot P4 that was stopped broadside-on across their path; and the two fully armed soldiers sitting in it. Military Police.

Gallagher brought the *quattro* to a cautious halt.

When facing armed men, never do anything suddenly unless it is part of an attack sequence.

O'Keefe.

"I know," Gallagher said softly.

"What do you know?" Rhiannon queried. She looked at him enquiringly before turning an uncertain gaze upon the soldiers.

He'd barely realized he'd spoken in answer to the ghost of O'Keefe.

"Just working something out," he said to her.

"You don't think they're involved do you?" She was beginning to sound worried. It was one thing to hurtle along alpine roads ahead of unseen and anonymous pursuers. It was even, admittedly, exciting. Another matter altogether when faced with armed soldiers who looked as if they meant business.

Gallagher kept his eyes on the soldiers. "They could be; but I have a feeling that even Fowler wouldn't go that far. But you never know with that conniving sod."

The two men, one black and the other white, seemed to be bona fide soldiers of France. It could also mean they were good actors. Both of them were looking at the *quattro* with interest. Gallagher hoped it was because they admired the car itself.

The black one had climbed out and was walking slowly forward, his assault rifle held at the ready across his body. A big pistol hung from his belt.

Gallagher, having no intention of giving the man any excuse, waited patiently, his mind swiftly analysing the situation. Without a weapon of his own, he was powerless to take them on, if they were fake. On the other hand, he would not have wanted a shooting match with Rhiannon in the car.

Turning round was out of the question. The

down and put up those traffic delay signs. The convoy is on the move."

"Yes, sir." The soldier cut transmission. 'We're to put up the signs now," he went on to Dujean.

"I wonder what that was all about?" Dujean said.

"When Security is involved, we keep out of it. I'm just an ordinary soldier. You should think the same."

"Nice car, though. And that woman! Lucky bastard."

"If Security want him, he may not be so lucky."

"I don't know. A car like that, a woman like that... Whatever he's into, it must pay well; better than anything you or I will make for a very long time, if we live forever."

"So who wants to live forever?"

They grinned at each other. A sound intruded upon their banter. A powerful motor was echoing up the climb.

"More company," Dujean said.

"Do we wait?"

"Might as well."

The Brabus Mercedes screeched to a halt. A window slid down.

"Why are you closing this road?" the cold-eyed man demanded imperiously in his unflavored French.

"We have orders to do so." It was again Dujean doing the talking. He stood as he had previously, his rifle held at the ready.

The cold-eyed man surveyed him expression-

wasn't sure he wanted to bring certain memories back to life.

"I killed someone," he said at last. "A Frenchman I once knew. He had been responsible for Lauren Tanner's death. I also made a fool of Galbin, who's a counter-intelligence Colonel. He does not forget such things in a hurry. The man I killed was dangerous to France in any case; but Galbin doesn't see it that way. The Department took the heat off me at the time; but I suspect if Galbin's involved in this, then it's Fowler who's set the hounds on to me. His way of telling me to do what he wants, or else. . . ."

"If someone killed me," Rhiannon began quietly, "would you go after them the way you did for Lauren?"

He glanced at her. The golden eyes seemed luminous.

"What a thing to say." He remembered how close she'd come to being killed, not so very long ago. He'd hunt the person down like a nemesis; but he didn't tell her that. What he said was: "Nothing's going to happen to you . . . not as long as I'm around. That's a promise."

She placed a hand on his thigh, and left it there. It was her way of telling him she trusted him implicitly.

At the Col, the white soldier was speaking into his radio.

"They've gone back down, sir. Dujean spoke to them."

"Now that we've done the security people's job for them," the voice said in the soldier's ear. "Go

"What? Behind us?" She turned to look. There was no one following. She looked at him again, puzzledly.

"The soldiers and that sign," Gallagher said. "Think about this. If you were going to close the road at the top of the Col, where would you put the first sign?"

"In that little town at the bottom, I suppose," she replied uncertainly. "At the junction of the road that leads up...."

"Exactly. You couldn't stop people from going as far as the Col itself, but you could warn them that the road was closed further on, preventing them from making a useless journey. Did you see any warning sign in Bargemon?"

"Well no . . . but I wasn't really looking."

"I was, and I saw nothing."

"Perhaps they forgot. Perhaps they don't put signs so far down. We've passed houses on the way. People have still got to get to them."

Speaking almost to himself, Gallagher went on: "They stopped us. They were armed, but made no threats. It just doesn't feel right. They turned us away, but for what reason? It's as if they were acting as beaters, pushing us into a waiting trap."

"But they looked like real soldiers."

"If they were, then it's Galbin's doing. . . ."

"Who's Galbin?"

"A little Frenchman you wouldn't like to meet. And if they're fake . . . it means some really determined and powerful people are involved. Neither choice looks good. But don't worry. They're not going to have it their own way."

"Tell me about Galbin."

Gallagher took his time before replying. He

Gallagher took the left fork, the quicker route. He'd have to return to Bargemon at the bottom of the incline to turn left for Fayence, then up again through Mons to join up with the N85 some thirteen kilometers after that. It was a long detour, with twisting roads all the way. Normally, he would have enjoyed the prospect; but under the circumstances, it would be using up precious time; time they could ill afford to spare.

"There's a whole area back there," he now answered, "that's France's answer to Salisbury Plain and the Welsh mountains rolled into one. It's a very big area—something like thirty miles from east to west, and perhaps fifteen from north to south at its widest point. That's as the crow flies. It's a hell of a lot of ground on foot. There are just two public roads that pass through it, and they're in the north-south direction, at this end of the zone. It sounds quiet, but there must be some kind of big exercise going on, otherwise they wouldn't have blocked them."

"How much time will going this way cost us?"

"Hard to tell. It's a long way round, and the road's the sort of stuff I like driving this car on; but as we're not exactly doing it for fun, I'd have chosen another occasion. Still, we're well ahead for the moment. If we don't come up against any other obstacles, we should maintain our lead."

"And the people you think are following?"

"Perhaps the soldiers will shoot them for us."

He grinned briefly at her. Then abruptly, his expression changed, becoming thoughtful.

"What's wrong?" Rhiannon asked, looking at him worriedly.

"The soldiers."

indeed if things went wrong. The soldier's smile therefore, did not make Gallagher feel relaxed. He'd seen situations go off the rails too many times at check-points. A smiling soldier could mean anything from a serious attack of nerves to the anticipatory pleasure of having to fire the weapon. Rarely did it mean genuine friendliness.

Gallagher said, in French: "We have a long way to go. Is the other road also closed?" He had no intention of using it.

"Monsieur speaks French," the soldier said, pleasantly surprised. He was still showing his friendly face. "That road is also closed," he went on. "It is temporary, but this one . . . it is for the whole day."

"What's the reason?"

"I am afraid I cannot tell you, Monsieur."

Gallagher nodded. It was the same everywhere. The anthem of the checkpoint. I cannot tell you. I don't know. You will be told in due course. None of your business!

"You must go around," the soldier was saying.

Again, Gallagher nodded. No point trying to argue it through and waste more time. He waved his thanks and began to turn the car around. The soldier stepped back a few paces to watch, still on the alert.

Gallagher felt an itch between his shoulder blades and half expected to hear a bullet crashing through the rear window. Nothing happened, and he took the *quattro* back down. The soldier stood in the road, watching them all the way.

Rhiannon let out her breath as they came to the fork and said: "My God. I was afraid even to breathe! What was that all about?"

maneuver would not be fast enough and the slightest miscalculation could mean a very rapid descent off the mountain. A fast reverse was possible, with a quick change of direction at the fork which was less than quarter of a mile back down the road. One branch of the fork curved downward into a four-kilometer hairpin which rejoined the route up the col in a T-junction. The other went more directly to the junction. It was a much steeper route, and was half the distance.

If things looked like becoming sticky, Gallagher decided he'd try the reverse maneuver and take the left-hand fork down; the steeper descent. Should the soldiers decide to follow, they would have to choose the same route if they wanted to catch him. But once the *quattro* was on its way, they'd have little hope of doing so.

In the event, it did not work out like that.

The cooler air of the mountains had caused Gallagher to raise the windows. As the soldier came up, he lowered his window in preparation to speak to the man.

The soldier had been making for the left-hand side of the car, realized his mistake and moved over to Gallagher's side.

"A beautiful car, Monsieur," the soldier began in accented English. He smiled.

"Thank you. What's the problem?"

"Problem? Ah . . . *oui, problème.*" The soldier pointed briefly to the sign. *"Interdit, Monsieur.* You mus' go back. No *passage."* He peered in at Rhiannon, and smiled at her.

Gallagher cast a fleeting glance at his mate still sitting in the vehicle, but no doubt on full alert. The one in the Peugeot would shoot very fast

lessly. "We cannot go back. It is a detour of over 45 kilometers, while it is only 10 to get from here to the junction with the D21. We are traveling with friends and have fallen behind. They are in a black Audi with English plates."

"I am sorry, Monsieur. We have orders to close the road. If you do not wish to detour, you can wait here for the road to re-open; but it will be three hours, at least. As for your friends, they have already been and have taken the detour."

Suddenly, the front passenger door and one of the rear doors of the Mercedes were flung open. The cold-eyed man and the one at the back had climbed swiftly out. Before either Dujean or his companion realized what was happening, two silenced pistols coughed at them.

Dujean's rifle clattered to the ground as his crumpling body slammed against the Peugeot P4, knocked there by the force of the bullets ploughing into him. His fellow soldier died where he sat, behind the wheel of the patrol vehicle. The whole episode had lasted less than five seconds.

The men from the Mercedes moved swiftly. The rifle was picked up and put into the Peugeot; then Dujean's body was lifted into the seat next to his comrade. The cold-eyed man then released the handbrake of the P4 and with the help of the other killer, pushed the vehicle off the road.

They didn't even wait to follow its tumbling progress down the steep mountainside. They did not see the two bodies flung from the plunging, disintegrating wreck. They did not see the ball of flame bursting into sudden life. They were already in the car, and it was accelerating across the high plain toward Broves.

"Those killings might have been a mistake," the driver said. There was a distinct lack of emotion in his voice. The deaths did not worry him, only their effect upon the job they had to do.

"This was not the time to have a nice conversation with them," the cold-eyed man said.

"Well, you're in command."

"Precisely."

They had spoken neither in French, nor in German.

About two kilometers from the Col was a four-way junction with a triangular patch of ground at its center. Coming from the west and going round it to turn left and northward, was a slow-moving stream of military vehicles made up mainly of armored personnel carriers. Controlling the traffic at the junction was a group of military police, commanded by a young captain.

There were four Peugeot P4's parked strategically at the junction. The captain sat in one of them with his driver, looking bored. Now and then he'd raise himself in his seat to stare approvingly or disapprovingly at his men as they worked to keep the vehicles moving. It was on one such occasion that his attention was drawn to the fast approaching blue shape.

He stared at it for brief seconds before yelling: "What's that civilian car doing here? Sergeant Blois! Stop it!"

The sergeant was a short distance away, sorting out an APC driver who had misjudged the turn and was chewing up the verge with the vehicle's six fat wheels. The sergeant turned to look, decided his captain's order was both pointless and suicidal.

It was obvious the car had no intention of stopping. It was also abundantly clear that the sergeant, while his men might have thought many uncomplimentary things about him, was never going to be accused of being keen on suicide. He stayed where he was and like all good sergeants, used his head.

He made a stopping motion with his hand to the flustered APC driver. The demented noise of the vehicle died appreciably; then it stalled. The roar of the approaching Mercedes could now be heard above the general din of the closest vehicles. There was the narrowest of gaps between the stalled APC and a lumbering AMX-30 main battle tank. Beyond the tank was a string of softer vehicles. There was just about enough room.

The blue Brabus shot through the gap without slackening speed. The sergeant could scarcely believe it.

"Blois!" the captain was yelling. "Why didn't you do as I ordered? I told you to stop him!" And before the sergeant could answer, he grabbed at the handset of the P4's radio and snarled in to it: "Dujean! Lacombe! Are you two sleeping out there? Why did you let that maniac through? You nearly caused a serious accident." He clicked at the handset impatiently. "Lacombe! Do you hear?"

The faint static of silence greeted him.

"Dujean!" he called into the set once more. "Lacombe!"

When his efforts were again rewarded by silence, he replaced the handset impatiently and called to Blois: "Sergeant, take over. I'm going to see what those two are up to." Again, without waiting for a response, he went on to his driver: "Start up. Let's go and see what Dujean and Lacombe are doing over there."

The driver obeyed, and the P4 pulled into the road and bounced away at speed, toward the Col.

The sergeant watched it depart impassively, then turned to the driver of the APC. "Are you going to get this moving? Or do you want me to hold your hand?" His expression was not a friendly one.

They saw the pall of smoke long before they got to the spot where Dujean's and Lacombe's vehicle had been pushed off the road. The P4 screeched to a halt. The captain climbed out to stare at the distant smoke.

"What were those two playing at?" he wondered aloud.

"Captain!" the driver called urgently.

"Yes? What is it?" The captain had replied testily, thinking of all the sorts of trouble he was going to get into for this. He turned to the driver, who was pointing.

"Over there, sir. I think it's blood."

"Over there" turned out to be less than two meters from the captain's polished boots. The captain walked over, and stooped. He stared disbelievingly at the blood, then made a decision. He ran back to the P4, and grabbed the handset.

"Get me Blois," he snapped into it. He waited impatiently while the sergeant was called, then: "Sergeant, who's at la Colle?" A pause. "Tell them to block the road. You heard me! Block the road and stop that blue civilian car. Use all means. Yes. You heard me correctly. *All* means! Yes. Even if it means shooting." He cut transmission before the sergeant could say any more. "Why is Blois always so insubordinate?" he snarled savagely.

The driver, a philosophical and prudent man, did not make comment.

At la Colle, the road split left to become the D37, while the right fork continued as the D25. Just before the fork itself, two Panhard M11 armored cars stood diagonally across the road, nose to nose, blocking it completely. On the roof of each cab was mounted a heavy machinegun, while on the rear of each vehicle was also mounted a single-tube anti-tank missile system.

Each weapon was manned and outside the armored cars, four more soldiers stood, two on each side of the road, armed with submachine guns.

In the distance, the blue Brabus Mercedes hurtled toward them.

Just after passing the little church of St. Romain, about a kilometer from the roadblock, the man at the wheel of the Mercedes said tightly: "I had a feeling this would happen. A reception committee."

The cold-eyed man said in equally chilling tones: "Forget your feelings and just drive the car. When I tell you to, give us a broadside stop, with my window facing them."

"As you wish."

The cold-eyed man did not comment. Instead, he reached for the door panel and pulled at the armrest which also doubled as a grab handle. A hinged section came open to reveal a rifle with a retractable metal stock, clipped into place. The weapon was based on the Heckler & Koch G41-

TGS, an assault rifle with a 40mm grenade launcher attached beneath the barrel.

He pulled off the G41, picked up a round from within the door recess and loaded it. He did not extend the stock.

The car was fast approaching the roadblock. When it was a hundred meters away, the man said: *"Now!"* and hit the window switch.

The driver was very good at his job. Even as the window began to slide downward, he had gone into action. The Mercedes seemed to brake and swing at the same. From its headlong rush it had snapped sideways to come to a full halt, broadside-on to the roadblock.

The window was down and the cold-eyed man had poked the twin snout of the rifle through, the gaping maw of its grenade launcher settling on the armored cars. The first round wheezed off and he calmly but swiftly loaded another, just as its predecessor exploded smack between the noses of the two vehicles, spraying the immediate area with fragments and felling the exposed soldiers. The force of the explosion also lifted the fronts of the cars briefly to send them crashing into each other, dislodging the other soldiers from their perches.

By now, the second round had slammed into one of the cabs, through an open-flung door. The subsequent explosion seemed to rip the armored car apart as fuel lines ruptured and the petrol ignited. A double explosion rolled across the Plain of Canjuers and a gush of flame whose heat could be felt in the Mercedes reached for and found the second Panhard. Pieces of metal clattered on the road a short distance from the blue car. Two soldiers, the only survivors, darted away running for dear life, seeking cover. They had submachine guns with them.

The cold-eyed man had no intention of giving them time to position themselves. The Mercedes was not armored and machine gun bullets could do a lot of damage. Such an eventuality could not be tolerated. Another grenade was already within the launcher tube. He followed the running soldiers, tracking them with the muzzles. They made it easy for him by running together.

He fired.

The grenade exploded at their feet, hurling them into the air and tearing at their bodies. By the time they had collapsed to the ground, the man had hauled the rifle in and was returning it to its hiding place. The window slid shut.

"Go!" he commanded the driver. "There's room over to the right. Over there." He pointed to the burning armored car. "Just next to it."

The flames were now licking at the second Panhard.

The driver said, even as he began to turn the Mercedes: "That second car...."

"If you do as I tell you instead of wasting time, we'll be well past before it explodes." The man's voice was harsh, almost scornful of the driver's apparent timidity.

The Mercedes surged toward the flames. The cold-eyed man relaxed in his seat, satisfied with the way things had gone. As always, the surprise attack with relentless force had succeeded.

It was a tactic they had all been taught, and in which he believed. Totally.

The blue car rushed safely past the burning armored cars and the dead and dying soldiers.

None of the occupants took a second look at the scene of devastation.

They continued along the D25 for about two kilometers before pulling off the road near some woods. The driver remained where he was while his passengers got out swiftly. What they did next was unhurriedly, yet quickly executed. It was obvious they'd had plenty of practice.

When they re-entered the car, it no longer carried German plates. Even the international sticker had been changed from the D for Deutschland, to an F for France. The license plates, now also French, sported the *Département* digits of 56, denoting it had been registered in Morbihan. Close inspection of the car's documents would have shown them to be perfectly in order.

The Brabus Mercedes moved back onto the road and headed for the D21. The change of plates had taken less than a minute.

Instead of going on to Fayence, Gallagher decided to cut across the dogleg at Seillans, where the D53 began. This was just as twisty as the other roads in the area, except it was even narrower.

"I thought we were going through Fayence," Rhiannon said.

"I'm giving our pursuers more choices. They can't cover every road, whoever they may be. Even Galbin will have his work cut out."

He glanced in the mirrors. Normal traffic. No overt sign of pursuit.

She was looking at him. "You seem thoughtful."

The road began to climb in a series of hairpin bends toward le Cunier.

He said: "I was just thinking how strange life can be. The last time I was in France, I was also fleeing pursuit. This very area too. But I was going the other way. The same man was after me."

"That was the time Lauren was killed."

"Yes."

A silence descended between them merging, it seemed, into the powerful throb of the car.

Then some minutes after they'd passed le Cunier, Rhiannon said: "Stop. Over there." She was pointing to the right.

"What?" He glanced at her. "Why?"

"You've passed it. Stop and go back."

He slowed down. Perhaps she needed to go to the toilet. There were plenty of bushes around. He stopped the car.

"Plenty of screening for privacy. Will this do?"

"I'm not talking about that." The golden eyes had a strange look to them.

"Then why. . . ."

"Exorcism," she said. "I want to lay a ghost, if you'll pardon the unintended pun. I want you to make love to me, back there behind the bushes. Like a cat, I'm laying my scent down. This is my territory now; not any bloody ghost's."

"Rhiannon . . . we've got people chasing us. . . ."

"We don't know that for certain. And even if they are, you've just said not even Galbin can cover everywhere. There was a hidden turning a couple of hundred yards back there. . . ." Her voice faded. The eyes stared at him.

"You're really serious about this," he said.

She nodded. Her eyes never left his face.

"Right," he said, and put the car into reverse.

The road sloped downward, but there wasn't far to go. He found the turning. It was more of an overgrown cart track. He eased the *quattro* off the road until it was virtually hidden from view. The day had again become warm and the sun was high and bright in a cloudless sky; but in the gloom of the turning, it felt appreciably cooler. From the road, the black car had all but disappeared. Any pursuit vehicle tearing past would miss it.

Rhiannon said: "Even if you think I'm being irrational. . . ."

He smiled at her as he switched off. "Be as irrational as you like. The reward's worth it."

"Then you don't mind?"

"Of course I don't mind." It was probably safer off the roads for the time being.

"And the people following us?"

"If they really are, let them chase themselves. We'll stay here for a while. They might even think we're miles away and may well believe they've lost us for good."

"So I did have the right idea." She was smiling now. "We've got no food, though. . . ."

"Who needs food?"

". . . but I've got a couple of apples in my bag."

"You would."

She took his hand and put it to her left breast. He felt its heat through the thin material of her blouse.

"Just so you know what you're in for," she said.

Above them, out of view, a growing sound beat upon the day. The helicopter passed almost directly overhead. They tensed briefly, then relaxed as it kept going, heading northwest.

"Not for us," she said, looking briefly up at the roof of the car.

"No. Not for us."

The Gazelle helicopter, on a routine training flight, crossed into the military zone on a heading that would take it over la Colle. A student pilot was being given a visual flight rules cross-country test. The instructor, in the left-hand seat, made the student keep low, allowing him to pop up only long enough to check his bearings. So far, the student had navigated without error.

"You've done very well today, Berland."

"Thank you, Major."

"Don't thank me as yet. Wait till you've completed the mission. Much can still go wrong between now and that time."

"Yes, Major."

"Now, Berland, I want you to pop up and tell me if la Colle is where you expect it to be."

Berland obeyed and brought the helicopter up to check his reference point. He did well. La Colle was dead on course.

Then they saw the smoke.

5

Gallagher and Rhiannon had found a tiny clearing on sloping ground, not far from the car. From where they lay, they could see its black shape through the undergrowth, a panther waiting patiently for unsuspecting prey.

The clearing was itself well secluded, with only the small patch of sky above the tree tops to break its cover. About them, unseen woodland creatures, at first made silent by their approach, scuttled in fits and starts. Now and again, the odd inquisitive insect would dart toward them to investigate, then dart away once more. Within the clearing, there was a sort of twilight.

Rhiannon said: "This is nice. A little world of our own." She lay back on the beach towels they'd brought from the car and stared up at the window of blue sky. "Do they still have wolves in places like this?"

"The odd rabid dog, perhaps," he told her gleefully, and growled as he nibbled at a full breast.

The thin, loose blouse she was wearing was

hardly a barrier, but she said: "Why don't I just take it off?"

She did so very slowly, the golden eyes continuingly fixed upon his. The tiniest of smiles played at the corners of her mouth. The blouse at last came off, to be followed by her bra, displaying the wonders of her breasts to him.

"You do the rest," she said, eyes appearing to shine at him.

She had kicked off her flat-heeled shoes and her toes curled and uncurled in slow rhythm as she waited for him. He unzipped her jeans with his own deliberate slowness, drew them down over the curving swell of her hips, down past the strong rounded thighs, down the glorious legs, and off. He placed the jeans with the same deliberate slowness, next to the discarded blouse and bra. He left the knickers on.

"You're torturing me!" she said in a small voice.

"Good." He leaned over to kiss her gently, then drew back to remove his own clothes. When he was fully naked, he reached for her knickers.

He drew them as slowly down as he'd done with the jeans but this time, his thumbs stroked the insides of her thighs as they went. A shiver shot through her and her entire body arched briefly, trembled, then relaxed again. She began to moan, and then her body began a slow undulation.

"I can't wait!" she told him softly. "I . . . I . . . can't. . . ."

Neither could he. Entry was smooth and a shock of ecstasy went through them. She was unbelievably hot inside and he felt the curling of her legs about him as if in a dream.

Her whimpers and squeals silenced the woodland creatures into immobility; then a long, drawn-out gasping wail rose from the clearing, punctuated by low sounds of pleasure.

A sudden, expectant silence descended; and the woodland creatures once more commenced their scuttling.

The two bodies lay in damp embrace, in the twilight of the clearing.

The instructor said: "Take her down, Berland. I don't like the look of this."

Even as Berland started to bring the Gazelle in for a landing, the instructor was reporting into the radio the scene that greeted their eyes. Before long, Sergeant Blois knew the worst, as did his commanding officer.

At the Col du Bel Homme, the captain listened to the report coming in, and saw the shape of his nightmare.

"Mr. Haslam," Prinknash began as the white Jaguar left Bargemon and took the road up the Col, "we don't know they went this way."

"I know this area quite well," Haslam said calmly, successfully controlling the irritation he felt. "Gallagher's trying to shake the dust of France off his feet as quickly as possible. We already know he's heading north. That means Switzerland in as straight a line as possible from St. Tropez. Going through here will cut out a lot of mileage.

"Up ahead is a military training area, and only two roads are open to public access. This is the way Gallagher will have gone, as will our friends in the blue car. So keep going, Sergeant. There's a good lad."

Prinknash took the long way up the Col and, ten minutes later, they saw the patrol vehicle straddling the road.

"MPs," he said. "Now what?"

The Jaguar came to an unflurried halt and the captain, a wiry man with a tight, angry face, strode up. He glanced pointedly at the license plates, then moved to stop by Haslam's window.

He looked down, without bending. Haslam found himself looking up the captain's nose.

"This road is closed," the captain said in English, clearly hating the need to speak the language.

"Why?" Haslam inquired mildly in French.

The captain seemed to jerk even further upright at the use of his mother tongue and decided to speak rapidly in it, to confuse this foreigner who thought he knew how to speak French.

"Military reasons," the captain said. "What is your business here?"

"I was not aware it was forbidden to use this road," Haslam countered smoothly.

The captain's eyes danced with manic displeasure as he realized that Haslam was indeed fluent in the language. It was like a personal insult. He decided to be totally uncooperative.

"It is now forbidden," he informed Haslam stonily. "You must return the way you have come and find another route. But first, I must ask for your papers."

"Do you have the authority?"

The captain, already thoroughly angered by the loss of his men and not a little worried about his career prospects, placed his hand meaningfully on the pistol at his belt.

"I have plenty of authority."

Haslam had decided it was time to end the game. "Very well. May I get out?"

"Yes. But be careful. My man is also armed." The captain stepped back a few paces.

"I'm sure he is. I shall be most careful."

Haslam climbed out unhurriedly. He towered over the captain.

"This is a matter of security, Captain," Haslam began, "and I have the cooperation of your own security services. I am following a blue, German-registered car."

The captain's eyes jumped again. "A *blue* car?"

"You look disturbed, Captain."

"A *blue* car?" The captain's eyes had reddened with approaching rage. "What do you know of this car?"

"I think," Haslam said calmly, "you would do wise to refer me to your Colonel."

The captain's eyes were having a bad day. They jumped for a third time.

"You . . . you know the Colonel?"

Haslam merely stared at him.

"I . . . I must check. Please remain where you are."

"I have no intention of leaving."

The captain hurried back to the P4 and grabbed the radio, while his driver stared emptily at Haslam. The captain spoke rapidly, and waited.

The captain replaced the handset, and came back.

"It appears that you are correct, Monsieur,"

he said to Haslam with less hostility. "You may go through. However, I should warn you that there is a military convoy on the road. Also . . . there has been an incident."

Haslam waited.

The captain pointed down the steep slope. "Down there at the bottom are two of my men and their vehicle. The rescue team is on it's way, but it won't do my men any good. The blue car was responsible."

"What?" Haslam stared at him in disbelief.

The captain gave a fleeting, bitter smile. "At the end of this road, at la Colle, you will see two more vehicles . . . destroyed. Those were armored cars. Eight more men died."

Haslam was still looking at the captain in disbelief. "How could an ordinary motorcar take on two armored cars and *eight* soldiers, and still win?"

"Perhaps *you* can tell me, M'sieur," the captain said tightly.

Haslam said: "I'm very sorry about your men, Captain, but you'll have to take your questions to your Colonel. I am unable to tell you anything."

"You mean you won't."

"I am as much in the dark as you are."

"And if you were not?"

"I still could not tell you."

The captain turned his mouth down cynically. "It is to be expected. Goodbye, M'sieur." The captain gave Haslam a dry salute and returned to his vehicle. It began to move out of the way.

Prinknash said, when Haslam had re-entered the Jaguar: "Being saluted by the Frogs, are we, Mr. Haslam?"

"Prinknash."

"Yes, Mr. Haslam?"

"You continue to amaze me."

"Oh look," Rhiannon said. "We've got a peeping tom."

Gallagher rolled off her quickly, senses alert, eyes tracking. He felt suddenly vulnerable, but could see no one within the immediate vicinity of the clearing. The undergrowth betrayed no hurried movements. The remote, on top of the pile of clothes and within easy reach, had been silent. No one had been near the car.

"You've frightened him," she went on. "He's run away."

He kept his eyes on the undergrowth. "Who ran away? Exactly what did you see?"

Then she giggled. The tone of her voice should have warned him.

He turned to look down at her. She lay on her back, her naked body displayed wantonly, her smile teasing.

"Alright. You've had your fun. What was it?"

The giggles returned, causing the smooth surface of her stomach to ripple suggestively. Response stirred within him.

"It was a lovely little squirrel," she said at last. "He was just by your toes, watching us very sternly." She stared at his lower body pointedly. "You were a bit vulnerable there. He might have been looking for winter stocks."

He crouched over her, framing her within the cage of his arms and legs. "A punishment is due, methinks. I'm going to keep you here till dark, and ravish you."

"Yes, please. Oh yes!" The giggles were gone, the voice now thick and low. Her body moved beneath him.

She gave the long, drawn-out "oooh!" that always electrified him, as he entered her, and shuddered with the pleasure of it. The body movements subtly grew in urgency.

The darkness, he was thinking, would hide the *quattro* well. Then he was vulnerable once more as the soft heat of Rhiannon took possession of him, drawing him deep into her.

"Ravish me!" she breathed in his ear. "Ravish me!"

The D21 terminated at the end of a two-kilometer straight where it joined the N85, the Route Napoléon, going toward Digne. The blue Mercedes had pulled off the road, just before the junction itself and the men inside had a good view of the passing traffic. They had already spent an hour waiting for their quarry. They, too, had spotter cars, but none had relayed a sighting.

The driver said: "We can't remain here forever. Someone's bound to get curious eventually."

They all knew he was thinking of police. So far, two motorcycle patrolmen had gone past, but they had not stopped to ask awkward questions. Either they hadn't been told of the incident with the army, or the French license plates were working as efficiently as they were meant to. Hiding in plain sight was sometimes the most effective camouflage.

The cold-eyed man said: "We wait. They don't know they're looking for three men. No one who's come up against us is still alive to talk about it."

But he did not look pleased.

The white Jaguar was hurrying along the same road. It had been held up in its passage across Canjuers by the convoy and by the vehicles of the medical teams that had gone to la Colle. Prinknash glanced at the blue Mercedes as they went past.

"Isn't that. . . ." he began.

"Keep going!" Haslam snapped at him. "Don't even slacken speed before the junction." He had noted the apparently casual glance that one of the occupants had given them.

The Jaguar stopped briefly at the junction before turning left toward Castellane and Digne. A kilometer later, they came to a crossroad.

"Take the left turning," Haslam said. "It's sharp and doubles back slightly. That should give us cover. Anyone coming from the south will have gone past before they see us. That's assuming they're looking."

Prinknash found a suitable place to stop, with the Jaguar's nose pointing toward the main road.

"It looked like the same car," Prinknash began, "but I don't think it was."

"What makes you come to that conclusion?"

"It had French plates. Even in France, there must be a lot of Mercedes-owning people."

"I'm sure there are, but that was the same car. There can't be that many *exactly* like it around."

"But the registration. . . ."

"And there was I, thinking you were a real policeman, Prinknash. The switched plate is one of the oldest tricks in the book. Which, I suppose,"

Haslam added thoughtfully, "may be precisely why they did it. So obvious, they expect everyone to miss it."

"Do we wait here?"

"Right first time, Prinknash. We wait."

London, 1600 hours.

Fowler left the austere cubicle he liked to call his office and made his way down the corridor in answer to a summons from Winterbourne. It was going to be yet another skirmish, but Fowler was unperturbed. He'd already primed Gallagher; and even if Gallagher did suspect this, it would not get him off the hook.

Fowler smiled as he pushed open the paneled oak door to Winterbourne's office.

The huge room could not have been more different from Fowler's. Seeming acres of plush red carpet separated Winterbourne's massive pedestal desk from the door. Its surface gleamed and upon it were the barest of essentials: a desk-top intercom and a row of telephones. At its precise center was a large ornately bound writing pad, thick with virgin paper. Winterbourne, a portly man much shorter than Fowler, stood away from the desk, looking down at the sleepy anonymous square through one of the huge windows.

Far too much glass, Fowler had always thought.

It tended to make him feel that any reasonably competent sniper could take out Winterbourne, from a number of vantage points. Fowler again smiled, this time at the possibility of such an event actually coming to pass. Winterbourne would probably die at 90, in his bath.

Winterbourne finally deigned to turn round to face Fowler and clasped his hands behind his back, legs spread. He tried to look stern and only succeeded in looking more like the petulant cherub he appeared to be impersonating.

"I asked Mrs. Arundel to buzz you over an hour ago, Fowler," Winterbourne began, getting the first shot in.

Fowler usually held his own fire, to later disintegrate Winterbourne with a well-aimed broadside. Winterbourne never seemed to learn.

"Several urgent reports required my immediate attention, Sir John," Fowler explained calmly.

"Could you not have called in on your arrival from Heathrow? You were here thirty minutes before I asked Mrs. Arundel to contact you. The Minister wants to know what you've been up to in France."

"The Minister would also like to know about this. I've been working on it since my return." Fowler handed Winterbourne a thin red file he had brought with him.

His face unsuccessfully trying to mask the chagrin he felt at having yet again played into Fowler's hands, he took the file with some reluctance and began to read.

"We picked that up from some French traffic," Fowler said, administering the *coup de grace*. "I've been waiting for it to be decoded."

Winterbourne looked up from the file. "Who are the people in the blue car?"

"The French clearly don't know."

Winterbourne's eyes were baleful. "I'm not interested in what the French know or do not know. I'm asking *you*, Fowler."

"I don't know, Sir John. I can only hazard a guess at this juncture."

"Please dispense with the semantics," Winterbourne said impatiently. "I'm certain you've got some idea. You've *always* got some idea."

"With respect, Sir John, I'd like to wait a little longer before committing myself to a definite...."

"My God, Fowler! I'm Head of this Department. I'm supposed to have the facts at my fingertips. The Minister...."

"The Minister would appreciate it much more if you gave him hard information rather than vague conjectures. That's why I advise less haste. I'm trying to get you something worth giving to him."

Winterbourne didn't look as if he believed Fowler, but knew when he'd reached an impasse. He shut the file and handed it back as if wanting to get rid of it quickly.

But he wasn't quite finished. He'd go down fighting.

"Well? Did you manage to persuade him?" The question was asked with the deliberate intention to goad.

"Persuade whom, Sir John?"

"Your precious Gallagher!" Winterbourne was nearly shouting now. "The reason you set off on that jaunt to the south of France ... at public expense, I might add. I shall have to justify it to the auditors...."

"The trip was made at my expense, Sir John," Fowler interrupted mildly. With a manor house in a prime location in the Cotswolds, Fowler was sufficiently well-heeled to be able to live quite handsomely without his salary. "I knew how reluctant you were to sanction the trip," he continued, "and not wishing to create any possible problems for you with the auditors, I chose to go independently. If the journey subsequently turned out to have been a mistake, then taxpayers' money would not have been wasted."

"And has it? Has it been a wasted journey?" Winterbourne wanted some blood; at least.

But this too was to be denied him.

Fowler gave one of his most fleeting smiles. "Let's say we're monitoring the situation. Now if you'll excuse me, Sir John, I have some urgent work that needs to be attended to."

Fowler went out, leaving Winterbourne to stare at the closing door. Winterbourne stood where he was for long seconds before turning again to look down on the sleepy little square.

"Damn that man," he said tightly.

The junction of the D21 and the N85, France. 1700.

The men from the Brabus Mercedes had taken turns to leave the car, to stretch their legs and ease the boredom of sitting in the vehicle while waiting for the black *quattro* to go by. They had walked down to the small river, the Artuby, that flowed beyond the other side of the road. One had taken a pair of binoculars with him to scan the surrounding area. The broken image of the white Jaguar had shown up through the partial screen of distant foliage. The three men were now all back in their car.

"See if it's still there," the cold-eyed man ordered. He had also checked the image himself when his colleague had mentioned it.

The one in the back raised the binoculars to

his eyes and focussed on the spot where he'd first seen the white image.

It was no longer there.

"It's gone," he said.

"Let me have those," the cold-eyed man said. Taking the binoculars, he climbed out of the car and after checking that no traffic with curious people was in the immediate vicinity, took a look through them.

The white car seemed to have gone.

He got back in, passed the binoculars back. "You're right," he said.

If the man in the back felt annoyed at having his abilities doubted, he said nothing about it; neither did his manner give any indication.

The driver said: "Who do you think it was?"

"Could have been the white car with English plates that passed earlier," the cold-eyed man replied. "Or it could have been somebody out for a quick time with a woman, or any number of other people. We'll check it out when we go past . . . just in case."

"They could have been there for as long as we have."

"Then why move?"

"Perhaps they saw us looking."

"That's over a kilometer away. Nearly two. There was no one outside the car. No one with binoculars to spot us."

"If they were waiting," the driver persisted, "were they after us? Or the black car?"

The cold-eyed man shrugged. It didn't really matter. There was really only one target. The important one. Nothing was going to prevent him from completing that mission.

* * *

Haslam, in shirtsleeves, was lying in cover on a patch of dry ground. He was also looking through a pair of binoculars, at the distant car.

Earlier, he had left the Jaguar to carry out a covert scrutiny of the Mercedes. He had seen the men take turns at leaving the car to go for short walks by the river. He had seen one of them scanning the area and, even in the act of moving deeper into cover, had seen the sudden freezing of the watcher and had known the Jaguar had been spotted.

He had waited until the one with the binoculars had returned to the blue car, before telling Prinknash to reverse a short distance until the Jaguar was more securely hidden behind a screen of thick roadside foliage. He had also shifted his own position.

Now as he lay, hidden from the road by the white flank of the Jaguar and well-screened from scrutiny from the Mercedes, he allowed his mind to go back to a time of his youth. He was nineteen again, peering from cover through a pair of naval binoculars at a small unit of German soldiers. Next to him was a young French girl, his guide. He was already in love with her. The only woman he would ever truly love. She was seventeen. Eventually, the *Milice* had caught up with her and had handed her over to the Gestapo. . . .

Thereafter, individual members of the *Milice* had become his targets. His cold rage had turned him into something of a monster; a killing machine. In all his years with the Department, no one had managed to surpass this destructive efficiency.

Until Gallagher had come along.

He did not agree with the way in which Fowler would go to great lengths to keep Gallagher within Department control; but he could understand Fowler's motives. Even so.

He sighed, and pushed the memory of the seventeen-year-old girl out of his mind. His job was to make sure the men in the blue car did not get close enough to Gallagher.

For the time being.

By twilight, both cars were still waiting. For the men in the Mercedes, it was an intensely frustrating time. Their spotter cars had relayed no sightings, and the cold-eyed man had become dangerously quiet. The other two dared not say a word to him. They were not cowards. Each in his own way was as murderous as the other; but each also pragmatically respected the power of the organization behind the man in command.

As for Haslam, he was quite contented to continue waiting, although the approach of night would make things appreciably more difficult. Prinknash moaned about being hungry. Haslam ignored him. Across the river, the sudden flare of headlamps would warn him when the blue Mercedes decided to leave.

6

Gallagher lay back in his seat and listened to the woodland noises of the night. It was pitch black outside. Beside him Rhiannon, lying in her own fully reclined seat, breathed softly in contented sleep.

They had made love for the rest of the day, revelling in the enjoyment of their bodies. At twilight, announcing a lack of desire to share the tiny clearing with the night-time creepy crawlies as she'd called them, she had decided they should return to the car. They had reclined the Recaro seats fully, and had again made love. Now she slept, well sated.

Despite the exertions of their energetic lovemaking and having had just the one apple since their hurried departure from Ramatuelle, he did not feel particularly hungry. Instead, he felt refreshed, senses fully on the alert. Lying there in the dark, he had tuned himself to the fine, preaction pitch that had served him so well in the past.

His hearing had become acutely perceptive of every sound about him. His eyes could distinguish shapes even in the intense gloom and his reactions, when the time dictated, would be very swift. In that specially controlled state, Gallagher came very close to being a creature of the wild.

He reached forward to turn on the ignition, to activate the electrics of the leather upholstered seat. The instrument panel went through its prestart routine and the time glowed 20.30 at him. The 15-switch panel fixed to the right hand wing of the seat squab gave off its own dim glow. He pressed one of the buttons, and the back of the seat began to rise to the accompaniment of a soft whirr.

Gallagher released the switch and the whirr stopped.

The sound had woken Rhiannon. Now she yawned, stretching like a very contented cat. When they had put their clothes back on, she had drawn on a lightweight sweater over her blouse and an arm brushed briefly at Gallagher's face as she stretched. It felt like a small, furry animal.

"Gosh," she said, her voice still full of sleep. She yawned once more. "It's dark out there. Have I been asleep long?"

"An hour at least."

"What about you?" She began to move her seat upward. "Did you have a little nap?"

"No. I was alright."

"You should have woken me."

"I like watching and hearing you sleep."

She gave him a quick kiss, pleased by his words. "I'm starving," she said. "One apple's not enough for a. . . ."

"Lustful woman?" He grinned at her in the dark of the car.

"Any complaints?"

"Not from me." He assured her.

"Doing it in a *quattro* is fun."

"I'll keep that in mind." It had not been their first time.

She said: "You've got something else on your mind too."

"That obvious?"

"There's something different about you. I know the signs. The part of you that sometimes frightens me is coming back. Do you still think we're being followed?"

"My instincts tell me they're waiting... somewhere out there." He clipped on his belt and started the car. The deep rumble of the twin exhausts growled out a challenge into the night.

He heard Rhiannon's belt click home as he turned on the lights and eased the *quattro* out of its temporary lair.

He turned right, in the direction of Mons. There was no traffic, and the lights pierced the darkness with brilliant stabs of white.

During the course of the day, they'd heard cars and lorries going past, but those had been few and far between. On one occasion, however, one car had seemed to be going even more slowly than the rest and Gallagher had grabbed his underpants and trousers to crawl through the undergrowth for a surreptitious look while he'd warned Rhiannon to get ready for a quick departure.

But it had been a false alarm. The culprit had turned out to be an open-backed van carrying young trees. They'd heard it whining its way upward as they had continued to enjoy each other.

That had been the only tense moment; but Gallagher had no intention of allowing himself to be lulled into a false sense of security.

He checked the fuel gauge. No petrol necessary before Switzerland; but they'd need some food before then. The thing was to obtain a meal of some sort without attracting undue attention from unseen watchers.

"How hungry are you, really?" he asked Rhiannon.

"I can wait for a while."

"An hour? Two hours?"

"An hour's fine. Maybe a little longer than that, but two would be pushing it. I've had a lot of exercise today," she continued meaningfully. "I need fuel."

He smiled in the glow-lit gloom. "I'll see what I can do."

"You'd better, or I'll just fade away. Then where will you be?"

He knew without looking, the kind of expression she had turned to him. Despite Fowler and unseen pursuers, he felt good. Being with her vitalised him.

"I don't think I'd like to answer that."

The D53 skirted the edge of the military zone before joining the road from Fayence which twisted its way northward via Mons, eventually to join up with the N85 some 30 kilometers later, at the Col de Valferrière. They made good time. Traffic was less than expected and Gallagher drove fast along the mountain road. The wider N85 allowed him to increase his speed and they were approaching the junction at le Logis du Pin where the Mercedes was still waiting, when Rhiannon saw what she was looking for, just off the road to the right.

"This will do," she said. It was a small hotel with a restaurant sign.

But he didn't slow down. "Too exposed," he said as they shot past.

They might have made it unseen, the blackness of the car merging successfully with the darkness, the glare of its lights making it indistinguishable from head-on. But the unexpected took a decisive hand in the game.

Expect the unexpected. O'Keefe's oft-repeated exhortation which Gallagher had made one of his firmest rules. Sometimes, however, the unexpected could come from directions so bizarre, no amount of preparedness could shield you from it.

At the very moment that the *quattro* passed, someone in the hotel car park decided to switch on his lights and begin to maneuver his car. In turning, the beams captured the *quattro* for fleeting moments, like a bomber caught in the vengeful beam of a searchlight. Then the blaze of lights left the black car.

But the damage had already been done.

All three men in the Brabus had seen the dark shape flit in and out of the lights.

"That's the car!" the one in the back said excitedly.

"Control yourself," the cold-eyed man snapped. "We've all seen it."

"You were right," the driver said.

"I'm always right. Being right means successful missions . . . and this one's going to be. Get moving before we lose him."

"You saw how he went past. It will take a lot to catch up."

The driver started the engine, turned on the lights.

"You've got enough power under that bonnet," the cold-eyed man said, "to take this thing over 250 kilometers an hour. Get after him! And don't tell me it's night. I can see that for myself."

The Brabus Mercedes, after having waited all day, set off in pursuit with a screech of tires.

Haslam had been standing outside the Jaguar looking through a pair of night glasses, and had seen the distant lights come on.

He got in quickly, dumped the glasses on the rear seat.

"We're in business," he said. "They're on the move."

A short while later, bright headlamps hurtled past, trailing a powerful roar.

"That has to be Gallagher," Haslam said. "So he's been laying low all day. Cunning." There was approval in his voice.

"He's bloody motoring," Prinknash said. "We'll never catch up." The AJ6 engine burst smoothly into life as he turned the ignition.

"We're not meant to. Our quarry will be along any minute now."

"I thought we were trailing Gallagher."

"Oh, we're trailing him. You can bet on it."

A short while later, glaring beams of light swerved from side to side as something slower was overtaken, then another fast shape sped by.

"There they go," Haslam said. "Alright, Prinknash. Hang on to them."

"That might take some doing."

"Then do your bloody best."

Prinknash trod on the accelerator. The Jaguar spun its rear wheels viciously until traction took over and 221 Coventry horses hurled it off after the Mercedes. He hauled straight across the traffic as he turned left, collecting a few irate blares from the horns of the other cars.

"Piss off!" he snarled as he began to chase the fast-receding rear lights.

"You're such a friendly soul, Prinknash," Haslam said.

Gallagher had seen the violent swerving of the first set of lights pulling into the traffic, but had said nothing to Rhiannon. Now, as he swung the *quattro* down into the first half of a tight double hairpin bend, he saw a second set of lights chasing in and out of the following traffic.

Rhiannon said: "You're giving the mirrors a lot of attention. What's behind us?"

"I'm not sure," he replied. "There seems to be a game of tag going on."

She looked back and upward, and saw the first set of lights speeding downward. They were a few bends behind. She continued to look, and saw the second set, further away, but also traveling fast. She looked forward once more. The road ahead was empty for the time being. The *quattro* seemed to be traveling faster.

"Do you . . . you think they're following us?" she asked in a voice that did not want her fears confirmed. "This is mountainous country. I remember reading once about crazy drivers in France who made a habit of bumping other cars off the mountain roads."

"No one's going to shove us off the road."

She gave another quick glance behind. The first set of lights did not seem to be catching up.

The *quattro* swept into an upward curving hairpin, then it was climbing steeply toward the Col de Luens, at over 1000 meters. Then it was downhill all the way to Castellane. Once on the other side of the Col, Gallagher reached for a row of switches specially mounted above the central grilles on the dashboard. He pressed one.

The rear lights went out. The all-black tail of the car was now invisible. He sped on toward Castellane.

"We can't keep up with him," the driver of the Mercedes said. "He knows we're following." The back end of the car fish-tailed slightly as he went into another bend. "That car of his sticks to the road like glue."

"You'd better not lose him," the cold-eyed man warned. There was an ominous edge to his voice.

The man in the back said: "What about the one behind? Do you think it's the same car we saw earlier?"

"It must be," the cold-eyed one said. "They must have known we spotted them so they moved out of sight. No matter. If they get too close, they'll wish they hadn't."

The Mercedes sped on through the dark. Some minutes later, just as it breasted the Col, a car going the other way came too far across their side of the road. The man at the wheel of the Brabus was forced to brake hard, at the wrong moment. The Brabus began to slide at high speed. The driver was quick and caught it in time; but the car stalled, right on the peak of the Col.

Swearing viciously at the departing car, the driver turned the ignition. The engine refused to start.

"We're losing time!" the cold-eyed man told him savagely. "Get this thing started!"

The man in the back said: "That other car's catching up."

"Don't state the obvious," the cold-eyed man said, before rounding on the driver once more. "What have you done to it? Get it started!"

The starter whirred uselessly.

"I haven't done anything to it," the driver snapped angrily. "The engine's hot and flooded. It will start soon."

"Assuming someone doesn't hit us first . . . probably the car that's racing up behind." The cold-eyed man pulled swiftly at the paneling in the door and snatched out the G41-TGS lookalike. This time, he did not load a grenade round. Instead he cocked it and selected automatic rifle fire. He lowered his window.

The driver, still trying to re-start the car, glanced at him and said: "What are you doing?"

"What do you think?" came the sharp retort. "If you start this thing in time, they'll live a little longer. If not. . . ."

"All this killing is unnecessary. . . ."

"We are *all* trained to kill. Nothing gets in the way of a successful end to this mission. *Nothing.* You would do well to remember that."

"Are you threatening me?"

"I never threaten. I act."

"We are of the best," the man in the back said calmly. "Shall we save our aggression for those against whom we intend to use it?" As the most junior of the team, he was not sure whether he had spoken out of turn, but felt the situation warranted it.

The two in front nodded silently. The crisis was over; for the time being. The team would work smoothly, for the sake of the mission. When the time came for reports, however. . . .

The lights behind were now getting very close and the cold-eyed man had poked the snout of the rifle out of his window.

Prinknash saw the car in the middle of the road at about the time the winking flashes began to come from it. As the first bullet struck and starred the windscreen, he reacted instinctively and pulled over to the left. This was unfortunate, for it presented the other car with a better target.

Something at once heavy and fiery slammed through the window and into him; then he felt another heavy blow.

"Oh Jesus!" he heard himself scream as he tugged again at the wheel, this time to the right.

Something was wrong with his arms and legs. A sufficient amount of his training remained long enough to enable him to bring the car to an untidy halt, half on and half off the road. He thought he could hear a loud horn.

Then the dark of the night seemed to get darker.

* * *

The Mercedes came to life just as the Jaguar crunched to a halt, its windscreen shattered, its horn wailing into the night, and one of its headlamps pointing crazily off the Col. The other had been shot out.

The cold-eyed man replaced the now-warm rifle as the car began to move. "That should keep them busy," he said emotionlessly.

"We've lost the black car," the driver said. He expected to be blamed.

"We'll find him again."

The apparent calmness with which this was said did not totally reassure him as he sent the Brabus roaring down the Col toward Castellane.

Haslam was completely unscathed. He unclipped his seat belt and eased Prinknash's hand off the horn lever. The wailing stopped. He could feel the warm stickiness of blood.

He checked Prinknash's pulse. It was weak, but still there. Prinknash would live; provided help could be got to him in time.

Haslam quickly grabbed the handset of the radiophone and got through to Fowler on a specially allocated, secure frequency. He gave a very brief report on what had occurred, together with his position. He broke transmission and settled down to wait, after doing what he could for Prinknash. There was a first aid kit in the car, but Prinknash needed more than first aid. Haslam could feel, in the gloom of the car, great splashes of blood on various parts of the pale upholstery.

He had reclined the seat to make Prinknash more comfortable. The younger man breathed shallowly, but made no other sound.

Haslam left the single headlamp on, like a forlorn beacon.

Gallagher took the *quattro* over the right hand of the twin bridges that crossed the Verdon into Castellane, followed the one-way traffic system to the left before turning right again for the town center. He had decided not to stay on the N85, intending to branch off to the right on the N555, after leaving the town. That would give their pursuers another choice to make.

Rhiannon, who had been looking back, said: "No one seems to be following. What do you think happened?"

He had seen briefly in the mirrors, the strange cavorting of the two sets of lights, and had mentioned it to her.

"Not sure," he answered thoughtfully. "Could be two different sets of people following us and they had a slight disagreement."

So much the better, he thought grimly. Let them kill each other off.

Rhiannon said: "Two *different* sets! I'm frightened enough as it is, Gordon. What do they want with us? What *could* they want?"

"I don't know, Rhiannon. I don't know. And that's the bloody trouble. As I've told you before, they all apparently seem to think I've got something they want. The truth is, I haven't and until today, I knew nothing of its existence. But don't worry," he added. "I'm not going to let anything happen to you. That's a promise."

She placed a hand gently on his thigh as the car cruised slowly through the town. "I'm sorry."

"For what?"

"For being frightened."

"Stay frightened. It's healthy." It also meant she would move that much more quickly if the need arose.

Never be ashamed of being frightened, sir. You'd be surprised at how fast you can shift when you know you'll cop it if you don't.

O'Keefe.

Gallagher turned right onto the N555 just out of town. The road began to climb and at the top of another Col five kilometers later, he glanced in the mirrors to see if there was any pursuit.

Nothing . . . so far.

The road curved downward, skirting the shore of the Castillon dam. By the time they had reached the junction with the N207 another 13 kilometers later and had turned left onto it for St. André-les-Alpes, there was still no pursuit. The N555 recommenced at St. André, while the 207 went sharply left. Gallagher again took the 555. This would take them north, by-passing Digne completely. The road seemed much narrower than the D roads they'd been on, but appeared less twisting. He let the *quattro* have its head.

"There should be lots of little places along this route," he said, "where we may be able to grab a quick bite, if we don't leave it too late."

"What about the people behind?"

He took another glance at the mirrors. "We're still clear. Nothing coming up fast. We'll give it a little longer."

The black car roared along the dark alpine road.

"Would you like some music," he asked.

"No," she replied. "Let's keep it like this."

"Fine," he said.

They traveled in mutual silence, listening to the engine: it's cadenced sounds and the muted whine of its powerful turbo.

"This is music," she said once, punctuating a long silence.

He smiled, but did not comment.

Just before Col d'Allos, a series of tight hairpin bends took them up to over 2200 meters, where they found a small relais. It was open. The *quattro* pulled into the car park. There were three other cars.

"There you are, madam," Gallagher said, as he cut the engine. "Food at 7,000 feet. If anything's coming up fast, we'll see it from a very long way off. We've got half an hour, I think."

The engine ticked to itself. The cooling fan continued to whirr. Outside, a slight wind caressed the car.

Rhiannon looked about her. It was a very clear night and she could see clusters of lights of the towns and villages in the distance, like bright flowers in a dark field.

"So beautiful and peaceful," she said quietly.

But in the dark, and the beauty, marauders waited. She shivered slightly.

Gallagher saw, and said: "It can be very cool this high, even in August. Shall I get you a thicker sweater?"

She shook her head. "No. Thanks. I'll be fine. Let's go and find some food before I start on my fingers."

They left the car and before entering the

building, Gallagher had a careful look at the other three vehicles. Two Citroens with French plates, and one Porsche 944 Turbo . . . with British plates.

It was unlikely, Gallagher reasoned, that their pursuers—whoever they were—would have had the entire region of France so tightly sewn up, that any stopping place was suspect. At the same time, it wouldn't do to be too complacent.

"Let's go in," he said to Rhiannon. She had wrapped her arms about her. "You are cold," he added with concern, putting a protective arm out to hold her close.

"I'm fine. Really." But she stayed close against him as they walked. "Are those cars alright?"

"I think they belong to innocent citizens going about their lawful business."

"But just in case. . . ." she began.

"We'll watch our step and be ready for a fast exit."

She nodded, and put an arm about his waist.

The occupants of the cars were readily distinguishable. The large family group seated round two tables placed together and talking in French, could only have come from the Citroens. Further away in a corner, a youngish couple were having an intimate dinner, oblivious to the world about them.

"The Porsche?" Rhiannon suggested.

Gallagher said: "Looks like it . . . although we haven't heard them speak."

He had chosen a table that gave a good view of the car park and of the approach from Allos itself, 15 kilometers away. There were weak lights on the outside of the building, enough to see what went on in the parking area. The table, however, was sufficiently out of possible direct line of fire. No other diners were in the place.

Rhiannon was studying the menu. "What's *pistou?*"

"A vegetable soup. Lots of basil and garlic." Every so often, Gallagher would give the car park and the approach road a quick scrutiny. He saw nothing to worry him.

"I don't mind garlic," she said, "but I'll give it a miss tonight." A soft rumble came from her. "Oh dear. My stomach's getting impatient. What about *algo-s . . . saou*, I think it is."

"Another soup. Fish. Try it. I think you'll like it."

"Alright, and I'll go for the chicken. Even I know what *poulet* means. If we were in Spain, now that would be different. I could regale you with wonderful bits of Spanish you wouldn't find in a dictionary."

"Then thank heavens for France," he said, smiling. He was pleased that she was still cheerful, despite her fear of whoever was continuing to pursue them. "Shall we order?"

They had an undisturbed meal. Rhiannon ate heartily, and Gallagher wondered if the massive appetite had been brought on more by fear than hunger.

It was nearly 1100 when they left to return to the car. The car park had received no new visitors. The mesmerised couple were still enraptured by each other and had eventually confirmed themselves as British, by briefly talking loud enough to be heard; speaking in southern counties English.

It still didn't mean anything, of course. Anyone on a job like this would be adept at faking accents.

Gallagher took heart from the fact that the remote had remained silent.

They entered the car. Gallagher turned the ignition and the engine burst into powerful life with a brief roar. In the relais, the young woman was walking past a window just then. She paused to look. Rhiannon saw her.

"We've got a spectator," she said.

Gallagher did not turn to see who it was. "Which one?"

"The woman from the Porsche . . . if it is their car."

"Keep an eye on her until we're out of sight. We'll see. . . ."

"She's turned round to talk to someone. It's the man. He's just come to the window. Perhaps she was just going to the loo and called him to come and admire the car. If they've got a Porsche, they probably like checking out the opposition."

"Let's hope that's all it is." He put the car into gear and moved off slowly. "What reaction?" He turned on the main beams.

"The same." She had turned round to continue looking at the window. In the gloom of the car, she could not be seen properly. "I really think they're just interested in the car."

"Time will tell."

They had reached the road and Gallagher turned right, to take the 20 kilometer twisting slope down into Barcelonnette.

He put his foot down. The *quattro* leapt away, a night creature unleashed.

"They were still looking," Rhiannon said, settling back in her seat.

Haslam was still in the wrecked Jaguar. A helicopter with paramedics had arrived to take care of Prinknash and had gone, its mission completed. Prinknash would be well looked-after. There were also two police cars and two motorcycle patrolmen directing traffic, all with their blue beacons and orange flashers working overtime. There was not much traffic to direct. Haslam, again on the radiophone to Fowler, had been left to talk in private.

"Prinknash's gone," Haslam was saying. "They've done a good job. He'll be alright. Sorry, Adrian."

"Not your fault, George. No one expected an assault team."

"What's going on?"

"Who knows? The whole thing's still opaque."

"They're after Gallagher. He's on his own now."

There was a long pause. "He can look after himself when he needs to."

"He's got the girl with him. Talk about innocent bystanders."

"Can't be helped, George."

It was Haslam's turn to pause. He swore under his breath.

"What was that?" Fowler queried. "I didn't quite catch it."

"Not important."

"You don't sound too happy. Are you alright? Are you sure you weren't hurt?"

"I'd know if I'd been hit by one of those bloody things," Haslam said testily.

"That's alright then. Nothing for you to do but to get back as soon as possible."

"There's a tow-truck coming for the car. I've got to wait."

"Of course. Make sure you take everything sensitive out of it first. That includes the radio-phone, naturally. Especially that. Someone will be out to claim the car tomorrow. Don't take it too hard, George. You've done a good job."

"You could have fooled me," Haslam said. "Out."

He cut transmission.

The Brabus Mercedes was parked in a side road off the N85, not far from Chateau-Arnoux, a mere 25 kilometers from Digne. It now sported Norwegian plates.

The cold-eyed man said: "He must have stopped again. If he's trying to get out of the country as quickly as possible, this is the fastest way."

"He could have turned off," the man in the back suggested cautiously.

"It doesn't really matter. The quickest way out is through Geneva. To do that, he must go via Gap to Grenoble, then it's autoroute all the way. That's the sensible, efficient way."

The driver said: "But we now know he's unpredictable. He may not choose the sensible way."

"Even in that car," the cold-eyed man said, "he'll be wasting time on the back roads. It doesn't matter if we miss him here in France. We shall know if he crosses into Switzerland. Someone will be watching the border. We'll follow him wherever he goes."

"Do you think the English were following us in order to help him?"

The cold-eyed man gave a short but chilling laugh. "That was their mistake. They can't help him now. Let's go on to Gap."

7

At about the time that the Brabus Mercedes was setting off for Gap 64 kilometers away, Gallagher was just leaving Barcelonnette on the N100, in the direction of Serre-Ponçon which was itself not far from Gap: but he would not be going that way.

Le Lauzet-Ubaye was 21 kilometers from Barcelonnette. The road was clear and he covered the distance at high speed. He saw nothing in his mirrors to give him cause for anxiety. Two kilometers after Ubaye, he turned right onto the N854. Here the road once again twisted, climbed and swooped downward as it bordered the headland of the huge lake formed by the Serre-Ponçon dam.

The N854 joined the N94 at the Serre-Ponçon bridge. This road too, led to Gap. As Gallagher turned left onto the bridge, a motorcycle policeman, looking up at the sound of the deep rumble from the exhausts, gaped when he saw the car. He spoke urgently into his radio, then mounted his bike to follow.

Gallagher saw the single headlamp in his mirrors.

"Too good to last, I suppose," he said.

The tone of his voice made Rhiannon ask urgently: "What is it?" She glanced round, saw the glare of the headlamp. "Police?"

"It is, but he's not flashing his lights . . . not yet, anyway. I'd better keep the speed down, just in case he's hoping to book me. Damn! This will cut into our time."

The *quattro* cruised over the bridge with the motorcycle trailing a steady distance behind.

At Sisteron, the Brabus Mercedes had lost precious time after having been baulked near the N85 underpass exit by a convoy of lorries feeding in from the right off the rue Saunerie. As a result, it was some 14 kilometers from Gap, approaching from the south when Gallagher, coming from the east, was just 10 kilometers away. Gallagher's route, cutting through the north-eastern corner of the town, would also enable him to get onto the Grenoble road much more quickly.

The lorries had made overtaking difficult for the Mercedes and on one occasion, the driver had thought they would have been run off the road. None of the lorries had sported less than sixteen wheels.

"Wretched lorries," the driver now said angrily. "We've lost too much time. He might get to Gap before us."

The cold-eyed man said nothing for a while.

"Those lorries have given me an idea," he said at last.

He did not elaborate.

* * *

"Oh-oh," Gallagher said. "Here he comes."

The motorcycle had followed them for 18 kilometers from Savines. Now, as they went through tiny la Bâtie, the policeman chose to accelerate.

"We haven't been speeding," Rhiannon said. "He can't pull us up for anything."

"That's not what's worrying me."

"You think he's received orders from the man you told me about? Galbin?"

"God knows. A motorcycle copper must have something better to do at this time of the night . . . unless he's acting under specific orders. Well, it looks as if it might take us a little longer to make it to Germany. I daren't risk trying to outrun him. We could, but the bastard would probably shoot."

The noise of the motorcycle under hard acceleration swelled above the sound of the *quattro*. Its lights were winking like a Christmas tree.

As the machine drew level, its rider's helmeted, be-goggled head turned briefly to stare hard at the occupants of the car; but instead of swinging in front to force Gallagher to stop, it continued accelerating, roaring on ahead. Soon, it had gone from view.

"What do you think he was up to?" Rhiannon asked puzzledly.

"I wish I knew. Bloody Fowler! Bloody Galbin!"

"It may have nothing to do with them. A curious policeman. That's all."

She was so innocent, Gallagher thought. Fowler's hand was writ there. He was sure of it. "Fowler's in deep."

"What will we do?"

"Keep going," Gallagher said bitterly.

"You can't let him win!"

Gallagher gave her a quick glance, and smiled. "Listen to you. Quite the tigress."

"You've got to do something, Gordon."

How little she knew or understood about Fowler! Which was just as well. He couldn't tell her that Fowler would think nothing of endangering her, if Fowler thought it would help secure his cooperation.

"I'll do something," he said. "Fowler won't always have it his own way."

They drove on in silence, and went through Gap fifteen minutes ahead of the Brabus Mercedes.

"We've missed him," the driver said.

The Mercedes was waiting in a side road at the bottom of a climb, six kilometers outside Gap.

"Looks like it," the cold-eyed man said. He seemed unusually calm.

They'd been waiting over half an hour.

"We know which way he's headed," he went on. "We won't lose him, and he can't lose us. Let's go."

The Mercedes pulled into the main road and turned north for Grenoble.

Gallagher drove fast along the autoroute. They had got to Grenoble without incident and had passed Chambéry with still no signs of pursuit, despite a stop for petrol just after that. Annecy was now over to the right, as they sped past on the final leg. The border was only 50 kilometers away.

He glanced at the timer. 0220, it said. They'd

made good time. At this rate, they'd reach the customs post well before 3 o'clock.

Rhiannon had reclined her seat a little and was seemingly fast asleep.

"Rhiannon?" he called softly.

"Yes?" She sounded wide awake.

"I thought you were asleep. You've been quiet for the last hour."

"I thought I should give you time to work things out. I know you like to have periods of silence with the car. You use it as a sort of mobile thinking room."

He made no comment, driving on within his silence and thinking about what she had just said.

"I'm glad I met you," he told her after several minutes had passed.

Her hand rested on his thigh in the now-familiar message that was one of assurance, as well as her expression of absolute trust in him.

"Are we close to the border?" she asked.

"Less than fifty kilometers?"

"And no one's behind us?"

"Only the ordinary traffic, such as it is. But as we're passing everything in sight, we can hardly say they're following."

"As long as we're not caught for speeding."

"I'm not much over the limit, anyway. Even so, I doubt if we'd be stopped."

She raised the back of her seat. "Galbin? You really think he's waiting up there?"

"Your guess is as good as mine."

The cold-eyed man said: "Take the next exit."

The Brabus was just approaching Annecy. The driver glanced to his right, surprised.

"We're not going on?"

"We are, but not this way."

"But. . . ."

"Please do as I say. We'll cross at Chancy."

The driver turned off the autoroute and took the N508 to Bellegarde, 18 kilometers from Chancy.

0245. The Geneva border post.

Gallagher said: "Well . . . here we go." He began to slow down.

Rhiannon was sitting tensely in her seat. She had adjusted the back so that it was now bolt upright.

There were two cars up ahead. Not much of a queue, but a border guard was waving the *quattro* into another lane. A little man was standing outside the post at the end of that particular lane.

"Behold," Gallagher said. "Colonel Galbin."

"He doesn't look like much."

"Neither does a krait, but you wouldn't want to tangle with it. He usually has a big bruiser in tow; an ex-Legionnaire para called Lefevre. You definitely wouldn't want to meet *him* on a dark night."

He brought the car to a halt. Just beyond the post were the Swiss guards. So close. . . . The guard paused, hands on hips. Then he jerked an arm in an imperious, beckoning wave. Gallagher drove on, slowly. Rhiannon said, in an urgent whisper, as if the guard could hear: "You're not going to try to drive through!"

"And give them a chance to shoot? I'm not that crazy. But you never can tell. Borders are dodgy places these days. They always were, come to think of it. It only seems worse."

She looked about her anxiously, as if expecting a hail of bullets.

They drove slowly past the guard who looked stolidly at them.

Gallagher could now see Galbin's expression clearly. "He doesn't look very happy. You'd have thought he'd be gloating. Instead, he looks as if someone's spoiled his night out."

Gallagher brought the *quattro* to an unfussed halt, for the second time. Galbin was directly opposite his door. He lowered the window. Galbin came forward slowly, placed a hand on the roof, and looked down.

"Good evening, Monsieur Gallagher," Galbin began. "We meet again after all this time."

"Time flies, Colonel Galbin."

No get out of the car, get your hands up, or any such overtly hostile command. What the hell was going on?

"You have enjoyed yourself in France?"

"Very much, Colonel. Thank you."

"And the young lady?"

"She loves France." This was bloody bizarre.

Galbin, Gallagher thought, was looking more and more constipated, and his voice sounded as if he were trying to bite his words off before they escaped.

"I am very pleased," Galbin said. "France is a very beautiful country. We do not like it when people use it as a battleground. That privilege is reserved for us."

And now it came. Galbin's attempt at a joke was as real as his forced bonhomie.

But Galbin, to Gallagher's astonishment, was saying: "Well, Monsieur Gallagher, enjoy your holiday. Perhaps we shall see you in France again soon." It was almost a heartfelt plea. "Goodnight, Madame. Goodnight, Monsieur." He gave the roof of the car a single tap, and walked away.

Almost in a daze and expecting something deceitful from the little Colonel, Gallagher put the car into gear and drove off cautiously.

But nothing happened. They made it to the Swiss post. Their documents were quickly scrutinised and they were on their way again within less than a minute.

Gallagher gave a sigh of relief as they headed into the city, making for the autoroute to Lausanne.

Rhiannon was almost hysterical with her own sense of relief. "What happened? Why did he let you go? He looked as if it was the last thing he wanted."

"He's been leaned on. It's the only explanation."

"You've got that much pull?"

"Not me. Fowler. Fowler got Galbin's bosses to lean on him."

"So Fowler never really intended Galbin to get you after all."

"Don't sound so relieved. We're not out of the woods yet. Fowler went to a great deal of trouble to put Galbin on to me, only to pull the plug on the poor sod at the last moment. From my reading of the situation, that's even more bad news. He wanted me to leave France and he got me chased out, though perhaps not by the route he'd intended. He's given me a warning, showing me what he can do. The French must owe him a favor. Fowler can and will manipulate anyone to get what he wants."

"You're not going to let him get away with it, are you? Say you're not."

"I'll give him a fight, if that's what you mean."

Easier said than done, he didn't tell her.

"There's one other little problem we haven't solved," he said.

"What's that?"

"We still don't know who's been following us, and why. Somehow, I don't think those lights we saw before we stopped at the relais were Galbin's people. Perhaps I ought to go to the airport at Cointrin and put you on a plane home. It might be safer."

"Don't you dare," she said.

Despite everything, he was glad she didn't want to leave.

"Alright," he said. "We'll go up to Germany. I have an old friend who has a nice, secluded chalet in Bavaria. Haven't seen him for a while, but he's always been on to me to use it. Now's the time to take him up on the offer."

"Oh good! Our own bit of forest to make love in."

He smiled, and probed the *quattro* deep into the city.

The Brabus Mercedes was approaching the border at Chancy.

The cold-eyed man said: "Have your pistols ready, but keep them well out of sight. We don't want any shooting if we can possibly help it. While we might get the French, we don't need trouble with the Swiss as well."

The man in the back said: "Seems quiet." There were three cars and a lorry ahead of them, but nothing behind or coming up from la Joux, the village they had just passed through. "Will they have put any extra men here?"

"There must be nearly forty border crossings around Geneva. It would take a very big operation to seal them all effectively, and quickly, in the time they've had. They'll therefore concentrate on the main routes. That's why I decided we should come this way. We'll pick up the target again. Just be prepared for trouble here, if it should come."

The Mercedes had now stopped behind a big BMW with Swiss plates.

The driver said, idly: "What does TC on our plate mean?"

The cold-eyed man stared at him.

"You know these things," the driver said defensively.

"So should you."

"I'm not a team commander."

"Now will you ever be unless you're prepared to know your theater of operations."

"I didn't know Switzerland was part of the theater."

"*Everywhere* is a theater. But as we're carrying Swiss registration, it would help to know where we're supposed to have come from." The cold-eyed man turned briefly to the one in the back. "Do you know?"

"Ticino. The Italian canton in the south east." He sounded smug.

The driver said sarcastically: "Well done. I

hope they don't decide to check the numbers too closely."

"If they do," the cold-eyed man said, "you might have to do a little shooting, like the rest of us."

The driver said nothing. The lorry was crawling away and it was now the turn of the BMW. Behind the Mercedes, a small coach was drawing near. It seemed full of passengers.

The BMW was waved through to the Swiss post, where it was waved on. The Mercedes got a cursory glance and it, too, was waved on. The border guards were more interested in the coachload of people.

At the Swiss post, the Mercedes was again waved through.

"And so," the cold-eyed man said, "Switzerland. We'll change again to Norwegian plates at a suitable distance from this area."

"They had a couple of special police," the man in the back said. "I saw them in the shadows."

"So did I. They obviously decided to cover everywhere, but gave priority to the main routes, as I thought they would. I hope they have a pleasant wait." The cold-eyed man made a sound that could have been a short laugh; but there was no humor in it.

0330, the main Geneva border post.

Galbin was looking like a man who already knew he'd lost twice.

"Check all the posts," he said to Lefevre. "Find out if any German-registered blue Mercedes has tried to sneak through."

"We would have been informed. . . ."

"Don't argue with me! Just do it!"

Lefevre went to the office that had been rigged as a communications and co-ordination center, to run the checks. A small computer with printer had been fed all the information on Mercedes sightings at the various posts, with their license numbers.

Lefevre said to the programmer: "Anything?"

The man, a CRS officer in partial combat gear, shook his head.

Lefevre said: "Call me up all Mercedes sightings within the last forty-five minutes."

The man tapped a few keys and a list, by time, position and nationality, came on-screen. Lefevre studied it carefully. There were thirty-nine. Most of them had come through on the autoroute.

"I never thought blue was such a popular color," Lefevre said drily. "Can you give me a model breakdown?"

"Yes," the man said and tapped a few more keys.

The list, suitably amended, came up again.

"Delete the coupés and sportscars."

Again the list came up. This time, it had shrunk to twenty.

"Now give me the last half hour."

The list was now fifteen. Lefevre stared at it, thinking. Something was showing up, but he didn't know what.

"Let's see the German cars."

Five Germans, but a constant had disappeared.

"Let's see the license districts." When that came up, he read aloud: " 'M—München, HH—Haupstadt Hamburg, EI—Eichstatt, Nü—Nürenberg, Nü—Nürenberg.' Must be traveling together and anyway, they came through here. No MZ for Mainz anywhere. Try the full fifteen again. Thanks. Let's see now . . . wait a minute. I said fifteen. You've given me sixteen."

"Late entry," the man said.

"Anyway, it's Swiss," Lefevre said, disappointed.

He paused. Something was calling to him. What the devil was it? Galbin wanted answers. Without them, anyone was a target for his wrath. Lefevre sometimes got tired of being the nearest. If he could come up with a clue. . . .

"Go back to the full list," he said, "then run through to the last fifteen minutes. I want to see what happens to the Germans."

The Germans had disappeared, but a blue Mercedes had passed through the one point where no others had. Chancy. But it was Swiss.

"What's this one at Chancy?"

"The late entry," the programmer replied. He stared at Lefevre. "But it's Swiss."

"I know, I know. It can't be possible . . . but the timing's about right."

The man continued to stare at him. "You believe they *changed* plates?"

"These people are professionals. Who knows? I'll have to tell the boss. I hope I'm wrong, because it would mean we've lost them and all this has been for nothing. It won't help his temper."

"Better you than me."

"Thanks," Lefevre said drily and went out to give the bad tidings.

"Check with Chancy," Galbin said quietly when Lefevre had told him. "Ask them to describe the car in detail, and its occupants."

Lefevre returned to the communications office and got the programmer to call Chancy. The programmer fed the information into the computer as it came through on his headset.

Lefevre watched the words come on-screen, not liking what he saw. When the call was finished, the programmer turned to him.

"Were those the men?"

"Powerful car . . . three tough-looking men. They could have been genuine Swiss; soldiers on leave, maybe. But I've got a feeling in my gut, and I don't like it one little bit. I'll lay bets we'll not hear from them again . . . not in France, anyway."

"Are you going to tell him?"

"Can you give me a print-out of everything we've just done?"

"Easily."

"Then I'll take that, let him read it, *then* tell him what I think has happened."

"It's your neck. Just give me a moment and I'll have it set up."

The CRS man ran the program and set it to print. It didn't take long. The programmer ripped off the two sheets of print-out and handed them over.

"You could be wrong," he said to Lefevre, "and that could put you into deeper water with your boss."

Lefevre said: "I've hunted men long enough to recognize the signs. If I had corns, they'd be itching."

"Good luck," the programmer said as Lefevre turned to go.

He grinned without pleasure. "I may need it."

Galbin studied the print-out in total silence,

then listened as Lefevre put forward his theory. Galbin still did not speak. Instead, he turned to stare at the near-empty swathe of road, the flimsy sheets still in his hand.

"Perhaps we should tell the Swiss," Lefevre suggested tentatively.

Another minute of silence passed. At last, Galbin turned round, eyes malicious.

"No," he said, in the same quiet voice he'd used previously. "They're after Gallagher. Let them find him. Perhaps, with luck, they'll succeed in killing him. Get him out of my hair." He smiled suddenly.

Lefevre could not remember having seen such an ugly grimace upon his superior's features.

"Fowler would not like that," Galbin continued. "And our friend Gallagher . . . least of all." He turned to look at the road once more. "Tell the men to pack up."

The eyes went dead, the lips tightened; then he wheeled, and stumped out.

Gallagher passed a swift glance over the timer. 0400. A quick scrutiny of the mirrors showed only the continuing sparse traffic well into the distance and retreating. Nothing coming up fast.

He still felt the uneasiness that had begun on the beach at Pampelonne. All his instincts told him the pursuit was still on. Galbin had only been part of the picture. Galbin was now neutralised; but there were others. He was sure of it.

"We'll have an early breakfast just before we get to Basel," he said to Rhiannon, "and fill up with petrol. Then it's non-stop till we get to Ingolstadt."

"Is that where your friend is?"

He nodded. "We should make it by 9:30, give or take a few minutes. Once in Germany, we'll really be able to put on some speed."

She glanced behind. "There doesn't seem to be anyone following."

"For the moment."

She looked at him worriedly, but made no comment.

At five-thirty, they stopped for a hot coffee and hot roll breakfast and to fill up the tank. During the refuelling, Gallagher carefully studied the vehicles that came in, but still saw nothing to overtly cause concern. His personal antennae, however, continued to quiver.

They drove on through Basel and crossed into Germany where the unrestricted autobahn allowed Gallagher to push the speed up to a cruise of 200 kilometers an hour. Roughly equivalent to 125 mph, this was well within the car's maximum of 165, giving him more than enough reserves with which to cope with the unforeseen, while cutting down the transit time to Ingolstadt.

On this the first leg to Freiburg, he took the speed to 130 mph, as the day prepared itself for sunrise.

The small BMW with the Geneva plates had reported the *quattro*'s departure from that city. It had not attempted to follow. Just past the Solothurn interchange 32 kilometers north of Bern, another BMW, this time with the ZH index letters denoting a Zurich registration, had also observed the passage of the black car.

Like its sister BMW, it had not attempted to follow.

Half an hour after Gallagher had crossed into Germany the Brabus Mercedes, now carrying Basel-Stadt plates, followed.

Early September

8

The Freiburg exit came up well before six o'clock, because of their high cruising speed.

"At this rate," Gallagher said as he turned off the autobahn, "we'll make it even earlier than I thought."

He intended to take the non-autobahn route to the Donauschingen interchange. It would mean 60 or so kilometers of slower road, but they would be able to make up for lost time on the autobahn north to Stuttgart. Then it would be right on the E11 for Munich and Ingolstadt; fast roads all the way until the Ingolstadt exit. He wondered if their unseen pursuers would follow.

His glance in the mirrors showed no car frantically scurrying off the autobahn in his wake.

Rhiannon said: "Would they really have followed us all the way through France, through Switzerland, and now into Germany?"

"That depends," he told her, still unsure of the reasons for pursuit. "They may be after the same thing as Fowler, or it may be something else entirely. They're a mystery to me, as are their reasons. It all depends on how fast they're prepared to go to get whatever it is they're after. All I know is that I haven't got it."

"Or what they're prepared to do," Rhiannon added quietly, suddenly glancing round, as if expecting to see someone traveling bumper to bumper with them.

"I'm confusing the trail as much as possible. If they did follow us this far, they'll think we're heading north toward Aachen and into Belgium, to take the ferry home. If it's Fowler's people, however, they'll know I won't go back until I'm good and ready. They *might* think we're coming this way, but I doubt it."

"They don't know about your friend?"

"They know about him," Gallagher said thoughtfully, ". . . well, Fowler might, if he digs deeply enough into the files."

"This . . . person . . . it is someone you've worked with before? Is that why you think Fowler might know?"

"It was some time ago. He might not make the connection."

"But what if he does?"

Gallagher gave a brief grin. "There are no Galbins here to set on me."

Rhiannon smiled. "In that case, I'm looking forward to our little forest." She leaned forward to glance up at the lightening sky. "It's going to be a nice warm day for the first of September." The glance paused upon him, turned again to survey the rear window, before settling upon him once more. "And if there are no interruptions, I'll make it hot for you."

"Promises, promises," he said.

* * *

The Brabus Mercedes had pulled into the Bühl petrol station on the autobahn, just before the Baden-Baden exit. This had put it 95 kilometers beyond Gallagher's own exit at Freiburg. The driver and the cold-eyed man were standing a little way from the car, while the one from the back seat attended to the refuelling.

"We've lost him again," the driver said. "Since we left the Swiss border I've been cruising at 200 kilometers. Not even a sighting in the distance. He's got to stop for petrol somewhere."

"His car is very fast," the cold-eyed man said, "and he knows how to handle it."

"Even allowing for that, he's not exactly invisible. We know he left Switzerland."

"We'll find him again." The cold-eyed man seemed unperturbed.

"We can't ask at every petrol station, and we can't cover every road in Germany with spotter cars. . . ."

"We'll find him again." The cold-eyed man's interruption had been delivered in a hard voice that brooked no further argument. He walked away from the driver and back toward the car. Refuelling had been completed.

He re-entered the Mercedes as his colleagues went off to pay for the petrol. The driver joined him silently.

"We'll take the Baden-Baden exit," the cold-eyed man said, "and find ourselves a little back road. We need a change of plates." The car still sported its Ticino registration. "And before you ask why we're leaving the autobahn, we know he has not gone on to Karlsruhe on his way north; at least, not by autobahn, or the spotter would have seen him. We must assume he's no longer traveling on the faster roads for the moment."

"The spotter at Karslruhe is our last one until the others come up."

"It will make things a trifle difficult," the cold-eyed man admitted, "but not impossible. We must be fluid in the execution of the mission."

"But he could have got off anywhere."

"You do like to argue, don't you? Or is it because you are unhappy with the mission? Would you like me to replace you?"

The driver's own highly developed sense of survival picked up the threat swiftly. Replacement would be rather more than simply that.

"We are encouraged to think independently," he said. "My words were not meant as criticism. I was, if you like, thinking aloud."

The cold-eyed man seemed to give the apology deep consideration.

"You are a good driver," he said at last. "One of the best. I personally requested you. Keep to the driving. I'll do the rest."

The man from the back seat returned, and climbed in.

"Let's go," the cold-eyed man said.

The Mercedes left the petrol station and a few kilometers later, it turned off for Baden-Baden where they later found a deserted road on the outskirts.

The cold-eyed man pressed a hidden switch beneath his seat. A flush-fitting panel beneath the rear seat sprang open on the right hand side. He pressed another switch and this time, a left hand panel sprang open. Both he and the man in the back got out quickly.

Within the secret cavities were the license plates of several nations, so well fashioned that they were indistinguishable from the real thing. Their method of fixing was by tiny but powerful electro-magnets which were switched off for release. The plates themselves were fitted with dummy studs to match exactly the various fixing patterns of the different countries. The recesses in the seat were scanner shielded.

When the car set off again, it once more carried German plates. This time, the index letter was S for Stuttgart.

Gallagher pulled into the Edenbergen station just outside Augsburg, to make a phone call. Fifteen kilometers further was the Dasing exit for Ingolstadt. He parked the *quattro* nose-on to a row of yellow telephone boxes.

He studied the immediate area carefully before climbing out.

"Won't be long," he said to Rhiannon as he left.

Two of the boxes were occupied; one by an American soldier in fatigues. Gallagher could see his small, drab-colored supply truck parked a short distance away. Another soldier was in the cab. Perhaps they had broken down.

Gallagher wrote him off as a possible threat. The soldier was very young and looked exceptionally green. Hardly an assassin in disguise. But he remained aware of both soldiers, just in case. The other booth was taken by a young girl who seemed more interested in the soldier than in the call she was supposed to be making.

Gallagher went into the box he had chosen, three along from the girl's. He had a good view of the parking area. He could also see if anyone interesting came off the autobahn. He inserted five Deutschmarks in one-mark units and dialed the number he wanted.

He leaned against one side of the cubicle and glanced round as if casually, while waiting for the digits to sort themselves out. Rhiannon smiled at him from the *quattro*. The soldier was still talking, the young girl definitely trying to give him the eye; but he seemed too preoccupied to care. The second soldier in the cab of the waiting lorry was now reading what looked like a glossy magazine.

Then a voice was saying: *"Ja? Hier ist Talheim."*

Gallagher said, in English: "Greywolf."

An exclamation came down the line. *"Lieber Gott . . . !"* Pause. "Is that really you?"

"Of course it's me."

"My God. For four years I hear nothing, now this! Where are you? In Germany?"

"Not only in Germany, but in Bavaria. Very close, in fact. I'm at the Edenbergen service station."

"On my doorstep!"

"Practically."

"Then naturally, you must stay with us."

"No questions, Freddy?"

"Why ask questions when I am soon to see you?"

"Pragmatic as ever. Oh by the way, I've got company."

"Female, of course."

"Of course."

A cheery laugh exploded in Gallagher's ear. "The kind of company we like, eh? You know of course this will break Eva's heart? I am only the second choice."

Eva was Talheim's wife and if nobody else could see the sun shining out of every orifice in his body, it was not for want of trying. To say that Eva Talheim was in love with her Freddy was to say that Isolde had a passing fancy for Tristan; or that Juliet saw Romeo as a one-night stand. She was crazy about him.

"And pigs fly," Gallagher said.

Another laugh. "So how long will you be?"

"As fast as it takes."

"So. You have a fast car?"

"Pretty fast."

"Alright. It is now eight o'clock. I will see you perhaps in forty-five minutes. *Ja?*"

"About then."

"You know where we are."

"Yes. See you, Freddy."

" 'wiedersehen, Greywolf."

Gallagher replaced the receiver thoughtfully, then left the phone box. No one to cause alarm had come into the parking area. The soldier had finished his call, but had been accosted by the girl. Perhaps she wanted a lift.

"Was it alright?" Rhiannon asked as he took his seat behind the wheel.

"It was fine. He was there, and is expecting us."

"Wasn't it too early?"

"Early? Freddy and Eva get up with the lark.

Outdoor types, those two. Or used to be. They now run a restaurant, so perhaps they've changed. Anyway, running a business like that still means getting up early."

"And who's Eva? Someone you used to know?"

"Miaow," he said. "Eva is Freddy's wife, and they're crazy about each other. You'll like her."

"A blonde, Bavarian goddess, I'll bet."

"No. A raven-haired Czech goddess. Ouch! That hurt."

She had pinched him. "Serves you right."

He grinned at her as he started the car and headed for the autobahn.

As it left, the girl turned from the soldier to stare at it speculatively.

"No point thinking about it," the soldier said. *"He* wouldn't have given you a lift. He's got someone with him. She wouldn't have let him."

"It is a very nice car." The girl was German.

"I'm sorry I can't give you a lift. Regulations."

"You are going to München. I am going to München. What is difficult?"

"Regulations," the green young soldier repeated. "But if you'd like, I'll come back in a car."

The girl was skeptical, scornful. "I must wait until you go to München and back? *Komisch!* I will get a lift soon."

"Look. Let me talk to my buddy. Perhaps we can think of something. We've got to wait for another truck that's broken down. Why don't we have a coffee while we wait? I'll buy you breakfast if you'd like."

The girl, who knew she'd hooked her fish, said with apparent reluctance: "OK."

* * *

The first time Talheim had spoken to Gallagher of Ingolstadt, he had called it the city of famous names. As Gallagher now manoeuvred the *quattro* through the narrow cobbled streets of the Altstadt—the older nucleus of the city itself—he had to agree. He had never seen such a high concentration of streets honoring poets, writers, composers and philosophers, and other historical superstars. Schiller, Goethe, Wagner, Hindenburg—they were all there.

He stopped the car in a narrow cul-de-sac on one side of Talheim's coffee shop restaurant. The coffee shop was on the ground floor and was very popular with the older teens. At the moment, however, it was not yet open for custom. He had reversed in, just in case a hurried departure became necessary.

"This is it," Gallagher said as he cut the engine. "Not even nine o'clock."

"You've been driving for nearly twenty-four hours. You must be tired. Are you alright?"

"I'm fine. I'll probably go out like a light later on though. Well? What do you think of Ingolstadt?"

She had been looking about her during their drive through town. "It's lovely in this part."

"There are lots of nice places around here and as for out in the country. . . ."

"Gordon!" she interrupted in a rising whisper full of urgency.

His head had been turned, checking behind her seat for loose articles in the rear footwell. The tenseness in her voice made him look quickly round, straightening in his seat.

A tall, well-built man with neat blond hair was approaching the car slowly. He had a slight limp and favored the left leg as he walked. He was dressed in an open-necked white shirt and dark trousers.

"This one's on our side," Gallagher said to her. "You're looking at Hans-Joachim Georg-Friedrich, the Count von Eugen-Talheim. In a fit of egalitarianism he decided to dispense with the 'von.'"

"*Three* double-barrelled names?"

"He is a Count," Gallagher answered, as if that explained it all.

"What's a German Count doing running a restaurant?"

"Which is what his family's been wanting to know for years; but I can only give you his own reply: Why not? The family were not all that happy about his marrying a Czech either; but that mattered little to him. You will have gathered that Freddy doesn't always do what others would like him to."

"I think I can understand why you two get on."

"Are you trying to say I'm the same?"

"Why don't you ask Fowler?" She was smiling. "I'm glad you make life difficult for him."

As long as he doesn't make life even more difficult for us.

Gallagher did not voice his thoughts. Talheim had reached the car and was looking pleased to see them. Gallagher climbed out, and they shook hands warmly.

"Four bloody years," Talheim said. "Well

... you're looking fit." He spoke English with an Oxbridge accent, but with Germanic inflections.

"You don't look so bad yourself."

Talheim's very deep blue eyes were full of wry humor. "Ah . . . but I collected a limp since we last saw each other."

"So I've noticed. What happened?"

"I didn't get out of the way fast enough. Some patch of foreign field has a sliver of Talheim bone."

"Does it hurt much?"

"Only when I try to run. Actually, there's very little pain. Twinges at odd times. I can walk without the limp when the occasion warrants it."

"So you're still in. . . ."

"Time to talk later. You must introduce me to that lovely young lady you're hiding in your powerful machine." Talheim gave the roof of the *quattro* an appreciative stroke. "Very nice." He pulled Gallagher's opened door wider and poked his head into the car. "Hello. I am Freddy, and I can see why Gordon is hiding you from me." He stuck out his hand and grinned at her.

"Rhiannon," she said as they shook hands.

"Ah! The name of legend. Gordon is a very lucky man."

"Thank you. Keep telling him that." She smiled at him.

"And she has a wonderful smile. Gordon, I shall keep her."

"You've already got a wife, you old wreck."

Talheim sighed. "There you are, my dear Rhiannon. He has reined me in. Come. Come and meet Eva."

The morning sun was already warm, but it had not yet penetrated the cool shade of the cul-de-sac. They walked into a pleasant rise in temperature as they rounded the front of the building.

"How did you know we were the ones arriving?" Rhiannon asked of Talheim.

"I heard the car. That sound, I thought, could only be Gordon's car. I know what pleases this man."

"Oh," she began innocently. "You'll have to tell me all about his murky past."

Talheim feigned horror. "Not for ears such as yours, my dear."

"With friends like this," Gallagher said, "enemies I don't need."

"You poor, poor man," Talheim said unrepentantly. "Here you are, my dears. In you go."

Eva Talheim was tall and willowy with rich black hair, high cheekbones, and the palest of skins. Her eyes were great pools of jet, her smile ravishing.

"Gordon!" she squealed as they entered. She pronounced the last syllable of his name as it was written. "Freddy would not tell me." She glanced reproachfully at her husband before hurrying forward to press her entire body against Gallagher and to kiss him fully on the mouth. "He would not say who was on the telephone."

"What can a poor husband do?" Talheim said good-naturedly to Rhiannon.

"Hmm," Rhiannon said.

Eva smacked Gallagher on the shoulder. "Four years! You should have shame. Not once do you come to see us." Her English was a mixture of Czech and German overtones spiced with American.

"I sent you cards," Gallagher offered lamely.

"Cards!" Cards were dismissed as being of little consequence.

"This is Rhiannon," Gallagher said quickly, feeling heat between his shoulder blades.

The dark eyes turned to Rhiannon. "A very beautiful woman, Gordon," Eva said going up to her. "He is a very lucky man," she continued to Rhiannon. "Does he deserve you, you think?"

Slightly unnerved by the approach, Rhiannon said: "That's for him. . . ."

"Ha! Never give a man such decisions. Only you can decide." Eva grinned suddenly, and kissed Rhiannon on both cheeks. "Welcome to Ingolstadt. Pay no attention to me. Freddy calls me his crazy Czech. Perhaps I am."

"Well. . . ."

"Don't deny it. Of course I am. I am married to a crazy German. Come. You have been driving for a long time, I think, so you will want to freshen yourself. We keep a small apartment here for when we are too late to go home. It has a bath *zimmer* . . . room? . . . yes, a bathroom. We will leave those two for now, then we shall have breakfast."

She led a bewildered Rhiannon out.

"She'll be alright," Talheim said.

"I'm sure she will."

Talheim looked about him. They were in the coffee shop. The chairs were up-ended upon the tables. The polished wooden floor gleamed. Within the confines of the building, Gallagher could hear snatches of conversation in German and the sounds of movement as Talheim's staff prepared for the day's business. The smell of freshly baked pastries and bread filled the place.

"Let's go upstairs," Talheim said. "The tables have all been laid, and it will be quieter. No one will come up for a while."

They went up the bare but polished wooden stairs and found themselves a corner that gave them a view of the small cobbled square at the front of the building. Any car entering it would be in full view.

Talheim said: "Now, Gordon. What's the real reason?"

"We're on holiday."

"And?"

"No 'and.'"

"Take a good look at me. You see a thirty-six-year-old man . . . not a thirty-six-minute infant. Of course there is an 'and.'"

"We really are on holiday. We'd like to use your chalet by the river for a week or so . . . if that's alright with you."

"You have an open invitation to use the chalet. You know that. But I think . . . I *know* there's more." The deep blue eyes looked at Gallagher unwaveringly. "I am always glad to hear from you, Gordon. But a phone call early in the morning when you're only a few kilometers away. . . . After four years? Are you back in the business? I thought you had left for good."

"I have."

"Then?"

"Sometimes, it is difficult to shake off the past."

Talheim nodded sympathetically. "I can understand that."

"You as well?"

"From time to time, they ask me to do a little consultation. . . ."

"Consultation," Gallagher said drily.

"*Ja*. That's what they like to call it. Eva, of course, hates when that happens."

"I don't blame her."

"Did you get the leg on one of those 'consultations'?"

Again, Talheim nodded. "*Ja*. She was not very pleased." He smiled. "And Rhiannon? Does she know about what you used to do?"

"She knows. Not details, of course. But she got involved in a job the Department threw at me. That's how I met her. She was a completely innocent bystander, if such beings exist. These days, the lines get blurred. Innocent bystanders get it in the neck all the time."

"And now something new has happened and you want to keep her safe."

Gallagher nodded. "We really were on holiday when this blew up. Literally." He related all that had occurred since Pampelonne, with the important exception of Borodin and Windshear.

"And you have no idea what they're after?"

"None at all." Which was true enough.

"You'll need some help."

"No. All I want is your chalet for a while."

"What if those people succeed in finding you?"

"Then I don't want you in the crossfire. Eva would never forgive me if anything happened to you. I feel badly enough as it is, bringing this your way."

"Nonsense. You helped me to bring Eva out. I can never repay you."

"We've had this out before. You owe me absolutely nothing; and we agreed not to bring that up again."

Talheim raised his hands briefly in surrender. "Alright, alright. But I still think you need help. There are some good weapons at the chalet." He smiled sheepishly. "Even now, I do not like to be unprepared. I also think I shall come up from time to time . . . to fish. There's a good reach by the chalet."

"To fish," Gallagher repeated sceptically.

"Of course." Talheim grinned. "What else?"

"I appreciate. . . ."

"Then we shall say no more about it. No. No more arguments, Gordon. Rhiannon must be kept safe. I heard about what happened to Lauren Tanner. . . ."

"How?"

"Some of my lines of communication are still open. I'm very sorry about what happened. You cannot afford to lose this girl as well."

"As if I don't know."

"So. You need help, and I shall give it. Understood?"

"Freddy. . . ."

"Understood?"

Gallagher nodded, at last accepting defeat.

"Good," Talheim said. "I shall not interfere. I shall merely be on hand to lend assistance if it's needed. Now let's arrange your accommodation for the night. You can stay here in the town apartment, or you can come up to the house with us tonight. We shall be finishing early. As you've been driving since yesterday, use the apartment anyway if you'd like to sleep after we've had breakfast."

"Thanks. I think I'll do that. First, I'm taking the car off the streets. I'm going to take it to the people who modified it, for a routine check. I'll leave it there till we're ready to go back to England."

"They're in Ingolstadt, these people?"

"Yes. In Kälberschuttstrasse. I'll borrow an ordinary car from them for the period."

"If they haven't one available, you can borrow mine. It's not a powerhouse like yours, but it's quite serviceable."

"And what will you do for transport?"

"We've got another. Now let's go down to breakfast before Eva comes looking." As they went down, Talheim continued: "When you announced yourself as Greywolf, you gave me quite a shock. I thought you'd gone back into the business." The blue eyes regarded Gallagher calmly. "In or not, you're still Greywolf, I think. It's still in you. My family, as you know, have hunting grounds in the forests of this region. I was brought up to understand the instincts of the hunter and hunted. You were always the most instinctive of hunters, even when you were being pursued." Talheim gave a short laugh. "I ought to know. I've seen you at it. Oh yes. You are still Greywolf. That will never change. I would not like to have you on my tail. It is little wonder that Fowler hates losing you."

"I think she's in love with you," Rhiannon said thoughtfully.

"Wrong," he said.

They were lying in bed in the Talheim apartment. It was four in the afternoon. After breakfast, Gallagher had taken the car to the Treser people who had originally worked their magic on it and had left it there. They had lent him a substitute, a small saloon that was unobtrusive, but which had also had its engine transformed. It would do.

He had returned to the cobbled square and on entering the apartment, had discovered he needed to sleep. Both he and Rhiannon had gone to bed and had succumbed. Now at four, they had come awake; then she had greeted him with those words.

"Wrong," he said again.

She leaned across him, her body hot against his, her breasts spreading warmly upon his chest.

She rubbed herself against him. "You deny it?"

"Absolutely."

She went into her squirming act once more. "Sounds like guilt to me."

"If you keep doing that," he warned, "I won't be responsible for my actions."

"Why do you think I'm doing it?"

"What if. . . ."

"She comes in? Serves her right."

He stared at her. "You're never jealous."

"Who me? Whatever gave you that idea?" The golden eyes looked into his. "She told me about how you and Freddy got her out."

"Eva talks too much. . . ."

"Shhh! Don't interrupt . . . or I'll do this." She squirmed.

"Ooh," he said.

"What's the matter. Don't you like it?" Her smile teased him.

"You know the answer to that."

"I can feel it. Are you going to behave until I've finished what I've got to say?"

"Do I have a choice?"

"No."

"Thought you'd say that."

"Eva said," she continued, eyes fixed upon him, "that you didn't have to help. It was a personal thing for Freddy. He'd had no official backup. You waited at the border, on the German side, to give him cover in case he ran into trouble. . . ."

"Even then," Gallagher said, "the Czech border guards were trigger-happy. They used to shoot at people in Germany. A few hikers have been shot at and wounded, and one or two killed. Freddy wanted me there to keep any nosey guards' heads down. Hardly tough work."

"But it didn't go like that, did it? Freddy got caught in the wire, just as a patrol turned up. They started shooting at him. Although Eva was safely across by then and Freddy called to you to leave with her, you went to get him out. The way she tells it, it sounds horrific. The guards were firing all the time and running toward the spot while you and Freddy struggled to get him free of the wire. She still can't understand how both of you made it without being killed."

"Luck," he said. "It was a very dark night."

"Rubbish. You're her big hero, you know."

"Freddy's the real hero. He got chewed up by that wire, and never once did he cry out. You ought to see his back some time. It looks as if he escaped from a shark."

"She says you killed three of the guards. . . ."

"They didn't leave me much choice."

"I wish you didn't have to do that kind of thing anymore."

"I don't. . . ."

She kissed him suddenly. "Let's not talk about it." Her squirming had gained a new intensity. Then she was straddling him and her upper body was rising high in the bed.

They were well insulated from the restaurant, and few sounds reached them. Despite the warmth of the day, they had kept the bedroom windows closed, to keep their own sounds in.

He felt her descend upon him, and the furnace within her seemed to completely take him over.

"I love you," she whispered repeatedly with increasing urgency until at last with a sharp cry, she collapsed upon him.

Her body gave a tiny shudder of pleasure as he stroked her gently. He would keep her safe.

The Brabus Mercedes had been all the way to Munich, and now it was heading back. The spotter car at Karlsruhe had seen nothing so the cold-eyed man had ordered the driver to take the Munich autobahn. But that had proved fruitless, despite having taken the blue car to near its maximum speed.

They were passing a lay-by just before the Adelshausen exit, when the cold-eyed man glanced across the other carriage-way.

"Take the next exit," he commanded the driver quickly.

"What. . . ."

"Just do it! When you've managed that, get back on to the autobahn, heading back for Munich, then pull into that parking lot across the way. I've seen something."

The driver complied, screeching the car off the autobahn and screeching it back on again. Two kilometers later, he pulled into the parking area. There were a couple of cars whose drivers had pulled in for a rest. One of the drivers had reclined his seat and was fast asleep. Further along, were two US Army trucks. Two soldiers were leaning against one of them. Another soldier was poking beneath the second one.

As the driver slowed the Mercedes down, he said: "Two cars and two army trucks...."

"Stop by the trucks," the cold-eyed man said.

"The *trucks?*"

"Don't worry about these soldiers. They're just supply men. No trouble at all if they get awkward."

"I wasn't worried about them. But why the trucks?"

"We passed them some time ago. They've been on this road for quite a while. They may have seen something. Right. Stop here."

The cold-eyed man got out and began to walk toward the trucks. The two lounging soldiers had straightened and were looking at him with wary interest.

He stopped before them, and smiled. "Good afternoon," he said in English, speaking with a Germanic-American accent.

"Good afternoon," one of the soldiers replied. "Can I help you, sir?"

"I hope so," the cold-eyed man said. He thought he detected a touch of guilt in the soldiers' expressions. The one beneath the other truck had paused to look. "I am looking for someone," he went on, and heard a sudden gasp from the cab of the closest truck. He immediately realized what was worrying the soldiers. He wanted to laugh.

They thought him a *policeman*. The gasp in the truck had come from a woman. He decided to use the knowledge.

Before either of them knew what was happening, he reached for the cab door handle and yanked the door open. A young girl stared at him from the embrace of another soldier. She was partially undressed.

The man gave them the benefit of a long stare before slamming the door shut. By now, the engineer soldier had crawled out from beneath his own truck, looking greasy. He stared at the man.

The cold-eyed man said: "I hope you all realize she's under age." He enjoyed the look of sudden fear in their faces. "But I can overlook that if you can be of assistance to me. Use all your powers of recall. It might help you." He waited to let his words sink in. "I am looking for a black car," he went on. "It's a very distinctive one. Once seen, you're hardly likely to forget it . . . if you try hard enough. There are two people in it. A man, and a woman. . . ."

"I've seen that car, sir," came an eager voice from the cab. The young soldier was getting hurriedly down, adjusting his clothes. "We were waiting for our buddy here, back up the road. His truck was giving some trouble. We saw the car . . . that is, I saw it and . . . and the young . . . er . . . lady in there. . . ." His voice died uncertainly.

The man said, in German: "Is that correct, Miss? Did you see that car?"

Her head rose slowly above the door to look out at him. She was completely unrepentant.

"Yes," she answered. "It is as he says."

"Do your parents know where you are?"

"What business is that of yours?"

"I can make it my business," the cold-eyed man lied, "but I am after bigger game."

"You policemen are all pigs!" She screamed in English.

The soldiers looked alarmed, clearly fearing possible criminal charges.

The cold-eyed man looked at the young soldier, then at the girl. "You two had better tell me all you know. I might forget what I've just seen."

"Don't trust him!" the girl said; which was good advice, if for the wrong reasons. "Never trust a policeman."

"I'll help you, sir," the young soldier said quickly. "I saw as much as she did."

"Du kerl!" the girl shouted at the soldier.

"He was making a phonecall," the soldier began, ignoring the girl. "I saw that too."

"Was he now," the cold-eyed man said softly. "Alright. I want to know everything. *Everything.*"

The soldier told all he knew, to the accompaniment of a string of German expletives from the girl.

When it was all over, the cold-eyed man said: "Thank you for your help. If I were you, I'd get rid of her as soon as you can."

"Yes, *sir!* Thank you, sir!"

The cold-eyed man walked slowly back to the Brabus. He did not smile as he heard the soldier say to the girl: "Right. We're leaving you here...."

"What?" came an outraged screech. "You cannot do this!"

"I'm sorry, but you've...."

"You Yankee shit! You bastard...."

"I'm not a Yankee. I come from...."

"*All* Amis are bastards!" the girl screamed.

The sleeping motorist, woken by the noise, peered up to have a look, and promptly went back to sleep.

The cold-eyed man entered the Brabus.

"What's going on?" the driver asked.

"They picked up that girl. . . ."

"You mean. . . ."

"Of course I mean. They were at it, or very close when I went up to them. They mistook me for a policeman and as I did not point out their mistake, co-operation was easily achieved. They have seen the car."

"Ah!"

The cold-eyed man related what the young soldier had said.

"He could be well on his way to Austria by now," the man in the back suggested.

"Possibly," the cold-eyed man said. "But I think not. He made a phone call from the Edenbergen autobahn services. Why make a call to Austria from there? He could have done that from France, or Switzerland, any time he chose. I think he made a local call. We'll concentrate on an area within a 100 kilometer radius from Munich, but not taking in the southeast where it crosses the Austrian border."

"That's still a lot of area," the man in the back said.

"The others will be here to help us. I'll call them in."

"And if we find nothing?"

"We draw another circle, this time centered on Nürnberg. I am convinced he is in the area. We'll just have to work at it. That's what we're here for." He pulled out a detailed map from the door panel and studied it carefully before returning it to its hiding place. I'll put a car each at Augsburg, Ingolstadt, and Landshut, working within a 50-kilometer radius from each point. The circles will sometimes overlap, giving extra coverage. We'll take Munich and the rest. We'll flush him out."

"How long do you give it?"

"If he is in there, three days should do . . . working round the clock. Alright. Let's get going."

The Brabus roared past the trucks on its way back onto the autobahn.

The girl was still screaming at the soldiers. She had not left the truck.

Moscow, the same day, 1900 hours.

The black limousine cruised at high speed along the empty outside lane, swooshing past lesser vehicles. In the dying light of the day it gleamed darkly, and those who saw it knew there was someone important inside. Only VIP's used that lane.

In the back, Skoryatin relaxed as the car sped him toward his destination. Next to him was Natalia Kamapova. They were both in uniform.

"I am very privileged to be accompanying you to such an important meeting, General," she said. The classic face gave him an almost regal smile. There was a freshly scrubbed look about her, as if she had recently stepped out of a bath: but she'd been working all day, as Skoryatin well knew.

"If you're going to be permanently on my staff," he said benignly, "you may as well come in at the deep end. We do not carry passengers. Your work over the past three months has impressed me. I have every confidence in your ability to cope with the situation."

"Thank you, General."

"Do not thank me, my dear child. You've earned it."

She gave him a smile of pleasure, and the remainder of the short journey was made in silence.

The street lights had come on by the time they had arrived at the venue for the meeting: an anonymous, architecturally ugly building behind a black iron fence. The car drove slowly through the open maw of massive iron gates that shut immediately behind it.

Skoryatin looked at Kamapova. "If I didn't know better," he began lightheartedly, "I'd say those gates make me feel as if we are never going to get out again. The KGB, of course, would like that very much. Eh?" He laughed suddenly at the expression on her face. "A joke, my dear Kamapova. A little joke. There are as many of our people here as there are KGB. It would be very expensive for them if they were foolish enough to try anything. Do you know what this place is?"

"No. No, General." The beautiful face looked at him questioningly.

"We call it neutral ground. When we wish to discuss matters in a semi-official manner. We come here. Many problems get solved in this way. It's a useful place. It is not our building; neither is it theirs."

"Do these meetings always work, General?"

"Not always. But then, nothing else in this world of ours works all the time. The man we're going to see. . . ."

Kamapova dared to interrupt. "I'll . . . I'll be sitting in with *you*, General?" The eyes were wide with uncertain surprise.

"I thought it would be a good way to start you off. You clearly expected to be left outside the discussion chamber. Is that it?"

"Yes, General. I thought. . . ."

"Do not worry. The KGB won't feel deprived. I've given them advance warning of your presence. They'll also have an aide for Ulvanov. I was going to tell you about him."

The car had stopped, and the driver awaited Skoryatin's order to get out and open his door.

"Ulvanov was less than . . . cautious," Skoryatin went on, delivering a full assessment of the KGB man within the brief pause, "and was unfortunate enough to find himself dispatched to a less hospitable place than Moscow. However, it appears that he has been forgiven and is once more at the helm. But he does not love us. He believes we had something to do with it."

"Did we, General?"

Skoryatin looked at her with amusement. "My dear child. Most certainly not." He told the lie with practiced skill. "It is no secret what we of the GRU think of the KGB, but. . . ."

Kamapova's eyes were darting in her face, hunted animals looking for somewhere to hide.

Beautifully done. They'd trained her very well indeed.

Skoryatin smiled at her, and said: "In case you're wondering about it . . . no, this car has no surveillance equipment aboard . . . except my own, naturally." He pressed a switch by his right hand, near the window lift. A low hum filled the car. "Clean," he went on. "Any planted listening device would have altered the frequency, causing an undulation in the tone. This car, and all my other staff vehicles, are protected in this way. They are also electronically swept several times a day." She might as well know. "We were not responsible for Comrade Ulvanov's dismissal. He did it all by himself." The switch was released, and the hum died.

Skoryatin rapped once on the armored dividing glass panel that separated the driver from his passengers. The driver understood the signal and climbed out to come round to open Skoryatin's door. The General got out.

"Thank you, Yuri."

The driver, a sergeant, bowed his head slightly. "General." The two of them were old comrades in arms. Sometimes, they had quiet drinks together where only first names were used. At all other times, the sergeant strictly observed protocol, even when addressed in the familiar. It was the General's prerogative.

"Let the captain out, will you please, Yuri?"

"Yes, General."

"And wait here for us."

"Yes, General."

There were four guards at the entrance to the building; two KGB, and two GRU. They watched with surreptitious appreciation as Kamapova climbed elegantly out, their eyes seemingly glued to her legs. The eyes were quickly averted when Skoryatin glanced at them.

He hid the smile he felt coming behind a stern expression. The soldiers saluted smartly. He acknowledged them curtly as he and Kamapova marched through. Two more guards within the building opened the huge double doors for them.

The place owed its origins to Czarist times and was much more opulent inside than would have been expected, given the dullness of its exterior. Skoryatin and Kamapova walked up a large, curving staircase, then along a short corridor to the room where the meeting was to be held. Neither carried documents of any kind.

There were guards outside that door too, again made up of KGB and GRU. One of them opened it. The other saluted. Skoryatin and Kamapova entered. The door shut softly behind them.

The large room with its polished floor was bare, save for the long table and four chairs at its center. Two men sat at one side of the table. Heavy curtains were drawn at one end, and the single bright chandelier bounced its light off the gleaming surfaces of the wood-paneled walls. At the center of the otherwise bare table was a square silver tray upon which was an exquisite glass decanter with a silver neck. Within the decanter was a clear liquid; and at each corner of the tray stood an empty glass. The junior officers, it seemed, would also be invited to drink.

Unusual. Such overt hospitality was to be viewed with the utmost suspicion. Skoryatin was not fooled.

Ulvanov and his aide now stood up as Skoryatin and Kamapova approached the table.

"Vladimir Mikhailovich!" Ulvanov greeted warmly. "It is good to see you again."

"It is very good to see you too, Dmitry Vasil'evich," Skoryatin said with equal warmth. "You're looking well."

Each man knew the other was lying. Skoryatin wished Ulvanov had remained in semi-exile, while Ulvanov was himself consumed by the fire of the need for revenge. His pallor betrayed the rigors of his punishment. His eyes could scarcely hide the burning hatred within them. Skoryatin knew all this, but he offered himself with apparent willingness to Ulvanov's spread arms, for the classic Russian welcoming embrace.

Kamapova stood demurely to one side while her chief greeted his KGB adversary. The KGB aide looked at her as if unsure whether he should give her a smile. He was a lean, close-eyed man with lank thinning hair.

The embrace over, Ulvanov was hospitality itself. "Please sit down, Comrades. Ah, Vladimir! Things must be looking up with the GRU. Such a beautiful aide! And may I present Major Drubiyev."

Ulvanov being overtly complimentary. He must be sure of himself, Skoryatin thought.

"The rewards for being a seasoned old soldier," Skoryatin joked. Might as well play the same deceitful game. "And you Dmitry Vasil'evich . . . congratulations on your promotion."

"My own reward. Yes . . . it feels good to be made Colonel-General, despite my little . . . but temporary fall from grace." There had been a subtle stress on the "temporary." "Back with my old Directorate, as you see."

They all took their seats at the table, the KGB pair facing their GRU counterparts. There had been no recognition in Ulvanov's eyes, of Kamapova. Skoryatin would have been surprised if such a lapse had occurred. Ulvanov's deviousness would not have allowed him to make such a crass error. There would be absolutely no hint of Kamapova's connection with Ulvanov. Skoryatin knew he would have to rely on his own instincts.

Physically, they were both big men, but very different; Ulvanov seeming almost barrel-shaped despite the past months of less than comfortable living, with a uniform that appeared to be refusing to fit him properly. Skoryatin, by comparison, appeared sleek. His uniform could have been tailored in Savile Row, so well did it clothe his frame. Skoryatin had spent a considerable time in the West either clandestinely, or on more relatively open postings to various diplomatic missions. Ulvanov held the view that Skoryatin had been tainted by Western values. Skoryatin was well aware of this; but it did not worry him. His own record was sufficiently impressive.

Ulvanov could only snipe, for the moment. He would never cease in his quest to eliminate his GRU opposite number. His was the much bigger organization, with the all-embracing power that could reach out for every citizen of the USSR. The GRU, for all its apparent autonomy, was still the Army, and therefore subject to far greater pressure from above. But it was not a cringing lap dog. It could bite, with great savagery, and even the KGB was not immune. Ulvanov had found that out, to his cost. The quest for revenge would be his raison d'etre.

And that, Skoryatin thought, would make him weak.

Ulvanov said: "I see you have not had much success with the salvage of the Tu-22P."

Skoryatin ignored the intended slight upon his capabilities. "The NATO forces have been keeping a close watch on our movements over the past months. They are even keener to see what we salvage. I have advised the secretary that hurried recovery would be unwise. He has agreed. In the meantime, we have a standing patrol to ensure the West do not get any ideas about a recovery of their own."

Skoryatin had no intention of allowing the aircraft to be salvaged, by any side.

"But the weapon," Ulvanov said. "The weapon must be salvaged. Afterward, the aircraft itself can be destroyed. We possess others but, as you know, only one operational weapon. That must be recovered at all costs. It would not do for the West to get their hands on it."

Skoryatin knew that Ulvanov's true interest lay in far more than the recovery of the sunken weapon. It was indeed vitally important that the terrifyingly lethal missile should not fall into the hands of the West; but Ulvanov was after much more. Ulvanov was after a target he could not see; something he thought more dangerous than the deadly weapon lying in its cold grave in the Greenland-Iceland-UK gap.

In a way, he was right . . . but it all depended on the point of view. To Skoryatin, people like Ulvanov were far more dangerous to world stability. To Ulvanov, Skoryatin was. Ulvanov was racked by suspicions and hatred, and having no proof upon which to base an accusation that would stick, would go to any lengths to nail his supposed target. Ulvanov would also have to be careful. A second mistake would mean total ruin, with no hope of reinstatement.

Skoryatin, well aware of Ulvanov's problems, had no intention of making life easy for the KGB general.

Skoryatin said: "What about the crew? Are we

to leave their bodies in the wreck when we eventually destroy it?"

"We know the cabin is intact. That can be brought up. Should this prove to be difficult, then it must be destroyed with the rest of the aircraft. The Americans are waiting like carrion to attempt their own salvage. Remember the last time. They went after one of our submarines then."

"We have sent submarines to the area of the wreck," Skoryatin said, "but they have been ceaselessly shadowed by NATO hunter killers. It will not be easy. There is also the problem of letting the Navy know what is actually in that weapon. They may not want to go near it, for fear that it might have ruptured. My Spetsnaz will have to do the actual work if a seabed retrieval becomes the only option. There are some highly skilled submersible operators among them whom I do not intend to commit, until I am quite certain they stand a chance of success. The secretary has my full report."

"Yes. I know." Ulvanov tried to disguise the chagrin the maneuver caused him and was only partially successful. It would be difficult to move against someone who had already made his position plain to the secretary. Neither cowardice nor dereliction of duty was a charge that would have the slightest chance of clinging to the eel-like Skoryatin. The measures would have to be far more drastic. Ulvanov had a mission that was already running, with that end specifically in mind.

"The KGB can provide people who could be trained," Ulvanov said. "They would be chosen from special units whose skills are already exceedingly high. They have, on occasion, worked with your own excellent troops, Vladimir Mikhailovich."

"And very good they were too, Dmitry Vsail'evich," Skoryatin said with a straight face. On those memorable occasions, it had taken firm control to prevent a mutiny in those GRU units forced into the unwelcome alliance. Not those bastards again, had been the general cry. The GRU personnel had felt insulted.

"With respect," Skoryatin continued, "this is a highly risky operation. Men and women could be killed. I would not like to jeopardize the lives of your own specialists."

"They would be quite prepared to die for the Motherland on such an operation, vital as it is to our defense integrity."

And blame me for it, Skoryatin thought, unimpressed by the outwardly generous offer that was full of hooks upon which to impale him.

He said: "You can, of course, have the suggestion mentioned to the secretary, but I would be duty bound to register my objections . . . with the reasons for doing so."

Ulvanov gave in gracefully; an event which was highly suspect.

"They are there at your disposal," he said, "should you want them."

"I shall keep that in mind," Skoryatin said accommodatingly, determined more than ever to watch his back for incoming knives.

"And now," Ulvanov was saying, "let us bring a little ease into these proceedings." He reached for the glasses on the silver tray and placed one before each person, beginning with Kamapova. He picked up the decanter and began to pour. "I know you like tea, Vladimir Mikhailovich, but as this is our first meeting since my . . . return, I thought we might have a little celebration." He put the decanter down and raised his glass. "To success."

Every other glass was raised. "To success," they repeated in unison.

Each mind held a different definition of success.

Later, as they traveled back in the Moscow evening, Skoryatin reflected that not once had his proposed trip to the Far East been mentioned; a sure sign that Ulvanov knew, even though it was not common knowledge within the GRU.

Skoryatin smiled to himself. Things were going exactly to plan.

"Cordial meeting, wasn't it?" he now said to Kamapova.

He could not see her eyes in the gloom of the car, but he could sense her confusion. The eyes would be looking uncertain.

Which was as he expected.

London, 1700 hours.

The intercom in Fowler's spartan office buzzed urgently.

"Yes, Mrs. Arundel."

"Sir John's on his way," the disembodied voice said in hushed tones, as if afraid of being overheard.

"Thank you," Fowler said and smiled briefly as the connection went dead.

Delphine Arundel, once a colonel's wife, had been widowed by Northern Ireland. In her thirties, she was a highly attractive woman and Department gossip had it that she was soft on both Gallagher and Fowler and couldn't decide. There was little evidence to substantiate this, though there was once an occasion when she was heard yelling at Fowler for the way he always got Gallagher into trouble. Fowler had apparently taken the dressing-down meekly. She despised Winterbourne. To many Department personnel, that was a plus. She was, however, very discreet about it.

Winterbourne entered the office looking furious. "What's this about Priknash being severely wounded and a Department vehicle being written off in France?"

"It's true, Sir John." Fowler did not rise from his chair.

"Why wasn't I informed? The Minister appears to have known about it for hours, and *he* got it from one of his backbenchers who just happens to have a line into a sister Department. *They* apparently got it from the French. Now everyone wants to know what we're supposed to be up to."

Fowler said: "Someone ought to do a clean-up job on the French section responsible."

"Is that all you've got to say?" Winterbourne demanded angrily.

"For the moment, Sir John, yes. A report of the incident was prepared for you as soon as I received the information. As you were at your club when it came in, I thought it best not to disturb you there. Besides, I could hardly have told you on an open line."

"There's a secure line to me at the Club. You know that!"

"We do have strong evidence of supposedly secure lines installed in similar circumstances by other Departments going suddenly open. I don't want that to happen to us."

Winterbourne's cherubic face looked more bad-tempered than ever. "Are you suggesting my line's *not* secure?"

"I'm making no such suggestion, Sir John. I'm merely advising caution. An approach like this from the Soviets is far too important a chance to ignore."

"It could also be another of their wretched games of multi-layered disinformation." Winterbourne sounded almost hopeful.

"I don't think so."

"If you're wrong. . . ."

Winterbourne left the words hanging, but Fowler knew exactly what the unspoken threat was.

"Then I shall carry the responsibility," he said calmly.

Winterbourne did not look satisfied. It was as if he felt that even Fowler's acceptance of responsibility for anything going badly wrong was still a reflection upon him.

"Where's the report?" he demanded tightly.

"With Mrs. Arundel. She hasn't seen it, of course. I put it in your outside safe myself."

There were two safes whose contents were solely for Winterbourne's attention: one in the outer office with Delphine Arundel, the other in Winterbourne's sanctum. The electronic combinations for both were supposedly held only by Fowler and Winterbourne. As Head of Department, however, Winterbourne could change the combination of the inner safe without Fowler's knowledge and had done so immediately on taking up the post. He was the only Department Head known to have exercised that privilege.

Winterbourne said: "If there are going to be any more casualties on our side, it had better be only Gallagher."

"I'll give him your regards next time I see him," Fowler said imperturbably. "He's certain to appreciate your concern for his health."

Winterbourne glared at him, stifled a retort, and backed slowly out of the room. The door slammed shut.

Fowler continued with his work as if Winterbourne had never been.

In Ingolstadt, the burnished clock on the wall of Talheim's restaurant began to chime the evening hour of eight. Gallagher and Rhiannon had been given a table in a secluded corner. The table appeared over-laden with food and at its center were two wooden slabs shaped like artists' palettes, each with a dozen circular depressions within which stood glasses of wine. Each wine was different, and ranged from full-bodied red to the palest white.

Gallagher and Rhiannon had both expressed horror at having to drink it all.

Cheerfully, Talheim had told them: "Eat, *and* drink. You're not driving anywhere tonight. Besides, this is my restaurant and you're not going to insult me by refusing, are you? Plenty of time to get to the chalet tomorrow." And he'd left them with a conspiratorial wink.

They decided they might as well tuck in.

At about the same time that Gallagher and Rhiannon were doing justice to Talheim's generous table, the car that had been detailed to search the Ingolstadt area pulled to the side of the road near a large international hotel on Goethestrasse. The two men inside were fed up. For three hours, they had scoured the city, hunting the black *quattro*, hoping to see it either parked somewhere or cruising through the traffic. They hated having to report failure.

The passenger picked up his radio and got directly in touch with the Brabus Mercedes, which was itself cruising through Munich. Reception was perfect, and fully screened from electronic snooping.

"Nothing," was all he said as opening gambit.

"I expected that." The voice of the cold-eyed man in Munich came through, devoid of emotion. "He's not likely to park on a street corner waiting for you. Search again, then widen your territory gradually, taking in each small town, village, or hamlet. Check isolated buildings and farms. His contacts could be living anywhere."

"We'll need to sleep sometime."

"So do we all." The cold-eyed man broke contact.

"Once more round the city," the man in Ingolstadt said to the driver as he put the radio away. There was grim resignation in his voice.

It would have given him some consolation to know that the reports from Augsburg and Landshut were also negative. The Brabus in Munich was not having much luck either.

It would have been some consolation, but it would not have made him feel any the better for it. He intended to succeed where the others had failed.

The car pulled into the road and began its second cruise.

At about midnight, it moved hesitantly into the cobbled square and stopped. In Talheim's restaurant, lights were being switched off.

"This is ridiculous!" the man in the passenger seat began exasperatedly. "It's the second time tonight you've boxed us into this place."

"It's this lousy traffic system," the driver grumbled. "All these narrow one-way streets."

Each was in a prickly mood. They had counted ten *quattros* during their patrol, but only one had been black, with a German license. A middle-aged business type had been driving it. They'd also seen several other models from the same manufacturer.

The driver began turning the car round and its lights briefly rested upon the small saloon Gallagher had borrowed.

"Everywhere you look in this damned town," the driver said, "you see these cars. They're like flies. You'd think they made them here."

"They do," his companion said savagely. "Now keep your mind on what we're supposed to be doing, and try not to bring us here again."

The driver misjudged his maneuver and nearly went into another parked saloon.

"Watch it, will you!" the passenger snapped testily.

The driver halted, reversed, and slowly eased his way past. As he did so, the last light was switched off in the restaurant, and a man and a woman left the building to walk to the car he had just missed. The headlamps framed them fleetingly, as if in a still shot.

The men in the car glanced only cursorily at the newcomers and drove away.

Talheim stood by his car and watched the retreating tail lights.

Eva said: "What's wrong?" She spoke to him in German. Sometimes, they conversed in Czech, in which Talheim was quite fluent. "Do you recognize that car?"

"No," he replied in a soft voice. "I don't."

"Then why are you looking at it like that?"

Face made yellow by the streetlights, he smiled sheepishly at her. "Old habits are hard to break."

She glanced back at the darkened restaurant.

"They'll be alright," he assured her. "Let's go home. We've got an early start in the morning."

Their home stood in wooded grounds on a hill outside the village of Lippertshofen, about 10 kilometers to the north of the city. They joined the Nördliche Ringstrasse, the peripheral road, intending to go left soon after onto Gaimersheimer Strasse, their route home. Just before they turned off, they passed a car, cruising slowly.

Talheim slowed down after taking the turn. The other car went steadily past. It stayed on the ring road.

Eva saw him studying the mirror. "What are you looking at?"

"That car we just passed looked like the one we saw by the restaurant. It was the same number." Talheim resumed normal speed.

"Perhaps they are lost."

"Perhaps."

His obvious skepticism made her say: "You think they are something to do with Gordon?"

Instead of replying, he said: "If this had happened in Prague, what would you have thought?"

"But this is not Prague," she told him reasonably.

"Then try to place yourself there," he said. "You had very sharp instincts then, because of the danger. Seeing the same car twice in such a short time *at night* especially, would have made your alarm bells ring. They do not ring now, because you feel safe."

"And if Gordon had seen it?"

"His alarm bells would be ringing. I am certain. Mine are beginning to tinkle. If you see that car in the square again, you must let me know as soon as I've returned from taking them to the chalet. I also think it would be a good idea to make sure the pistol is fully loaded . . . just in case."

A fifteen-shot automatic was always kept at the restaurant. Talheim had long made sure that she knew how to use it. You never knew who would come calling one day. Both their backgrounds ensured they did not take too much for granted.

"Alright," she agreed reluctantly. She did not like guns.

"I could be wrong," he said, in an attempt to reassure her. "Perhaps they are lost." He paused and when she had said nothing, went on: "Gordon does not want us involved; but if he needs help. . . ."

"Then you must give it." She stroked his upper arm briefly, gently, to show her support.

"You crazy Czech," he said to her fondly.

She smiled in the gloom of the car to hide from herself the anxiety she felt.

* * *

Gallagher came awake at six o'clock, feeling refreshed. A good intake of mineral water had ensured the non-existence of a hangover. He climbed out of bed, pulled the white quilt over a still-sleeping Rhiannon, went into the bathroom to get a large towel which he wrapped about him, then returned to walk to the window.

He peered out.

The window overlooked the cul-de-sac where he'd left the borrowed car. There was no one about. The car seemed alright.

He studied the immediate area carefully. Nothing to worry about. Up above, a cloudless sky heralded a bright, warm day. Down in the cul-de-sac, where the early sun's rays had not yet made an entrance, all was still and in shadow.

Gallagher liked this part of the day, whether in the city or the country, or even out on his own in hostile territory. This was the period when the world waited poised, as if for flight, to see what the coming hours would bring. He savored the moment, knowing the spell was soon to be broken. The still-distant sounds of the new day's traffic would, before long, find its loud way into the relative quiet of the little square.

He looked down the cul-de-sac once more.

"See anything?" a voice groggy with sleep and contentment asked from behind him.

He turned. Rhiannon's tousled head peeped from beneath the quilt. An eye studied him from behind a curtain of hair.

"I thought you were still asleep," he said.

"Not much chance of that with you clumping about."

"Gross exaggeration. You never heard me."

Which was true enough. Even when relaxed, Gallagher tended to move with the quietness of a stalking cat.

"I've been watching you for some time," she admitted. She brushed her hair from her face and sat up, baring the upper half of her naked body. "And you can put that look away. I'm still trying to recover."

He grinned at her. "I don't know what you mean." He approached the bed.

She dived back beneath the quilt, laughing. "I meant what I said!"

"Of course you did." The towel dropped to the floor and he climbed in. "Once more before breakfast." He reached for her beneath the soft warmth of the duvet.

"Oh well," she said, "I might as well surrender."

The word ended in a shuddering gasp as he entered easily into her.

"So who's surrendering to whom?" he asked.

"Hmmm," she said, and locked herself about him.

By seven-thirty, they were showered and dressed when the buzzer sounded.

Gallagher picked up the entryphone.

"Freddy," Talheim announced. "Would you like breakfast in the coffee shop with us? There are fresh rolls."

"We don't want to put you to any more trouble. We can. . . ."

"It is no trouble," Talheim interrupted. "Are you dressed?"

"Yes."

"Good. We'll have some time before opening for business. Come down in five minutes."

"Right."

"By the way, did you two sleep well?"

"Very well, thanks."

"Aha. I can tell by your voice. . . ."

"Behave yourself, Freddy."

Talheim laughed. "Five minutes."

As Gallagher replaced the entryphone, he called to Rhiannon who was in the kitchen about to make coffee. "Forget the coffee. We've been invited to breakfast in five minutes."

"They're back early," she called in return.

"As I've said . . . crack of dawn merchant, our Freddy."

At breakfast, Talheim said: "We saw a car out in the square last night, as we were leaving."

Gallagher looked at him expectantly and said nothing.

"We saw it again," Talheim went on, "on the ring road, going slowly." He shrugged. "It may be nothing, of course. They may have lost their way in the traffic system. . . ."

"They?"

"There were two men. I've given it some thought. They're the kind of people you and I would recognize. Eva too, I think, given her experiences with the secret police in her old country."

Gallagher looked at her. "Eva?"

She nodded slowly, with a reluctance that showed she wanted to be wrong. "I must agree with Freddy. I don't want to, but thinking back . . . It is as he says. There are some kind of people you can recognize, even if you do not know them."

"What were they driving?" he asked Talheim.

"A dark coupe model. An Opel. Yes . . . an Opel. I'm certain."

"Registration?"

"German. The index letters show it as Karlsruhe. Could be a hired car, could be genuine . . . or it could be false plates. Could they be German, those men? Perhaps from the East?"

"Your guess is as good as mine. East German, Brits, Americans, Russians . . . take your pick."

"Perhaps I am wrong. . . ."

"I've never known you to be, Freddy."

"In that case, we must get to the chalet as quickly as possible. Eva and I will see if the car returns, and let you know. There is a cordless phone at the chalet. Very handy. There are, as I've mentioned earlier, some weapons there too, just in case."

"Freddy. . . ."

"No arguments, Gordon. Let us be sensible about this. Until we are sure these men are not the ones we think they may be, it is best to be prepared. *Ja?*"

Gallagher nodded slowly. *"Ja."*

He looked at Rhiannon. The earlier sparkle in the golden eyes had been replaced by a haunted look.

In Munich, the Brabus Mercedes had been in contact with the other three cars. All had so far reported failure.

The cold-eyed man terminated the last conversation with a grim expression on his face. He had told the cars to continue their search.

"Perhaps he's not even in Germany," the driver tentatively suggested.

The cold-eyed man gave the driver a hard stare and said nothing.

He didn't have to.

10

Gallagher followed Talheim's car off the narrow paved road and onto gravelly forest track. Plumes of dust rose behind each vehicle and he let Talheim get further ahead to minimise the dust cloud before him.

They had left Ingolstadt soon after breakfast, before the start of the day's business at the coffee shop, and were now entering the Hienheimer Forest 60 kilometers later. Talheim had deliberately taken a roundabout route—putting an extra 15 kilometers on the journey so far—so as to confuse possible pursuit. Throughout, Rhiannon had been virtually silent.

Talheim took a left turn into an unpaved avenue of tall trees. They were now in the forest proper, and light came from above the treetops. A sort of twilight had enveloped the road and the rising dust plumes, combined with the darkly green borders of forest, gave the whole scene an air of mythic mystery.

Rhiannon said: "I feel like Little Red Riding Hood."

"And the wolf's right next to you." He pretended to snarl at her.

"Pussycat, you mean."

"Right," he said. "You'll pay for that later."

"Promises, promises." But she was smiling again.

The avenue of trees ended abruptly as Talheim led them into another turn, this time to the right. The track took them through low vegetation. It climbed gently for a kilometer or so before sloping equally gently downward. They passed a single parking area but met no traffic. Another turn, and the track began to climb steeply this time; then Talheim slowed right down and appeared to have stopped. They were once more within a landscape of tall trees.

Talheim blinked his left indicator once as Gallagher pulled up behind him and began to turn.

The narrow track was almost invisible from the larger forest road, and anyone driving past would have missed it. There were no overt indications of its existence, save for the barest hint of a thinning of the grass verge.

Talheim's car seemed to have been swallowed by the forest itself. Gallagher inched after him. It was like driving through a tunnel; except that this one appeared to close in on the car. Foliage whispered against the bodywork and it was so dark, Talheim had switched on his lights. Gallagher followed suit.

Rhiannon said: "Forget what I said about Red Riding Hood. I think the Wicked Witch is waiting at the other end."

"Frightened?"

"You've got to admit, this is spooky. Where's

this friend of yours taking us?" She added, only partly joking.

"It's wait and see time."

"Do you trust him?"

He glanced at her. "How can you doubt that after what Eva told you?"

"People change. You ought to know. It was your line of business once."

"Not Freddy."

"You had another friend. . . . He changed, didn't he? And you had to kill him."

Dalgleish.

"That was different. Terrible psychological things had been done to him."

"He had changed, and would have killed you."

She was perfectly correct, of course; but he didn't want to think of Talheim leading him into a trap. Twice before, he'd been betrayed by a good friend and colleague. He did not want a third occurrence. It wouldn't do to have to kill Freddy as well.

Then Rhiannon was saying: "Ooh! This is lovely. It's simply lovely."

They had broken out of the tunnel into the bright daylight of a large clearing, in the middle of which was a small lake about 200 meters across. A short distance from its northern shore was Talheim's chalet, the only building there.

The house was A-shaped, the steep slopes of its roof reaching to the ground, in the style of many holiday homes in the Bavarian area: but there was an outstanding difference. The entire roof housed rows of solar panels.

The two cars pulled up before it, their lights

now switched off. Talheim climbed out, came round as Gallagher and Rhiannon also got out.

"Freddy, this is quite beautiful," she said, looking about her. "What a perfect hideaway!"

He smiled. "That was what I thought when I leased this land and built on it."

Gallagher was also looking about him. "Solar panels, fully self-sufficient for power. I have a feeling you got some help with the lease, Freddy. Official help. I think the guns you've got in there have a more serious purpose than just for your own protection. How am I doing?"

Talheim's eyes were speculative. "Not badly. Yes. I have sometimes used this place in a more ... official capacity, but not very often. But tell me, you were not sure whether I was leading you into a trap, *ja?*"

"Freddy...."

"In your place, I would have felt the same. Now do not look so embarrassed. In our business, survival is paramount. After all, you're not much use if you've been taken out."

Gallagher moved away to inspect the exterior of the chalet.

Watching as Gallagher walked slowly round the building, Rhiannon said: "You really don't mind?"

"But of course not. And you, Rhiannon, I think you were a little worried in the tunnel, perhaps?"

"I ... I suppose it's because...."

Talheim patted her on the shoulder. "Do not worry. I would have been surprised if Gordon had not felt some doubts."

"But you two are friends. In the car, he tried

to assure me he trusted you completely, but I know he was considering what action to take . . . just in case."

"Even friends must be careful."

"But he trusts you. I know he does."

"And I trust him. It does not mean we have to be careless."

She shook her head slowly. "I hate the kind of business you and Gordon are involved in."

"We are no longer involved. We are out of harness."

"I'd like to believe that, but I do know better."

"Come, come, Rhiannon. Enjoy the peace of this place for as long as you would like . . . a week, a month, six months . . . it is yours and Gordon's for as long as you wish. Look over there. You are high above the valley: 500 meters. Sixteen hundred feet up. Enjoy it and do not worry about the world outside. Many times, I come here in retreat. Eva and I bathe in the lake and pretend we are the only two people in the whole world."

"A nice fairy tale."

"Perhaps . . . but for the time we are here, it seems real. And so, it works. Come. Let us join Gordon."

Gallagher came round the front as they arrived.

Talheim said: "Found any bugs?"

"Only those that crawl. We'll take it."

"Why, thank you, sir. That will be ten million deutschmarks in advance."

Gallagher smiled at Rhiannon. "See my banker. She's got all my money."

"You two are crazy," she said, smiling back at them.

"But of course," Talheim said. "Only crazy people do what we used to. Let's go in."

The chalet had an open porch and was on two levels. The entire front was made up of double-glazed panels and the sliding door could only be opened by a push-button code. Talheim punched it in on the small keyboard attached to the door, and a large panel slid open automatically. He told them the code as they entered.

The two bedrooms and the bathroom were on the upper level. The whole place was paneled in pine, and the furnishings would have been at home in a luxury apartment. A central, spiral staircase led up to the bedrooms. Next to it was a large, four-sided bookcase that rose from floor to ceiling. Every shelf was full. There were no other partitions, and the two short corridors formed by the stairs and the bookcase led from the lounge area to the spacious kitchen-diner at the back.

Talheim led them to a large cupboard in the kitchen. He opened it to display a control board.

"The power supply," he said. "As you can see, everything is labeled. You can read enough German, Gordon, to know what it all means." He shut the cupboard. "So. That's everything. You've seen the phone. If you need anything at all, call us. We've brought enough food for a week, at least, and there are stocks of non-perishables already here, if you do not wish to go out to do shopping. Call us, and I'll bring something up."

Gallagher said: "There shouldn't be any need. We'll be fine."

"Alright. Now we must unload the cars and get all that stuff in the freezer. It's warm out there now."

Half an hour later, preparing to return to Ingolstadt, Talheim said: "I must show you where the guns are." He glanced briefly at the ceiling. Rhiannon was upstairs. "She might be upset if she saw them, so now is the time." He went to the bookcase, removed two thick biographies of Beethoven from a middle shelf. "Remember these books." There appeared to be nothing but more wood behind the two volumes, but Talheim pressed against it with outstretched fingers.

A three-inch square moved inward, then was released. It was once more flush with the rest of the paneling. That particular side of the bookcase had sprung open like a door. Talheim returned the biographies to their place, then pulled the case fully open. Behind it was a well-stocked guncase.

Gallagher stared at the weaponry displayed, conscious of Talheim's vague smile of satisfaction. In addition to two gleaming examples of highly expensive hunting rifles, there were two Heckler and Koch assault rifles, a G41-TGS with its integral grenade launcher, two massive SIG-Sauer P226 automatic pistols, and a smaller Walther. There was plenty of ammunition for all the weapons. Talheim certainly took his self-protection seriously.

Gallagher said: "Bloody hell, Freddy. You could repel a small army with that lot."

Talheim pushed the bookcase shut. "We're a long way from immediate help out here. The kind of people this is meant to stop would do the job very quickly, long before help arrived. Best to surprise them. By the way, pressing the switch also unlocks the guncase: and clicking the bookcase home secures the whole thing."

They went outside.

Talheim continued: "The power storage system's under the house, but you won't need to check it out. It looks after itself. If there are any anomalies, call me. If you'd like to go down to the river, the Altmühl's two kilometers to the north. There's a path at the back of the house beyond the clearing. Your nearest place of any consequence is Essing . . . if you do decide to go shopping after all. It's across the river and is four kilometers by car." He grinned suddenly. "There's another lake, bigger than this one, not far from here. *Wolfsee.* Appropriate for a grey wolf. Well . . . I must be going. Eva will begin to wonder what's taking so long. Enjoy yourselves. I'll look you up from time to time. Goodbye, Rhiannon," he called.

The full-length window above the porch was slid open and she appeared within its frame.

" 'Bye, Freddy . . . and thanks. I'm going to love it here."

"The pleasure is mine. Look after this crazy man."

"I will." She waved at him.

To Gallagher, Talheim said in a quiet voice: "Keep her safe. Use any weapon you like, if the situation demands."

Gallagher nodded. "But I hope it won't be necessary."

"Just in case."

"Alright, Freddy. Just in case. Thanks."

Talheim shrugged. "So what are friends for?" They shook hands. *" 'wiedersehen."*

"Auf wiedersehen, Freddy," Gallagher said.

He watched as Talheim returned to his car and drove away. He remained where he was, listening as the fading sounds of the departing vehicle were gradually absorbed by the powerful silence of the forest. Something jumped in the lake, sounding abnormally loud. Talheim had had it stocked.

"Fish for supper?" Rhiannon called down.

He looked up at her. "Something else first."

Her smile told him she knew exactly what he meant. "I think," she said, "I'm going to like it here."

"Oh lucky me," he said, and hurried into the chalet.

Two days later, their luck ran out.

Gallagher was lying on his front, his bare upper body propped by his elbows, camera to his eye. Next to him was the radiophone. Further ahead, close to the edge of the lake, Rhiannon lay face down on a large towel, feet toward him. She was completely naked.

"What are you doing?" her voice came to him.

"Take a look."

She raised her head to do so, twisting her body slightly.

He triggered the shot. "Perfect," he crowed.

"Don't you dare!" she squealed at him.

"Too late."

She was on her feet and coming at him. "I'll do you!"

He took another shot and, laughing, began his retreat. Then the phone warbled. They both stopped to stare at it, voices dying in mid-laugh.

Gallagher picked it up. "Yes?"

"Did I interrupt anything?" came Talheim's suggestive voice.

"Would I tell you?"

Talheim laughed. "Message from the car people," he went on. It had been deliberately arranged that all messages went via Talheim.

Gallagher said: "Anything serious?"

"I don't think so. It's to do with the electronics. They wouldn't tell me. What have you got on that thing? Anyway, they would like you to come down and see them today. Rhiannon can stay here with us until you're finished."

"Hang on." Gallagher turned to her. "You heard. What do you want to do?"

"I'll be alright here. You won't be long, will you?"

"I don't think I like that idea very much." He said into the phone: "Rhiannon says she's alright here...."

"Then I must come up."

"There's no need...."

"There is every need, Gordon. I will be with you soon."

As the call ended, Gallagher said to her: "Well, he's coming up."

"I'll be alright. No one except Freddy and Eva knows we're here."

"You don't seriously think I'd leave you by yourself in the middle of this forest...."

"I'm not a baby."

"I can see that."

"Put your eyes back. I'll be alright," she said again. "You don't have to worry. We've had two lovely, peaceful days here. We can relax."

"That's when we'd be at our most vulnerable. Anyone who comes looking won't be a baby."

The golden eyes surveyed him for long moments. "I make you vulnerable, don't I?"

"Nonsense. Of course you don't."

She nodded slowly, as if confirming something to herself. "Of course I do."

"If you want to see it like that . . . we all make each other vulnerable in some way. I'd rather be with you, than without you."

She smiled. "You've just earned yourself a prize."

"As long as we're dressed when Freddy gets here. Wouldn't want to shock the poor man, would we?"

She pulled him down to the ground, sinking slowly beneath him.

"We've got plenty of time," she said softly.

The dark green Opel Monza was cruising along Kälberschuttstrasse, the men in it racked with frustration. They felt certain they had closely scrutinised every town, village, hamlet and isolated building within their designated search area. They had used day binoculars, and infrared glasses, to no avail. They were convinced that their quarry was long gone, and that their commander in the Munich car had got it wrong. Neither of them would dare say so to him. It was safer to plod over old ground until he decided to call off the search. Besides, the failure would be on *his* head.

The driver of the Monza saw movement in the corner of his eye, across the road to his left. He glanced over, more out of an involuntary reaction than curiosity, and nearly jammed on the brakes. His training made him continue at the same steady speed, to slow down gradually, and to pull over to the curb and stop without fuss.

His colleague said irritably: "What do you think. . . ."

"Look behind and across the road to that car engineering place and tell me what you see."

The other complied. "I don't believe it!" he said in a hushed voice after a brief pause. "So simple."

"And so brilliant. Another few seconds later and we would have missed it."

They were looking at a low building with a shallow roof, in front of which was a large parking area where eight cars were neatly parked, four to each side. They were all Audi models, with a variety of body modifications. A ninth was being driven across the wide apron to turn right, and eventually disappear behind the building.

A black *quattro*.

"Are you sure it's the right one?" the driver's colleague asked tentatively, as if afraid they'd got it wrong.

"British plates."

"There could be other British customers."

"At this very moment?" The driver was skeptical. "I think it's our man."

"I think you're right."

The driver said: "Clever. He leaves his car here for servicing, then goes to ground. The question is where. At least we know he's in the area."

"Assuming he hasn't gone on to Munich to catch a plane."

"So what do we do? Warn them in Munich about his car?"

"No. Not yet. Let's be sure."

"We should. . . ."

"If we're wrong, would you like to be the one to say so?"

The driver thought of the cold-eyed man in Munich and decided on discretion. "Alright. We say nothing for the time being. But what *do* we do?"

"We wait a little longer . . . for the time being. He may be in there . . . On second thoughts, let's do a circuit. When we return, pull up a little further from the entrance then raise the bonnet. We're going to have a little engine trouble."

Ten minutes later, they were back. Another car had arrived and was parked nose-in, on the right side of the apron.

The driver, who had climbed out of the Opel to raise the bonnet, remarked as he pretended to be studying the engine bay: "I think I recognise that little saloon out there."

His companion joined him after a short pause, feigning a look of concern. "Are you certain?"

"Not a hundred percent, but as near as makes no difference. It was in that little square you got so worked up about."

The other chose to ignore the jibe. "How can you be sure?"

"The wheels. Our lights were on the car for some time as I tried to turn round. I remember thinking how nice those wheels looked."

"There could be many cars around here with wheels like that."

"Perhaps. But how many have you seen on that particular model?"

"You could be right, I suppose . . . and you could be wrong."

"You can pass the chance up if you like. It's your decision." The driver was getting his own back for the night before.

His companion stared at him expressionlessly, recognising the unspoken threat. "I have an idea."

The passenger went back to pull at the door upholstery. Like the Mercedes, it too possessed a hidden compartment. From the bottom, beneath a neatly stowed automatic pistol and a cut-down assault rifle, he took out something that looked like a 5-mark coin. Its surfaces were perfectly smooth. He placed it in a trouser pocket.

"I'm going over there," he told the driver. "Open the radiator cap. We need some water." Without waiting for comment, he began walking toward the building.

He had nearly reached the small Audi saloon, when a man in overalls approached from one side of the building, heading for one of the cars. The mechanic paused uncertainly to stare at the newcomer, then changed tack to approach him.

"Can I help you?" the mechanic began in German.

The man smiled sheepishly. "We need some water for the radiator. I'm afraid my driver forgot to check it this morning. Such a silly oversight. Do you have any?"

"Of course. Wait here. I'll bring some."

"Thank you."

The mechanic hurried away.

Casually, the man wandered closer to the small saloon and made a great show of admiring it. When he was certain he could not be observed, he placed the false 5-mark coin beneath a rear wing.

It clung to the metal. Uninterruptedly, it seemed, he continued to admire the car.

The mechanic was soon back with a plastic jug, with two liters of water.

"Thank you," he said again as he took the water and hurried over to the Opel.

The mechanic followed as far as the entrance to gaze with idle curiosity.

The driver said: "Well?" He began pouring the water. Most of it went on the ground.

"I've planted a bug. If it's the right car, we're in business."

"And if it's not?"

"I'll wring your neck."

Wordlessly, the driver handed back the now-empty jug which the man returned to the waiting mechanic.

"Vielen dank," he said.

"Bitte."

"Auf wiedersehen."

" 'wiedersehen."

The man returned to the Opel. The bonnet was already down and the driver back behind the wheel.

"Let's get out of here," the man said as he climbed in. "That mechanic is still looking." He turned on the car radio. A red light began to blink, and a soft beeping came out of it. "Well, the bug's working. At least, that car's not wired up. Let's see where it leads us. Don't go too far."

The driver started the Opel and drove off.

The mechanic stared after it.

Gallagher came out of the building soon after and walked toward the small Audi. The *quattro* would be ready in another five hours. No point hanging around. He saw the mechanic with the empty plastic jug making for one of the other cars and gave him a wave. The man waved back and grinned.

Gallagher climbed into the borrowed car and headed back for the chalet where Rhiannon and Talheim were waiting. He toyed with the idea of dropping in to see Eva but decided it would be better to go straight to the chalet, to enable Talheim to return to the restaurant.

He drove on, completely oblivious of the bug and the unwelcome company he was towing behind him.

The driver said: "Where the hell is he going?"

"Just hope, for your sake," the other began ominously, "we're not tailing some traveling salesman. Just hope our target's not still back there, waiting for his car."

They were following at a good distance from their quarry and had not seen who was driving.

"We've been through this area," the driver said after a while, defensively. They were passing through Laimerstadt, close to the Hienheimer Forest. "Could we have missed something before?"

"Looks like he's gone into the forest over there. Better follow, and just keep hoping."

The driver did not miss the implied threat. He said nothing and continued to tail the distant car.

Rhiannon had put on some clothes before Talheim's arrival at the chalet. In a loose white frock, barefoot and bare-legged, she sat on the ground near the lake, knees drawn up close together, arms clasped about them.

A short distance away, Talheim sat on a collapsible stool, fishing. So far, he'd been unsuccessful. The surface of the lake was remarkably still.

It was so quiet in the clearing, they heard the faint sound of Gallagher's car when it was still some way off.

"Your man returns," Talheim said, "and I still haven't caught a single fish. I was hoping for a few."

"Never mind, Freddy. I couldn't eat them anyway. They're like friends to me now. It would be like eating a pet."

Talheim was unrepentant. "Have you any idea how much trouble I had stocking this? I've had some good dinners from this lake, but I think they're getting to know me."

"Perhaps they go into hiding."

"Ha," he said, and continued to fish.

The sound of the approaching car gradually increased in volume and presently the Audi came through the green tunnel to stop near the house.

Rhiannon stood up as Gallagher climbed out and hurried to meet him.

"I must be terrible company," Talheim called without looking round. "She has been impatient for your return almost as soon as you left."

"Should you be talking so loudly?" Gallagher said as he came forward with Rhiannon, arms about each other's waist. "You'll scare the fish."

"What fish?" Talheim said disgustedly. "Rhiannon's right. They've gone into hiding. What was wrong with the car?"

"Nothing wrong. I'd asked for a few mods to the alarm system and they wanted me to check it out before setting it up for good."

"And?"

"It's perfect. The car will be ready for collection about five o'clock."

"So you'll be going back. I might as well wait here."

"I can't keep you away from the restaurant for the whole day, Freddy," Gallagher said. "Eva won't forgive either of us. Rhiannon can come down with me this time."

"To tell you the truth," Talheim began conspiratorially, "I'm determined not to be beaten by those fish. I'm happy to stay."

"Let me have a go with that rod."

"Think you can do better?" Talheim surrendered the rod with an amused smile.

"Who can tell? The fish don't know me, do they?"

The driver said: "I can't understand it. First we get a strong signal, then it fades . . . but he's nowhere to be seen. Cars don't disappear into thin air."

The Opel Monza had criss-crossed the forest for nearly three hours, trying to locate the source of the signal. It had gone along the roads to Echendorf and Buch, through the Buchertal and across the river to Nusshausen, and back again, retracing its journey. Each time, the signal had gone through its modulated response. Eventually, the search was narrowed to an area within the bounds of that particular route.

But the men could see no access to it. Solid forest greeted their probing eyes.

The passenger said: "I think you were right about him; but I also think the bastard saw me plant the bug. He led us to this forsaken place, went in there to dump it, then drove away, leaving us to chase our tails. That's what I think. I'd like to get my hands on the shit."

"So do we go back into Ingolstadt and wait for him to pick up his car?"

"If he hasn't picked it up already. *Shit!*" The passenger thumped at his door with a clenched fist, giving vent to his sense of frustration. "We were so close."

"Do we tell Munich?"

"No!" came the snarled response. "We damn well *don't* tell Munich. We've lost him, haven't we?"

"Alright," the driver said stolidly. "We don't tell Munich . . . but we've got to do something."

"I know we've got to do something! I'm tired and I want to sleep. Look. Just stop here for a moment. I want to think this out."

The Monza came to a halt at a junction with a long forest track, not far from the Wolfsee. The driver switched off the engine. From their seats, they could see a substantial stretch of the track, in both directions.

It was four o'clock.

"Alright," Gallagher said in defeat, handing the rod back. "I can't believe I've spent nearly three hours trying to haul one of your bloody fish out of there. Are you sure it's *fish* you've got in that water, Freddy?"

Talheim grinned triumphantly. "They're certainly there. Go and get your car. When you return, I shall have beaten them."

"You hope," Gallagher said sceptically, moving toward the Audi. "See you later."

"Fish for supper," Talheim said as a parting shot.

"This I'll have to see." Gallagher turned to Rhiannon who had accompanied him to the car. "I'll be back very soon. All I've got to do is pick up the *quattro*."

"Fly back then."

He kissed her. "At your command."

"I can hear a car!" the driver said.

"The signal's getting louder too!" his companion exclaimed.

They both stared at the radio, then the driver looked up and down the track. Nothing.

"Where's it coming from?" he asked, mainly of himself.

The passenger said: "Start up. Come on! Start up and move back a little."

"Why...."

"Just do it!"

"Alright, alright." The driver started the Monza and began to reverse slowly.

"That's it. Stop here."

They could still see the track, but were less conspicuous. A vehicle coming along it would not spot them until too late.

The sound of the approaching engine grew louder; but there was still no sign of its source. Then a couple of minutes later, they saw the small saloon emerge, as if being given birth by forest, to turn right, going away from them.

"How did he manage that?" the driver asked in surprise. He put the Monza in gear, intending to follow.

His colleague placed a restraining hand on his

arm. "Wait. Let him get well out of sight." The man pointed to the radio. "We know where he'll be. I want to check what's in that patch of forest."

"But how did he get in? There's no road, and that little car's not exactly a tank."

"I'll soon find out." The passenger drew an automatic pistol from beneath his jacket and climbed quickly out. "Wait here."

He ran at a crouch across the track and into the edge of the forest. He made his way to where he'd gauged the car to have made its exit. It was some distance from the junction and it took him a good five minutes to find the freshly depressed foliage. He found the hidden tunnel soon after.

"Well, well," he murmured softly.

He walked cautiously along the tunnel, crouching as he went, to clear its leafy ceiling. He slowed right down as it began to get lighter and by the time he had come to its end at the clearing, another fifteen minutes had passed. He stayed near the mouth of the tunnel and studied the two figures by the lake.

"Well, well," he said again. "A nice little hide-out indeed." He backed into the tunnel, then turned to retrace his steps quickly.

11

"I was just about to come looking for you," the driver said.

"In which case, you might have spoilt everything."

"You've been gone over half an hour. He's got well away from us now. He'll have picked up his car by the time...."

The passenger grinned without humor. "No need. He'll be coming back." He didn't get into the Opel.

The driver looked at him, waiting.

"There's a way in! And in there is a lake and a house ... and by the lake are two people: a man fishing, and a young woman."

The driver peered at the mass of forest. *"In there. Fishing?* Have you gone mad?"

"Not unless I'm seeing things. I don't know who the man is, but the young woman is definitely our target's piece of stuff. If we take her, all we've then got to do is wait for him to fall into our laps. Since we're not supposed to kill him until he's talked, what could be better?"

"You're certain this is going to work?"

"Not afraid, are you?"

It was a calculated insult, and the driver's glare showed clearly what he thought of it. He said nothing.

"Alright," his companion said. "I take it back."

"We should warn Munich."

A sigh. "How long have we been out in the field together?"

"On and off . . . three years."

"Then you're well aware that units like ours are fully autonomous. We *co-operate* from time to time with other units, when a special operation requires it. Munich is only in nominal command. That cold bastard in the Mercedes was sent out to *co-ordinate,* not to command fully. When this is all over, we've got to remain here to continue our role as good German citizens. I'm not going to let him take the glory. *We* found the quarry, after *he'd* lost him."

The driver said: "What about the man in there?"

"If he tries to play the hero . . . we kill him. Take your pistol. We shouldn't need more than that." A joyless smile. "They're not expecting our sort of company."

"I've never seen such hopeless fishermen," Rhiannon said, staring pointedly at the bare ground next to Talheim. "You ought to give it up, Freddy. The fish have beaten the two of you hands down."

As if to underscore the point, at the far side of the lake, a fish jumped cleanly out of the water for a fleeting instant; the first to do so throughout the entire day. Its fat body gleamed in the sun before it slammed back with a loud plop into the water. The disturbance died almost as suddenly as it had begun. The surface was smooth once more.

Rhiannon was almost laughing. "I think it was trying to tell you something."

But Talheim did not respond. "Go into the house," he said quietly.

"What. . . ."

"Keep your voice down! And *don't* . . . don't turn to stare at me. Do precisely what I tell you. Stand up and walk casually back to the house. When you are inside, I will call out, asking where is that drink. You will answer you're making it and won't be long. Try to keep your voice calm. Please do not interrupt. Now go. Leave the rest to me."

Trying to keep the sudden fear from her face, she did as he had instructed. He continued fishing as if nothing had disturbed him. After she'd been in the chalet for a few minutes, she heard his call.

"Rhiannon! Where's that drink? Are you manufacturing it?"

"I'm making it. I won't be much longer."

"Oh never mind. The fish are very stubborn today. I'll come and get it."

From within the house, she watched as he laid the rod down and began to walk toward her, limping much more heavily than she could remember having seen.

From the cover of the forest, the driver said: "A cripple. You're right. It should be easy."

"Of course I'm right. I'll take them from the

front. You go round the back to cover me, just in case."

The driver nodded, and they split up, moving swiftly to their positions.

In the chalet, Talheim said: "Come. Quickly!"

The pronounced limp had magically disappeared as he went to the bookcase. He moved a different set of books and pressed the switch hidden behind them. Another shelf swung open to reveal a door. He pulled it open. Lights came on, showing a short fight of steps.

"In you go," he said to Rhiannon. "There's a comfortable room down there, fully air-conditioned. Bolt the door after you. It cannot be forced open from outside. It is a safe place, and there's plenty of food to eat. If Gordon or I do not knock after one hour, there is another door. It leads to a passage that eventually comes out in the forest behind the house. That exit is well camouflaged, and no one can find it by accident. Now go."

She hesitated, eyes wide. "But what's happening? Why should I go down there?"

Talheim spoke quickly. "There are men in the forest. They do not as yet know that I've seen them...."

"I can't leave...."

"You will only get in the way. Like Gordon, I work better when I do not have to worry. I know what I'm doing. Gordon will soon be back. Together, we shall handle this. Now quickly. You *must* go."

He almost shoved her down the steps and pushed the door shut. He heard the bolts go, nodded with satisfaction, then pushed the bookshelf back. He quickly went to the one which hid the guncase case and opened it. He selected the G41-TGS and a P226, taking plenty of ammunition for both. The pistol came with a holster and he strapped it about his waist. He loaded the G41 both with bullets and a grenade.

The bookcase once more looked innocent. Talheim waited for the men to make their move. The longer they took, the closer was the time Gallagher would return.

From behind the house, the driver idly wondered why the man and the woman had not yet returned to the lake. He grinned. Perhaps they were having a quick one before her boyfriend returned. It would be interesting to catch them at it.

He peered from cover and saw his partner working round to the front. They'd have to move quickly to capture the woman before the target returned, or the whole thing would be ruined.

He flattened himself behind a tree and waited. The forest seemed to have gone quiet, as if watching every move he made. He shivered suddenly.

This was ridiculous, he thought. How could he shiver on such a warm day?

Rhiannon stared about her. Talheim was right. It was a very comfortable room; luxurious, in fact. A bedsitter like that would have cost a fortune in London. She inspected her temporary hiding place.

There was a good pine bed fully made, two expensive-looking armchairs and a settee, a dining table, a fully equipped small kitchen, a shower room and toilet. The living area was richly carpeted, while the kitchen and dining space had been floored with terracotta tiling. The whole was a long open-planned design, with a ceiling-high, deep red leather-upholstered room divider on castors. All lighting was sunken, with rotary switches.

There was, as Talheim had said, a good stock of food in the cupboards and in the tall fridge-freezer. She wondered who really used the place, and why.

She paused, listening for gunshots, but could hear nothing. It was probably sound-proofed. There was even a television. A radio-phone was next to it. If she were forced to go out the way Talheim had said, she would take the phone and call Eva.

She stopped thinking about such an eventuality. It would mean that both Gordon and Freddy would be dead.

She hugged herself tightly and stared up at the ceiling.

Talheim saw the man working round the edge of the clearing in preparation for heading toward the chalet, and smiled grimly. He knew the precise route the unknown man would take: via the car to use it as cover, then a quick dash to the side of the building.

"You won't make it," he said tightly.

He decided to use the rifle section of the G41. The grenades would be for later. He had identified two people stalking in the forest. Were there more? At least one would certainly be at the back. He'd have to watch for that. In the meantime, he'd hold them at bay till Gallagher returned.

No point trying to get a message through by

phone. Eva would be taking it, would get worried and. . . .

More complications. Better to sit it out.

The man made his dash to the car. Talheim scanned the lakeside. No other movement. Only two, after all?

He went swiftly out of the chalet, keeping low, weapon ready. Once outside, he dropped to the floor of the porch, stretched out on his stomach, and took up a shooting position. He waited for the man to come out from behind the car.

Thirty seconds later, the man rose, pistol in hand, to make his dash. He was well exposed, caught out of cover before he realized his danger.

He was quick. He wasted no time getting over the considerable shock he must have experienced. Instead, he shot at Talheim. His reflexes were commendably swift. The G41 barked at exactly the same time.

Talheim's aim was true. The bullet took the running man squarely in the chest, pushing him upright before slamming him over onto his back. He landed heavily on hunched shoulders. His legs thrashed wildly as he tried to get up. The thrashing slowly decreased in intensity until at last, the body lay still in a cranked position for some moments, before flopping over onto its side. A dark redness spread flowingly across the front of its shirt.

Talheim felt a sudden wave of sharp pain followed almost immediately by a strange numbness in his left leg. It felt wet, too. He shifted himself slightly, to inspect the damage.

"Schiess!" he said, at once annoyed and surprised.

It was the same leg that had been hit before, giving him the limp. The now dead man's reflexes had almost been too good. Eva would not be pleased, he thought drily.

He moved his foot gingerly, then tried shifting the leg. Both worked: but the pain had come back.

"Schiess!" he said again. At least no bones had been hit. The bullet appeared to have gone right through. Perhaps the wound looked worse than it was.

He lay down the G41, removed the belt from his trousers, and used it as a makeshift tourniquet. It would have to do for now. There was at least one other man to take care of.

Using the rifle as a prop, he attempted to stand. It was not a good idea. The pain hit him in another savage wave. He would have to do it the hard way and crawl around.

"Schiess!" he said for a third time, disgustedly. Imagine allowing himself to have been caught out like that.

From his position in the woods behind the chalet, the driver was having almost the same thoughts. He had heard the sharp explosive sound of the rifle, had seen the effect on his colleague. He now stared at the dead body, thinking bitterly how they had allowed themselves to be suckered.

"You wouldn't listen!" he muttered with a harshness born of frustration, at the body in the clearing. "I said we should have warned Munich and waited."

Waiting for reinforcements would have made the job less hazardous. The way the people in the chalet had got themselves under cover had not been carried out by innocents or cripples.

The driver's mouth thinned into a grim line. They had obviously been spotted, and the fake cripple had fooled them into complacency; and complacency had exacted its own penalty. They had been warned about this so often during training that the driver was astonished at his dead colleague's lack of caution. To be foolish was not to be brave. There was no glory in a useless death.

The driver was in a quandary. Munich had to be warned; but there would also be questions as to why he had not given covering fire. How could he convincingly argue he had not wanted the action carried out in this way, without raising the suspicion that he had been less than supportive when the shooting had begun?

He looked about him, carefully surveying his immediate surroundings. Was he being stalked even now? He was not afraid; but he had no intention of dying in this forest either. The advantage was now firmly in the hands of the people in the building. They knew their terrain.

The driver made his decision. He would make a break for it and warn Munich; but he would also try to keep the people here. That meant destroying their transport. How he wished for a couple of grenades!

They could walk out, of course; but that would take time, even on familiar terrain. They would be even further delayed if he could wound one of them.

Having convinced himself he had found the answer, the driver began to work his way round toward the front of the chalet and closer to the car.

* * *

Rhiannon heard nothing that could tell her what was going on above her head. She paced the room slowly, from time to time looking at each of the exits, wondering what she would do if an hour did pass without news from either Gallagher or Talheim.

She shook her head vigorously, as if trying to force the thought of their deaths out of her mind.

She again stared up at the ceiling.

Talheim lay on the porch, breathing slowly and deeply. The pain was just about bearable; provided he didn't try anything too energetic. One attempt at crawling after the remaining attacker had been quickly abandoned, after the leg had made its displeasure painfully felt. Instead, he had formed a sort of barricade with the porch furniture, and waited behind that. He had plenty of ammunition. Rushing the house would cost dearly.

He glanced at his watch. Nearly half an hour had passed since he'd shot the man by the car. A few squadrons of flies and assorted insects were hovering above the body, as if wondering whether it was safe to land.

What had happened to his companions? It didn't really matter. The longer they took, the closer came the time for Gallagher's return. Gallagher would have to be warned, so as not to drive straight into a cross-fire.

Movement.

Talheim scanned his field of fire slowly. He decided to use the grenade launcher. There was no reason for whoever was out there to suppose he had one. He waited for the person to betray himself. He knew just what he had to do.

The movement came again: a fleeting one among the trees. One particular tree became the focus of his attention. He aimed the G41 and fired almost at the very moment of aiming. The grenade left the tube and hurtled into the forest. It exploded against the tree with a loud roar and a billow of vivid flame bordered by a sudden ring of dense smoke. Vicious splinters of wood hurtled from the center of the blast, spraying the immediate area lethally. A scream rose from within the dark of the forest.

Talheim smiled grimly. Wood sometimes made very effective shrapnel. He waited as thick, black smoke rose through the trees and into the hot sky. There were no foresters' watchtowers sufficiently close to take note of the beacon. In any case, he did not want foresters wandering into this. They'd only be killed by the people in the forest before they could get anywhere near.

Talheim thought he saw hurried movement, deeper in the forest . . going *away*.

The driver ran, now and then stumbling as he made his way through the gloom, heading for where he'd left the Opel. Blood coursed down one cheek from a deep gash that went from just beneath one eye to his chin. There was a sogginess in his shirt too.

He had not been hit by the grenade, whose unexpected arrival had shaken him. Splinters of wood had, however, lacerated him. One had pierced his stomach like a stiletto; and he had pulled it out with a scream as he ran. He still had his gun, but his sole desire was now to get to the car, to warn Munich.

He ran on, now and then smashing painfully into the trees in his way, bouncing off them, staggering, then running on.

Through his labored breathing, he cursed his dead colleague for the bungle.

Gallagher saw the man stumble out of the forest just as he was turning the *quattro* onto the hidden track. He did not pause but instead accelerated through the tunnel, knowing there was trouble up ahead. He could smell burning.

At the mouth of the tunnel, he stopped the car and got out swiftly, going for cover. But Talheim was shouting.

"Go after him, Gordon! *Hurry!*"

Gallagher paused, saw the body by Talheim's car. Good Christ, he thought, and felt the fear for Rhiannon's safety rise in his throat. He saw the smoke, and the shattered tree.

"Where's Rhiannon?" he yelled.

"She is fine. Now hurry! Here. Take this with you." There was a strange catch in Talheim's voice.

Gallagher felt another fear. "Freddy!" he said anxiously, and ran swiftly at the crouch across the clearing, feeling horribly exposed to fire.

But nothing happened, and he made it to the porch. He saw the blood on Talheim's leg.

"For God's sake, Freddy, what's happened here?"

"Plenty of time to tell you later," Talheim answered quickly. "Rhiannon is safe and I am alright." He poked the G41 at Gallagher. "Take it.

It's loaded . . . with bullets and a grenade. Get the bastard. Better do it before he gets out of the forest area. I don't think the police would like you shooting up the villages."

Gallagher took the weapon. "You mean they'd like me using this in here?"

"Probably not, but hurry, or you'll miss him altogether. He's probably calling up his friends, if there are more of them. And don't worry about Rhiannon. I've got her safely hidden. *Now go!*"

Gallagher ran back to the *quattro,* drove into the clearing to turn it round, then headed it back through the tunnel, engine growling deeply. The gray wolf was on the hunt.

The snout of the *quattro* poked out of the forest and paused. Gallagher looked left, then right. He saw the plume of dust and set off in pursuit.

The driver looked in his mirror and saw, through the veil of his own wake, the second billowing tail fast approaching. At the moment of his exit from the forest, he had first heard, then seen the black car go in. He knew it was now coming after him, and again felt the shiver he had first experienced near the clearing.

He had warned Munich and even now the Brabus and the other cars were hurtling to his aid; but they would be of little use if the black car caught up with him first.

He felt a sob of rage and frustration escape him. It was all his dead colleague's fault.

"You should have waited, damn you!" he snarled.

He glanced in the mirror. The black car was drawing inexorably closer.

* * *

Gallagher briefly glanced at the instrument panel and saw the digits still counting their way upward. The car felt revitalised, seeming to possess limitless power. It surged toward the fugitive Opel, a ravening beast tearing after its prey. The green glow of the figures showed 160 kph, nearly 100 miles an hour. The figures continued to count upward. The Monza was being reeled in.

Then Gallagher was stamping on the brakes. The Opel had suddenly swung left, fish-tailing onto another track. His left hand reached for and swiftly rotated the differential switch. Soon the lights on the central console came on to tell him the diffs had locked. He could now spin all four wheels under power.

Foot off the brakes. Turn coming up. Power on, speed rocketing upward. Into the turn. Car sliding in nicely. Hold it! Nose pointing straight down the track. Reverse rotation of diff switch. Lights going off. Opel dead ahead, trailing dust and gravel. Watch out for windscreen. Speed continuing to build. Foot down.

Gallagher's eyes had become lifeless. The fine tuning of his senses for combat had taken place. The rigorous training he had endured, despite his having left the Department's employ for some time, always returned to him at such moments. It would never truly leave him; but would always be there, ready to take over.

The man ahead, and his dead comrade, had tried to endanger Rhiannon. Talheim had been shot in the attempt. Gallagher thought of what had happened to Lauren Tanner, and the nightmare returned to sear through his mind. How many others were there? And who was running them? Why were they after him in the first place?

Bloody Fowler. What did that conniving sod have to do with it?

The dust cloud behind the Opel appeared to be curving to the right. Gallagher played with the gears, followed the weaving car out of the T-junction and onto the new track. The *quattro* roared in pursuit, eating up the distance between them.

Another T-junction. The Opel went wide as it again turned right, losing ground. It seemed to stagger, corrected, hurtled on, practically hidden by the cloud in its wake. Attuned to his own machine, Gallagher continued to shorten the distance inexorably.

The lorry was trundling its way peacefully along the track, its driver relaxed, hands casually resting on the steering wheel. Then his entire manner underwent a sudden transformation. He stared apprehensively at the boiling clouds of dust racing toward him.

What were those fools up to? There was no room to pass at that speed. Were they trying to kill themselves? They would kill him too, if he didn't do something quickly.

He began to turn the wheel to the right, trying to get as far as possible off the track, without smashing into the trees bordering it. He shook his head slowly in despair. Crazy people with too much money, racing each other in their fancy cars.

The driver began to get worried. They were already too close. *They would definitely hit him!*

He tried desperately to find room where there wasn't any. He opened his mouth to scream.

Gallagher saw the truck looming out of the dust and instinctively prepared himself for evasion. The Opel seemed to be carrying straight on, heading for the inevitable collision. Already, Gallagher's eyes had searched out possible avenues of escape. He could see none.

Then the Opel, as if only just becoming aware of its danger, lurched untidily to the right. Gallagher barely had time to wonder about it when he saw the turning. He didn't follow. Instead, he weaved into it and out again. The truck hurtled past with a frightened blaring of its air horns.

Gallagher was stabbing hard at the brakes. Another turning had appeared on the right. He swung the *quattro* into it. The car slid neatly in, without fuss, and barely a reduction in speed. Beyond the trees, he could see the moving dust cloud. The track he was on appeared to be taking him closer; then he realized what was happening: the two tracks would eventually meet. He increased power, and began to draw ahead.

The merging of the tracks, he judged, was about 500 meters away. He could see the meeting point. At his present speed, he would be there in ten seconds. He floored the accelerator. The rush of air into the charger came through with a gasping roar that sounded like a challenge. The car surged forward. The dust in its wake rose like trailing cloud of a cavalry attack. The Opel began to fall further behind.

He reached the meeting point of the track a

good 100 meters in front of the Opel, and began to pull away.

He knew exactly what to do. It would be risky, but it should work.

The driver of the Opel was confused. He had expected the black car to either ram into him, or at least chase him bumper to bumper. Instead, it had slid in front of him and was pulling rapidly away, smothering his own car with the dust of its wake.

Peering through the whirling curtain, he instinctively slowed down. Why chase him, only to pull out in front at this stage?

He cut his speed further, trying to work it out.

Then he saw why. The dust cloud ahead of him appeared to have come to a halt and was settling. Though he had cut his speed, he was still traveling fast enough to cover the intervening distance quickly. Within the cloud was the black car, broadside on, blocking his path completely.

He felt a wave of despair. There was no way off the track. The fork was far behind him. He saw the man standing outside the black car, and the weapon aimed straight at his windscreen. He had been neatly suckered.

He made his decision. If he was going to go, he'd take the bastard with him.

He stamped on the accelerator. The Opel Monza surged forward.

Gallagher knew his maneuver carried the risk of just such an eventuality; but he had expected it and was ready. The Opel was still a good 500 meters away. He held his ground and did not fire. He wanted the target to get closer. It would have to be finely judged.

Fractions of seconds seemed like years as the hurtling mass of metal tore toward him. A matador, he thought, must feel like this when faced by an enraged bull in a dusty arena.

Now!

He fired the grenade and without waiting to see its effect, threw the G41 into the car, climbed in and without wasting time with his seatbelt, turned the *quattro* away from the approaching bomb on wheels.

He had left the engine running, and his escape was as swift as he'd planned it.

The driver of the Opel actually saw with absolute clarity for a split second, the shape of the grenade as it rushed toward him. Then the windscreen was shattering and the world had turned into a place of intolerable pressure and a sea of fire.

He did not even hear the explosion.

Gallagher stopped the car a safe distance away and climbed out to look.

The first explosion had lifted the Opel completely off the ground and, while in the air, it did a full 360 degree roll. Then the second explosion, generated by the fuel in its tank, simply tore it apart. Its wheels flew off in four separate directions, one landing on the track to come rolling toward him. When all momentum was gone, it stood upright momentarily a few meters away, as if observing him, its tire smoking. Then it flopped wearily onto its side.

The rest of the car scattered itself over a wide

area of forest and track, its residue sending a black pall into the clear sky.

Gallagher stared at it for some moments before slowly getting back into the *quattro*, to make his way back to the chalet.

Talheim was still where he'd left him, and the body by the car had collected more flies.

Propped against the glass sliding door, Talheim said: "Did you get him?"

Gallagher nodded and handed back the G41.

Talheim felt the launcher tube. "Warm. So you used it."

Again Gallagher nodded, saying nothing. He stared at Talheim's wounded leg.

"I thought you would. I don't think those people quite realize who they're playing with. Oh, don't worry about the leg. Nothing serious."

"Where's Rhiannon?"

"As I said, somewhere very safe. Better get her out, and I am afraid you'll have to leave here quickly. I'm certain they'll bring up reinforcements. They'll be after blood now."

"We can't leave you here."

"I'll be alright. I'll give you half an hour, then I'll call some people I know. If our dead friends' pals turn up, they'll get a hot reception."

"Freddy, I'm sorry about all this. Tell Eva...."

"Don't waste time! Get Rhiannon out and hurry. Eva will understand. And as for me..." Talheim grinned, painfully. "We've been there before, Gordon, you and I. Now get yourselves out of here."

Talheim told him how to find Rhiannon. She came rushing up the steps to throw her arms about him.

"Oh Gordon! I couldn't hear a thing down there. I was so worried. Are you alright? And Freddy?" She noted the expression on his face. "What's happened? Is Freddy. . . ."

"We're leaving."

"But Gordon. . . ."

"Get your things. Hurry." He spoke more harshly than he'd intended.

"What's happened to Freddy?"

"You'll see. Please. Go upstairs and get your things. And mine as well," he added, "if you wouldn't mind. I'm going to see to Freddy."

She gave him a look that was at once puzzled, and frightened. "I can smell smoke. And . . . and what's wrong with Freddy?"

"Come on, love," he said gently. "Up you go. It's not as bad as you think." Only bloody worse, he thought.

Her frightened look didn't go away, but she did as he'd asked.

He went outside to Talheim. "You're bound to have something here that we can use on that wound."

Talheim nodded. "The bathroom cabinet has enough for our present needs. There's a more comprehensive supply in the room below but I'll be alright till my people get here."

"Your people. Have you been lying to me, Freddy? Are you still active?"

Talheim looked at him sheepishly. "I have contacts."

"And the rest. Right. Let's see to that leg."

By the time Gallagher had attended to it, Rhiannon had come down with their gear. She stared at Talheim's leg and the blood on the porch; at the still smoking tree; at the dead body by the car. She said nothing, but went pale beneath her tan.

She looked at each of them slowly. "I'll put the things in the car," she said at last. "Is it open?"

Gallagher nodded.

Talheim watched as she walked to the *quattro*, laden with the bags. "Don't lose her," he said.

"I don't intend to."

"Although she knows about you, she is still shocked by the realities of what can happen. It is not an easy thing to come to terms with. It is easier for someone like Eva who has had to live on the edge of survival from childhood. Those men, whoever they are, must have a very strong purpose driving them. This attack says it all. Now that we have killed two, they will want revenge as well. Be careful, Greywolf. And take very good care of her."

Rhiannon was making her way back.

"You can count on it," Gallagher said, watching her.

"Those men . . . they won't care if she gets in the way."

"I know that only too well."

"So what are you going to do?"

"Take her back to England. It's the only thing. Then there's someone I'm going to see about all this."

The grimness in his voice made Talheim say: "Not in your old Department, by any chance?"

Gallagher's smile was fleeting. "I wonder what gave you that idea."

Their conversation died as Rhiannon joined them. She squatted on her heels to give Talheim a hug.

"I'm not going to ask daft questions, Freddy . . . but look after yourself."

He smiled at her. "I should get shot more often."

Her own smile was shaky. "Eva would never forgive you."

"She's going to give me hell as it is." Then he added in a stage whisper: "And make sure you don't let him get away."

"He's stuck with me."

"That's what I like to hear. Now come, you two. Leave this place."

Rhiannon stood up and went to wait in the car.

Gallagher said: "Don't leave it too long, Freddy. Get those people of yours here."

"I know what I'm doing. Now come on. *Raus.*"

"Alright, you bloody useless fisherman." Gallagher gave Talheim's shoulder a brief squeeze. "You never even caught one."

"I caught something else instead."

"See you, Freddy."

"And you, Gordon."

"He'll be alright," Gallagher said in the car as they made their way back through the tunnel.

"Was that for my benefit?" she asked. "Or yours?"

He glanced at her, his smile acknowledging the accuracy of her instincts.

"Both," he said.

The Brabus Mercedes was heading for Hienheimer Forest when the cold-eyed man noticed the helicopter, a speck in the distance. It was heading for the same area.

He picked up the radiophone. "Abort," he said. "Abort. We'll meet in Nürnberg."

The driver stared at him. "Why call the cars off?"

The cold-eyed man pointed to the aircraft. "We've lost this round. There'll be company waiting. Head for Nürnberg."

A silence descended upon them as the driver changed direction. They had all heard the frantic last call from their colleague in the Opel.

"I am being pursued!" he had shouted. "My partner is dead! Need help!" He had then given the location for the second and last time.

No more messages had come through.

"What now?" the man in the back asked at last.

"He may still be in there," the cold-eyed man said, "or he may have gone on. I'll alert the other locations. We'll find him again."

There was the chill of death in the cold-eyed man's voice.

12

"I've lost count of the number of times that I've driven through Belgium from Germany," Gallagher began with resignation, "and each time, it's somehow managed to rain."

The spots of drizzle that had threatened just as they were passing Aachen had turned into a downpour now that they were negotiating the circuit round Brussels.

He had driven at high speed, keeping the digits on the 230kph mark—nearly 144 miles an hour—as often as was possible on the unrestricted German autobahns. They had left Talheim at the chalet just before six o'clock, and despite a stop for petrol and the necessarily much lower velocity on the speed-limited Belgian roads, the peripheral autoroute around the capital city had been reached by ten.

The yellow glare of the road lights, made baleful by the deluge, gave the interchange the look of a futuristic terminal. Gallagher took the route to Ghent. There was barely any traffic.

Most of the journey had been made with a minimum of conversation. He had played tapes on the Blaupunkt Toronto, now wired through to six speakers, and Rhiannon had seemed content to recline her seat and listen to the music, sometimes changing the tapes when she wanted particular ones. He had left her to it, knowing that what had occurred at the chalet was still on her mind.

It was on his, too, and thoughts for her safety were paramount. He had kept a careful scrutiny of his mirrors; but nothing had appeared in them; except those vehicles that had appeared there briefly, after he had streaked past.

"Perhaps it's a special welcome that's been reserved for you," she now said, easing the back of her seat upright.

"Then tell whoever is responsible I'd prefer some dry weather for a change. When it's pouring like this, the road surface between Bruges and the Zeebrugge can sometimes be like a shallow river. I don't want to cut our speed too far, but at the same time, I don't fancy aquaplaning either. Are you hungry? We can stop off in Bruges. . . ."

"No. I'm fine. We can eat on the ferry."

"The ferry it is." He could just make out the ghost of a smile on her face. "Are you alright now?"

She nodded. "Yes. I'm okay."

"Once we're past Bruges, we'll be on the home stretch." He stared through the rainswept windscreen. The wipers worked furiously. "I wish this rain would fall somewhere else though."

But the rain stayed with them and just after Bruges, he saw the great spray of water on the long straight that led to Zeebrugge.

"That's all we needed," he said with a groan. "Bloody trucks."

This being the ferry route, it was to be expected; but he had hoped to have missed meeting a convoy. It would slow them right down if they could not pass quickly.

"We'll have to get past," he went on. "We might miss the boat otherwise and be forced to hang around till the next one. I can think of better places to spend the next few hours than a ferry port."

"Do you think those people are still after us?" she asked, trying to sound calm.

"I've checked the mirrors all the way. Nothing so far. They probably think we're still near Ingolstadt . . . assuming Freddy's people got there in time."

"Do you . . . do you think they have? Freddy's people, I mean."

"Bound to. He knew what he was doing. He's been in worse situations."

"You're really worried about him, aren't you?"

"It shows?"

"Your voice. It's all in your voice."

"He'll be alright," Gallagher said after a while, hoping that would indeed be so. "Let's concentrate on getting past those things up ahead."

He had pulled into the outside lane, to give himself plenty of time for the maneuver.

Rhiannon leaned forward to peer at the road through the rain-drenched windscreen.

"You were certainly right about the water," she said. "There's enough here to ski on. All you'd need is a rope to attach to one of the lorries for a tow all the way to the ferry terminal."

Given the state of the road surface, she wasn't far wrong, he thought.

"The lane's clear," he said, "so now's as good a time as any."

The *quattro* surged forward as he began to overtake. The two lorries, massive eighteen-wheelers, were traveling almost nose to tail, throwing up enough water to rival a fleet of fire engines.

As he began to pass the first one, Gallagher felt as if he had taken the car through a waterfall. For the briefest of instants that seemed like a year, the view both ahead and behind was totally obscured. The drumming of the water sounded like rapid machinegun fire. Then they were through.

"Someone ought to do something about the spray thrown up by monsters like that," he said. "Now for the next one."

But Rhiannon was screaming: *"Gordon!"*

The second truck had suddenly pulled into the fast lane; and the one now behind had speeded up. The full glare of its headlamps had been turned on. Its air horns were blaring.

The rear window was a blinding area of diffused light, patterned by streaming rivulets: and ahead the windscreen, deluged by pounding gallons of water thrown up by the massive wheels of the other truck, could barely be seen through. The truck stubbornly refused to move over while from behind, its companion drew ever closer.

Gallagher swung the *quattro* into the inside lane. The truck in front blocked him by moving back, while the one in the rear tried to crowd him.

He pulled out into the outside lane. The truck in front heaved its bulk at the car, forcing Gallagher to abort; but the other truck continued to move up, horns still blaring.

"Gordon!" Rhiannon was saying in a high, fearful voice. *"What are they doing?"*

He knew exactly what they were attempting.

"Sandwich," he said grimly. "We're the meat."

"Oh my God," she said in a voice full of fear. "Not again! They can't be the same people. They couldn't know...."

"Not the same people, perhaps... but some of their friends."

"But how could they know we'd be here, and be *waiting?*" Her voice had risen, and her eyes stared at the ghostly juggernaut in the rain.

It didn't matter how they knew. What mattered was survival.

"We'll get out of this," he told her. Trouble was, he couldn't see how.

She calmed herself down; but her eyes were still wide with fear. Then suddenly, she grew angry.

"Bastards!" she said. *"Bloody bastards!"* she shouted at the trucks.

"That's more like it," he told her. "Stay angry."

He moved the *quattro* over to the inside lane for a second time. The truck in front again moved to block him. He moved back. It followed. All the while, speed increased, and the one behind continued to creep up. The digits showed his speed to be 130 kph, just over 80 miles an hour. Surely the trucks would have to be hauling off soon.

But the one in front was baulking him, making sure the other would catch up. Then would come the crunch. Literally.

"Sod it," Gallagher said, and dropped speed abruptly.

The truck in front seemed to race ahead and its tail of spray went from the car's windscreen, allowing him to see more clearly. But the one behind had caught up.

Gradually, he let the speed build again as he moved into the inside lane. The truck with the lights fell behind.

"What . . . what are you doing?" Rhiannon asked uncertainly.

"They're trying to kill us. Fine. Let's see how they like a taste of their own medicine."

"You're going to kill *them?*"

"It's either that, or we'll soon become another accident statistic. Rather them than us."

She said nothing, but stared at him as if seeing him for the first time.

"There's no choice, Rhiannon."

"I know," she said. But it was not approval.

The truck had moved in front once more. Gallagher booted the *quattro* forward. It launched itself as if wanting to plane. The truck began to move to block him, putting on speed. He hit the brakes just when it seemed the car would be shouldered off the road. Rhiannon held on tightly to the door grab-handle.

The car seemed to squat on the wet road, like a cat digging its claws into a cushion. The truck behind was taken by surprise and appeared to dip forward as its driver trod on its brakes.

"I think I've got them," he said.

He tried the maneuver again. Again, the truck dipped obligingly.

"I'm going to try for it next time," he told her. "They seem to be waiting for something, and I don't think we ought to hang around to find out. I'm going to have to do it quite fast, but don't worry about the speed. Okay?"

She nodded.

He put his foot down. The turbo roared and the car surged forward. The truck began to move out in front. The one behind had fallen behind, but it had begun to accelerate in response. Gallagher flicked the switch that would disable his brake lights, and let his speed continue to climb.

Once more, they had entered the truck's powerhouse of spray. The one behind was coming up. The one in front had again settled in the outside lane.

Gallagher waited his moment.

Rhiannon had turned to look fearfully at the blaze of light.

"Gordon," she said in a voice that was trying hard not to scream. "He's close!"

"I know. I want him closer."

Ahead, he could almost believe he was flying through a rain cloud. The truck was barely visible.

Then he was hitting the brakes and snapping the car out of lane. It moved under full control, changing direction with utter stability. The inside lane was clear.

Gallagher floored the accelerator. The *quattro* launched itself forward, gathered speed and hurtled away. It cleared the nose of the truck just as the driver woke up to what had happened. The truck tried to swing in but was already much too late. The driver, however, had overdone it. The eighteen-wheeled monster began to jacknife.

The one behind, having had no warning of the car's braking, was much closer than he wanted to be. He had no room for maneuver. He trod on his brakes, but on the soaked road, his momentum became his enemy.

His truck ploughed into the one that was now directly across his path. Both vehicles, like great dinosaurs, began to twist about each other, sliding with horrendous metallic noises that sounded like roars of combat. Then a huge explosion rolled into the night.

Gallagher saw the vivid glare, heard the rolling sound, and knew he had succeeded. The lights at the Blankenberg junction were green and he maintained his speed.

Then Rhiannon was again shouting his name.

"I've seen him," he said.

Another truck, coming from the direction of Bruges, had deliberately jumped the lights in an attempt to block their path, but was not quick enough. It carried on and slammed into a fourth truck coming from Zeebrugge. A second explosion rent the drowned night. Flames added their brightness to the dark.

"Whatever they were planning," Gallagher said, "we've stopped this lot at least, for good."

He drove on to Zeebrugge. They made it in time to the ferry.

The crossing was without incident; but Rhiannon did not sleep, neither did she choose to eat, making do instead with just a cup of coffee.

The journey from Dover up to London was equally without incident. It was as if no one had been chasing them since France. London was dry. There had been no rain for days.

When at 0630 they eventually arrived at his maisonette in Holland Park, they went straight to bed where Rhiannon lay wide awake, holding on to him and shivering. Long-delayed reaction had at last taken hold of her. They lay thus for hours, during which time the phone rang several times. Gallagher ignored it, letting the answering machine do the job. He had deliberately not checked it on his return. The calls could wait.

At ten o'clock, Rhiannon at last fell asleep. He watched her for some moments, then got out of bed without disturbing her to turn down the volume of the phone's buzzer. He went back, and he too fell asleep.

He awoke at two o'clock, feeling refreshed. Rhiannon was still sleeping. Again without disturbing her, he climbed out, had a long bath, put on some clean clothes and made himself a light meal. When he had finished, she was still out to the world. He continued to ignore the phone, leaving it on mute, though the warning light had blinked several times.

He looked in on her once more, decided she would be alright, wrote her a brief note to say he was going out for a while, and left the house. She would be quite safe and if she also chose to go out, knew how to set the security system.

He got into the *quattro* and drove to the garage in Cobham to have it checked, to see how the new modifications installed in Germany had settled in after the recent high-speed dash and arguments with the homicidal trucks.

He also intended to see Fowler; but that particular visit was not going to be a pleasant one. At the garage in Cobham, he decided to make a remote call to the answering machine while he waited for the car. There were several photo assignments waiting, a few social invitations; and a call from Fowler.

"If you're back in one piece," the mild voice said, "do come and see me. You'll need my help."

Gallagher replaced the phone slowly. "Bastard," he said.

"Bad news?"

Gallagher looked up. One of the garage firm's directors, a man he always dealt with, had entered the office he'd been loaned from which to make his call.

"Irritating would be a better way to describe it," Gallagher replied.

The man, familiar with Gallagher's sometimes mysterious comings and goings, did not press further. He well remembered how once Gallagher had brought the car in with blood all over the passenger seat. The expected descent of a battalion of police upon the garage premises had not materialised. Ever since, he'd learned to leave such queries that rose in his mind strictly unspoken.

"The car's perfect," he now said. "Nothing wrong."

Gallagher stood up. "Now that's good news."

"It's waiting outside."

Gallagher smiled. "Thanks for the fast service." They shook hands and he went out to the car.

He took the high roundabout out of Cobham, went right and down onto the wide lanes of the A3 for London. There was not much traffic and the *quattro* cruised smoothly at 70 mph.

A couple of minutes later, a glance in the mirrors betrayed the presence of a white speck in the distance. As the speck grew with the assurance born of the knowledge that the speed limit could be broken with impunity, Gallagher did not need to identify the long snout. A police Rover was on his tail.

He glanced at the speedometer. The digits sat firmly at 70. This was not Germany where a patrol car could be passed at high speed without the attendant feeling of being haunted. The wide road was virtually empty. Gallagher always felt that limits increased rather than decreased accidents. It encouraged bunching. Meeting a moving phalanx of metal, waiting for an accident to happen was the stuff of nightmares.

The Rover was closer and still in hot pursuit. Gallagher maintained his speed in the inside lane. There was no one ahead of him. Suddenly, the Rover darted from the outside lane to swoop into station behind the *quattro*. The convoy traveled for a good three miles, the police car making no move to either overtake or flash its lights to order Gallagher to stop.

He decided if the patrol car wanted to follow him, that was its business. There was only one occupant in the Rover.

A mile later, the policeman appeared to have decided the game had lost its allure. The expected flashing of the blue beacon at last came. Gallagher pulled over, determined to be pleasant, despite his intense irritation. The last thing he wanted was a run-in with a policeman looking for something to do. They'd be there all day and he had better things to do with his own time.

The Rover pulled up almost on the bumper, and the patrolman got out, approaching on the passenger side. Gallagher lowered the window. The policeman rested a hand on the car and peered in.

He smiled. "Squadron Leader Gallagher? Sorry to have sat on your tail like that, sir. Wanted to make sure I'd got the right car."

As soon as Gallagher had heard the policeman use his old rank, he knew what was coming next. Fowler. It could only be Fowler. Gallagher was not one of those people who hung on to his rank once out of the service; and Fowler knew it. A needle if there ever was one.

"Got a message for you, sir," the policeman was saying. "Headquarters want you to contact them." The policeman added a little joke. "Not at war, are we, sir?"

Headquarters. Fowler's warped sense of humor. Bastard.

"Not as far as I know," Gallagher replied.

The policeman grinned. "As long as it stays that way. I've still got a lot of loving to do."

"So do we all, officer. And thanks for the message."

"My pleasure, sir." The policeman saluted and went back to his patrol car. He waved at Gallagher, then sent the Rover squealing up the road, accelerating to a speed that most motorists could only dream of doing without being caught.

Gallagher continued on his journey, deliberately keeping his speed below 70. Fowler could bloody well wait.

* * *

Fowler said: "Glad you could make it." The eyes behind the glasses appeared to gleam with amusement. "And in one piece too."

Gallagher looked at him stonily. "The police car was your idea, was it?"

"A simple reminder."

"Of what? Your ability to screw up my life? To place innocent bystanders at risk? Or to use policemen as messenger boys?"

"To remind you," Fowler said calmly, "that you're not out of the woods yet. As I was quite certain you had received my telephone message and had chosen to ignore it, I felt a little encouragement was needed."

"It was a wasted effort. I was coming to see you. . . ."

"I'm flattered. . . ."

"To have this whole stinking business cleared up. We were nearly killed in Belgium. . . ."

"And in Germany, by all accounts."

Gallagher paused, staring at Fowler coldly. "You've got a bloody nerve, Fowler."

Fowler said: "Sit down, Gordon. Have some tea. Arundel's on her way. Biscuits too. Your favorites. She heard you were coming."

Gallagher remained standing.

Fowler picked up some transcripts from his desk and began to leaf through them. He didn't seem to mind that Gallagher had chosen not to take a seat.

As he sorted the sheets of paper, he continued: "You appear to leave a trail of death and destruction in your wake. In France, an assorted number of French army vehicles and ten dead. Soldiers.

One Department car, and Prinknash shot in. . . ."

Gallagher's eyes had narrowed while Fowler read the list. Now he cut in to say: "Now it's my turn to feel flattered. You're not trying to say *I* was responsible? Anyone shooting Prinknash up gets a handshake from me, but sorry . . . Not guilty."

"Then Switzerland," Fowler went on, as if Gallagher had not spoken, "mercifully escaped your attentions. In Germany, two dead, a blazing vehicle that had been blown apart, and a patch of smoking forest. You want to be careful. The Germans are very partial to their greenery these days. Talheim gets shot. Then it's on to Belgium where *four* lorries managed to pound each other to pieces. Six dead, one of whom was an innocent bystander. . . ."

Gallagher heard himself say: "Which one?"

Fowler looked up at him. "Do sit down, Gordon. You look as if you'll need to. Which one? A driver on his way off the ferry to Brussels. His truck was hit by another that had jumped the lights, in pouring rain. He lived long enough to tell the police. But you were there, so you know."

Gallagher had sat down.

"What are you really saying, Fowler?"

"*I* know, and *you* know, that none of this was directly your fault. A hit team is running amok for reasons we can only speculate. What is certain is that the police forces of several countries may persuade themselves you were responsible, in the absence of the real culprits. . . ."

"You're sure you don't mean *you* will persuade them?" Gallagher asked softly.

Fowler smiled fleetingly. "Ah. I see. You believe I am about to coerce you. I don't have to.

Those men are professionals: but even professionals give in to revenge. They won't leave you alone. As for your young lady, do you want her continually put at risk? You need our help."

"And what if I refuse this marvelous help?"

Fowler sighed. "Then matters could become quite tricky. You'll have no umbrella over here when they come to strike and, of course, should you for example manage to use one of their weapons against them, you may find that somewhat difficult to explain away. It's not as if you're . . . er . . . on strength, so to speak. And as for Europe, there are now quite large chunks of it where the reception from certain of their departments could prove a trifle chilly . . . unless of course we put in a good word. . . ."

"You conniving sod," Gallagher said bitterly. The hazel eyes regarded Fowler lifelessly. "I'd expect a little shame, at the very least."

"Knew you'd see it my way." Fowler reached into a desk drawer and took out a large brown envelope which he placed before Gallagher. "One valid passport in the name of Paul Renwick, return tickets to Bergen in Norway, and all the money you should need . . . in cash. Instructions in there will tell you where to go for your first meeting. You'll receive further instructions from then on. Your hotel's booked for three days. This shouldn't take longer. You fly from Gatwick tomorrow morning. You'll be back before you know it."

"I'd prefer not to go."

"I'm sure you would, but Borodin will be waiting. Not making that rendezvous could cost us a lot. I'd not be very pleased if you missed it. After all, he did ask for you. He'll see no one else. You're stuck with it, I'm afraid."

"You look very sorry, Fowler."

"I do understand the reasons for the sarcasm," Fowler said mildly, "But it's quite unwarranted. I do really wish you had not been dragged into this."

"I've seen more genuine tears on crocodiles."

A soft knock interrupted them.

"Come in, Arundel," Fowler called.

Delphine Arundel entered with tea and biscuits for two, on a wooden tray. She plonked it down on Fowler's desk, the action clearly showing her disapproval.

"How are you, Gordon?" she asked in a warm voice, obviously pleased to see him.

"I was better before I came in here, but I've just improved."

"Still able to say the right things, I see." She smiled at him, then gave Fowler a cold stare.

Fowler said: "Arundel quite clearly does not approve of my hauling you in like this, Gordon, although I've explained there was no choice."

"Do you believe him?" she asked.

"No," Gallagher answered.

"That makes two of us," she said and, with another hard stare at Fowler, she went out.

Fowler said: "Very protective toward you, is Arundel. I expect I'll have my head bitten off." He didn't sound particularly worried.

"I think I'll skip tea," Gallagher said, rising.

"Arundel will be disappointed."

"She'll understand." Gallagher picked up the envelope. "You've had this all worked out, haven't you? My tickets are ready, hotel's booked, rendezvous set. You've had it all set up, even before you came to France with your little story. Don't even try to explain." Fowler had been just about to speak.

As Gallagher moved to the door, Winterbourne barged in.

"Ah! Gallagher," he began.

"Goodbye," Gallagher said harshly, and brushed past.

Winterbourne stared after him, before continuing into Fowler's office. "There are times," Winterbourne began in an outraged voice, "when I wonder why that man ever held the Queen's commission . . . even if it was in the Royal Air Force. No offense meant, Fowler."

Fowler, who knew better, said with masterly equanimity: "No offense taken, Sir John. But I do know of some people who are far less deserving of holding a commission than Gallagher."

Winterbourne looked at Fowler as if trying to decide whether the barb had been aimed his way.

Gallagher saw the white van with the checkerboard sidestripes and the man hovering near the *quattro*. The all-new private wheel-clampers about to spring into action.

"Don't you bloody dare," Gallagher snarled at him.

The man, in a pale blue zipped jacket and jeans, said: "Just doing my job, mate."

"Piss off!" Gallagher said. "I'm just leaving."

A uniformed policeman came out of the van, putting on his cap as he did so. He laid a restraining hand on the man's shoulder.

"Ease off, Mick. Not this one. Sorry, sir," he

went on to Gallagher. "Mick here's new to this and doesn't know the form just yet."

But Gallagher wanted to give vent to the anger he felt. The man called Mick was, for the moment, a convenient target.

"Your job depends on people buying cars," he snapped. "Imagine what would happen if we hung on to our money."

"Why wouldn't people want to buy cars?" the man called Mick asked, genuinely astonished.

Gallagher stared at him, resignedly noting the incomprehension. "Think about it," he said. "If you can."

He got into the *quattro*, and drove off.

The wheelclamp man watched the departing car. "Did you see that?" he asked the policeman. "No keys. So who is he, then?"

"Don't ask questions, Mick. There's a good lad."

Haslam entered Fowler's office.

"Was that Gallagher's car I've just seen leaving the square?"

"It was indeed, George." Fowler had a peaceful expression upon his face.

"You're looking smug," Haslam said. "Things going well, are they? He's agreed to go?"

"Not so much an agreement as an acceptance of reality."

"Which you no doubt helped him to see."

"Cynicism in your old age, George?"

"I've been cynical since birth. How did he take it?"

"He displayed some anger, but rather less

than I'd expected." Fowler seemed thoughtful now.

Haslam said: "Dangerous."

"What do you mean?"

"Gallagher marshals his anger and forges it into a weapon. When he doesn't *look* angry, that's when he's at his most dangerous. Let's hope he never finds out what you're really up to."

"And what am I up to, George?"

Haslam looked skeptical. "You may be able to fool Winterbourne, and even Gallagher; but you've got to be up very early in the morning to pull a fast one over me."

"Meaning?"

"Meaning you're not really interested in the list, if it does exist. You're after bigger game. You're after Borodin, whoever he may be. A great coup, if you can pull it off. A top dissident in Soviet Intelligence. . . ."

"You're wrong, George. I'm not after Borodin. Others may be, though."

"The Russians, naturally."

"And the rest."

"The Americans?"

"Why not? They'd love something like that. They need a big success."

"But do they know about this?"

"Who can tell?" Fowler said with a touch of bitterness.

Haslam knew what he meant. *"Winterbourne* would tell them?"

"I wouldn't put it past him. Close relationship and all that rubbish. He's after an Ambassadorship to Washington. He'll do anything to get it. He seems to think that's where the seat of power is."

Haslam gave a tight grin. "What a child."

Fowler said: "There are a lot like him about. My job is to find out why Borodin is prepared to risk himself to come West and to ensure no one takes him."

"I see. So you expect Gallagher to help him if he gets into trouble."

Fowler smiled. "Gallagher is our knight errant. He doesn't trust me. . . ."

"Oh the poor deluded fool."

"That's enough sarcasm from you, George. I've already had it from Gallagher. To continue . . . he doesn't trust me. . . ." Fowler ignored Haslam's amused stare. ". . . and will do all he can to ensure he pays me back for what's happened. If he does find a list, he'll not turn it over to me. He'll quite probably not give it to Borodin either. After all, Borodin could be a fake. No. I suspect Gallagher will destroy the list . . . if he finds one. If Borodin *is* genuine, however, I believe Gallagher will help him out of trouble, should he get into any."

Haslam said: "You're able to read Gallagher that well?"

Fowler sighed. "No, George. I can't. I'm making inspired guesses and hoping they'll turn out to be correct."

There was a moment's silence, then Haslam said: "It's good to see you looking worried for a change."

"You say the nicest things, George."

Gallagher returned home to find Rhiannon gone. Her note was next to the one he had left. She had decided to go to her flat, then would pay a visit to the gallery. She'd call him later.

He studied the note with a feeling of disquiet. She was not due to return to work for another few days. Perhaps she needed time on her own to get over what had occurred on the continent. He could understand that. A holiday that had promised so much had been turned into a murderous shambles.

All because Fowler had stuck his oar in.

Bastard, Gallagher said in his mind.

He stared at Rhiannon's note. The feeling of disquiet would not go away.

Haslam entered the room in the private wing of the small hospital where injured Department personnel were taken for repair. Strictly speaking, Prinknash did not qualify; but he had been seriously wounded and Fowler had insisted, against Winterbourne's wishes, that Prinknash should be taken there.

Prinknash was sitting propped up in bed, right leg encased in plaster and suspended off the bedclothes.

"You look uncomfortable," Haslam said with a brief smile.

Prinknash had been intently studying a magazine full of naked blonde young women. He hastily placed it beneath his pillow.

"Make you go blind," Haslam continued, looking at Prinknash's guilty face. "Someone smuggled it in?"

"Er . . . no, Mr. Haslam. I found it in the bedside cabinet."

Haslam shook his head slowly. "The things

people take into hospital. Well, Prinknash? Are they treating you well?"

"They're treating me like royalty, Mr. Haslam. Very nice hospital, this. Not your average National Health job, I'll bet. Where is this place, Mr. Haslam?"

"Somewhere to look after our wounded," Haslam replied, clearly intending to say no more in explanation. "The leg's alright then?"

Prinknash nodded. "At least they didn't have to take it off. Three bullets those bastards put in me. One bruised a bone as it went through. A little closer and it would have shattered it. The doctor said I might have lost the leg then. Bastards. Bloody Frogs."

Haslam said: "The French didn't shoot you."

"Happened in Frogland, didn't it? I'll tell you, Mr. Haslam. I'm glad to be back . . . even like this. Good old England. No place like it. Best country in the world." Prinknash looked at Haslam as if daring him to disagree.

Haslam said: "There are times when it can be . . . and at others . . . the very worst. There were also times, about which I would agree with you wholeheartedly." He sounded as if mourning the passing of someone very close.

"Like when we had the Empire? You'd know about that, wouldn't you Mr. Haslam. Those must have been the days."

Haslam stared at Prinknash. "I wasn't thinking about the days of Empire. I was thinking about something else entirely."

"I . . . I don't understand, Mr. Haslam."

"I know you don't," Haslam said. He tapped Prinknash on the shoulder. "Look after that leg.

Oh yes . . . enjoy your magazine." He smiled and began to walk toward the door.

"Thanks for coming, Mr. Haslam," Prinknash said.

Haslam paused, looked round. "In a few more days, you'll be moved to another hospital. Not as salubrious, I'm afraid, but you'll be able to receive more visitors: family and so on. They've been informed you were injured on duty. No need to tell you they cannot be told what specific duty."

"No need, Mr. Haslam."

"Good man." Haslam nodded, and went out.

13

Gallagher watched as the warning light on the phone began to blink. He had not yet opened the envelope Fowler had given to him and, thinking it could be Fowler on the phone, left the answering machine connected. He turned up the volume.

Someone began to speak. It was Rhiannon.

"So you're not back yet," her voice said. There was a quality to it that made him pause as he had begun to reach for the phone, to take the call himself. "I . . . I don't like talking to these things, but I suppose I might as well now I've made the call. I . . . I hope you won't think me an awful . . . coward; but . . . but what has happened over the past few days has frightened me. I . . . I want to spend a few days by myself . . . oh dear, I'm not doing this very well. Oh, Gordon . . . I . . . I don't want anything to come between us, but I keep thinking about the kind of work you used to do . . . I'm not like Eva, I suppose. She seems able to cope with Freddy getting shot . . . I . . . oh damn! I know I'm not doing this right. Call me when you get in. Please?"

The call ended. Gallagher felt a knot in his stomach. Rhiannon had been crying. He was sure of it, though she had valiantly tried to disguise the fact. Was this Borodin affair going to drive her away from him? Was he to lose her, after all, just like the others? He wanted her out of harm's way; but if she chose to leave. . . .

He didn't want to think about it. He stared at the phone and did not call her. Instead, he began to open Fowler's envelope.

Everything within it was as Fowler had said; but there was a note too, in his handwriting.

"Take a camera with you," the note began. "Look like a tourist, if you can. In case you've been wondering how you were traced to Talheim's chalet, a bug was placed on the car loaned to you. A mechanic found it while inspecting the car. Someone rang Talheim's number about it, and one of his former colleagues went to pick it up. The information was passed to us. Good luck."

Gallagher tore the note into little pieces and dumped them in a bin. Good luck indeed. Sod you, Fowler.

He was angry with himself. He had been careless, and Talheim had collected a bullet because of it.

Still in his foul mood, he inspected the passport the Department had provided. It was genuine. This was no makeshift document and was similar to the ones he had used during his own time in harness. Even his photograph was a recent one. He didn't bother trying to work out how they had done it. That would have been a waste of time. It could have occurred at any juncture during the past year when Fowler had been in contact. It was amazing what a decent long lens could do these days.

Paul Renwick, the name on the passport, was apparently an advertising executive. Gallagher put the passport down and pulled out a type sheet of paper with the instructions for the first meet and information about his hotel. That was all. The typed sheet went the way of Fowler's note. His ticket told him his flight was leaving Gatwick the next morning at 0930. There was a generous amount of cash. Fowler was certainly not being mean. Borodin was clearly important to the Department.

"That's not a thought that makes me happy," Gallagher said aloud.

He didn't call Rhiannon.

In the morning he called a cab, then securing the house, waited outside for it to arrive. The *quattro* was also secured, its alarm systems activated. Leaving it in full view in the car port should help convince any interested watchers he was still in town. He had deliberately packed a small travel bag and had put his favorite Nikon in it. He was dressed in a casual lightweight suit but wore no tie. In case Norway turned out to be suffering an early onset of winter, he had packed a sweater and a zipped leather jacket. He shouldn't need more, he hoped.

The cab arrived and he got in, making no overt move to check his surroundings. As the cab pulled into Holland Park Avenue and headed toward Marble Arch, he said to the driver: "Take me down Oxford Street first. There's something I've got to pick up."

The cab took the requested route and when it had gone far enough along Oxford Street to suit his purposes, he asked the driver to stop.

"I won't be long," he said as he climbed out.

"It's all the same to me, mate," the driver said. "It's your money."

"Er, yes."

Well it was Department money; but that was hardly the issue. Gallagher walked up a narrow street that went round the back of the as yet unopened shops, to exit into Tottenham Court Road. He walked its entire length, then doubled back. As he approached the spot where he'd left the cab he speeded up and got quickly into it.

"Victoria Station, please," he now said to the driver.

The cab set off immediately. Gallagher took a quick look through the rear window. No sign of another car pulling away from the curb in an attempt to follow. By the time the cab had arrived at Victoria, there was still no evidence of a tail.

The fast train to Gatwick carried no passenger that appeared to have an interest in his movements. At the airport, he did not let his guard down. No visual evidence of a tail did not necessarily mean one did not exist. People had died forgetting that.

He checked in, then went to a phone. Rhiannon should be up. She wasn't.

"Yes?" she said groggily.

"It's me," he said. "I'm sorry I woke you."

"It's alright. I had a bad night, I wasn't really asleep. Why didn't you call me? I've had a terrible time wondering. Are you angry with me?"

"Of course I'm not," he replied gently. "I just wanted to give you the time...."

"That doesn't mean you couldn't call me to talk.... Where are you anyway? I think I can hear airplanes. Gordon...."

"I'm going away for a short while. I'll call you when I get back. We'll have a long talk then."

"Going away?" Alarm sounded in her voice. "Where? Gordon, you're not...."

"Don't worry. I'll be back before you know it...."

"Oh Gordon, no. You can't. Please...."

"Rhian, I've got to go now, or I'll miss...."

"Don't hang up, please! Gordon...." The forlorn voice faded.

"I must." Gently. "See you when I get back." Slowly, he replaced the receiver. Suddenly, he felt the anger boil within him, despite his determination to control it. "You bastard, Fowler," he snarled quietly to himself.

Then his feelings were once more under firm control as his flight was called.

Iturup, the Kuril Islands. 2100 hours, the same day.

The lights of the airbase were all out. An intelligence exercise was being held. Normal operations, however, were being continued. That was the ostensible object of the exercise. At one end of an unlit runway, a 46½-meter-long Ilyushin Il-76 AWACS aircraft waited for take-off clearance. Like the base itself, the Il-76 was showing no lights. Take-off would be done on instruments.

Sitting at one of the operator consoles was Skoryatin. He was there in his capacity as observer, to monitor the crew's performance. They did not know him as the powerful General of the GRU. They knew he was GRU; but as Colonel Igor Taginiev. All of them looked upon him as a snooper with steel-rimmed glasses, who was out to make trouble for any unfortunate deemed to have performed less than satisfactorily.

They would do their best to ignore him, of course; which meant they'd spend as little time as was politely possible looking at him. That suited Skoryatin perfectly.

The four powerful jet engines began to spool up and the huge aircraft, with its high T-tail and disc-shaped radome fixed to its spine, started to roll along the darkened runway.

Skoryatin involuntarily tensed himself for the take-off. He hoped the pilots knew their job. He had no intention of being spread all over the invisible ground. There were important things to do.

The Il-76 heaved itself with a great roar into the night. The twenty wheels of its massive undercarriage thumped into their housings as the pilots cleaned up and went into a steady climb, heading north-west across Sakhalin and deep into the airspaces of the Far Eastern and Transbaikal Military Districts. Their task for the mission was to sniff out any intrusions by American spy planes and to direct fighters on to them: supposedly.

Skoryatin relaxed in his seat. His mind was very far from American spy planes for the time being. He was thinking of Kamapova successfully kept out of the way by the man who was impersonating him. Kamapova had been told that the Comrade Colonel-General was making surprise inspections of the island units and would be away for some days. It had been arranged that she saw his form entering an armored vehicle. It has also been arranged that she would be kept fully occupied by the resident GRU Colonel.

Skoryatin had planned to be back well before she began to get too nosy and tried to go off after him.

He smiled thinly. All was going well.

One of the crew members saw his smile, misunderstood, and looked worried. The operator became more diligently interested in his monitor screen.

Bergen Approach, 1230 hours.

Gallagher heard the wheels clunking out of their wells and like many, even non-current pilots being flown by others, imagined himself on the flight deck and hoped the pilots knew what they were doing. He glanced out of the window and Norway greeted him with a spectacular view of a shoal of small islands of varying sizes, beneath the aircraft's path.

As the BAe 1-11 descended, the islands seemed to gather speed in the opposite direction and one view in particular fixed itself in his memory: it was of a red-topped house perched upon a tiny patch of ground, scarcely bigger than itself. Then it was gone and the 1-11 was flaring out, groping for the runway. The pilots made heavy work of it and the wheels slammed into contact.

Thank you, Gallagher said in his mind. *I like having my spine rattled.*

A middle-aged woman sitting next to him said: "That was a bit hard wasn't it?" She was trying to sound nonchalant and failed. The landing had scared her.

He smiled encouragingly. "Not as hard as some I've sat through." Which was true enough, except that they hadn't been on airliners.

The aircraft came to a halt a short distance from the low terminal building and he walked with the other passengers, mainly tourists who seemed to be traveling together, along a marked path on the tarmac to the terminal. Bergen was pleasantly warm.

As he entered, Gallagher looked about him and was amused by an advertisement that greeted his eyes. It was for a Chinese restaurant. Come to Norway for a Chinese take-away.

He didn't dwell on his weak joke for long. His eyes scanned his surroundings but detected nothing to give alarm. There had been no one on the aircraft either, to cause him anxiety. Perhaps whoever his pursuers were, they still hunted for him in London.

Paul Renwick's passport gave him no trouble and he walked through the building to the open parking area. Two single decker buses were waiting in the sunshine. A man was ushering the tourists into one. Both vehicles bore the name of the hotel he had been booked into. He went up to the still empty bus and spoke to the driver in English, giving the hotel's name. The driver nodded, and Gallagher climbed aboard. Soon, more of the tourists had piled in, and the bus set off. As it began its journey into town, Gallagher looked to his left and saw beyond the car park itself the hangars and light aircraft of an aero club.

He settled in his seat and wondered what Bergen had in store for him.

Bergen. City of the seven mountains; the Fjord Capital, over 900 years old, home of Edvard Grieg. Gallagher looked out of his hotel window and decided he was going to like Bergen.

It seemed to him to be the epitome of a Scandinavian city: neat, clean, uncluttered. On this day it was also bright and warm. Cities had a general atmosphere about them, above and beyond their good and bad points. Paris was exciting, rude, chic; Berlin was exciting too, but dangerous; New York, dangerous *and* frightening; poor old London had had its spirit stamped upon, and something mean and ugly had taken its place. Bergen, however, seemed friendly. He hoped it would remain so.

The hotel the Department had booked him into was very comfortable indeed: a worrying factor. With Fowler prepared to shell out the money so freely, it was difficult not to feel like a condemned man. He looked along the cobbled thoroughfare of Torgalmenning toward the medieval wooden buildings of Bryggen and decided to dispense with such gloomy thoughts.

He glanced at the small travel clock he had brought. Forty-five minutes to his first rendezvous. It was time to get moving. He had changed into jeans and a clean shirt, and his leather jacket. On his feet were black ankle boots of soft leather with grip soles. He picked up the Nikon and went out. Time to play the tourist.

He left the hotel, turned left for the few yards to Torgalmenning, then turned right along it for Bryggen. He crossed over to the wide central divider that had been made into a pedestrian precinct with thick wooden benches and tables, where one could sit and watch Bergen life pass by. At one end of the precinct was a massive plinth with the bronze figures of Bergen's past installed about its base. As he passed it, two women sitting at a nearby table were conversing in bemused American voices. Perhaps they were lost.

Gallagher had been surprised by the number of American voices he had so far heard, now and then punctuated by a few British. As far as the Americans were concerned, it was perhaps not so surprising. Many modern day Americans were of Scandinavian descent and a good proportion of those had come from Norway. This was the old country, the land of their forefathers to be visited at least once in a lifetime.

It was also NATO country and he had scanned the faces he had seen for anyone who looked likely to be following him: but as yet there had been no alarm. The more the situation remained like that, the more he'd like it.

Following his instructions, he continued along Torgalmenning until he came to the open air market at the tip of the Vagen, a long harbor that was itself an arm of two adjoining fjords. The market sold mainly fresh fish of a wide variety; but there were fruit stalls as well. Gallagher had been told of a particular stall where he should linger briefly.

He identified it, and wandered over to stand close by. He felt slightly uneasy, in case he was being set up for target practice. It would be so simple. Then he told himself he was being paranoid.

With good bloody reason, he thought drily.

Playing the tourist, he began to fidget with the camera. From where he stood, he had a good view of the long harbor. To his left, at moorings that looked like a terminal, were three, twinhulled fast passenger boats with rakish superstructures. They were secured neatly in line astern, with a boat-length space between the first and the second. Perhaps one had just left, or was on its way in. They were very sleek-looking vessels. Two had blue hulls, and the other, smaller than its sisters, was red. All had white superstructures.

Over to the right were a pair of iron-hulled oil rig support ships and beyond them, a cruise ship. The harbor itself had many inlets along which many small craft—sailing boats, motorcruisers, and speedboats—were moored. Other inlets betrayed their presence only by their entrances. Gallagher had no doubt there were even more craft tucked away in them. Like most of the points of habitation in western Norway, Bergen was a city of the water.

Closer in to his right, a tall three-masted ship was moored. Gallagher decided it was time to give his role a little authenticity. He focussed on the ship and took a few shots. He then moved away from the stall.

There were plenty of people about, but the market was not crowded. No one approached him. He sauntered through and continued on his way.

His route now took him into Bryggen and went up a fairly steep incline. Now and then he paused to inspect shop windows, some of which displayed a remarkable variety of mouth-watering pastries. No one appeared to be tailing him. Eventually, he came to the point he'd been making for:

the Mount Fløien funicular station. FLØIBANEN, the sign on the building said. Well, he'd made it to the right place.

He followed the next part of his instructions, entered and walked along the tunnel to the ticket booth and bought a ride to the top. He climbed into the car which was soon filled with other passengers. It began to crank its way up the almost precipitous climb. A quick glance of his fellow-passengers still brought no tinglings of incipient alarm. They appeared to be mainly Norwegian judging by the conversation. There were the usual, ubiquitous Japanese faces.

A girl with shoulder length, fine blonde hair and lively blue eyes was looking at him interestedly. Her tight jeans and equally tight white T-shirt accentuated the pleasing fullness of her body. Over the T-shirt was a denim jacket and on her feet were trainers. She was dressed like an American, but did not look it. Across her chest was the legend, in bold black letters: STOP ACID RAIN.

She smiled almost shyly at him, a dimple appearing in her left cheek. He smiled back, wondering what pithy comment this would have elicited from Rhiannon. The thought made him hold on to his smile for a while longer, before memory of their recent parting slowly killed it. He turned away from the girl in the T-shirt just before that happened, to look back down the narrow gauge track with the thick cable running alongside. Could it snap? he wondered.

The car stopped at various places on the way up. Gallagher read them in his mind as they approached: Promsgate, Fjellveien, Skansenyren.

The girl in the T-shirt got off at Skansenyren. It was one more stop to Fløien, the end of the line. The Japanese were still there, with their batteries of cameras.

Gallagher walked out of the terminal building and onto the curving pathway that was bordered from the steep drop by a stout metal barrier. There was a small souvenir shop at the side of the building over whose entrance was hung the small flags of twelve nations, six of which were Scandinavian. The larger flags were of Britain, the US, Germany, and Japan. The Japanese were already in the shop.

Gallagher looked out at the magnificent panorama of Bergen spread out beneath him and wondered where his contact was. The curving track went round to his left where it became a short stretch of loose, slate-gray gravel, to end at a low white, wooden building. Though the main part of the structure appeared to be on level ground, the front section was upon an extended patio which was higher closer to the barrier, to compensate for a gentle slope. Great windows looked out upon Bergen; but the place itself was closed. It seemed forlorn and the worse for wear.

He returned his attention to the city. Out on the water, a creaming wake marked the return of the missing catamaran.

"Beautiful, isn't it?" English spoken with an American accent, but the speaker was not American.

Gallagher turned. The girl with the T-shirt was smiling at him. He had heard the soft footsteps but had assumed it was just another tourist moving round for a better view.

Never assume, sir. Assuming can get you killed.

O'Keefe.

"Do you like Bergen, Mr. Renwick?" She pronounced it as it was written.

"Renwick," he corrected in his surprise, making the "w" silent. *"You* are my contact?"

The smile widened. "I am. Yes." She extended her hand.

Good God. She looked so young to be in this business. No more than eighteen. He shook the hand. It was warm and firm.

"I am sorry about the name," she went on. "I'm sometimes a little shaky with English."

"Sounds fine to me."

The one-dimple smile came on again. "Thank you. By your expression, I think I know what you are thinking. You're thinking . . . oh no! They have sent me a child." Her smile was infectious.

Gallagher said: "I'm not thinking that at all."

"My name," she began formally, "is Kirstin Størvaag, and I am over twenty-one."

Not by much, he didn't say.

"Please," she was saying, the dimple prominent once more, "let us move away from here. I have somewhere a little more private.

As they walked, he noted the fine blonde down on her cheeks. She was quite tall, the top of her head reaching the level of his eyes.

She took him to a side door in the white building and produced a key. He didn't ask how she'd got hold of it. It was none of his business. She unlocked the door, and stood by for him to enter. She followed him in, locking it from the inside.

The place had the air of disuse its sad exterior

had promised. They entered a vast room that looked like a dining area, with tables lining the walls like files of dead soldiers. Chairs were upended upon them.

Kirstin went up to one of the four tall windows that looked out upon Bergen, far below. A table was close by.

"We'll take this one," she said. "We can see out, but the people outside cannot, unless they come close."

No one had so far shown the slightest interest in their actions. They took two chairs off the table and sat down.

"This used to be a restaurant," she told him.

"Why did it close?"

She shrugged. "I have no idea. I am not from Bergen."

He did not ask where from. "Why did you get off the cable car?"

"To see if anyone would follow. No one did, as you know, and no one was waiting. We are alright up here." She reached into the bag she had brought with her to take out and hand him a small envelope. "Your train tickets. You must take the Oslo train at 1510, but you will not be. . . ."

"Today?"

The blue eyes looked at him. "It must be today."

"But my hotel. . . ."

"You are not to check out. They should not ask, but if anyone does, you are going on an excursion. The main tourist season is over for the summer, but there are still excursions. It will not seem suspicious to anyone really interested in what you are doing. Okay? So . . . you do not go to Oslo but get off at Myrdal. This is a normal tourist route. The train will arrive at 1705. You will have five minutes to change to the small mountain train to Flåm. Again, you will not be going all the way. You must get off at Dalsbotn. Do not miss your stop. I shall be waiting there for you. Okay?"

Gallagher nodded. He put the envelope into an inside jacket pocket.

"You are very efficient."

The dimple came on. "Thank you. But I have a small confession to make. I have never been given such work before. I work mainly in an office; but I am a good driver. My superiors decided I should be your guide as well as driver."

"I am sure everything will go smoothly."

Give me strength, he was thinking. *They've sent me a baby.*

Her smile told him he had said the right thing. She stood up. "We must go now. You cannot miss the train. Look for number 64. That is the one you must take."

He got to his feet. "Right." He paused, looking out of the window. A Japanese couple was approaching.

Kirstin looked anxiously at him. "Are they...?"

"Who knows? Let's see what develops."

The couple had come onto the patio and the man came right up to the window to peer in. He carried the inevitable camera, slung from his neck. He pointed to the camera, indicating he wanted to come in to take a picture.

Kirstin made a vigorous, negative motion with her hands. "Come," she said quickly to Gallagher. "We must get out."

He followed as she hurried off, and they left

the building. She made for the patio. Gallagher tagged along.

The Japanese couple were still there.

"I am very sorry," Kirstin said to the man in deliberately slow English. "This place is closed. We are here on official tourist business. I am very sorry," she repeated. "I am not authorized to let anyone go in."

The man bowed slightly to her. "So sorry," he said. "So sorry."

She gave him a quick smile and set off for the cable car terminus with Gallagher.

"I will not be coming down with you," she said. "I shall make my own way and see you at Dalsbotn. For the moment, we must not travel together." She stood back as he went through the gate near the souvenir shop, the dimpled smile sending him on his way.

It stayed in his mind as the car winched itself downward. As was his practice, he gave his fellow-passengers a quick scan. Still nothing to be alarmed about. The Japanese couple had not followed. It didn't mean anything, of course. Going in blind like this, it was safer to be prepared for any eventuality. Kirstin Størvaag herself could be a hostile; even if she did know the name the Department had give him; even though she had been at the very meeting place his instructions had led him to. But for the moment, he had to go along. There was no other option.

In his hotel room, Gallagher took a collapsible camera equipment case made of fabric out of his travel bag and together with the Nikon, put the tickets and some money into it. The passport went into the inner jacket pocket which could be pressed shut on velcro fastenings. The rest of the cash was distributed about his person. He left his suit, the shoes he had traveled in and the bag, in the wardrobe. The small clock was also left where it was. Nothing now in the room would give any clues to a possible snooper.

Leaving the hotel presented no problem. No one appeared to take the slightest notice. There was still a good forty minutes before his train departed and having no desire to hang about the station, decided to go for a short walk. He could always take a taxi if time became pressing.

It was about ten minutes later when he sensed he was being observed. He was in a narrow unpaved alley that was pitted with shallow depressions. Ahead, he could see the white steeple of a small church topped by a bluey-green spire. Across the alley was hung multicolored bunting and banners advertising various businesses.

He paused, looked about him confusedly, as if trying to get his bearings. As he turned, he saw the Japanese couple. They smiled at him. He smiled in return. They were not the problem. Behind them, some distance away, was a man who seemed too intent on a shop window. In a light gray suit, he stood side-on to Gallagher, hands in pockets. He was European.

Gallagher continued to rubber-neck like a lost tourist, before continuing on his way. Soon, he came to an even narrower alley that was little more than a wide path. Neatly cobbled with a darker pattern running along the middle like a dividing line, it led up an incline to what seemed like a car park at the far end.

He turned into it. Cream colored low buildings

encroached on either side. Close to the corner, someone had laid out a display of bunches of flowers in open wrappers. Next to them was an open crate of peaches. He walked past, hurrying now toward the car he could see at the exit. He hoped it was not a blockade.

It wasn't.

He turned left at the top and walked quickly to a group of four cars parked close together. There was sufficient cover behind them. When he got there, he sat on the ground and began to fiddle with the camera case, as if looking for something. All the while, he kept a surreptitious watch on the exit.

He didn't have to wait for very long. The man in the gray suit appeared, paused uncertainly, glanced briefly at the parked cars, then directed his scrutiny further afield. He did not look pleased with himself. At last, he turned and went back down the narrow alley.

Gallagher gave it another five minutes before he stood up to go in search of a taxi. He found one almost immediately. As it took him to the station, he wondered who the man was and how he had known where to find him.

Was the gray-suited man one of Kirstin Størvaag's colleagues, acting as backup? Or was she, in fact, guilty of betrayal? He didn't want to think so. But if the man had not been from Norwegian Intelligence, then he could only be one of the team of people who had been in pursuit since France.

Gallagher tightened his lips grimly. In which case, so much for Fowler's passport. Someone was leaking all down the line.

And I'm pig in the middle, he thought savagely.

The clock hanging from the girdered arch of the platform shelter showed it to be 3:08 when he arrived. Two minutes to departure. Perfect. He hurried to the train and climbed aboard. It was very crowded and began to move as he searched for his seat. One had thoughtfully been reserved for him in First Class. Kirstin Størvaag's doing?

It was conveniently by a window and he settled in as the train gathered speed out of Bergen. There had been no time for a pursuer to climb aboard.

The man in the light gray suit walked out of the station and went unhurriedly over to where the Brabus Mercedes was parked. The car had been driven almost non-stop from Germany and had crossed the Danish border with Flensburg plates. Here in Norway, it still carried them.

The man opened a rear door and climbed in.

From the front, the cold-eyed man said: "Well?"

"The train left ten minutes ago."

"If you hadn't lost him, *you* could have been on board."

The man in the back decided to be brave. "We're not dealing with an amateur. He registered me very quickly and took immediate action."

The cold-eyed man said: "If you had caught that train, we would have been certain of his destination. As it is, he could be going all the way to Oslo, now that he's seen you."

"Look . . . despite the hitches we've had. . . ."

"Hitches? You call losing half the team

hitches?" The cold-eyed man turned to fix his stare upon his colleague.

But the man in the back was still feeling brave. "Despite our hitches," he repeated firmly, "our information has been mostly correct. We were told he would be coming to Bergen, and he was here. Why don't we try the other location ... even though he does know someone's following him? He may not be able to change his plans at such short notice...."

The cold-eyed stare had not shifted. "You wouldn't be thinking of making a bid for the leadership of this team, would you?" Softly, dangerously.

The other shook his head. "I wouldn't dream of it. You're in command, as far as I'm concerned. We've lost personnel from other teams, while under your command. I'm trying to save our necks."

The cold-eyed man pondered upon this for long moments. "Ten minutes ago, did you say?"

"Twelve now."

"What about the hotel?"

"He wouldn't leave anything there for us to go on, even if we did get into his room without a nosey hotel staffer putting his snout in."

"Alright. We'll go to the next location. You'd better be right."

"The decision is yours."

"Of course." Drily. The cold-eyed man turned to face frontward once more. "Let's head for Gudvangen," he told the driver. "There's a ferry to Aurland at 1700. We can't afford to miss it. So make this thing move, but don't pick up Norwegian police on the way. Taking care of them would slow us down."

The Brabus began to move, heading for the E68 which would eventually take it to Voss and on to Gudvangen.

The cold-eyed man said: "I want you two to remember... when the mission is over, I want this one to myself. Do you understand? No one is to take him."

The man in the back, pushing his luck, said: "And if he's shooting at us?"

The cold-eyed man made no reply.

14

As the train made its way toward Voss, Norway unfolded its magnificent scenery before his eyes. Pushing out of his mind the thoughts of the true reason for his being where he was, he admired the awe-inspiring vistas as they sped past.

The railway track skirted the shore of a long fjord, on the opposite side of which great masses of land seemed to rise straight out of the water. He carried an impression in his mind of vivid green, and the smooth slate of the surface of the water. A photographer's paradise. No wonder the tourists were going mad with their cameras.

He resisted the impulse to do likewise, preferring to commit what he saw to memory, for the time being. Perhaps when Fowler was not directing certain aspects of his life, he would return to see it all properly.

The train made it to Voss on time, at 1621. From his seat, Gallagher looked out on the open platform. Directly in vision was a pillar with a sign that said this was platform 10. Beyond the platform, a slip road appeared to go down into the main street which was a short distance away. Across the street was a big hotel and a service station beyond which were the waters of a wide lake. Movement in the air caught his eye. A floatplane was curving in to land; then there was a slight jerk as the train began to move. Barely two minutes had passed.

When the train reached Myrdal, he got out quickly, not wanting to miss his connection. He need not have worried. The little train was waiting. A group of people off the Oslo train began to climb aboard. They were mainly American. Presumably, they were going all the way to Flåm.

He gave them a fast scrutiny but saw no one who seemed a likely pursuer. Their Norwegian guide was talking to them, explaining that this was a most unique railway line which plunged nearly 3000 feet down to the end of the line on the Aurlandsfjord, in only just over 12 miles. He assured them they would see most spectacular scenery of the deep, narrow valley. They were not to worry about the gradient. Each carriage had five separate braking systems, any of which would bring the train to a halt.

The look on some of the faces clearly said they hoped he was right.

The little train set off on time. The guide continued to talk his charges through. Gallagher sat back and enjoyed the scenery, which was as spectacular as the guide had promised. The train made its way down, through long snowsheds and tunnels, sometimes popping out in mid-air it would seem. Every now and then it would stop to enable the group of tourists to click away at everything in sight with their cameras. Steep rock faces were coursed by waterfalls. Streams and rivers rushed by. Cavernous valleys gave the impression of being taken to a magic kingdom.

But above all such thoughts, Gallagher kept his mind alert. This was not the best place in the world to be caught off guard and possibly end up being tossed off the train.

He again made a scrutiny of his fellow passengers. The guide was walking along the carriage, pausing at each seat to talk to its occupants.

No, Gallagher told himself. There was no threat there.

Dalsbotn came up without incident. The train had popped out of yet another tunnel and there it was, virtually at the mouth.

Gallagher was the only person to get off and as the train moved away, he could see why. He was in the middle of nowhere. The stop was graced by two wooden buildings: a tool shed, and the other, scarcely bigger, seemed to be the waiting room. This was a simple hut with a flat roof that sloped gently toward the back, but was in pristine condition and painted cream, with brown doors. A single bulb in an all-weather casing hung from the eave. Above the door, a fixed sign proclaimed: DALSBOTN.

He'd come to the right place; but there was no sign of Kirstin Størvaag.

He looked about him, not liking the feeling that was surfacing in his mind. The "platform" upon which he stood was a short length of hardpacked, chalky earth raised about a foot off track level and bounded by a concrete border. The twin rails of the track went into a gentle curve to the left and downward out of sight. He could still hear the noises of the train, growing fainter.

A dirt road went off the track to the right, and upward. There was a house up the slope among the trees; but no movement. To his left, continuing off the earthen platform, the unpaved road with its gravelly surface wound downward and as he moved to get a better look, he saw that it went down fairly steeply in a series of tight S-bends. On the left side of the road, where there were occasional precipitous drops, a low metal barrier fixed to wooden posts had been erected. Two taller posts at the start of the descent bespoke of a double gate: but only one of these still remained: a simple rectangle with a diagonal beam, to which was attached a strip of chicken wire.

Gallagher went up to it. The section of barrier closest to it had been dented. He peered down the drop. There was no vehicle at the bottom. He hoped the dent had been made by some other driver and not Kirstin Størvaag.

All around were high mountains with steep slopes of thick vegetation and dark rocky outcrops. A faint roar came from a distant waterfall that chucked itself powerfully off a high mountain to his left and, far below, the river Flåm added its own voice to the background noise. Yet for all that, the entire area appeared shrouded in a profound silence. Telegraph poles, carrying power and telephone lines, marched from the platform to the house on the slope before cutting down into the valley, across the bends of the road.

Studying it all, Gallagher decided he could get to like it; if only his presence did not also bring with it a pursuing danger.

Where was Kirstin Størvaag? Had she set him up, conning him into dumping himself in the middle of the Norwegian mountains ... to await what?

Already, he had begun to assess the situation, in case he found himself having to fight for his survival. At least, there was plenty of cover. But where was the nearest proper road? The nearest town or village? If he were still here by nightfall, he could always sleep in the hut. He wasn't sure it would be wise to go up to the house. Was someone up there even now studying him through binoculars? The gloomy thoughts did not make him feel any better.

He was extremely vulnerable. A rifle shot could echo suddenly through these mountains. But would anyone be close enough to come and investigate? Even if someone did, it would already be too late.

Then he heard a new sound, growing louder. A car, being driven very fast. On such a road surface, the driver was either good, or foolhardy.

He moved back until he was behind the hut, out of sight of anyone driving up the road. He waited as the sound of the car grew louder. It was a powerful engine, and the driver seemed to know what he was doing. The gears were changed smoothly, the revs barely altering in response.

Soon, in a cloud of dust, the silver snout of a Saab Turbo 16S came through the broken gate. The car drove right up to the hut. Gallagher had drawn back to keep out of sight. He heard the engine slow to a tickover. A door was opened, then shut with a soft but solid clunk. Footsteps.

He waited.

The footsteps paused on the platform, then

there was the softly grating noise of shoe on gravel as the whoever it was moved around tentatively. The hut was inspected.

"Mr. Renwick!" She pronounced it properly too. "Mr. Renwick are you there?"

Gallagher shut his eyes briefly. *That's right,* he thought with resignation. *Shout it to the mountains.*

He moved out of cover. "I'm here."

She jumped. "Oh!" Then she looked embarrassed and confused all at once. "Mr. Renwick, I'm so sorry to be late. . . ."

"Don't worry about it." He went toward her. "I haven't been here very long."

"It was the ferry, you see. . . ."

He stared at the Saab. By what route had she got here? "Ferry?" he repeated puzzledly.

"Have you been to Norway before?"

Gallagher had flown over Norway several times during NATO exercises, sometimes mixing it with Norwegian Air Force F-16s in mock air combat; but his ground experience of the country was strictly limited. Landing at Bodø didn't count.

He told her nothing of this. "No," he replied instead.

"You cannot help noticing," she began as they walked to the car, "that here in Norway we have plenty of water. Most of our communication system relies on it. Many roads can only be joined by the fjord ferries. I went by helicopter to Kaupanger, and then a ferry to Revsnes. The car was waiting for me there. I then drove across the mountains to get here." They reached the Saab and paused. "I would have arrived on time, but the helicopter missed the ferry and I had to wait fifteen minutes for another." She sounded displeased with herself, as if her lateness was somehow a sign of chronic inefficiency. "It was decided that taking such a route would confuse anyone following either of us." She smiled. "There were no helicopters chasing me. I think we have succeeded."

He didn't have the heart to tell her about the man in Bergen. If she knew nothing about what had occurred, informing her would probably scare her silly; after she had first berated herself for incompetence. If she were involved, then his knowledge was best kept to himself for possible future use. It made him one up: for the time being.

She opened her door. "Please get in," she said. "We should be going."

He got into the passenger seat and clipped on his belt. After the *quattro,* the Saab seemed much narrower and higher. It was, however, very comfortable and gave him the impression of being deeply cocooned. It felt very solid, and the curve of its windscreen and dashboard gave it the air of a fighter cockpit. Gallagher at first found its high stance disconcerting.

He watched as Kirstin snapped on her belt. The 16-valve engine revved smoothly as she sent the car hurtling down the gravelly slope. He couldn't dispel from his mind that this was a front-wheel-drive car and she was treating it as if all four wheels were driven. He also kept thinking of the barrier which now somehow seemed very frail as it sped past.

She went into the first tight bend with the skill of a rally driver, throwing the tail out, but holding it nicely on line. It didn't make him feel any better. Maybe that was how Norwegians drove when they were let loose.

"Do not worry," she said to him cheerfully. "I am a very good driver. You are safe with me."

Gallagher smiled weakly and watched almost mesmerised, as the scenery whipped past.

Now and then, he saw isolated houses, perched upon high ground. Other dirt roads branched off to meet them. Then mercifully, as the road descended, the bends appeared to become gentler until at last it became almost straight, with the shallowest of curves modifying its line. In the distance, the road again swung away out of sight.

"That's where we're going to stay," she said, pointing briefly ahead.

Midway along the straight, Gallagher saw a big cabin that had been built upon a concrete base, a few feet off the road. Behind it was a small hut with two doors. The cabin itself had a fresh look about it, as if it had recently been refurbished. It had been painted a deep brown, with its windows marked out in white. A brick chimney poked out of the spine of its roof.

She raced up to it, trod on the brakes, bringing the Saab to a sudden halt. Dust billowed upward from behind the car, as if trying to get away.

"There," she said proudly as she climbed out. "Our home for the night. Tomorrow, I shall take you to your meeting."

Gallagher got out gingerly, amazed to have arrived at all. He looked about him, studying the immediate environs. The cabin and the road, although flanked by steep slopes that rose skyward, were still high in the mountains. The river flowed with a heavy rushing sound that blended with the roar of the waterfall which was much closer, though still some distance away. He could see the rising curtain of fine spray caused by its pounding impact upon the rocks far below.

The brooding mountains, seeming close enough to touch, were flecked with patches of snow upon their bald peaks. On some, vegetation ended so abruptly, it was as if someone had drawn a line past which nothing dared grow.

Gallagher studied the road surface. There were tire tracks other than those of the Saab. Along its edge, closest to the cabin and for a short distance on either side, slabs of rock had been planted, perhaps as a guide for passing vehicles. The ground beyond the rocks seemed soft; but there was a hard-packed ramp that sloped down toward the rear of the cabin, to end in a grassy wilderness. Glimpses of the river could be caught through the slender trunks of saplings on its bank, perhaps forty meters away. Across the road, glistening streaks on the steep incline showed how far the run-off water from the mountains had come. Difficult terrain upon which to dodge a pursuer.

"Do many people come up here?" he asked. "There are these tire tracks, and the houses further up."

"In the summer season, there are walkers. Not many. Most tourists like to stay near the fjords. But Norwegians who have holiday homes around here like to go walking and fishing. The fishermen usually stay further down. Nearer to Flåm, there is good fishing. The tire tracks are from the people who live up here. They will not disturb us."

"I wasn't thinking about them. What's in the hut?"

"It is a wood store. There are logs for the fire. There are also some logs inside, but I do not think we'll need them. You have brought fine weather with you. No rain in Bergen, and up here, it is bright and warm, even in September."

That's not all I may have brought, he didn't say.

"Of course," she was saying, "we have the Gulf Stream. It keeps our coast warm, and even in the winter, the fjords can be free of ice."

Gallagher was not thinking about ice-free fjords. He looked up and down the road, and again studied the immediate terrain.

Kirstin looked at him, eyes questioning. "There is something wrong?"

He did not make an immediate reply as he continued to look about him. Then he said: "Nothing wrong. How far is it to Flåm?"

"From here? About seven kilometers by this road. Do you wish to go there?"

He shook his head. "Is the surface like this all the way?"

"It becomes a normal road at Lunden. That is the last stop before Flåm itself. Flåm is at the head of Aurlandsfjord. The road then goes to Aurland, then over the mountains. In some places, at the top, the surface is again like this. It is also narrow."

The only escape route then, unless. . . . "Are there ferries?"

"Oh yes. There is a ferry from Aurland, and sometimes from Flåm. You think there is going to be trouble?"

She was either very good at her deception, or she was truly green and innocent.

"It is always safer to be prepared for trouble," he told her, "even when you don't expect it." If she had spoken the truth, that gave two possible escape routes.

She smiled suddenly. "I was told you were very good and that I should listen to you. Perfect at the job, they said."

"I don't know who 'they' are, and I don't think I want to . . . but you're looking at the world's most imperfect man."

"I don't believe you. You don't make mistakes they said."

"Bully for them. And I do make mistakes. Sometimes, very bad ones."

The blue eyes stared at him. "I still don't believe you. Other people force you to make mistakes. I shall try not to get in your way."

He made no comment. Misguided hero worship was the last thing he needed. If the man he had seen in Bergen had friends—and he'd bet on that—and if somehow they managed to follow him up here, she would have to function without his having to think about her . . . or she'd be dead; always assuming, of course, she was not playing her own little game.

He said: "Take me on a short drive. I want to see what's further on. But take it slowly."

She said, as they entered the car: "Is my driving worrying you? I'm a very good. . . ."

"Driver. I know. But I want you to go a little less fast because I want to check a few things out. I'm looking for something special."

The Saab lunged down the dirt road. "Will this do?"

Gallagher refrained from closing his eyes in despair. "I meant a little slower."

"Okay." The Saab appeared to slow down barely perceptibly.

Gallagher gave up. Behind the wheel, Kirstin Størvaag seemed to operate in two modes: very fast, and stop.

"What are you looking for?" she asked.

"I'll know when I see it."

If she could arrive in the mountains with a car, so could whoever was following him. Mountain roads were dangerous. It should be possible to spring a nasty surprise. All he needed to find was the right place.

The road had now become almost level with the river which appeared to have widened and grown sluggish. At one stage, the road was virtually the riverbank. Again, slabs of rock had been planted at the roadside to deter wandering vehicles, though only on short, intermittent stretches. There were deep rock pools in the river, and in the middle of the stretch they were passing, Gallagher saw a small island, lushly covered with vegetation. High river level would probably cover a good part of it; but at present, the water here was too shallow for his purposes.

A short distance further down, he saw a split in the river. The natural protrusion of the land had been buttressed by stonework and masonry, and two simple wooden bridges, perhaps three meters or so in span each, had been laid across each arm of the river fork, to allow a path to the waterfall which could now be seen in all its glory.

"Stop," he said.

The Saab came to a halt with a brief sliding of wheels. He got out and went to the river's edge. He looked up at the waterfall. It spilled forcefully beyond the bridges. The river had again gathered speed, and the roar of the waterfall had been joined by a more ferocious and powerful sound. Gallagher thought he knew what that meant. Rapids. Rapids meant a waterfall further on. Perhaps the entire river had itself become another fall: that would mean a chasm. He hoped it was deep enough.

He re-entered the car. "Does the river drop suddenly on its way to Flåm?" he asked her. "Or is it a steady descent all the way?"

"Oh no. Not far from here is a very steep drop. The road bends away from it and there is a low barrier; but it is still very dangerous if you make a mistake."

Better and better.

"Take me there . . . but take that bend very, very slowly, won't you. Please?"

She smiled as she put the Saab into gear, the dimple prominent. "You are not afraid of my driving, are you, Mr. Renwick?"

"Call me Paul," Gallagher said, "and I'll call you Kirstin. If you're going to drop us off this mountain, we might as well be informal about it."

"Alright," she said, and the Saab shot off.

Before long, Gallagher saw what she meant. "Stop here," he said again.

This time, she brought the car to a halt in an almost leisurely manner. She smiled at him triumphantly.

"Keep it up," he said as he got out. But his

mind was already upon the ambush he intended to spring, should the need arise. The location was perfect.

The road was now hugging the mountainside, for the river had carved its way downward, biting deep into the earth. On both sides, the ground rose precipitously; but opposite, it reared from the river far below, its flanks thinly covered with slender-trunked trees. The river curved to the left, widening as it flowed toward Flåm.

Along the road, seeming to overhang the far river and supported by tall girders, was a massive pipeline Gallagher judged to be over a meter in diameter. In places, between sections, it was clad with slats of wood, as if a master cooper had gone to work on it. Here and there, thin streams of water squirted weakly out, betraying the presence of minor perforations in the pipe itself.

Further on, a vertical structure rose from the pipeline. Cylindrical, it looked like an inspection access of some kind. Motioning to Kirstin to follow in the car, he began walking toward it. The Saab rumbled slowly after him, like a hunting dog.

As he walked, he peered down, beyond the pipe. Vicious-looking black rocks, polished to a gleaming obsidian, broke the white tumble of the water. The supporting girders, like spindly legs, rose upward to the large pipeline. Gallagher could hear the water rushing through it mutedly. From the tower, a fixed metal ladder descended to the river. The pipeline went beyond the tower then dropped to what seemed to be a pumping station, at river level.

He walked on. The valley had widened and was spread below him. He arrived at the bend Kirstin had spoken of. It curved right and as he turned into it, he saw that the pipeline and the road behind went out of sight fairly quickly. A car tearing down that road would be in serious trouble indeed, if it suddenly came upon an obstruction hiding round the corner. On the narrow road with its loose surface, any misjudgement at the crucial time would lead to a very nasty drop onto the unforgiving rocks below.

The Saab burbled behind him. Gallagher raised a hand briefly, indicating to Kirstin he wanted her to stop. He looked thoughtfully about him. Someone had been digging at the mountain side. The corner was being widened and enough space had been cleared to enable the Saab to turn round. He waved to Kirstin, describing a circle with his hand to show he wanted her to turn. He had found what he'd been looking for.

There were no roadmaking vehicles by the freshly gouged earth, but the workmen had left four oil drums, each with a yellow-painted band about the middle, standing on end at the base of the new cliff face created by the digging. Gallagher wondered if they were empty and went up to check. Slitherings of loose earth made him approach cautiously. Not fun to be covered by a sudden landslide.

He gave each drum a tap with the edge of his fist. Each boomed hollowly. He felt pleased. Empty drums would be a lot easier to position. Kirstin was watching him puzzledly from the car, but he chose not to enlighten her.

He went back to the corner to gaze down upon the river. It was as if he were hovering, looking down from the sky. The river flowed on, bisecting a fair-sized village of neat houses in the distance. Across the gorge, the steep slope was marked by footpaths winding upward. There were actually houses up there. He wondered what it was like trying to make the climb when the snows came.

He returned to the car and got in. Kirstin had parked it tail in.

"Do you wish to go on?" she asked.

He shook his head. "I've seen all I want to for the moment. This is really very beautiful," he added.

"Perhaps you will come over again, when you have more time to appreciate it."

"I think I will." Rhiannon would love it.

"You will not be disappointed." She smiled quickly at him, not knowing his thoughts. "So it is back to the cabin?"

"Yes, thanks. This will do for now."

The place was spartan but remarkably clean, and not at all like a house that had been unattended for some time. The living room-cum-dining room-cum-kitchen was open plan, taking up almost the entire ground floor. A fixed structure like a long step ladder led up to the upper floor where the two bedrooms were separated by the most basic of partitions, with doors with simple latches to give some measure of privacy. There was a small shower room and a toilet with a plastic sink on the ground floor.

"Not a luxury hotel, as you can see," Kirstin said, "but we have everything. There is electric light, and we have water. The beds are comfortable. Plenty of food in the refrigerator. You are hungry? I shall make us something to eat."

Gallagher said: "Now you've mentioned it, I am. Are you expecting anyone else?" he asked her suddenly. "This place looks well-prepared."

She was not taken aback. Perhaps she was a good actress. "I was here last week, getting everything ready. There may be the man you are going to meet. I am not sure whether he will return with us. I have been told that is up to you."

Bloody Fowler. Probably after a snatch. Send Gallagher in like a beater to flush out the prey, then nab him. Big feather in Fowler's cap, as a high-ranking Russian gets picked up.

Gallagher began to wonder if Borodin—whoever *he* really was—had asked for a meeting at all. Perhaps this was all an elaborate defection attempt, and the bastards who'd been chasing him since France had somehow got on to it and were under orders to stop the defector . . . and whoever was going to meet him. Great.

"Thanks for nothing, Fowler," Gallagher said bitterly.

Kirstin stared at him. "Who is Fowler? What do you mean?"

"You wouldn't want to know. Is the ground hard behind this cabin?"

"Yes."

"Hard enough for the car?"

"I think so."

"Check. If it is, drive the car round. It will be less exposed than where you've left it."

"You are really expecting trouble."

"Just being prepared. You never can tell."

She nodded. "I shall move it." She paused. "There is something else I must show you."

While he watched her, she went to a tall cupboard that appeared sturdier than the others in the place and unlocked it with a key she carried. As the thick doors swung open, Gallagher stared at the gleaming weaponry within. He went up to the cupboard.

There were three weapons: a brand new Beretta AR 70/90 assault rifle with a folding stock; a Socimi 821 submachine gun, so light it could be fired one-handedly; and the big SIG Sauer P226 automatic. The Beretta was itself so new, he doubted it had been as yet issued for standard service.

Kirstin was saying: "I was told this particular automatic is your favorite pistol."

"Someone's been saying a lot of things to you." The bloody long arm of bloody Fowler. "Can you use any of these?"

She seemed startled. "I am not very good with guns. I was told they are for you, if you should need them."

Oh bloody wonderful. "I try not to use guns if I possibly can," he said. "I also try not to get involved in these little games . . . not that it ever does me any good."

She was looking confused. "But. . . ."

"Is there anything else you've still got to tell me?"

"I am sorry, Mr. Renwick. . . ." She'd gone all formal again. ". . . but I do not know as much as you think I do. I was told to be your driver and guide. Normally, I am a linguist, and I work in an office. Because I am a good driver, I was given this assignment."

"What languages do you speak?"

"All the Scandinavian ones, of course, including Finnish. I am also reasonably good with French, German, Dutch . . . English, of course . . . and Hungarian."

"Interesting group. What about Russian?"

"Russian? Yes. Yes. I can speak Russian . . . a little."

Surprise, surprise. Her "little" Russian would be quite substantial. Of that he had no doubt. Borodin was obviously going to be brought here. Gallagher knew it would not be left to him to decide. Kirstin Størvaag was far too junior to be the debriefing officer. Who then? Fowler, in all probability; plus his Norwegian counterpart . . . plus an American or two?

But would the Norwegians agree to the snatching of a heavyweight Russian on their soil, even if he were a genuine defector? Gallagher gave up on it for the time being. Other matters were more pressing: like keeping himself and Kirstin Størvaag alive.

He said: "Let's not go back to being formal. Give me the key and I'll move the car. You get on with the dinner. I want to have a little look around the place."

She gave him the ignition key. "And the guns?"

"They're with us. We can hardly throw them away."

Gudvangen, 1900 hours.

The Brabus was parked by the ferry terminal. The cold-eyed man was leaning against it, barely able to contain his anger. Inside the car, the driver and the third man sat quietly, as if afraid their very movement would give their senior colleague an excuse to explode into uncontrollable rage.

The driver felt the most vulnerable. Some 21 kilometers after Voss, he had taken a left turn off the E68 and they had found themselves on the road to Viksöyri, going away from Gudvangen. It had been a stupid thing to do; a simple misreading of a roadsign. By the time they had turned round and rejoined the correct road, it had already been too late. They missed the ferry.

The next and last one of the day was not until 2010 hours. They had more than an hour to wait, to add to the one and a half hours they'd already spent hanging around.

The cold-eyed man's eyes were poisonous.

An airfield well above the Arctic Circle in the 14th Military District of Siberia. 0200 hours.

The Il-76 taxied to its allocated refuelling point. It had been in the air for ten hours, had crossed five time zones and into the airspace of two Military Districts. It would stay only long enough to take on fuel before setting off on the long flight back.

As the aircraft came to a halt, the commander left the flight deck to speak to his passenger who was getting ready to leave.

"I hope you have found it interesting on this flight with us, Comrade Colonel," he said to Skoryatin. "It has been our privilege to have you aboard. I am only sorry we could not find an American spy plane for you."

"It was still a most interesting exercise, Comrade Major." Skoryatin knew the man was trying to ensure no adverse reports were made about him and his crew. "You proved that operating across the Military Districts causes no insurmountable problems. Your control of the fighters in each District was most illuminating. I have judged your part of the exercise to have been a success and I shall say so in my report. As for the American spy planes . . ." Skoryatin smiled conspiratorially. ". . . well . . . we can't expect them to come out and play all the time, can we?"

"No, Comrade Colonel Taginiev. I suppose not; but we would have made it hot for them tonight."

"I'm sure you would. Now I must be off. I've another plane to catch. The exercise continues. I wish you a safe flight back."

"Thank you, Comrade."

Skoryatin left the big aircraft and walked in the biting cold toward a waiting crew vehicle. After he had climbed in, it sped across the airfield toward the other aircraft, an electronic intelligence gatherer that was a version of the Ilyushin Il-18.

The Il-76 commander watched the vehicle disappear into the darkness before returning to the flight deck. The second crew, who had been carried on this particular flight, were already taking up their positions.

He said to the co-pilot who had flown with him: "I'm glad that's over. He can get in somebody else's hair now."

"At least he's a real soldier," the co-pilot said. "We might have been saddled with a KGB snooper."

The fake Colonel Taginiev scrambled aboard the Il-18 ELINT, and it was moving almost before he had settled in his seat. It took to the air on its four turboprops, long before the massive Il-76 would finish refuelling. It's flight would take it westward into the 5th Military District of Leningrad, to Severomorsk. With its range of over 4000 miles it would land, disembark its passenger, take off once more for a two-hour patrol, before returning to base. The crew were not told of the strange Colonel's business and to a man, none wanted to know. The aircraft would cross three more time zones on its way.

The time was 0215.

At the time that the Il-18 was winging itself into the air, it was 2115 on the Aurlandsfjord. It would be another 25 minutes before the ferry would disgorge its passengers and vehicles at Aurland. On the upper deck, the cold-eyed man stared unseeingly at the pinpricks of light on the high ground rising out of the fjord. His temper had not improved.

In the cabin in the mountains, Gallagher pushed his empty plate reluctantly away.

"That," he said, "was a fantastic meal. The trouble with you Norwegians is that you make everything look so good it's difficult to know when to stop."

Kirstin looked pleased. "It was nothing much. The stocks here are very basic, and most of it is tinned. If I had some truly fresh food . . . ah . . . I would show you." She smiled. "Perhaps you should catch us some fish tomorrow."

The mention of fish made him remember Talheim's chalet and brought thoughts of Rhiannon to the fore. He had been trying to suppress them for some time. They distracted, and that was the last thing he needed.

"Perhaps," he said. He glanced out of the window. "You can never see darkness like this in a city."

She was staring at him. "Are you okay? Did I say something wrong?"

"No," he answered. "You said nothing wrong. And I'm fine." He stood up and began to clear the table.

She placed a hand on his. "Leave them. I can do it. I know where to put everything. Remember, I prepared this place. That is . . . I did most of the work."

She took her hand slowly away. The warmth of it remained. He went over to the cupboard and took out the guns. One by one, he checked them minutely, while she busied herself with clearing up. Every so often, she would glance at him.

The guns were in perfect condition. There was also a good supply of ammunition. Even so, defending this place against a concerted attack was not his idea of a good time.

She said: "You handle them like a man who has lived with guns."

"I haven't lived with guns."

"Then a man who was well trained to use them . . . more than an ordinary soldier."

He said nothing.

"And I don't suppose your name is really Paul Renwick."

"Is yours Kirstin Størvaag?"

"Yes."

"You said you were not from Bergen. Where then?"

"You have not answered me."

"Does it matter what my name is?"

She paused for thought on that one. "I suppose not," she said eventually. "But it would have been nice to know the real one."

Again, he said nothing.

15

The Brabus Mercedes came off the ferry like a charging bull, its lights flashing briefly on the blue sign with the white letters that said AURLAND.

The cold-eyed man glanced at the sign as it went past. "This place can't be very big. It shouldn't be too difficult to search."

The driver said: "Where do we start? We know he didn't leave Bergen by car, but that doesn't mean he hasn't picked one up. He could be anywhere."

The cold-eyed man gave him a hard stare. The mistaken turn off the route had not been forgotten.

"Process of elimination," the cold-eyed man said tightly. "First, we make *sure* he isn't here."

The one in the back said: "He could have gone over the mountains."

"It was your idea to come here."

"But your decision."

"Don't play games with me. We search, then we try further up the fjord. We must cover all possibilities. We'll also try the mountain road beyond Flåm."

"At *night?*" The driver sounded anxious.

"What do you think this is?" The cold-eyed man snarled. "A holiday? If I were in his place, I'd have picked somewhere out of the way. There are bound to be isolated buildings up there."

"We can't try them all," the one in the back said.

"We're not going to try them. We'll simply keep to the road, patroling it all night, if necessary. It's the one he's got to use. As you so smugly pointed out, our information has so far proved mostly correct. We can't be given exact locations; but the general areas have always been the right ones. It is up to us to find the quarry. We can't do that by thinking only of the difficulties. And don't forget . . . he has already drawn blood. He must be made to pay for that."

An hour later, they were on their way to Flåm.

The man in the back said: "We've tried eight hotels and pensions of varying standards and one campsite, asking for a friend we're supposed to be meeting. All it proves. . . ."

"I know what it proves," the cold-eyed man interrupted. "He hasn't booked into any of them. The field continues to narrow. If we get the same response from those in Flåm, we'll know he's taken a house somewhere. What we've then got to do is either find it and keep it under surveillance; or watch the road. There are three pensions, one hotel, and a campsite to check out. Let's hope they haven't closed early. What's the matter?" he said to the driver. "Frightened of Norwegian roads? Let's have more speed!"

The Brabus roared its way along the narrow fjord road toward Flåm.

* * *

At fifteen minutes past midnight, it was picking its way through some roadworks in Flåmsdalen, on its way up the mountain road. It was still some distance from the pipeline.

The driver, guiding the car past a silent earth-moving vehicle said: "There's no surface to this wretched track."

"Don't even think of stopping," the cold-eyed man said warningly.

"I wasn't thinking of stopping. It's not my car."

A hostile silence descended between them. The cold-eyed man's demeanor had grown more and more unpleasant as their search continued to prove fruitless. The other two knew he needed some measure of success if he were not to go completely off the rails. It was not a good thing to have a mission go sour on you.

But they did not feel sympathy for him. He was a highly skilled professional: and their loyalty to him was strictly limited to keeping their own noses clean. The responsibility for the mission was his.

The cold-eyed man knew all of this, and it served to make his temper even worse. There was a rage within him; but it was cold and murderous, well under control, waiting to be unleashed.

Severomorsk, 0015 local time.

The Ilyushin Il-18 whispered down for its landing. The fake Colonel Taginiev disembarked and went to a waiting vehicle. The Il-18 did a quick turnaround and was soon lined up for take-off. Within minutes, it was airborne.

The small, four-wheel-drive jeep-like staff car sped toward some buildings on the vast base.

"Is everything arranged?"

"Yes, Comrade," the driver replied. "We've got to get you over the drop zone within two hours. Someone will be waiting with a car." The driver was a GRU major and a member of the dissident group.

"Do you know who I am?"

"No, Comrade . . . and it is better that I do not."

"Good. Good."

In the silence which followed, the fake Colonel Taginiev began to remove his flight suit, having gone into the rear of the speeding vehicle to do this. Civilian clothes were there. He got into them. By the time he was dressed, the staff car had stopped near a light aircraft. Skoryatin/Taginiev got out and quickly boarded the aircraft, which carried no markings. He put on a parachute. There had been no goodbye from the driver of the staff vehicle.

The pilot of the aircraft did not look round to check on his unknown passenger. He had been warned not to. He started his machine and began to taxi to his take-off point. He showed no lights. Those on the base who knew of the aircraft movement did not query its mission. They knew it was a GRU operation and that it was no concern of theirs. The virtually autonomous GRU had its own channels through which it operated. Careers were not worth risking in misguided attempts to find out more.

The aircraft began its take-off run and was

soon airborne. Its course took it westward. It would be keeping low all the way.

Gallagher lay on his back, fully awake. From the next room, where Kirstin Størvaag had gone to bed, came no sound. She must have at last fallen asleep.

They had decided to retire for the night just after ten. Nothing much had been said. Gallagher had given her the Socimi to take to the bedroom, in case circumstances warranted use of the weapons during the night. Even if she couldn't hit anything, the submachine gun would keep heads down. He had himself taken the P226 and the AR70/90.

She had moved about quite a bit in her room but at last appeared to have quietened down. He had dozed on and off, but always so lightly that any sound in the night would bring him awake. He was now fully alert, for on the sounds of the night, had come another.

The distant rumble of an engine.

He brought himself slowly upright in the bed, to listen. The noise was definitely growing in volume. To his ears, it sounded loud enough to wake the world. He got out of bed and dressed quickly. He did not switch any light on. Apart from acting like a beacon for whoever was coming up the road, it was not necessary. His eyes, accustomed to the dark, had all the illumination they needed from that which came in through the small window above the bed. Even in September the sky above the mountains seemed pale by comparison.

He picked up the automatic. It was fully loaded, and cocked. The rifle was also ready for action. He went to the window to look out, making sure he could not be seen if anyone decided to shine a light upon it. He could see the shape of that part of the road which headed toward Flåm. As yet, no glow betrayed the approach of the vehicle he could hear. In the next room, Kirstin Størvaag appeared to be still deep in sleep.

Almost without realizing it, he had begun to count off the seconds in his mind. When he got to 120, a glow appeared beyond the bend in the road. Headlamps.

He pressed himself against the bare wood of the cabin and kept his eye on the road. The glow soon became the multi-glare of a battery of head and spot lamps on the nose of the car. As it drew closer, the power of its engine became obvious. It was not being driven quickly. This was no local coming home after a heavy night out.

The mysterious car approached inexorably, then stopped directly outside the cabin. Gallagher was thankful he had decided to park the Saab out of sight. It worked, provided the observer was coming from Flåm. From the opposite direction, it was another matter entirely.

He waited, listening as the powerful engine ticked over ominously. He hoped if Kirstin came awake, she would have the presence of mind to do so quietly. He also hoped whoever was in that car would not choose to inspect the cabin. It wouldn't take long to spot the Saab.

The strange car remained where it was for what seemed an interminably long minute; then as if reluctantly making up its mind it began to move away slowly, before accelerating up the road. The noise of its exhaust seemed particularly loud, but there was no sound from the other bedroom.

She could not have slept through that, surely?

Gallagher left his bedroom to go swiftly into hers. She was still fast asleep, back toward him, the duvet tucked up to her chin. He sat on the edge of the bed, placed his hands upon the outline of her body and shook it gently.

"Kirstin!" he whispered urgently. "Kirstin!"

She moaned softly, moved sinuously beneath the bedclothes, but did not come awake.

He grabbed at her more firmly, and shook the body with more vigor. "Kirstin! Wake up. Wake up!"

Her body writhed beneath his hands, but she was still reluctant to open her eyes.

"I must remember never to put you on guard," he muttered drily and took drastic action. He put a hand over her mouth and nose.

She jerked awake with a stifled squeal. He took his hands away. She sat bolt upright, and the duvet fell away. She was naked; at least her upper half was. She made no move to cover herself.

"Paul!"

Amazing.

"So much for giving you a weapon with which to defend yourself. If I'd been one of those men out there, you'd be dead . . . and who knows what they might have planned first."

"Men? What men?"

"For all I know, it could be just one man; but get dressed. We're leaving."

"Now?"

"Yes. Now!"

"But. . . ."

"Look... while you were having your pleasant dreams, a car stopped right outside for at least a minute, before going on. It's just possible it won't come back, but if it does, I intend to be ready with a little reception. Does this road go all the way up the mountain?"

"It's supposed to go to Myrdal, but the surface is mostly like it is down here...."

"That's it. Up you get. Put some clothes on and be ready to drive. Bring that bloody gun as well."

"Yes, yes... I'm... I am sorry if I've...."

Gallagher stood up. "You're up now. That's all that matters. I'll be downstairs."

He went out of the room.

The cold-eyed man slammed his fist against the dashboard. "He's got to be here!"

The Brabus took a climbing turn at moderate speed. The driver said nothing. The cold-eyed man turned to look at the one in the back who seemed to be staring through the rear window.

"What are you looking at?" he snapped.

The man in the back did not seem to mind the tone of voice. He turned his head frontward, and said thoughtfully. "Something's teasing at me."

The cold-eyed man's hot glare seemed to light up the gloom in the car. *"Teasing* you? What are you talking about?"

The driver said: "What about this place? It looks more substantial than that rickety hut we just passed. More like the kind of place he'd choose."

Everyone looked. The Brabus had stopped again, this time at a junction, with a road forking off to the right. The car's lamps, on full beam, lit up a red-topped, two-storeyed house standing by itself at the end of the new road.

"Drive up," the cold-eyed man ordered.

"If he is in there," the one in the back began cautiously, "we shouldn't warn him. After all, we still need to know the contact. I'll go and have a look. Turn off the lights."

The driver hesitated, but the cold-eyed man nodded agreement. The lights went off. The man got out of the back, and as he straightened, unconsciously looked back. Something was troubling him. Then he gasped.

"What's the matter with you now?" the cold-eyed man asked impatiently from within the car.

"Lights! I've just seen lights and they're *moving!*"

"Are you sure? Where?"

"By that place we stopped at. I'm sure of it!"

"Get in!" the cold-eyed man barked; and to the driver: "Turn round. Hurry, damn you!" Then again to the man in the back: "If you're wrong...."

"I'm not wrong. I remember what was worrying me. As we moved away, I thought I saw the shape of a car...."

The Brabus was turning round with a great spinning of wheels.

The cold-eyed man interrupted: *"Then why didn't you speak up?"*

"I wasn't sure then. It could have been anything. Would you have liked it if I'd stopped the car only to find an upturned boat?"

The cold-eyed man said nothing.

"The lights made me certain," the man in the back went on. "Why would a car be moving off so suddenly? At this time of the night . . . up here?"

"For your sake," the cold-eyed man said, "I hope we're not chasing a bunch of Norwegians on a fishing trip."

"Fishing?"

"Who knows what these people get up to in this place," the cold-eyed man snapped sourly.

The Brabus set off down the mountain, soaring in pursuit.

Gallagher took a quick look behind and thought he saw the glow of lights swinging round, but wasn't sure.

Once awake, Kirstin had proved to be a very fast mover indeed. She had appeared downstairs fully dressed, much sooner than he had been led to expect by her seemingly determined drowsiness. He was still not sure about her. She had come down with the Socimi, carrying it as if it were plague-ridden.

When he had first checked out the guns, he had seen a powerful torch with an unusual, rectangular lens in the cupboard and before leaving the cabin, had taped it to the scope mount of the assault rifle. What he had in mind would be lethal to their pursuers; he hoped.

Kirstin drove the Saab in a manner that seemed even more terrifying in the darkness of the mountain valley, but she seemed able to keep the hurtling car upon the narrow road.

He glanced round for a second time. Yes. The flash of light was definite.

"Are they coming?" she asked. There was a tremor in her voice.

"Lights are following," he said.

"What if it's someone who lives up here? We'd be. . . ."

"It's very unlikely. That's the car that stopped outside. They saw our lights, which is exactly what I wanted. That's why I insisted we should leave when we did. It brings them back after us, but still leaves us enough time to prepare."

The pipeline was in the lights now and soon, the corner was approaching.

"Stop after the corner," he said, "in the same spot as earlier, but try to pull in closer. I want you well out of the way. Leave the sidelights on for a while. They'll give us sufficient light to work in."

She took the corner slowly and pulled into the recently widened area, parking the Saab well out of sight of any car coming down the road. They got out quickly and began to roll the drums to the corner. Gallagher had decided to modify his strategy, choosing to use the rifle *and* the drums. As a result, he lined them up well before the apex, but in a diagonal that led to the edge of the road and the chasm.

As they ran back to the car, she said: "I think you have done this before."

"With modifications," he told her. "But it seems to work." He took out the rifle. "I want you to remain with the car. Don't come to look. You'll only get in the way. If I don't make it, get the hell out of here. If you're too slow and someone comes after you, use that bloody machine gun. It's your best chance. It might slow them down long enough because whatever happens, they'll be on foot. Alright?"

She nodded.

"Now get in the car, and turn off the lights."

She paused, gave him a quick impulsive hug, then climbed in.

"What was that for?"

"Luck," she said, and shut the door.

The lights went off as he hurried back toward the tower. He judged he had about a minute at the most, before the pursuing car made its appearance. He also had every intention of surviving. His somewhat dramatic instructions to Kirstin Størvaag had been to frighten her into remaining where she was and not get underfoot. If she was indeed as incompetent with guns as she'd led him to believe, then she'd stay put. If she wasn't. . . .

He didn't want to think about it.

He reached the tower. There was sufficient cover for his purpose. A car traveling fast would not have time to take avoiding action by the time he was seen. For an ambush to work effectively, it had to be sprung with devastating suddenness.

Turn the adversary's nerves into a jangling mess, sir. While he's still trying to sort himself out, tear him to pieces . . . if you get my meaning, sir.

O'Keefe.

And the adversary was coming. Gallagher heard the powerful roaring of the car even as he saw the lights flashing round the bend before the stretch with the pipeline; and soon, they illumed the night with their blaze.

He pressed himself against the tower. It would have to be done very quickly, and at the precise moment. The car was traveling fast, much too fast for the road. From Gallagher's point of view, that was all the better. The moment would be soon.

He switched on the torch, with the rifle pointing upward. The powerful beam seared into the sky.

In the Brabus, they all saw the sudden flash.

"What the . . . !" the driver began. Then he saw the drums. *"Where did they come from?"* he screamed, and began to take avoiding action, instinctively veering away from the drop.

But he was already much too late.

The cold-eyed man, whose instincts were far more highly tuned than his colleagues', knew immediately what was happening and had begun to take his own avoiding action.

His hand was on the door, in the process of opening it.

Just as the car drew level with the tower, Gallagher brought the rifle down, pointing dead on target. The powerful beam of the torch hit the struggling driver right in the eyes, blinding him: and even as he squeezed the trigger and a burst of automatic fire barked sharply into the night, he could see the drivor raise a futile arm to block out the light.

Then window and windscreen were shattering; and the car was bouncing crazily off the hard, rising ground, to slam into the drums with a multiple bang that seemed to echo long into the dark mountains. He shifted his fire, shredding the tires. The Brabus seemed to be darting from side to side in agony, trying to get away from the hail that followed it. It cannoned into the low barrier, rising over it as momentum flung it over the side.

Its lights did a maddened cartwheel as it plummeted to the river below with a dying, enraged wail of its over-revving engine. A thumping, metallic crunching followed; then a silence.

Gallagher did not stay to watch, but ran back to the Saab as the sounds of the river took over once more.

He pulled open the door. Kirstin was staring at him.

"I heard it all," she said. "It . . . it was terrible." She sounded shocked.

"Come on," he said. "We've got to move." He put the Beretta behind the seats, then got in and shut the door. "Come on, Kirstin," he said gently. "Let's go."

"The drums. . . ."

"Are all out of the way. The car saw to that. Now let's get out of here!"

"Back to the cabin?"

"Forget the cabin. It's compromised."

She started the engine. "We'd better go to Aurland then. We must take the first ferry in the morning."

She had switched on the lights and had got the Saab on the move when a shot startled the night. She gave a sharp gasp. Both their windows were open and something buzzed in and out again.

"Kirstin!" Gallagher said in alarm.

"I'm alright. . . ."

The car continued to move, turning away from the direction of the shot. Gallagher had whipped round and was astonished by what he could see. *An indistinct shape was running and stumbling toward them!*

"I don't believe it!" he said, more to himself. "One of them has survived. *Shit.*" The Saab had gathered speed and it lunged forward as the turbo came on. It went fast into the downward sweeping lefthander. No other shots had come.

The cold-eyed man had raised his pistol to take aim, but had tripped over one of the drums. When he had stood up again, the fleeing car was out of range.

His body ached from the impact of his hasty departure from the Brabus. Miraculously, he appeared not to have broken anything, though he could feel blood on his face. There were lacerations, he knew, on his arms and legs. He had no idea what his clothes were like; but that would not deter him.

He went slowly back to where the car had gone over. His two colleagues were down there with it. He did not mourn them; but for the humiliation he had suffered, he burned with the thirst for revenge. Nothing would prevent him from getting it.

He made a decision and began walking. He had been trained in the harshest of schools. He had not suffered serious injury and was still operational. He had money and correct documents upon him. He had ammunition and his pistol. Emergencies such as this were planned for and he would find a telephone and make contact with others who could be of some help to him.

The mission was still on.

Gallagher looked at Kirstin with concern. He had asked about her condition several times, but she had replied on each occasion that she was alright. She drove the car with skill and did not appear likely to lose control of it. But every now and then, she would bite her lip, as if to stop from crying out.

"Stop," he said.

The Saab lost some speed, but it did not come to a halt.

"I'm alright," she insisted. "My shoulder's a little numb . . . that's all. I am okay. Really."

"Stop," he repeated. "I want to see for myself."

"But that man. . . ."

"Is walking. He's hardly going to catch up."

She thought about it, then: "Alright."

The Saab gradually lost speed and finally stopped near the river. The lights showed two big rocks in mid-stream, with a wooden walkway going from the bank to link them. The walkway also went round each rock. On the right hand side of the road and just ahead, Gallagher saw a great petrified fall of massive black boulders that seemed precariously balanced. Incredibly, there was a house directly at its base. Perhaps the fall was further away than it looked.

He got out of the car and went round to her side. "Right. Let's have a look. Better switch off the engine. We wouldn't want to wake the neighbors, would we?" he joked. "Although why we didn't wake the whole valley with our earlier racket, I'll never know. Norwegian valley people must be heavy sleepers."

"Only when they want to be," she said, smiling at him weakly. She pushed her door open, and climbed out.

There was a dark stain he saw, on her left shoulder. It had bloomed to reach halfway down the sleeve of her denim jacket. He helped her to remove it, betraying a bright red patch on her

T-shirt. There were streaks of blood down her arm too, but the bleeding itself appeared to have stopped. That at least, was good news.

"The T-shirt will have to come off," he said. "I want to look at the wound. We've got to dress it. Sit in the car with your feet on the ground. There. That's it."

"I have no brassiere on. We had to leave so quickly. . . ."

"I don't mind if you don't mind. I woke you up. Remember?"

Her smile told him she did remember. "Alright," she said, and began to remove the thin garment. "You will have to help. Moving the arm upward is painful."

As he reached forward, he said drily: "I'd hate to think of what a police patrol would say if they came along at this moment."

"They would probably laugh."

"Before, or after they locked us up?" He peered studiously at the ugly weal in the flesh of her shoulder, ignoring her bare, full breasts. "It doesn't look too bad. You were very lucky. The skin's broken but the blood's coagulated around the wound. Just as well we took the T-shirt off. It hadn't yet begun to stick. Is there a first aid kit in the car?"

"Yes. There is a panel in the side behind my seat, with a loop. If you pull it, the first aid box is in there. I will have to stand so you can. . . ."

"Don't worry. I'll go round the other side."

He found the kit and dressed the wound gently. When he'd finished, he said: "How's that feel?"

"Much better. You are a very gentle man."

"No I'm not," he said, putting the kit away. "Now we've got to find you some fresh clothes. Any in the boot?"

She nodded. "There is my small bag." The night was not cold, but the proximity of the river had a cooling effect and she had now crossed her arms about her upper body.

He found another denim jacket, a sweater, and another T-shirt. This one carried no message. There were other items of clothing too. He rolled the bloodied jacket and shirt tightly, and pushed them into a corner.

"Do not worry about the brassiere," she said. "I can do that later."

"If you say so."

He again had to help her with the T-shirt and the jacket. Her nipples showed stiffly through the shirt.

"Button the jacket," he said. "You'll catch cold."

"I am not cold," she said, "and it is easier when I drive."

"You're not driving. I am. You've got to rest that shoulder."

"I can drive. My shoulder is alright. You do not know where to go."

"You can direct me. You can always drive later if you feel up to it."

She seemed set to argue, then decided to give in. "Alright."

They changed seats and as he drove the Saab away, he wondered what the man they'd left behind would do next.

"You were very brave, Kirstin," he said to her. "You did well."

She said nothing for a while, and seemed deep within her thoughts. Then her voice came softly, seemingly from a long way off.

"Takk," she said.

The cold-eyed man kicked at the door. It shook, but didn't give. He kicked it again, harder this time. The sound echoed loudly. He knew he was angry and making too much noise. Putting his shoulder against it, he applied a continuing pressure. When he had just about resigned himself to going in through a smashed window, the door gave suddenly with a loud snap as the wood cracked at the lock.

He pushed it open and entered. He didn't expect to find anything that would give him much information about the people who had just left; but at least he'd be comfortable for the rest of the night. There was little chance of their returning, although he would have loved that.

He inspected the place from top to bottom. There was plenty of food, and the hastily vacated beds still carried a vestige of warmth; but of the people themselves, there was no clue.

He went into the rooms twice, stared at the beds, and resisted the impulse to put a bullet in each. Waste of ammunition, and most unprofessional. He returned downstairs, washed himself, then made a cold meal from what was available. He then went up into a bedroom and lay down to sleep, the gun in his hand.

He had chosen Gallagher's bed.

"Stop!" Kirstin said. "There is a telephone."

They had just passed the Flåm railway station

and were curving right for the road to Aurland. Gallagher pulled up near the box and she got out quickly. He watched as she entered, searching in a pocket for a coin. He half expected her not to have one, but she pulled it out with an air of triumph and slotted it in. She dialed, waited for the call to go through, then began to speak rapidly in Norwegian.

He heard her only vaguely and turned his head to the left, to look out on the dark waters of Aurlandsfjord. The long tongue of a pier was lit by street lamps and rows of discarded tires covered its flank. Tied up for the night, stern on, was the black hull and white superstructure of a ferry. In the far distance, pinpricks of light starred the mountain backcloth. Here, on the edge of the fjord, the sky seemed brighter.

He heard a sound and turned to look. Kirstin had finished her call and had left the box.

"There is a place in Aurland where we can stay until morning," she said as she took her seat. "We must catch the ferry at ten after nine, for Gudvangen."

"And then?"

"I shall take you somewhere else until it is safe to meet the man who is to see you. My superiors will get a message to him."

"And who might they be, I wonder?"

"Am I to answer this question?"

"No," he said. "I was not expecting a reply. Why a phone call? Don't you have a radio?"

She pointed to the glove compartment. "In there."

"Now she tells me."

"But it is tuned to a special frequency and can only be used when contact is made."

He put the car into gear. "Ask a silly question. Lead me to Aurland."

The drive took only a few minutes, and she directed him to a house on a steepish slope, within a short distance of the ferry embarkation point. She had a key for that too. The car was reversed out of sight, and they went inside. They took the guns with them.

"Like the cabin," she said, "this is also stocked with food, just in case."

"Was he to come here if something like this happened"

"I am not certain. I would have to be advised." she paused, looked at him anxiously. "Are you angry with me"

"Not with you," he replied. "With someone you don't know." He thought she seemed paler than before. "How's the shoulder"

"It feels alright. I can move the arm without much pain. I am fine."

"Then we should catch up on our sleep. I have a feeling we'll need it."

She nodded, and looked at the rifle and automatic in his hands. "Are you taking these to bed with you?"

"Yes. And you should take Socimi."

"You do not like guns, you told me."

"It's because they kill people."

"People kill people."

"Now you see the problem."

The Antonov AN-2 single-engined biplane had crossed the border unmolested. A brief electronic burst of a coded exit signal had ensured no fighters came sniffing round. The AN-2, though owing its genesis to the late forties, was in plentiful numbers in current service, and its manufacture had only ended in 1985. This particular aircraft was almost brand new.

Normally capable of carrying a crew of two and six fully armed paratroops, it was ideal for clandestine drop missions. Its max cruise of 258 kph also made it suitable for low level drops. This was not its first such mission.

The exit code had been given to the pilot by Skoryatin only after the aircraft had already taken off. The re-entry code would be passed on just before the drop was made. Should the pilot give the exit code by mistake, his chances of landing back at base in one piece would be very slim indeed.

After 1½ hours' flight at low level but at 0300 local Finnish time, the AN-2 swept over the vast waters and myriad islands of Lake Inari. Skoryatin, a simple jumpsuit over his civilian clothes, made preparations for leaving the aircraft. He also wore a paratrooper's helmet. He went to the cockpit to hand the pilot the re-entry code, and watched as it was entered on the transponder. Then he gave the man a tap on the shoulder and went to take up station by the door.

The pilot opened it remotely, and Skoryatin launched himself into the cold night air. The chute opened almost immediately. It was to be a fast drop. He landed as he had planned, near a footpath on the edge of some marshes, not far from Palomaa on the National Route 970.

He quickly released the parachute and hauled

it toward him. Working swiftly, he got out of the overalls, removed the helmet and wrapped both tightly within the folds of the chute. Not far from where he had landed was a fast-flowing river. He ran the hundred meters or so toward it and threw the parcel in. He watched it disappear, a smile coming briefly. What confusion it would cause ... if anyone ever found it.

He ran back to his landing point. The boots he had used for the jump were appropriate for the clothes he wore. As he arrived, a torch flashed twice with a pre-arranged signal. He waited. It flashed again; four times. An inversion of the first signal. It was correct. The torch then blinked at intervals, to guide him.

A minute later, the torch bearer said, in Russian: "I am glad you had a good jump, Comrade. Aren't you a little old for this sort of thing?"

"I was jumping out of airplanes," Skoryatin began cheerfully, "when you were a young pup. I'll still be able to do it when living in the West has long made you dissolute. Besides, I could not have risked an aircraft landing in case the pilot got it wrong and we had to leave the wretched thing here. Can't take too many liberties with the friendly countries. I'm glad you're the one who came."

They embraced briefly in greeting and though they had known each other for many years, no names were spoken.

"You're taking a great risk."

"As our friendly enemies the Americans would say," Skoryatin told him, "the stakes are very high."

The other nodded. "We'd better get out of here. The car's not far."

Skoryatin said: "From now on we speak Norwegian, or English."

"Fine," came the agreement, in English. The voice sounded American.

They came to the car, a dark Volvo with Norwegian plates. It was parked just off the main road, hidden from the view of any passing traffic. Skoryatin put the traveling wardrobe he'd jumped with into the boot.

"Perhaps you're right about my age," he said as he took his seat. "I feel as if I've been in the air for twenty years without a break." Skoryatin was very fit.

"There you are. I told you."

"Don't write me off so easily."

"That's one mistake I'd never dream of making."

They both knew what he meant, and chuckled. The man started the Volvo and drove onto the road when no headlights betrayed the approach of already sparse traffic. He turned left, heading for the junction with National Route 4.

"And what about you, my fine capitalist, fashion shop owner? Will you be able to leave Paris if the need arises? Will you miss the decadent lifestyle?" It was a teasing question, but quite serious.

"That won't be a problem."

"You hate Paris?"

"I love it, but being there has convinced me that what you're doing is right. I don't want to see either Moscow or Paris burned. I'm with you."

"For which I'm thankful," Skoryatin said

drily, "otherwise my reception might have been a little too hot for my health. You yourself have taken a great risk. You're sure your absence is safely covered?"

The man, who'd been stationed in Paris for many years, was KGB. A colonel.

"We're both survivors," he replied. "My cover's solid. I'm supposed to be nosing around in the south of France. As for the shop staff, they think I'm having an affair with a married customer, not touring Scandinavia in a hired car for this past week. When I've dropped you off I'll inform Oslo, and I'll be back in my shop and no one will be the wiser."

"Are you"

"Am I what?"

"Having an affair with this married woman?"

The man from Paris smiled in the gloom. "How can you ask such questions."

"Just be very careful, my friend. We are hunted by the West, as well as by our own."

They drove on in silence for a while, then the man from Paris said: "The hunters are having a bad time of it, according to my information. Someone's been taking them on at their own game, and winning." There was a note of surprise in his voice as he told Skoryatin what he knew.

Skoryatin nodded slowly in satisfaction. "It's all going well; but there's more to come. Before you leave, check with Oslo for an update and let me know."

"Right," the man from Paris acknowledged. "Your tickets are in the glove box, and all hotel and other travel arrangements made. Your flight leaves from Alta at 0805 for Tromsø, where it arrives at 0840. The plane departs Tromsø at 0900, arriving Oslo at 1050. Then at 1140, you leave Oslo for the flight to Sogndal. This gets there at 1245. You join a tourist bus from your hotel for the Kaupanger ferry which leaves at 1315 for Revsnes. The crossing only takes fifteen minutes. Your bus will then take you on to Laerdal for your meet."

"Very thorough. I'm impressed. Now if you don't mind, I think I'll get some sleep. Wake me just before the border."

So saying, Skoryatin reclined his seat, and promptly shut his eyes.

The man from Paris came to the junction and turned right, heading for Karigasniemi and the Norwegian border. After the crossing, his route would take him on to Karasjok, then left to Stornes where he would turn right onto the road to Alta. It was a journey of some 335 kilometers and he intended to make it to the airport by 0730, Norwegian time.

The road ahead was empty, and there was no one behind.

16

0730 hours, Aurland.

Gallagher looked out of his bedroom window and saw a wondrous sight. His position was on the outside edge of a bend in the fjord and on his left, to the east, the early sun's rays blazed whitely from behind a bank of thin cloud that capped a rank of peaks at the far end of the Aurland valley. The rays filtered through to caress the placid waters of the fjord, giving it the appearance of a giant mirror. Directly ahead of him, the probing tongue that went toward Flåm was still untouched by the light, adding an air of haunting mystery to the scene. At the top of the steep rock walls that rose from the far side of the water, a thin line of cloud, like a white headband, hung motionlessly just beneath the peaks. Nothing moved anywhere.

The day itself seemed to be waiting. He wondered what it would bring. Then he heard Kirstin moving around.

The waiting day no longer waited. It had started.

He began to get ready. The smell of coffee came to him and by the time he'd gone down to meet her, she was fully dressed, and a hot cup of coffee was ready for him. She greeted him with a cheerful smile. She seemed decidedly chirpier.

"Sleep well?" he asked.

"As long as I didn't turn on the wrong shoulder, I was okay. It bled a little, but I have put on a new dressing. A plaster is keeping it on. And I can move the arm. Look." She showed him, and appeared to have no trouble with it.

"Are you sure you're not pretending?"

"Look at my face. There is no pain on it. Now you must drink your coffee. We are to leave soon."

"I thought we were taking the ferry at ten past nine."

"I have made another telephone call," she said. "From here. There is a slight change. We are leaving the Saab. It will be alright where it is. We must get to Vangsnes, and if we take the ferry, we shall be too late for the Snøggbåt to. . . ."

"The *what?*"

For a moment, she looked puzzled. "The Snøgg. . . . Ah. I am sorry. It is the fast boat. Perhaps you saw some in Bergen. They are the catamarans."

He nodded. "Yes. I know the ones you mean."

"We shall be taking it to Rysjedalsvika. It gets there at *ti tjue* . . . oh I am again so sorry. I'm forgetting my English this morning. I mean ten-twenty."

"Don't worry about it," he said. "I wouldn't last five seconds with Norwegian. How far is it to Vang . . Vangsnes? Did I say that correctly?" He fought down his suspicions of the sudden change of plan and covered his reaction by drinking the coffee.

"Yes. That was fine." She didn't sound as if she had thought it a hundred percent so. "Vangsnes is only about 35 kilometers from here ... in a straight line, but over 80 from Gudvangen. So you see, we would miss the connection."

"And how do we get there?"

She gave him the one-dimpled smile. "Listen."

A sound had been faintly encroaching upon his awareness and he immediately recognized the whipping slash of blades through air. Someone was certainly pulling out all the stops.

"We must get ready," Kirstin said. "I have put the Socimi in my bag, and here is something for the rifle."

The something she picked up from the floor was a canvas case for a fishing rod. It seemed big enough for the AR70/90, if the magazine were removed.

"All people fish in Norway; in the fjords, the rivers, lakes, the sea. . . ."

"All people?"

"Well . . . perhaps one or two do not." She grinned at him.

"I'll remember that. I'll get my things. The chopper seems loud enough to wake the whole valley. It must be nearly here."

She went to a window. "It's just coming in to where the ferry makes its stop. It will not land unless the pilot sees us."

He went quickly up to his bedroom. It was as he had thought with the rifle. But there was plenty of room for the magazine, the SIG Sauer and all ammunition, in his equipment bag. He rejoined her, wondering what the good people of Aurland would say if they knew what was in the bags. He wondered too, if anyone had as yet discovered the wrecked car and its occupants, in the gorge.

"Right," he said to her. "I'm ready."

They left the house and made their way down to the ferry staging post. Triple signs, attached one above the other to three metal tubes, said KAUPANGER REFSNES GUDVANGEN in black on yellow, with the silhouette of a ship on a white background, on each. A few early motorists had already arrived, though the ferry had not yet come. They were staring at the helicopter, a twin-engined civilian version of the Bell Huey in red and white livery.

The aircraft was beginning to descend. The cars had stopped well enough away, but as the approaching helicopter's downwash raised a small dust cloud, windows were hastily wound up. A few stares were darted Gallagher's and Kirstin's way, then again to the helicopter.

The Huey landed and, crouching, they ran toward it and climbed aboard.

"Morn!" Kirstin called in greeting to the pilot as they took their seats and strapped in.

The pilot nodded, smiled, and lifted smoothly going into a straight climb to about 500 feet, before going into forward flight along the fjord. Gallagher watched fascinated as they beat their way between the high ramparts, and as the waters of the fjord widened increasingly beneath. He wondered what it was like taking an F-16 really low down. The Norwegian air force pilots must have some fun, he decided, doing a low level. Or frighten themselves silly if they overcooked it. Water could be just as unforgiving as solid rock, at the wrong speed.

Twelve minutes later, a tall statue on a headland caught his eye. Beyond it was a small church.

"Vangsnes," Kirstin told him. "The Fridtjov statue. We're nearly there."

The massive warrior, left fist on hip, right hand resting on the hilt of the broadsword planted at his foot, dwarfed the helicopter.

"How tall is that thing?" Gallagher asked as they went past.

"If you count the platform, 26½ meters . . . 95 feet to you."

"Oh we use meters too . . . sometimes."

"Now you are laughing at me."

"No I'm not."

She looked as if she wasn't sure, but something moving fast on the water caught her attention. "Look! It's the Snøggb . . . er . . ."

"It's alright. I know what Snøggbåt means now." He smiled at her to show he had said it in good humor.

The sleek catamaran, a single-decker, was cutting across the fjord from Leikanger.

"Normally," Kirstin was saying, "we should be waiting ten minutes before, and should book; but I think we shall find seats."

"I have that feeling too," Gallagher said drily.

"I *know* you are laughing at me."

"Not at you," he assured her. "Not at you at all."

"May I believe you?"

"You may." He pointed to the encased rifle. "What about this? Do we have to leave luggage in a particular place on the ship?"

"I do not think we shall have to worry about it."

"As long as I know."

The helicopter landed them with five minutes to spare.

"Tusen takk, Per," she said to the pilot. *"Adjø."* She obviously knew him.

The pilot gave a brief wave, nodded to Gallagher, then took his ship up, winging away toward the mouth of the fjord. Gallagher chose not to ask Kirstin about him or his subsequent destination.

"He does not know what this is about," she said without prompting. "Only that it is a government contract for the flight. We used him last week to try out the route."

Oh Fowler, Gallagher thought. *Duplicity is thy name.*

The name on the stern of the blue and white twin-hull said FJORDTROLL. He followed her to the embarkation point on the port side of the superstructure. It was roomier inside than he'd expected with seating, he judged, for well over a hundred passengers. They found seats without trouble. No one asked for money. Such matters had clearly already been dealt with.

Promptly at 0800, the boat throbbed to the increased revs of its twin engines as it moved away from the shore; then it was raising its prow out of the water, accelerating toward its next stop.

A great way to travel, he thought, as the catamaran hull skimmed along the vast waters of the Sognefjord.

After a while, Kirstin said: "Let's go outside.

I like being on deck on the fjords. At this time of the day, it will be perfect."

Probably bloody cold, he thought, thinking of the slipstream.

He tapped the rifle.

"We'll take everything with us," she said, glancing at it. "I think it will be alright."

No one told them not to take baggage out on deck. Either the crew had been forewarned, or they weren't bothered.

There was plenty of room on the open deck of the flat stern. No one else seemed to share Kirstin's yen for an open air morning sail. A waist-high railing bordered the deck. Gallagher went to one side and sat down with his back against it, the cased rifle across his knees, to stare out at the boiling wake beyond the stern. From a short white pole fluttered the ship's ensign: the Norwegian postal flag.

Kirstin stood against the railing, the breeze streaming her hair away from her face. She shut her eyes, enjoying it.

Gallagher continued to stare at the seemingly endless trail of white behind the ship and found himself thinking of Rhiannon. Her sudden presence in his mind filled him with unease; but it was not the unease caused by anxiety for her safety. It was something else.

And that created some confusion within him.

At about the same time that Gallagher had been staring out of his bedroom window in Aurland, the Volvo driven by the man from Paris arrived at the airport in Alta. The border crossing had been no problem.

Skoryatin got out and went to get his bag from the boot. The man from Paris got out with him and stood waiting as he lifted it out and shut the boot.

"You've done very well," Skoryatin said. "You must be tired. Get some sleep. I can catch up on mine on the plane."

"I'll be alright. I'll have some coffee and a quick bite, then it's on to Tromsø. I'll be leaving the car there for the hire people, and I'll take the 1430 to Oslo. I've plenty of time, and you'll be long gone. No one will see us together down there. I'll stay the night in Oslo, then it's back to Paris in the morning. I wish you well."

Skoryatin stuck out his hand. "We might as well do this the Western way." They shook hands.

"I'll call Oslo to tell them the package has arrived," the man from Paris said. "If there's any problem, there'll be a message at Sogndal."

Skoryatin nodded. "Alright. Be lucky."

"We all need to be," the man from Paris said, and got back into the car.

Skoryatin watched as it drove away, before going off to check in.

Things were still going according to plan.

Someone else had also got plans on his mind at seven-thirty that morning, but they were most certainly not working out as originally intended.

The cold-eyed man made himself a quick breakfast in the cabin so hastily vacated by Gallagher and Kirstin Størvaag and pondered on how best to make use of the day. During the early hours of the morning, he had been woken by the passage of a train and had fallen asleep once more. Then he'd come awake again, with the day well on it's way, but not knowing the exact time. He'd smashed his watch during his roll out of the car.

He was very good at judging how late it was, however, and was usually only five minutes out either way. He'd heard the train on two further occasions. He was sure of it. The thing was to get out of here, and catching that train seemed the best way. If the train went down the valley, it must also go up. He had to get in touch with Oslo. There was no telephone in the cabin, so that meant the train to the nearest place with one.

He'd had a shower. There was plenty of soap and towels, one of which he thought smelled of a woman. He'd checked his clothes and found that in the light of day, they did not look as bad as he'd at first thought. Certainly, they would not attract undue attention. There were slight tears, but these were practically invisible. The scratches on his face caused by his fall from the car were not unduly prominent. He'd found some aftershave which he'd patted onto them, after shaving with one of the disposable razors from the shower room. The subsequent stinging had revitalised him. He'd also put the aftershave on the lacerations on his legs.

His shoes were virtually unscratched and despite the ache he felt in the region of his ribcage, he did not think he'd cracked one. When he'd got off the ferry, he had decided to put on a holster for the pistol and was thankful he had made that decision. It would have been difficult to carry the weapon in broad daylight. As it was, his jacket hid it completely.

He left the cabin and began walking up the gravelly road. Somewhere up ahead, he was sure, there was bound to be a place where the train paused. He'd heard the application of brakes.

As he walked, his thoughts were not concerned with his erstwhile colleagues at the bottom of the gorge.

Iturup, the Kuril Islands. 1830 hours, the same day.

As personal assistant to a Colonel-General of the GRU, Kamapova was able to use her special clearance to gain access to a secure phone to make a call to Moscow. She was also able to do this unattended, in a small communications office. Her own personal beauty helped in no small measure to smooth the path through what could otherwise have been an obstructive bureaucracy. She used a direct link to the person she wanted.

"Comrade . . ." she began as soon as contact was made.

"Do not identify me," the voice at the other end interrupted, "even if this link may be secure."

"I was not about to, Comrade."

"Good." Approvingly. "Good. What warrants this call?"

"The quarry has been missing for a day, ostensibly on an exercise at the far end of the island."

"And is there an exercise?"

"A big one, Comrade, involving several arms of the services, and other Military Districts. . . ."

"Ah. That one. I know of it. Do you believe this to be a cover for something else?"

"The exercise is genuine, Comrade."

"But?"

"I feel this is the moment we have been expecting. I should have accompanied him, but he used another officer to divert me . . ."

"What exactly do you mean?"

"This officer spent most of his time showing me around. . . ."

"I want his name and rank when you return."

"Yes, Comrade."

"You will be pleased to know," the voice from Moscow went on, "that I agree with your reading of the situation. Information has come that the quarry is in fact in the West. . . ."

"The *West?*"

"You will not interrupt me again."

"I apologise, Comrade."

"Accepted. You are to return tonight."

Remembering the stern rebuke, Kamapova controlled the exclamation that had been about to betray her.

"There is a transport aircraft leaving within the hour," the voice continued. "Your passage has been arranged. Be on it. You will be in Moscow by midnight, local time. Someone will be at your apartment with instructions from me."

Before she could make comment, the link was terminated.

Kamapova left the office and returned to her quarters, to prepare for the flight back.

Sognefjord, 1019 hours.

The FJORDTROLL rumbled slowly toward the quay with hissing of its wash as its engines were throttled right back. It stopped just long enough for passengers to disembark and embark, before creaming away toward Bergen, the end of that particular run.

Gallagher looked at the departing boat and said to Kirstin: "I'd like to do that again . . . when I can really enjoy it. Are there others like it on other routes?"

"Oh yes," she replied. "Many more. Perhaps when you have the time, I can show you." Not waiting for his reaction, she continued: "It is time for the next part of our journey." She began walking.

"And where's that?" he asked, as he accompanied her.

"Not far," she said intriguingly. "A few meters only."

The few meters turned out to be 50, along the quay. Tucked into the side was a gleaming white Draco speedboat. It had a sleek prow and a steeply raked curving windscreen side panels that tapered to just past midships. The screen had an anti-dazzle strip across the top. At the neat stern were the bathing platform and ladder, beneath which, on the centerline, he could see the steering arm of a Volvo Penta duoprop marine engine. He could not see inside the boat because it was shielded by a white fabric harbor cover. Curving above it and secured to each side of the craft was the twin-tubed support frame for a small enclosed radar scanner that reminded him of an overturned cake tin. It, too, gleamed white.

"We're going in this?" he said to her.

She paused, to look at him. "What is wrong with it?" she countered.

He stared at the 5½-meter boat. "There's nothing wrong with it. It's a very nice piece of kit. You must have friends in the right places. Or is it yours?"

"It isn't mine; but it is ours to use for the present purposes."

"Which are?"

"To confuse those who are following us."

"Another fall-back position?"

"Fall-back . . . ?" A puzzled look came into her eyes. "Aah . . . ah yes. I think I understand. Yes. That's what it is."

"Can you handle it?"

"Can I handle . . . you mean this boat? Of course I can handle it. I am Norwegian."

"And all Norwegians," he began drily, "are sailors."

"Naturally. We begin very young. I could handle small boats with an outboard motor by the age of ten, on my own."

"I should have known better than to ask. What about your shoulder? If you're going to take me into that ocean of a fjord, I'd like to think you're fit enough to do it."

"My shoulder is alright. Do not worry."

"Who's worried?"

Her smile was all-knowing. "You prefer to work on your own."

I wasn't always like that, he didn't tell her, thinking of the long-dead O'Keefe; thinking about others who had died while with him.

He said nothing.

"I know you worry about my getting in the way," she said. And when he had still made no comment, added: "Come. Help me with the boat."

They removed the cover, and Gallagher saw it had been well-designed and fitted out. The sundeck aft was finished with teak strips, with low side and stern rails serving as grab handles. There was a

U-shaped sofa seat forward of the sundeck and forward of that were two comfortably upholstered bucket seats. The top of the comprehensively equipped and curved instrument panel was also covered in teak striping. The radar monitor was fitted to it, as well as a video echo-sounder and a VHF radiophone with a numbered keypad. A tan-colored tonneau cover was rolled neatly round its bracing strut which had been pushed forward against the top of the windscreen. This was no simple joyboat.

"What is this really? Someone's undercover boat?"

"I don't know," she replied, going back onto the quay to cast off the bow line. "You do the stern," she went on as she climbed back aboard. "I was told it would be here, and it is."

He cast off the line and gave the boat a push from the quay, then took his seat beside her. He put his bag and the cased rifle by his feet.

"I know," he said. "You're just the driver."

"Of course," she said, and started the engine.

It burst smoothly into life and the boat began to move. She opened the throttle gently, getting well clear of the quay; then she thrust it wide. The boat seemed to leap out of the water as it sped away. There was a huge smile upon her face.

"This is wonderful!" she said above the roar of the motor, the hiss of the boat's passage, and the rush of the slipstream. She had stood up to put her face into the wind. Her hair streamed behind her.

"We are on the biggest fjord in Norway," she continued. "Sognefjord. It is 204 kilometers long and at its deepest, 1,308 meters."

Bloody hell, he thought. "That's deeper than the North Sea!"

"Much, much deeper."

"Well don't sink us will you!"

She laughed. "Why? Can't you swim?"

"I just don't like getting wet with my clothes on."

She laughed once more and swung the boat west, toward the great mouth of the fjord. A black-hulled ferry was crossing to the far shore. The boat seemed tiny, Gallagher thought, in the expanse of the water; but the surface was almost like a millpond.

Kirstin appeared to be in her element and despite his thoughts of homicidal pursuers, he found he was enjoying the fast skim across the wide fjord.

"We're going over there." She pointed straight ahead.

Gallagher stared at what seemed like a collection of low-lying peaks, apparently floating on the horizon. As the boat sped on, they progressively grew taller.

"We have about 12 kilometers to go," she said, "then I will take you into the skerries. We shall hide there, and wait. There is food on the boat, and we have got all the water we need to wash in. Yes?"

He looked at the water speeding past. "I think you can say that."

She glanced at him. "I think you are having another little joke."

"No, no. It's just a way of saying things." He'd have to watch that. "How's the shoulder? I can help, if you'd like. Just give me the course, and I'll stay on it."

"It is alright. Also, I know these waters and the skerries. We would not want to go aground."

So he relaxed and let her get on with it. Indeed, she was very good with boats, just as she had said. He amused himself by enjoying the sight of passing coasters and as they drew closer to their destination, the peaks on the horizon gradually metamorphosing into islands. There were also many tiny lumps of rock, some a mere foot or two out of the water, which could give a lot of grief to the unwary.

Within twenty-five minutes of their departure, the speedboat was making its way through a narrow straight between two large islands, the one to starboard about five kilometers long.

"This group of islands," Kirstin said, "form the Kommune... that is District... of Solund. The main island here on our left is Sula. We are going north then round to the west, before going south again. That side is a little open to the sea; but there are the skerries, and plenty of inlets for us to hide. We can get out and into the fjord again by going through the Steinsund."

She played with the boat among the islets until eventually she found a calm haven within a barrier of mainly bare, low-lying islands. She shut down the engine, and Gallagher dropped the anchor into shallow water.

"We are fine here," she said.

It was wonderfully peaceful, and there was not another human being for miles. On one of the islands, bigger than the others and with surprisingly profuse vegetation, was a solitary small hut, a short distance from the water's edge. It was painted a dull red, and grass grew upon its roof. It seemed in good condition.

"Somebody's island?" he asked.

"Ours for now," she said. She began to do something with the radar. "I am setting the alarm," she told him, and when she had finished: "We now have a 360° protection zone, at a range of one nautical mile. That is enough, I think. If any boat comes into it the alarm will sound and flash."

Gallagher looked about him. Plenty of access through the various channels; but plenty of exits too. Kirstin knew the skerries. Hopefully, the kind of people who would come looking—assuming they knew where to look—would be in unfamiliar territory.

"A bonus point to us," he said aloud.

She was studying him, head thrown back a little. "You are thinking of how best to fight if we have trouble."

He nodded, and picked up the rod case which he unzipped, to take out the rifle. He got the magazine out of his bag, and snapped it back on.

"Nothing like being prepared," he said.

She stared at the rifle for some moments, then began to remove her clothes.

"I'm going for a swim," she said and nonchalantly walked stark naked to the stern. She climbed down the ladder and into the water. "I'm a mermaid," she called up to him, then began swimming away from the boat.

The plaster on her wounded shoulder was a pinkish smear on her skin.

"What about your shoulder?" he called back, standing up.

She paused, turned to face him. "The water is good for it. You should come in. It is warm."

"Two of us in the water would not be a good idea if anyone did come looking."

"Alright," she said, and proceeded to swim to one of the rocklike islands about 150 meters away. When she reached it, she climbed on and sat down in a pose reminiscent of the figure in Copenhagen.

From this distance, he thought, she did look like a bloody mermaid out there on that rock.

She waved. He waved in return; but he was thinking if anyone chose to turn up, there was no way she could get back in time. He should have ordered her not to go so far.

How could she beat a fast boat, even from a nautical mile away? Her shoulder would slow her down, whatever she liked to believe. She was trying to prove to him she was not a hindrance. He admired her for it; but that kind of courage was not all she would need for her continuing survival.

He did a slow scan of the area, checking each rock, each island that grew out of the water. Intending attackers would not necessarily come through the passages. Some could take cover from *behind* the islands, while others acted as beaters. . . .

But it was all so peaceful. Surely, they were safe out here among the skerries? Kirstin Størvaag sat on her rock, playing with her hair in the sun.

The time was exactly 1245.

At that moment, Skoryatin was walking toward the hotel bus that would take him through Kaupanger on the 30-kilometer ride to his hotel in Sogndal. He looked refreshed and at ease as he took his seat. He began to chat to a fellow passenger, who turned out to be an Australian with Norwegian antecedents.

"Oh really?" Skoryatin said in American accents as if this were the biggest news in the world. "My folks originally came from fjord country too, but that was way back; my grandfather's time. I like visiting the old country, but I don't get much time to do it. Last time I was here was twenty years ago. Things sure have changed. Norway's doing pretty well for itself these days."

The Australian had a look on his face that clearly said he wished he'd never brought up the subject. The prospect of being bored by chapter and verse of an American pilgrim's history was not something he was looking forward to.

Skoryatin bombarded the unfortunate man with his well-prepared story as the bus started on its journey.

The cold-eyed man had caught the 1100 train out of Flåm for Myrdal where he had made his call to Oslo. The silence that had at first greeted his report did not bode well for the immediate future. After being curtly asked whether he had sufficient funds, he was ordered to take the train to Bergen, and to check into an international class hotel where he would be anonymous. If his funds stretched to it, he should buy some clothes as soon as he arrived. He was to await further instructions. He would be met in Bergen.

As the Bergen train sped along its track, he stared uninterestedly at the passing scenery. He had been humiliated by the person on the telephone and the prospect of being downgraded on this mission did not sit well with him. Being told to wait to be met in Bergen instead of being given help, meant exactly that. Whoever was coming had been given control.

The cold-eyed man felt an all-consuming hatred for the person he'd been chasing since France and who had been responsible for his spectacular downfall. If nothing else were achieved, he was determined to have his revenge. The mission was no longer his.

Skoryatin was moving away from the reception desk where he had just registered, when the receptionist called to him.

"Oh, Mr. Thomsen! I forgot. A message has come for you."

Calmly, he returned to the desk. The receptionist handed him a white envelope with the name Henry Thomsen on it.

"Thank you," he said and opened it in her presence. The note said: "Telephone from Oslo. Your daughter cannot meet you today, but will see you tomorrow."

He folded the note, put it back into the envelope and slipped it into a jacket pocket.

"My colleague took the call earlier," the receptionist said. "I hope it is not bad news."

"Oh no. Not bad news at all. My daughter is at University in Oslo. We are planning to meet up while I am over here."

"So you have family in Norway?"

"Not where they originally came from, as far as I can make out. My grandfather came from Vestnes, in Møre og Romsdal."

"That is north of Alesund. Not far. You will be going there?"

"Maybe. It was a small family then. Maybe there is someone there who remembers."

The receptionist wanted to talk. "So you speak Norwegian."

Skoryatin gave a deprecating little laugh. "When I was younger, I could get by. Now, I am ashamed to say, I'm like a tourist. I can just about say *Snakker De engelsk*."

"Oh I think you are much better than that."

"You're very kind, Miss. But you should hear my daughter. You'd think she was born in Oslo." He smiled at her. "And thank you ... er ... *tusen takk* for your help."

"You're welcome, Mr. Thomsen. Do you still want the bus for Laerdal?"

"No. I'll wait for tomorrow. I think I'll take a walk around the town this afternoon. Thank you."

She watched him go thinking what a nice man. It was obvious he was disappointed about not seeing his daughter.

In his room, Skoryatin was quite happy about the way things were turning out. All the long months of planning were bearing ripe fruit.

"I'm the Artic Maiden," Kirstin said as she climbed back aboard.

Gallagher had watched as she had plunged off the rock and into the water, her naked body a white and blonde flash that had momentarily disappeared, to surface in a foaming of the water as she had pulled strongly toward the boat. The shoulder seemed to have given her little discomfort, though the plaster had now lifted at the edges. She would need a fresh dressing.

"I thought you were a mermaid," he reminded her as she came onto the sundeck. The boat dipped slightly in sympathy to her movements.

"Then I am the Arctic Maiden Mermaid Viking. I was born in the sea, above the Arctic Circle." She got down into the boat, picked up a towel and began to dry herself with quick, patting movements. Then she paused, one breast uncovered. "I am speaking the truth," she told him, noting his doubting expression. The dimple appeared briefly. "Perhaps I exaggerate. I was born on a small island about 100 kilometers off Bodø. That's like being in the sea."

He knew the island she meant, but only because he'd seen it when approaching Bodø during NATO exercises. He said nothing about that to her.

"You'll need a fresh dressing for that shoulder," was what he said. "Is there a kit on board?"

She nodded. "In the glove box."

She began to dress while he got the kit out. It was very comprehensive; almost as if whoever had put it there expected casualties. Gallagher did not like that train of thought at all. Kirstin had sat down behind the wheel, the upper half of her body still unclothed. She was peeling at the dressing and trying not to grimace.

"Let me do that," he said, and gently began to work at it.

At last, the plaster came off and he was able to look at the wound. It was not as bad as he had feared. The coagulation had remained intact, despite her swim. The dressing had kept it mainly dry.

"You were very lucky with that wild shot," he told her. "I think if he'd paused just a fraction of a second to align himself properly, you'd have had it." He began to apply the new dressing.

Her eyes were close to his. "I'd be dead?"

"Very."

She looked away, thinking about the possibility, while he continued to work on her shoulder.

"There," he said. "Finished."

She looked at it, moved the shoulder as if testing, then pressed her hand gently upon it, increasing the force until she reached a level that satisfied her.

"It does not hurt too much, but I will not be able to wear my BH."

"What's a BH?" he asked as she began to put on her T-shirt; then he got the message. "What a name for it."

Before she could comment, the radio began to blink and buzz. She picked up the mike quickly. "Størvaag."

There followed a rapid conversation in Norwegian, then she was nodding. *"Ja. Ja. Jeg forstår."* The light on the phone died. She put the microphone down. "Well you heard."

"I heard, but didn't understand."

"The car has been found. There were two men in it, and many weapons. The police were very surprised."

"I'll bet. Who found it?"

"An engineer going to do an inspection of the water pipe. The man you are to meet has arrived, but we are to remain here for now. The meeting may be arranged for tomorrow. We must wait until we are told when to leave."

He nodded and picked up the rifle briefly. He put it down again, where he could get at it quickly. He looked about him once more.

His senses were cast out beyond the bounds of the skerries, a web-like alarm system awaiting the first trigger upon its outer edges.

17

Moscow, 0030 hours.

Kamapova entered her small apartment to find the lank-haired KGB man who had been at the meeting between Skoryatin and Ulvanov waiting for her. She did not bother to ask how he had gained entry. It would have been superfluous.

"Welcome home, Comrade," he greeted, without the slightest manifestation of shame. "I trust you had a pleasant flight?"

It had not been up to airline standard, but she said: "Yes thank you, Comrade." She stared at two new suitcases by his feet. They appeared to be fully packed. "Whose are these?"

"Yours. You are going to the West. All the necessary papers have been seen to. Your tickets are on the table, as is the money you are likely to need. Your documentation is in the name of Ingrid Lander, a rich American divorcee of Scandinavian descent." He smiled thinly. "You are not too young to have been divorced. Your mother was a Norwegian who married an American businessman. Conveniently, both are dead. You are traveling aimlessly, trying to forget the divorce, though it's nice to have the money to do it with. Your next stop is Oslo. Your passport will show you have been to the Far East, having stopped in Thailand, Hong Kong, and Japan."

The smile disappeared from the KGB man's face as he continued: "This is a very important mission, Comrade. You will be eliminating a traitor. I am authorized to tell you that success will reap a great many benefits." He looked pointedly around the small room. "A much bigger apartment, for example. Accelerated promotion . . . I have been told Lieutenant-Colonel is highly feasible, plus a decoration of sufficient merit."

He made no mention of the price of failure. They both knew what it would be. Yet despite that, she felt excited. *Lieutenant-Colonel!* A bigger apartment, and more money to spend in the state store.

She looked at her visitor expressionlessly. "I am honored, Comrade."

"I am glad you appreciate that. All the necessary instructions are in an envelope by the other papers. Study them, then destroy them before you leave. Doing so is in your very best interests. I shall leave you to prepare yourself and get some sleep. Your flight leaves at 1135. You'll be going to Oslo then on to Bergen. You'll arrive there at 1705 local time. You'll know what to do. A taxi driven by one of my men will be waiting to take you to the airport in the morning. Is all this clear?"

"Perfectly, Comrade."

He nodded briefly. "Good. I shall now say goodnight."

"Goodnight, Comrade."

The beautiful face watched the KGB man leave, giving no indications of the emotions being felt. When he was safely out of the room, Kamapova permitted herself a wide smile of pleasure.

It was 2230 in Bergen, and the cold-eyed man also had a visitor. Their conversation was barely civil.

"They cannot do this to me," he was saying. "I have been responsible for this field mission from the beginning . . ."

"And have managed to lose all the personnel you were allocated," the other said unsympathetically. "You cannot be surprised if someone is sent out to take over. Be thankful you have not been recalled."

"Who is this wonder-person? What can he do that . . ."

"She."

"What? They're sending a *woman?*"

"Why not a woman, Comrade? Are you a westernised chauvinist, after all?"

"No. No. Of course not!"

"Then why the objection?"

"I object to being demoted."

"It could have been worse. It could still be."

"And I could order you to give me the help that I need."

"You could, but I would not accept any responsibility. I would make official note of my protest."

The cold-eyed man looked at his companion sneeringly.

"Much as I expected. Well I *am* ordering you to supply what I have asked for."

"I would have to check with Control."

The cold-eyed man pulled out his automatic.

The contact stared at him disbelievingly. "You are mad! You cannot do this! You cannot fire that thing in this hotel. The place would be crawling with police . . ."

"I said nothing about shooting you here."

"You *are* mad! You cannot shoot me just because I do as I'm told. They would come after you. You cannot jeopardize the mission because of a personal vendetta. It was you who allowed yourself to be outmanoeuvred. You are meant to be a professional. Try acting like one, or you'll be finished."

"I'm finished, anyway . . . and you know it. They'd punish me when I returned, whatever the outcome. I don't think long years of cold winters would suit me. . . ."

The other man stared. "You're going to defect?"

"Don't be stupid. I'm going after him . . . on my own, if need be."

"You can't. You haven't got the information. . . ."

"And I know who's going to give it to me."

"Don't look at me. I'm not going against Control's wishes."

The cold-eyed man smiled. His eyes were murderous. "You've been living in the West for some time now. I think you've grown soft. I wonder for how long you would last under one of my interrogations. I don't need any fancy little rooms. I can make do with what I've got. My own inventiveness."

The other had paled suddenly. "You wouldn't dare! You wouldn't risk it...."

"A man who knows he's finished has nothing more to lose," the cold-eyed man said harshly. "You've got plenty. Spare yourself. Give me the information I need and the equipment I've asked for. You can say what you like to the little Comrade when she gets here. Blame it all on me."

"You're insane! What do you think they'll do to me if I go against my orders?"

"Nothing as bad as what *I'll* do to you. You can tell them I forced you . . . at gunpoint." The cold-eyed man gave a nasty chuckle that carried the promise of death in it. "It's true enough. First, you'll give me the information, then we're going to go everywhere together until I get what I want. After that, you can do as you like. I'll leave you here in Bergen while I carry on with the mission. Alright?"

"You can't...."

The gun was poked gently at a left eye. *"Alright?"*

"Be reasonable...."

The gun tapped firmly against an ear, hard enough to make the man's eyes water.

"Alright?" came a third time. "I can do this for long, long hours you know. I can tie and gag you and go to work on all parts of your body."

"If you kill me, you won't get the information...."

"Oh you'll tell me long before that happens. You be reasonable, and tell me where they've gone, get me transport and weapons and some hired help, and I'll be on my way . . . *and* you'll be in one piece. What could be simpler? I do not want to kill you, Comrade, but you are leaving me no choice."

The gun was again resting against the left eye. A silence had descended, broken only by the shallow breathing of the by now very frightened man. He knew he was dealing with someone implacable.

At last, he said in a hoarse voice: "Al . . . alright."

The gun did not move away. "Don't try to do anything that might make me believe you intend to betray me," the cold-eyed man warned. "You will most certainly die if that happens. Think well upon it."

The man tried to nod, remembered the gun against his eye. "I'll . . . do as you say, but I cannot be responsible . . ."

"Haven't I already said you can blame me?" the cold-eyed man assured him, almost cheerfully. "Now come on. Start telling me the things I want to hear. Soft," he added contemptuously. "That's what you office boys are."

The man began to talk.

Gallagher looked out at the rippled surface of the water. A very light breeze had sprung up, barely strong enough to shift the boat on its mooring. Despite the lateness of the hour, the clear sky was a pale gray that was reflected in a way that fooled the eye into believing there were strange shapes moving in the shallows. The silhouettes of the skerries and islets were ghostly, indistinct presences, unmoving sentries in the dim sea.

They had rigged the tonneau. It had three transparent panels; a large rectangle for the stern, and one on each side. From his position, he could see no lights anywhere. It was as if they were totally alone in the world.

Wanting to assure himself that she could really navigate the skerries under pressure, he had asked Kirstin to take him on a fast ride through them. Though at times he had wondered about the wisdom of that decision as she had threaded the boat through hair-raisingly narrow channels at speed, he was left in no doubt that she would be able to get them out in a hurry. He hoped it wouldn't be at night.

At one stage, she had beached the boat on the large island with the hut, and he had left her on board while he had gone ashore to do a quick reconnaissance. He had taken the rifle, telling her to fire off the Socimi should anyone hostile appear. The island had proved to be virtually as bare as the others, save for the vegetation in the area of the hut.

No one had come to disturb them, and no messages had come over the radiophone. They had decided that they would be there for the night. Sleeping bags had been found in a compartment behind the instrument panel, as had a supply of food and water, with cooking implements that could be worked off the boat's power supply. Everything had been thought of.

Gallagher looked into the night, eyes searching, rifle at the ready. Kirstin was curled up in one of the bags, fast asleep. He would not disturb her, having decided to spend the entire night on guard, between snatches of sleep. It would be no hardship. He had done this before for longer periods, in far more precarious situations.

He stared at the empty sea. The boat rocked barely perceptibly.

The cold-eyed man had found his transport. He now knew where he had to go, and he had also got his hired help.

"So this is it?"

"Yes," the contact said.

"Living in the West clearly has its benefits."

"I have appearances to keep up."

"So it would seem," the cold-eyed man said sourly.

They were looking at the small boats moored to the long pier that came off the Market. Prominent among them was a long sleek craft that gleamed darkly in the harbor lighting.

"Let's take a closer look," the cold-eyed man said.

Reluctantly, the contact accompanied him along the pier toward the boat. It was a 10-meter high performance motor yacht with a sharp prow that rose smoothly to the steeply raked, wrap-around windscreen of the open cockpit. The stern was also raked at a sharp angle, with a platform well inserted into it, for access from the water. Wide fins rose from the sides near the stern, canted slightly inward, to cockpit level. Braced against them were the bases of the slim arch that carried the mid-mounted radar scanner.

"It looks fast," the cold-eyed man commented approvingly.

"It is. It's a triple screw, with three 350PS engines. She will do a maximum of 60 knots. She can outrun any patrol boat and any warship of whatever size . . . a very useful capability. We use her to explore the fjords. Good submarine country, the fjords."

"Well," the cold-eyed man said, "let's see what's on board."

The contact was nervous. "You won't forget I've got to be in Stavanger in the morning." A roundish man with balding head and a wide-spaced, pigeon-toed walk rather like that of a wrestler, he was in shipping; a good cover for his other interests. He seemed to be having trouble with his breathing.

"I won't forget," the cold-eyed man said. "Come on. On you get. You've got to show me where the weapons are."

They went aboard. The contact turned on subdued lighting in the cabin beneath the cockpit. It was sumptuously furnished, with air-conditioning.

The cold-eyed man looked about him, a grim smile upon his lips. "How many roubles did this cost?"

"It was budgeted for," the contact retorted sharply. "I don't like your tone. You are not here to question my activities. You should not be here at all."

"So you insist in reminding me. But I am here, and you're going to show me the weapons."

The contact went to a rectangular porthole and pressed firmly against the panel next to it. One of the dark red suede cushions of the cabin seating rose silently, to reveal a comprehensive collection of weaponry.

The cold-eyed man made him take each one out for inspection.

"Good," the cold-eyed man said approvingly when the weapons were all neatly stowed again and the cushion once more in place. "Now about the men you hired."

"Two sailors we have . . . er . . . used before. They will be here at 0600. Their nationalities will not concern you. Both speak English, the language in which you will converse with them."

"Do they know who you really are?"

The contact shook his head. "I am just someone who gives them slightly illegal jobs from time to time, for which they are paid very well. It ensures their loyalty as well as their silence." The contact smiled unpleasantly. "They were also involved in a brawl in Stavanger in which a woman was killed. I got them away. This also ensures their loyalty and their continuing silence. There are people in Stavanger, apart from the police themselves, who would dearly like to know their identity. The seaman's world can be a very closed one, and there is sometimes nowhere to run to."

The cold-eyed man nodded. "Very efficient, Comrade. And now, we must settle down for the night."

"What? I cannot remain here with you! I must get to Stavanger. I have things to prepare. . . ."

"You do not seriously believe I'm going to let you out of my sight before I leave, do you? Am I to sit here patiently while your cut-throats arrive to take care of me?"

"You defame me, Comrade! Those men are coming to help you. How can you say. . . ."

"Then you have nothing to worry about." The gun was pointing. This time, it was fitted with a silencer. "You sit over there, and I'll remain here by the exit and the light switch. If we are very quiet, we shall pass the rest of the night quite pleasantly . . . Comrade."

The contact sat nervously down, staring at the gun as if mesmerised.

Promptly at six the next morning the men, one white, the other black, arrived at the boat. They were big, tough-looking, their faces hard. The cold-eyed man watched them carefully as they came aboard. Both wore jeans and rope-soled shoes, tight T-shirts and yachting jackets. The clothes seemed of much better quality than he would have expected of such men. Their heads were bare.

"Hello chief," the white one greeted the contact. "Nice boat."

"This . . . er . . . this is the gentleman I spoke to you about. Give him complete co-operation."

The black one grinned. "Sure, chief. You know us. Cooperation guaranteed."

The cold-eyed man watched them closely. They had spoken with strong American accents. He was not sure what to make of it. Had the contact been in touch with American assassins? Was the contact possibly a *double* agent? Given the manner of his lifestyle, it was entirely likely he had been compromised.

The cold-eyed man felt happier about the decision he had taken during the night.

"The chief is coming with us," the cold-eyed man announced.

The contact was shocked. *"What?* But I told you. . . ."

"I've changed my mind," the cold-eyed man snapped, lying.

The two men looked at him speculatively. "I'm

Jim," the white one said, "and my friend here is John."

"Of course you are," the cold-eyed man said drily.

"And where are we going?" the one introduced as John asked.

"Hunting. Our destination is about 50 nautical miles from here. In this boat, that should take us only about an hour, give or take a few minutes."

Both men grinned. "We like to hunt," the one calling himself Jim said.

"Then I promise you some good sport."

Gallagher looked out at the brightness of the morning. The night had passed quietly. The radar alarm had been silent, and the calm sea and clear sky promised a warm day to come.

Kirstin stirred, looked up at him. "Daylight," she said, as if discovering it for the first time. "What time is it?"

"Six-thirty."

She stared at him. "You have been up all night? Why didn't you wake me?"

"I've had some sleep and besides, I want you fully awake if we've got to leave here in a hurry. I would not particularly enjoy being stranded on one of these rocks if someone's chasing us."

She sat up and peered out of the tonneau. "It seems clear. I hear no engines, and the radar is quiet."

"That means nothing in this game. Let's get the tonneau down." He wanted a clear field of fire if anything should happen.

She got out of the bag to help him. The tonneau was rolled back into its stowage position, the sleeping bags put away. "If you'd like a quick dip to wash away the sleep, go ahead. I've had mine while you were down. The water felt cold, but it's refreshed me."

"I never even heard you," she said in wonder.

"It takes practice. Well? Do you want to go in?"

"Yes." She stripped quickly and climbed over the side.

Gallagher had the rifle ready, eyes scanning. Then the radio-phone blinked and squawked at him.

"Mr. Renwick!" it said in English. "Be on your guard. We have heard that some people are on their way to you by boat! Be in contact when you have resolved the situation." The phone stopped blinking.

Shit.

"Kirstin!" he bawled. "Get back here!"

She had been swimming at a leisurely pace a few meters away. Her head had swiveled round when she'd heard the squawk, a startled expression upon her face. Now, she was ploughing back toward the boat.

She climbed aboard, her naked body dripping. It was a beautiful sight in the morning sun, but Gallagher paid scant attention.

"What has happened?"

"We're going to have some company. Get your clothes on and be ready to move. We may really have to test your skill among these skerries." He gave the surroundings another searching scan. "I knew it was too bloody quiet around here."

* * *

The sleek, dark blue craft was planing its way across the Sognesjö, heading for the Straumsfjord on the west coast of Ytre Sula. It was near its maximum speed, its engines running remarkably quietly, and had made better time than expected. The man called Jim was at the helm. Ytre Sula was just eight nautical miles from Gallagher's and Kirstin's hiding place among the skerries.

The cold-eyed man's contact was standing behind the cockpit, left hand gripped tightly to a side rail. On the starboard side was the cold-eyed man himself and next to Jim up in the cockpit was John. Neither of the two men had as yet been given weapons.

The contact said: "When this is finished, you must get me back to Bergen so that I can get to Stavanger."

"Of course," the cold-eyed man said accommodatingly. Then he pulled out the automatic and shot the contact.

The now unsilenced gun gave a sharp bark that snarled across the muted thunder of the triple engines. The men in the cockpit had turned instinctively to look. The boat, highly sensitive at speed, twitched and swerved alarmingly.

"Watch the *damn* wheel!" John yelled at his buddy. *"Goddammit!"*

Jim corrected swiftly, and the boat was once more on course.

The contact's body, slammed against the side rail by the force of the single bullet, had been pitched over the side by the violent maneuver of the vessel. A thin trail of blood marked his passing. He had died with his eyes wide open in hurt surprise.

The cold-eyed man stared past the churning wake. There was no sign of the body.

The man called John watched him. "I never liked the little bastard anyway. But is this what you've got planned for us?"

Jim's back had stiffened as both men awaited the reply.

"Not unless you give me cause. You have already been paid. All you've got to do when this is over is take me back to Bergen. I shall disappear, as you in your own interests, no doubt will."

"So what do we hunt with?"

"I shall give one of you a weapon in due course. The other sees to the helm. In case either of you entertains the idea of taking me, I should warn you that there are three 40-millimeter grenades primed to go off, should anything happen to me. The trigger is on my person. I shall press it long before I die. You would certainly not survive the explosion. I see this little lesson has sunk in. Good."

"Sonofabitch," the one called John said softly.

The thunder of the engines answered him.

The Draco lay still in the water, engine burbling at idle. Gallagher studied the radar. The remote keypad was on top of the instrument panel. He increased the range to the unit's maximum, 16 nautical miles. Nothing. There were shoals of islands and skerries in the way, so that was not surprising. He left it on that range setting.

Kirstin said: "Perhaps we should not remain here, just waiting for them."

"It's our best chance," he told her. "We don't know what they're using. If they've got a bigger boat—which seems likely—the skerries are to our advantage. Besides, I'd prefer not to be caught in open water. They may well be able to outrun us. I'm also prepared to bet they've got radar too. If we stay put, we'll be masked for as long as possible, whereas they'll be moving. We'll know about them first."

She looked worried.

As well she might, he thought. She could well be dead before it was all over.

"Anything on that radar?" the cold-eyed man asked of John.

John was staring at it intently. "No, chief...."

"Don't call me chief."

John glanced quickly at Jim, who shrugged.

John said: "Nothing so far, apart from the usual traffic. We're not into the area you want to go as yet. What are we looking for anyway?"

"You'll know when you see it."

The sleek craft hurtled on its way through the Straumsfjord and began curving to starboard on a track that would take it past the group of islands on the northern tip of Ytre Sula.

Distance from the Draco's position was now 4 nautical miles.

Gallagher stared at the radar. "Not a bloody sausage," he said to himself.

But Kirstin heard him. "A sausage?" She frowned trying to make sense of it.

"What? Oh. I mean there's nothing on the radar. They must be behind one of the islands, if they're coming at all."

During their exploratory trip through the

area, he had discovered that their island was part of a basic group of four. The other three were larger, the biggest of which was a good 2½ kilometers long. There were narrow channels between them through which the Draco could pass without trouble. Arranged as they were like loose pieces in a jigsaw puzzle, he intended to use them to confound his pursuers.

Their own island with the hut was shaped like a lobster's claw, their haven the inlet between the pincers, with the shoals of skerries spread around like an outer ring of defences. He hoped they would rip the guts out of the pursuing boat and intended to ensure that exactly such a fate would befall it.

Kirstin said: "How did they know where to find us?"

"That's easy," he replied grimly. "Someone told them." Someone had been telling them since France, he didn't add.

"But who would do such a thing?"

"Good question, but a bit harder to answer."

She sat at the wheel, hands lightly resting upon its rim. He looked at her, checking that everything was alright. Her appearance had been changed, for the little subterfuge he'd planned. Odd bits of clothing were always being left on boats, and the Draco was no exception. In a cubby hole, they'd found a grubby woollen hat into which she had tucked her blonde hair and pulled it low down on her head. His leather jacket had been substituted for the denim. From a distance and seen from behind in the seat, she could be mistaken for a man, even through binoculars.

He hoped. As long as she didn't turn round.

"Remember what I told you," he said to her. "Don't turn round to see where they are, whatever you do. Use the radar to check their distance, and the echo sounder to take them into shallow water. That will make them cautious, forcing them to fall behind. Maintain a sea distance of one nautical mile if possible, and never keep a straight course for long. They'll probably have much more speed, so weaving into dangerous water will hold them off. Right. Can you remember the rest?"

She nodded, gnawing a little at her lower lip.

"Are you sure you're alright?"

"I am alright. Yes."

"And for God's sake . . . don't get shot again."

She gave a weak smile. "I shall try."

He gave her unwounded shoulder a brief squeeze. "You'll be fine."

I wish I believed that, he thought anxiously. He was asking a lot of her.

"I've got something!" John shouted.

"What bearing?" the cold-eyed man demanded.

"Zero-three-zero. It's stationary. Could be some people out for the day."

"So early?"

"Why not?"

"We shall investigate."

But the investigation proved fruitless. They came upon a small fishing boat that was just raising anchor, circled it once, leaving a boiling wake while its startled crew looked on.

"We are wasting time!" the cold-eyed man snarled with rage.

Tense minutes passed, then John again shouted: "I've got another!"

"You had better be right. What bearing this time?"

"One-one-five. Again stationary."

"Alright. Find it."

The dark blue motor yacht had begun curving into the open waters of the Lågöyfjord. It now turned onto the new heading.

From the helm, the man who called himself Jim said: "That area's full of skerries. At this speed, we'll rip the bottom out if we hit anything."

"Maintain your speed, and keep on course," the cold-eyed man said emotionlessly.

"I thought you wanted to get back to Bergen."

"I do. And so will you . . . if you do as I say." The cold eyes surveyed each man in turn, lifelessly: then he went below to return almost immediately with a pair of binoculars. He raised them to his eyes. "Now we shall see," he said softly.

The boat rushed on at maximum speed.

Gallagher had seen the target blip on the radar almost at the instant that the Draco had itself been discovered. He now selected the range for two nautical miles, with twin range rings one nautical mile apart. The inner ring was the one-mile limit.

He had lowered himself to the bottom of the Draco. Now, he raised his head cautiously to see what was moving so rapidly. He saw the churning water and immediately ducked down once more.

"My God!" he said. "What the hell is it?"

"It is almost flying," Kirstin said. Her voice shook a little.

"Don't look anymore!" he told her urgently. "They may have binoculars on you. Get ready."

The blip had long crossed the outer ring and was now approaching the one-mile range. Gallagher checked the AR70/90. He was as ready as he would ever be.

The blip was almost on the ring.

"Go!" he shouted.

The Draco responded instantly as she slammed the throttle forward. The boat seemed to want to leap out of the water as it shot away, gathering speed with alacrity. Gallagher had to brace himself to avoid being tossed onto his back. He stayed low, out of sight, as the boat appeared to tilt skyward.

"They're moving!" It was John who again gave the alarm.

"I've seen them," the cold-eyed man acknowledged. "Do you still think they are ordinary people out for the day?" To the one called Jim, he said: "Don't lose them."

"The skerries. . . ."

"Don't lose them!" the cold-eyed man interrupted harshly. "I want that man alive. We'll cripple their boat, then we shall have them."

"What do we cripple it with?" John asked. "Our spit?"

The cold-eyed man stared at him. "The time has come to give you a weapon. Just remember which is the target."

"Oh I never mistake a target." John grinned.

"I am not in the mood for your stupid comments."

The cold-eyed man again went below. This

time, he returned with an M16A and an H&K G41-TGS with a 40mm grenade round already loaded. He handed the M16 to John.

"Pepper the boat," he said, "but don't hit anyone. Yet."

John eyed the grenade launcher. "And what's that one for?"

"None of your business," the cold-eyed man snapped.

Kirstin was performing extremely well. For fifteen minutes, she had led the dark blue boat round the eastern pincer of the island to head south through narrow channels and skerries, always keeping the range at the one mile Gallagher had told her to. On several occasions, the faster boat had been forced to alter course in order to follow, thereby losing ground. As yet, no shots had been fired at them.

In the bottom of the boat, Gallagher could only marvel at her control. Half-expecting to hear the sickening crunch that would tell him she had misjudged it, his admiration grew as the Draco appeared to be hurling itself with insane abandon through the maze of islands. At times he would glance up to see the slab shape of a rock whizzing by, perilously close. But each time, as if by a miracle, they seemed to miss.

After another couple of minutes, he called out: "Where are they now?"

"Exactly one mile, dead astern."

"It's time for the next phase. Get ready to weave when I tell you."

"Alright."

Gallagher got up suddenly, braced himself in a firing position against the stern deck, and loosed off a burst. He ducked down again, forcing himself not to stare in horror. The pursuing boat was a thing of awesome beauty. It seemed to be traveling on its stern and would be upon them any time now.

"Weave!" he screamed at Kirstin.

More in reaction to the pitch of his voice than anything else, she swung the wheel over. The Draco went into a skidding turn to starboard, straight into a shoal of skerries. She guided it neatly between two particularly nasty-looking groups, finding a safe passage where there appeared to be none.

The dark boat, baulking at following the maneuver, throttled back suddenly and swung away, looking for a safer route. It fell rapidly back to about two nautical miles.

"They fired at us," John said. He sounded aggrieved.

"I saw the flashes," the cold-eyed man said contemptuously. "They have panicked. There was little chance of a hit."

Jim said: "The guy knows his way around here. He knows if he goes into open sea we'll get him. He can dodge us here forever."

"He will not. You will go after him! If he can get through, so can we. What are you afraid of? This is not your boat, and you have been paid to do a job, so *do it! Get after him!"*

"What are they doing now?" Gallagher asked.

"I don't think they're sure of what to do. I've led them into some skerries and they're on the outside, trying to find a way in."

"Can we get out without closing the range?"

"Oh yes. I am about to go north again, back to the island with the hut. They will follow, but they must stay on the outside. It will cost them time."

"Good. We must now do the really dangerous part. I'll have just the one chance, so we must make it work."

"Alright."

Gallagher felt the Draco swing as she changed course. He peered at the radar. It was awkward to see properly from his position, but he was able to note the lengthening of the range. The blip had gone off the two-mile ring.

"Are they still in sight?" he asked.

"I've put an island between us. When they again have me in sight, I shall be turning round a point. I'll then be able to drop you off before they follow. Is that okay?"

"That's fine," he assured her. "You're doing very well."

She smiled, but he knew she was frightened. She was going to be alone.

When they rounded the point she had spoken of, the dark boat was still some distance away, though it had seen their route. There was a tiny gravel beach in front of the hut and Kirstin drove the Draco right up to it. As soon as the bow touched, Gallagher got up and jumped off. The beach was steeply sloped so that the stern drive of the Draco was still in deep water.

He turned and gave the bow a push as Kirstin engaged reverse. The boat pulled away, then turned to get quickly out of the inlet. Gallagher raced to get behind the hut and worked his way inland. The timing had to be exact. He heard the Draco accelerate along the planned route, a narrow channel along the southwest coast of the island. It was deep enough for the pursuit boat to follow, but sufficiently narrow to force it to slow down.

As he hurried, he could hear the smooth hum of the Draco's engine, but coming up behind was the low thunder of the dark boat.

But he was nearly there. He'd be ready.

"Now we have them!" the cold eyed man said.

The Draco was dead ahead. There was nowhere for it to turn, having been forced by the narrow passage to maintain a steady course.

"Open up!" the cold-eyed man ordered.

"The channel is deep, but we are still close to rocks on either side," Jim said cautiously. "Our slow speed is still faster than he's going at the present time."

"Don't argue with me!"

"It's your funeral," Jim said.

"Yours, if you don't do as I say." The cold-eyed man turned his attention to John. "Do *you* want to argue?"

"I'm not driving," was what John said.

During his reconnaisance, Gallagher had found the depression in the smooth rock that gave him a perfect field of fire across the channel, while leaving him well in cover. By the time those in the boat realized what was happening, it would be too late. They would not be able to maneuver out of danger without going aground. The only way out would be to increase speed and use that to get out of range; but Gallagher had the answer to that move. He settled down as the sound of the boat grew louder.

Then it was passing so close, it seemed as if he could touch it if he reached out. Its sleek prow was high off the water, as it hurtled in pursuit of the Draco.

Leading on the helmsman, Gallagher squeezed off a burst of three. The result was devastating. The helmsman took them all in the neck. He was slammed to the right by the force of the bullets and he fell against the wheel, spinning it as he slid downward. The other two men in the boat first turned startled faces in the direction of where they had thought the shots had come from, before shifting their horrified stares to what was happening.

The dark boat had responded instantly to the sudden change at the helm and had swung at speed, to ram itself against the unyielding rocks on the other side of the channel. A terrible crunching rent the air as the boat tried to climb out of the water, its raked prow probing skyward as it splintered with the force of the blow. The sleek stern dipped beneath the surface and upward momentum ceased.

The stern began to sink. The engines seemed to be howling with rage and pain. The shattered bow began to scream as it ripped itself to pieces on the way down; and on the edge of that strangely inanimate scream was another. This time it was human, and nerve-clawing. The scream died abruptly as the dark boat plunged deeply sternfirst, until the sharp tip of the prow disappeared. The water boiled violently and was still. There was no explosion.

Gallagher stood up, amazed by the effect of his short burst of fire, but was unmoved. Then he stared, astonished. *Someone had swum up from beneath the water!*

He was in full view, and the swimmer paused to look up. Gallagher found himself looking into the coldest eyes he had ever seen upon a human being. The man tread water, just looking up at him.

Gallagher would never be able to remember for exactly how long that tableau remained. It was as if all passage of time had been halted. The man's eyes held nothing in them.

There was a sudden inhuman yell and Gallagher saw that the swimmer, keeping himself afloat with a furious kicking of his feet and almost rising out of the water, was pointing a *gun* upward.

Gallagher's reaction was as swift as it was deadly. The AR70/90 barked two rapid bursts of three and the man in the water appeared to have lost his head. A dark bloom stained the surface. Of the man, there was no sign.

Gallagher stared at the water for long moments, but there was no further disturbance. It was as if the dark boat and its occupants had never been. He turned his back upon the once-more peaceful channel.

Holding the rifle across his chest, he trotted the 400 meters to the southern tip of the island where the Draco was waiting. Kirstin had again been able to beach it. He climbed aboard, and she eased it off, before turning to head for open water and the Sognefjord.

"You were very good," he said to her.

"And you," she said, "are very good. I did not think you would stop them. I was very frightened."

"So was I," he said.

She was silent for a while before saying: "I have told them on the phone what has happened. We are to return to Rysjedalvik. The helicopter will come to take us back to Aurland. We are to drive to Laerdal. The man you are to meet will be there."

"When is this to happen?"

"At three o'clock this afternoon."

She fell silent again. After nearly fifteen minutes had passed, Gallagher asked: "Is something wrong?"

She shook her head. But something clearly was. He had expected a reaction to what had happened: the fear of being caught, the subsequent destruction of the dark boat, and the eventual relief. But this was something else entirely.

At last, she said: "Your eyes. When you came aboard, there was something in your eyes I have never seen. It frightened me."

He found there was nothing he could say.

18

The journey to Laerdal was as spectacular as it was uneventful. The Saab clawed its way up the steeply winding road from Aurland, disclosing a panorama of fjord and mountains that spread as far as the eye could see. Kirstin drove fast, with a competence that was as good as had been her handling of the boat. She appeared to have conquered the effects of her ordeal. She was, however, much quieter than was normal for her.

The narrow road lost its hairpin bends but still climbed, meandering its way across a vast undulating and bleak landscape that was entirely treeless. But the image on the mind was vivid. The ground rose in massive mounds from the puny road and in the far distance, the snow-capped peaks seemed to have a blue tinge. Here and there, Gallagher saw lonely huts, huddled to the brownish slopes. Then the terrain changed again.

The road had become even narrower, its surface more indifferent.

Kirstin said: "Look over there."

The Saab was passing through a depression between two flanks of rising ground. On the left, a blanket of hard-packed snow reached all the way down to a small lake whose surface was thinly covered with ice at the edges, but rippled freely at the center. A power pylon stood in solitary majesty half-way up the slope.

"That lake looks bloody cold," Gallagher said.

"It is. We are 1300 meters up."

Nearly 4300 feet. No wonder it was bloody cold. To his right, however, the ground was virtually free of snow.

"The second meeting will be up here," she was saying.

Gallagher stared at her. "You've got to be joking. Up *here*? What second meeting?"

"It is what I have been told. First you meet him in Laerdal, then we come up here another day for the second." She shrugged. "That is all I know. Perhaps he will tell you more."

"He'd bloody better. No one said anything about *two* meetings."

A silence came as the road suddenly ran out of tarmac and became a gravelly surface. The hairpin bends seemed to have returned too. She hurled the Saab into it, apparently unworried. The road was descending and with the descent came the resurgence of vegetation. The bends seemed to have been carved through rock and to Gallagher, the car appeared to be missing the unyielding surface by inches. A roadsign suggested 50kph, but she ignored it, continuing to hurtle downward.

He was tempted to tell her to ease off, but kept his counsel. Trees were now on the forested slopes as Laerdal drew closer and the outside temperature had risen considerably. They had virtually traveled through two climatic systems, Gallagher realized, within a relatively short distance.

Out of habit, he glanced round. There was no traffic following. They had passed no vehicles, and none had come toward them; though they had seen a couple parked on the downward route, just after a bend.

"People out at the waterfalls," was what Kirstin had said about that.

Laerdal turned out to be quiet. There were a trio of cars and a van standing in the car park in the town center, and two tourist coaches. The tourists were straggling around, but the locals were conspicuous by their absence. Most places appeared to be shut. As the Saab pulled into a parking slot, Gallagher had the unnerving feeling of being on a film set.

He got out of the car and looked about him. The car park was itself at the center of a deep U-shaped plaza. On one side was a long, three-storied hotel, and on the other, a string of shops catering for various goods. All were closed. The base of the U was mostly taken up by a cafeteria. It too, was closed.

Beyond the entrance and across the road was a loose group of two-storied houses made of wood, pretty in pastel shades, with two-tiered verandahs supported by slender columns. There seemed to be no one in them.

He walked into the road and looked down it, both ways. Not a car in sight and no one, save for the odd wandering tourist. It was like being transported back in time. Laerdal, like so many of its sister towns, nestled deep within the embrace of a valley, at the end of its fjord. It was enchanting, scrupulously clean, and seemed preserved for ever.

"In the season, this is a very popular place." Kirstin had joined him. "It is very good for the salmon. Many people come here for the fishing. It was an Englishman who discovered this, in the old days."

They began walking along the quiet street. They came to a shop window and Gallagher stared at the sign hanging within. It was in English. "Here you can get the famous salmon fly," it said.

He smiled. "I see what you mean."

They walked on. A small gaggle of tourists was ahead of them.

"How are we supposed to know whom we're looking?" he asked her.

"We continue to walk together. He will find us."

"Do you know what he looks like?"

She shook her head.

"Great."

Another five minutes passed. They turned, began walking back the way they had come, pausing every now and then to look at a shop window. They passed tourists who smiled at them bemusedly. A few were clicking away with their cameras at the pretty houses.

Gallagher began to think he had been brought here on a wild goose chase.

"Hi there, darling!" an American voice said from behind.

Kirstin appeared to have stopped. Gallagher turned to see a big but athletic-looking middle-aged man giving her an embrace. She looked as if she were trying to make up her mind whether to be horrified or not. The man had a smooth face, with bushy eyebrows.

An American? Gallagher thought, immediately on the alert. What was going on?

His eyes began scanning, hunting out potential threats. He had chosen to leave the P226 in the car. It was probably, under the circumstances, not a wise decision; but he'd had enough of guns, and did not want to carry the thing around in this peaceful place if he could help it. The rifle and the submachine gun were well out of reach in Aurland. He wished he didn't now feel so vulnerable.

The man who had embraced Kirstin was now looking at him.

"I am alone," the man said. "There is no threat. You must be Paul Renwick." He smiled. "You are surprised. You're paying me a great compliment. I must sound genuinely American. I am Borodin."

He kept an arm about Kirstin and before Gallagher fully realized what was happening, the other arm had reached out.

Gallagher felt himself clasped by the shoulder.

"Let us walk," Skoryatin said.

To anyone looking, it was the perfect picture of a man greeting his daughter and her husband or boyfriend.

"You've been having some adventures, I've been told," Skoryatin continued.

"Is that what you call it?"

"Oh ho! You sound angry, my friend. You shouldn't be. I am most impressed by your capabilities. You have beaten one of the most cold-blooded killers in this business. You wiped out his teams, and got him in the end. Most impressive indeed. He was after me, you know."

"That's funny. I thought he was after me."

"Only because you got in the way. When he found he couldn't get rid of you, he clearly became obsessed. Very unprofessional."

"Why am I here?" Gallagher demanded, cutting across the pleasantries.

"You are still angry." Skoryatin sounded almost sad. "I can appreciate your feelings. Yes, yes. I can. You feel you have been put at great risk. . . ."

Gallagher gave a short, bitter laugh.

"I know how you feel . . ."

"Someone's been telling them how to find me. I'd like to know who was responsible."

"And then what?" Skoryatin had stopped, face close to Gallagher's.

"I have my suspicions," Gallagher said.

Skoryatin smiled suddenly, and began walking again. "We have perhaps twenty minutes, maybe less, before my bus leaves and I play the loud tourist again. I must tell you everything by then."

"Everything?"

"Everything relevant."

"Ah," Gallagher said sceptically, and left it at that.

Skoryatin looked at Kirstin, and took his arm from her shoulders. She winced.

"I'm sorry," he said apologetically. "Have I been too rough with my embrace?"

"She was shot," Gallagher said tightly, "in that shoulder."

"I am very sorry to hear that." Skoryatin appeared genuinely concerned.

"Your killer did it. Luckily, the bullet just grazed her."

"Very lucky indeed. He was never known to miss."

"It was at night," Gallagher said. "She was in a moving car, and I'd just shot *his* car from under him."

Again, Skoryatin smiled, as if amused. "I can see the recommendations were correct." He turned to Kirstin. "Would you excuse us, please, young lady? I'm sure you'll appreciate why. We'll walk on ahead. Pretend you're lagging behind to look into the shop windows."

She gave Gallagher an uncertain look, then said: "Alright."

As they moved on, Skoryatin continued: "I have taken great risks to get here. I cannot afford to have anything go wrong."

"Is all the smokescreen about a list really to cover your defection?"

Skoryatin stopped suddenly. *"Defection?"* he hissed sharply. His eyes narrowed, a strange wariness in them. "Who gave you such an insane idea? Why should I wish to defect?"

Taken aback, Gallagher said: "But there is no list. I've never seen the bloody thing. I therefore assumed this whole charade was a cover for. . . ."

"Not a *defection*. A kidnap attempt, perhaps?" Skoryatin's eyes were suddenly very hard. "Your people would not, by any chance be trying to use this. . . ."

"Don't look at me. I know nothing about such plans. And don't call them *my* people. I've been conned into this. I've been hounded from France to Scandinavia, and I still don't know what the hell for. So if you've got the answers, I like to know them; then I can go home and forget all about you."

Skoryatin began walking once more. Gallagher kept pace with him.

"Wonderful place, Norway," he said, going off at a tangent. "Look at this little town. So peaceful. A far cry from our kind of world."

"I wish you wouldn't keep including me," Gallagher said.

"She thought very highly of you." Skoryatin gave Gallagher a sideways look. "Irina."

It was Gallagher's turn to stop, memory of what had occurred on Skye coming suddenly back to haunt him.

"Come. Come . . . let's keep walking," Skoryatin said. "You knew her as Lucinda. I am glad you were the one with her at the last."

There was a brief silence, then Gallagher said: "You . . . you sound as if you were very close."

"We were. She was one of my best agents. Imagine all the others like her who would be at risk, if that list were to get into the wrong hands. . . ."

"But. . . ."

"Please bear with me. You may not believe you've seen it. You may, in truth, not have it . . . but you may *know* where it is."

"That's impossible! I assure you, if you've come all this way to retrieve this . . . this list, then you've made a wasted journey."

"Remember the man in the boat. . . ."

"How did you know so soon. . . ."

"Come now, Mr. Renwick, that is a silly question. I am here, therefore I must have been told what occurred."

"And what else?"

Skoryatin's smile came back. "You still do not trust me?"

"I've learned a long time ago that was a sure way to terminate a career, permanently."

"A survivor. I like that. Then let us agree to work for our mutual benefit. My group believes that a curb must be put on the more . . . shall we say . . . eccentric ideas of the hawkish people in both our camps. I have no desire to see Moscow turned into a pile of irradiated ash, any more than you would like to see London or any other Western city suffer the same fate."

"I'm not particularly keen on seeing Moscow go that way either."

Skoryatin seemed amused. "And I, I love London, and Paris, and New York, and Oslo, and all the others. I'd like to see them remain in one piece." He suddenly smiled, wickedly. "Washington I can take or leave." Then he was serious once more. "We may not be able to change human nature, but we believe we can sometimes curb its excesses.

"I believe that there are times when Western foreign policy defies all reason. In your mania for the need to eradicate the Red menace, you give your support to some of the most revolting dictators upon the face of this earth. Result? An uprising; and since you do not supply arms to those who do the revolting unless, of course, they are not Reds, *we* do. The country then falls into our sphere of influence. Your support of the wrong people actually costs you. Sometimes, you get a result that is even worse. Eventually, you will lose South Africa too, and we shall have access to the ports on the Cape, and a nice position from which to strangle your shipping should the need ever arise. We'll also have the minerals. In the event of war, we would be able to isolate the Falklands from our positions on the Cape. You would find it difficult to keep your line of supply open without a prohibitive cost. I have some KGB comrades who tell a private joke. The West is doing such a good job that all the nice postings are drying up. Why send people out when the job's already being done?

"My group, however, does not want that kind of scenario. It would make the world a far more dangerous place and all those cities we love would have to start numbering their days. We do not want our country weakened, but neither do we want it dead. We will therefore fight for its life, but we will not commit world suicide. Our group exists to ensure neither your hawks nor ours brings that day upon us all. Should the names in that group fall into the hands of our enemies, not only will they be liquidated, but the hawks will gain an insurmountable advantage. It would bring a new meaning to the term Cold War. That is why I have risked coming here, to retrieve it.

"The bomber in the waters off Greenland carries a crew member who was one of us. His name is on that list. You cannot begin to understand how dangerous this is for all of us. I have enlisted your help because of what Irina said about you. You, she said, can be trusted. You would not give the list to your people so that they could one day threaten us into working for them. We are not traitors. Everything I have just said to you is a measure of the trust I believe Irina had in you. I am doing as she would.

"She never told us your name. I am certain it is not Paul Renwick. She did not describe you. I will not break that confidence either. And as none of those who attacked you are still alive, *they* won't be saying much."

When Skoryatin had finished, they walked on in silence. Gallagher took a quick look behind. Kirstin was some distance away, looking somewhat left out.

He breathed a long sigh. "I'm not sure about all this. For Lucinda, I would help. In a way, she saved my life. But I really have no idea, not the faintest, about your list. How could your people have been so crazy, anyway, to make a record of something like that?"

"In any organization, there are always errors. What seems like a good idea at one time, becomes positively dangerous at another. Can you honestly say that your own Departments have never suffered such problems?"

Gallagher knew he could not.

"Do you have any clues as to its whereabouts?" he asked. "And what am I supposed to be looking for?"

"It is on the disk of a micro-computer . . ."

"Bloody hell!"

". . . and in her report, Irina mentioned a place called the . . . Table?"

Gallagher shut his eyes in despair. "The Table, if it's the same one I'm thinking about, is in one of the wildest places in the west of Scotland. It's impossible."

Impossible was not the word. The Table was in

the Quiraing, and the Quiraing, when lashed by a full-blown Skye storm, was not the best of places to hide something scarcely bigger than a book of matches. The night Irina alias Lucinda had died in there, a particularly ferocious storm had been in progress. It was a ludicrous quest. The list was probably safer up there. No one would find it.

He told the man calling himself Borodin precisely what he thought of the chances of a successful retrieval.

"Do it," Skoryatin said, "for Lucinda."

It was an unfair pressure, and it forced Gallagher into a corner. He didn't want to go. He didn't want to relive the nightmare walk with Lucinda bleeding to death upon his back, while he had been completely oblivious of the fact. He had even been talking to her.

"Many people will die," Skoryatin said, pushing his advantage. "If that happened, it would probably make war with the West far more likely. And don't tell me about Afghanistan. We have our idiots too."

Gallagher sighed once more. "How long have I got?"

"Three days, to get there and back."

"*Three!* Don't be ridiculous. You might as well ask me to look for a grain of white sugar in a snowfield."

"I must leave Scandinavia within four days. You must be back here within three. I cannot stay longer. If I am officially missed, the danger to our group will be just as acute."

"It's probably safer out there, if it ever *was* there. No one's ever going to find it."

Skoryatin gave him a neutral look. "If you

were one of the people on the list, would you bet your life on that?"

Gallagher remained silent.

Skoryatin nodded. "As I thought. By the way, I hope that young lady has not been issued with a camera to take pictures of me. That would not be very wise."

"If she had, I would have taken it away from her. Don't worry, I've been keeping an eye open."

Skoryatin smiled. "An honorable man. You should not be in this business."

"I'm not. I left some time ago."

"But they won't leave you alone."

"No."

"No one likes losing a good operative. I'd have hated losing you myself. Who knows what tricks I would have got up to to keep you on strength?" Skoryatin glanced at his watch. "Time for my coach. We'd better get back. The young lady must be quite lonely." He appeared to go off on another tangent "Norway has a most magnificent coastline. All these marvelous fjords. Over 21,000 kilometers of coast if you include them. Very difficult to defend. My Spetsnaz could enter the fjords in submarines and create havoc. Of course, this is not tank country so we would gain, and lose. I would rather not put the theory to the test. Find that list."

Kirstin was coming toward them.

"And here's your young lady. I'll leave you now. See you in three days."

Skoryatin went up to Kirstin, gave her another embrace as if saying goodbye to a fond daughter.

They watched him join the other tourists. He

was soon chatting with them and laughing. A few of them turned to look at Gallagher and Kirstin.

"God knows what he'd told them about us," Gallagher said.

"He is very nice," she said.

He's a bloody killer too, Gallagher thought.

Kamapova's flight landed on time at Bergen airport. In accordance with her instructions, she took a taxi to the hotel that had been booked for her through a spurious travel agency. She waited for half an hour in the hotel, before going out to find a public telephone. She made her call at precisely 1800. There was no reply.

She felt annoyance, but no alarm. Operatives became slack in the West, if some stories were to be believed. She had no intention of allowing inefficiency to ruin this important mission.

She tried again at 1830. There was still no reply. Her annoyance was crystallizing into anger. Where was he?

At 1900, she got a reply. Third time was the cut-off point. Had there again been no answer she would either have had to abort, or go it alone. New arrangements would have had to be made. She would have had to contact Moscow, a prospect she dreaded. It would have meant the end of her ambitions.

"Where have you been?" she snarled into the phone, the beautiful face distorting. "I have been calling you since six." She spoke in English.

"There is no need for that attitude." The voice on the other end was quite calm. "Meet me as arranged, in fifteen minutes." The line went dead.

Furious, she restrained herself from banging

the receiver down. It would not do to show such emotion. She was a professional. But her contempt for what she saw as sloppiness was such that she decided to ensure her contact knew it.

Gone was the virtuously demure GRU captain. In her place was a determined and hard individual. The game playing was over.

Fifteen minutes later, she was standing in the Market, near the beginning of the pier.

A man came up to her and said: "You are Mrs. Lander?"

"Yes."

"Where have you been recently?"

"Thailand, Hong Kong, Japan . . . and Moscow." The deliberate pause was the important signal.

"Welcome to Bergen, Comrade." The man spoke softly, with a touch of wry humor. "I am Scipio."

It was the codename her instructions had given.

"You were late."

"Remember where you are," he said firmly. "Such attitudes will be of little use to you here."

"I shall. . . ."

"Report me? Don't be a fool. Come. I'll show you the boat." Without waiting for her to comment, Scipio went onto the pier and began walking along it. She had no option but to follow.

"That's not the one I was told to expect," she said when she saw the white motor cruiser. She followed him on board.

"Engine trouble," Scipio explained. "This morning. It's a very temperamental boat. This is more reliable and will get you to Aurland in plenty of time. We'll set off tomorrow, taking our time about it, and stopping en route. On the second day, we'll arrive in Aurland. You'll spend the rest of the day studying your subject. On the morning of the third day, you go into action. I shall be waiting on the boat to take you back when it is all over. Understood?"

She nodded.

"Fine," he said. "The weapon is already on board. Return to your hotel. Meet me here in the morning at eight o'clock. Bring whatever you think will give the impression you're going on a boat trip. Do not book out of your hotel. You will of course bring a bag for the weapon."

Again, she nodded.

"Good. I'll see you in the morning."

He watched appreciatively as she climbed off the boat, her skirt hitching up momentarily to give a brief but generous view of leg. He continued to watch the graceful rythm of her body as she walked, a tiny smile on his lips.

She never once looked back at him.

Gallagher returned to Bergen that night and caught the 0740 flight to London the next morning. The 1015 Super Shuttle got him to Glasgow by 1125. He hired a car at the airport, choosing a stone gray metallic Porsche 944 Lux. It was Fowler's money and he decided if he had to go through with this, he might as well get as much enjoyment out of it as possible.

The weather was good for the 180-mile run up to the Kyle of Lochalsh and it took him three highly enjoyable hours to make it. He missed the powerhouse of the *quattro*, but the Porsche sang along the swooping coastal road and he temporarily forgot the true reason for his being there. September was a good month to be in Scotland; if it didn't rain.

It was raining in Kyle of Lochalsh.

Gallagher turned the Porsche left and down onto the concrete apron to await the next ferry. He had missed one and could see it making its way through the curtain of misty rain, looking for all the world like a midget aircraft carrier.

Ever since leaving Bergen, he had checked constantly for shadowers, but none had so far been detected. He looked now through the mirror, to see if anyone had pulled up behind him. A couple of cars had come onto the apron, one on each side of him. He made a mental note of them, in case they appeared again on his particular route.

The next ferry arrived and it was time to drive down to the precarious-looking ramp and onto the open deck of the little ship. Skye remained stubbornly hidden by the rain as the ferry ploughed its way across to Kyleakin. The two cars had kept station with the Porsche. One was now parked behind, the other alongside. Two men were in the one at the back, a grey Jaguar saloon. The one alongside was occupied by a youngish couple. It was a Vauxhall Cavalier.

Perhaps it meant nothing. Perhaps they were islanders, or people who simply liked Skye in September. He would look out for them.

A broad shaft of sunlight beamed down upon Kyleakin when Gallagher drove off the ferry and by the time he'd made it to Portree, the sun had chased the rain away. He headed northward into the Trotternish peninsula, remembering now the last time he had come. The somber mood stayed with him as he drove fast along the A855 toward Staffin.

He intended to spend the night in Uig and could have gone left on the A850, to join the A856 which would eventually take him to the small bay on the western coast; but he wanted to see if he had picked up a tail. He was cruising along the shore of Loch Leathan and looked up just in time a see a shaft of light descend out of low-lying clouds, to illuminate the weathered column of the Old Man of Storr in the distance. It was then that his glance caught movement in his mirror.

It was the Cavalier, traveling at speed. Gallagher gunned the Porsche, and it streaked away. The Cavalier had disappeared. The road was so narrow there were times when it seemed its edges were beneath the car.

When he got to Staffin, there was still no sign of the Cavalier. Perhaps it was a false alarm. He went on to Brogaig and paused at the junction that led to the Quiraing. Two of the road signs pointed back the way he had come; Kilmaluag, Flodigarry, Kilmuir, and Uig via coast. The sign he was interested in pointed the other way, had a blue border and said: Uig via Quirang. He drove along the familiar road, the strange mysterious landscape seeming to welcome him. Three minutes later, he was swinging the car into the steeply climbing bend to the spine of the razor-backed Quiraing range.

He brought the 944 to a halt in the small parking area of dark gravel adjacent to the road and climbed out. He stared reluctantly at the basaltic escarpments that hid Borodin's secret.

I'm bloody crazy to be here, he thought grimly. *I'll never find it.*

But he had made the journey, so he would have to try.

He heard a fluttering sound and turned to look. A Peregrine falcon had alighted no more than three yards from where he stood. The bird tucked its wings close and regarded him, cocking its head from side to side. It was totally unafraid and remained where it was for a full minute; then with a final look at Gallagher, it leapt into the air and disappeared into the Quiraing, in the direction of the Table. Involuntarily, he shivered. The place was getting to him already.

Gallagher did not believe in omens. Even so....

Another sound intruded; the sound of a car being driven fast. He ran to the crest of the bend to look. Coming from the direction of Brogaig was the tiny red speck of the Cavalier.

He ran back to the Porsche, got in and drove off toward Uig. The five mile journey took little time, and the Cavalier never came into distant sight in his mirrors. He was just going into the tight bend that swept down toward the bay when he was forced to alter his line to make room for another car going the other way: the gray Jaguar. The men in it stared at him in surprise as he flashed past.

They'd planned a sandwich. Bastards.

Gallagher found himself a little hotel, then decided to return to the Quiraing, to spend the rest of the daylight hours searching for the tiny disk. He would make the trip on foot. The weather, despite its notoriety, seemed set to remain stable for the next few hours. He decided to chance it. If the people in the cars wanted to follow him, they could sit and watch the Porsche. He had parked it in full view. The thing was to get away before they returned.

He walked along the River Rha, then climbed up toward the road, intending to use it while keeping a close ear for the sound of engines. Ten minutes after he'd joined the road, he heard them. He ducked into the deep cleft of a nearby mountain stream, trying to keep his feet dry as he waited. Two cars passed, going rapidly. He inched cautiously upward to have a look, keeping his head just above the level of the road surface. The Jaguar and the Cavalier were hurtling toward Uig.

"I hope you enjoy yourselves," he muttered and got quickly back onto the road when they had disappeared. He crossed over, and began the climb into the Quiraing.

London, 1500 hours.

Fowler was in Winterbourne's office. He stood silently while Winterbourne studied the folder he had brought. The cherubic face was gradually clouding over until it had become a dark red.

Winterbourne closed the folder with precise movements when he had finished reading. His angry eyes looked up at Fowler.

"How much of this am I to believe, Fowler?"

"All of it, Sir John. I'd hardly bring you reports that were untrue."

Winterbourne looked as if he didn't believe that for a second. "While Gallagher has been causing mayhem for the Norwegians. . . ."

"Not *for* them, Sir John."

"On their soil then!" Winterbourne almost

yelled. "Am I therefore to believe that you're prepared to let this . . . this Borodin, as he calls himself, go free?"

"There was never any intention to snatch him."

"Why not, man? Good God! A high-ranking Soviet in Intelligence would be an enormous coup for this Department."

"Better for us if he's over there. If we snatch him, we'll just get some out-of-date stuff. Waste of time. I'm after something else entirely; something that's important enough to bring him West."

"And which you still insist in keeping from me."

"I want to be sure, Sir John."

Winterbourne glared. "Of exactly what?"

Fowler remained silent.

Winterbourne said: "One of these days. . . ."

"May I take the folder if you're finished?"

Winterbourne's mouth snapped shut tightly. He picked up the folder and brusquely handed it over.

"Thank you, Sir John. I'll keep you informed."

"Do that, Fowler," Winterbourne snapped. "You do that."

Fowler went out, feeling the baleful stare upon his back. He returned to his small office to find George Haslam waiting.

Haslam said: "You look happy. Has Winterbourne been made a peer of the Realm?"

"Oh that they would!" Fowler said with feeling. "At least it would get him out of my hair."

"That bad, is it?"

"As bad as it can be."

"How much does he know?"

"Enough to do some damage. Now he wants a coup for the Department. Wants to boast about it in his club, probably." Fowler sighed. "I work for this country above and beyond party lines. No single party is the nation. My duty, therefore, is to the nation as a whole. I try to act in what I feel are its best interests, not what's going to give some idiot a decoration or a place in the Honors List. . . ."

"You're forgetting," Haslam interrupted quietly. "You don't have to convince me."

Fowler smiled fleetingly. "Of course I don't."

"Well?" Haslam said, glancing at the folder. "What do you think?"

"It's all up to Gallagher, George."

Gallagher returned to his hotel at sunset. Skye was putting on a show and a glorious fire stained the western horizon. He bought a drink and went onto the porch, to salute the dying sun. He sat down at a vacant table, from where he had a good view of the car park. Both the Cavalier and the Jaguar were there. No one was in them.

The cars had been parked well away from the Porsche, and Gallagher looked slowly about him, trying to spot their owners. None was in sight. It didn't matter.

His trip to the Quiraing had been fruitless. He had gone over the ground where Dalgliesh had been all those months ago. It was an insanely hopeless task. Anything could have happened to the disk. It had probably never been brought there by Dalgleish, no matter what Lucinda had believed.

He knew there were several recorded instances of people finding long lost articles in the most bizarre of circumstances; but he honestly thought this one was a washout. Nevertheless, for Lucinda's sake, he would give it one more try in the morning. Then it would be back to Norway to give Borodin the bad news.

He remained on the porch until the light from the sky was completely gone. As he stood up to go in for dinner, four people with drinks in their hands came out. They looked at him neutrally.

"Nice evening," he said.

They were the people from the cars.

He set off very early the next day. It was a greyish dawn as he eased himself out of the window of the ground floor hotel room. He had settled his bill the night before, saying he would be leaving after breakfast. He had made coffee in his room. That would have to do till later. He ran at the crouch to the car park and let down all eight tires of the two cars; then he got into the Porsche and drove to the Quiraing. He hoped it would take them all day to sort themselves out.

His second search proved equally fruitless. Borodin expected far too much. Three days was simply unrealistic. Such a job need three weeks, perhaps three *months* of meticulous scouring of the immediate area. Even then, success would not be certain.

He decided he was wasting his time and hurried back to the Porsche. The Jaguar and the Cavalier were not there to welcome him.

He headed back for Kyleakin, via Staffin, and caught the ferry across. No one followed him. Whoever those people were, he felt certain he had lost them now. No overt move had been made toward him, which could only mean they had been waiting for him to find the list. They would probably have assumed he would not have stayed at the hotel, had he been successful the night before. Now he'd left, they would no doubt think he had found it.

Shit, Gallagher thought as the Porsche streaked toward Glasgow. *That's all I need.*

At the airport he handed the car back to the rental company, caught the 1815 Super Shuttle to London and was able to make the 1945 flight to Bergen. By 0030 Bergen time, he was settling down for the night in his hotel bedroom.

He had seen no one throughout the journey whom he'd regarded as a possible tail; but it didn't mean they were not following. He had placed two chairs, one on top the other, against the door. They were balanced in such a way that even a surreptitious push would send one crashing. More than enough of an alarm.

Having failed to find the list it would be interesting to see how everyone took that piece of news.

0600 hours the next day, Aurland.

Kamapova left the boat and walked up to the house where Kirstin Størvaag awaited Gallagher's return. She knocked softly on the door. There was no reply. She tried again, this time a little harder. After another pause, she thought she could hear movement. She put her right hand into the bag she carried.

Kirstin heard the knock and climbed out of bed, drowsy with sleep. She was naked and, thinking it was Gallagher returning somewhat early, put on a light dressing gown and went downstairs. She was pleased he was back, and there was a smile upon her face.

She opened the door. The smile died.

"Get back in!" the unknown, beautiful woman ordered. "And don't make a single sound."

Her staring eyes looked down at the silenced pistol pointing at her.

Kamapova entered the house and shut the door quietly. The whole thing had been smoothly and quickly done.

She jerked her head toward a chair. "Over there!"

Kirstin sat down, staring at the gun. She held the dressing gown tightly about her, as if for protection.

Kamapova said: "I haven't the time to waste. I shall ask you questions, and you will answer them quickly. Is that understood?"

Kirstin stared at the gun, and said nothing. She seemed bewildered.

"It is no use trying to be brave," Kamopova said coldly. "I do not intend to spend much time on you. One way or the other, I shall have my answers. Do not force me to shoot you. I shall do so if I think it necessary." She paused. "Well?"

Again, Kirstin said nothing, though she was clearly frightened.

Kamapova stared at her closely, peered at something that could be seen beneath the shoulder of the dressing gown.

"Open the gown," she commanded.

Kirstin looked at her with revulsion.

"Don't be stupid, child," Kamapova said,

seemingly affronted. "I leave that kind of thing to others. Open the gown. That shoulder."

Kirstin bared the injured shoulder.

"Aha," Kamapova said softly, moving closer. Without warning, she grabbed an edge of the plaster and ripped the dressing off.

Kirstin gave a high involuntary scream which she cut off by putting her hand over her mouth. Tears of pain sprang to her eyes.

Kamapova gazed interestedly at the long scab. It had been healing nicely, but now its edges were raised and blood was seeping from beneath. She removed the silencer from the pistol and, using the sight, began to probe at the scab.

Kirstin flinched and tried to push herself far back into the chair.

"I will ask a question," Kamapova began caressingly. "You will answer. If you do not, I shall remove this scab so . . . !" She suddenly dug the sight into the wound and lifted. The seeping blood turned into a rivulet.

Kirstin screamed.

"I would not do that again," Kamapova warned. "I shall shoot you if you do. You will be dead, and I shall be out of here before anyone comes. Now. Shall we try?"

The tears were flowing freely down Kirstin's face, but she still refused to talk. In the end, she did; but that was only after Kamapova had removed the whole scab and had begun to rub the sight of the gun up and down along it. The shoulder was raw and bleeding profusely.

"That was very good," Kamapova said. "Now go and clean yourself up. You're leaving."

When Kirstin, eyes red from pain, had washed

the abused shoulder and had managed to put another dressing on it, she got dressed. Throughout, Kamapova watched her, but did not help.

They left the house and walked down to where the cabin cruiser was moored.

Kamapova said: "Don't think of doing anything stupid. I shall shoot before you've moved a few meters. Do you understand?"

Mouth grim, Kirstin nodded.

They got to the boat without incident.

"Company for you, Scipio," Kamapova said, as they climbed aboard.

Scipio stared appreciatively at Kirstin. "The kind of company I like."

"I thought you would."

He looked keenly at Kirstin's eyes. "What have you been doing to her?"

"Just getting acquainted."

Scipio gave a wry smile. "I see."

"Wait here until I return," Kamapova said haughtily, adding with palpable contempt: "Amuse yourself with her if you wish."

Scipio said, daringly: "I think you'd be more fun."

Kamapova's eyes blazed. "A mistake like that would be fatal for you." She got off the boat and walked back to the house.

Gallagher caught the 1150 flight to Sogndal, and the 1405 ferry from Kaupanger to Revsnes. Kirstin was supposed to meet him there with the Saab for the journey to the ice lake, where the meeting with Borodin was set for three o'clock. Again, no one appeared to have followed him.

He saw the car as soon as he got off the ferry,

but there was no sign of Kirstin. Perhaps she had gone to answer a call of nature. He stood by the car and waited, hoping she wouldn't be long.

A voice behind him said: "Mr. Renwick?"

He turned to see a ravishingly beautiful woman with a dancer's body and golden hair that seemed to flow past her shoulders.

Surprised to hear the fake name being used, he stared at her, senses on the alert, body still and calm. "Where's Kirstin?"

"We had to send her for medical treatment."

"What's wrong with her?" The senses had gone into high gear.

"The shoulder."

"It was alright when I left."

"I'm afraid it became septic. She thought it was getting better, but I suspect she didn't want to let you down, so she said nothing. I'm Ingrid Lundt. I'm here to take you to the meeting. I've been fully briefed." She smiled and offered her hand.

Gallagher shook it. "How do I know you come from Kirstin?"

"I'd be very surprised if you were not suspicious," she said easily. "But I have got the car, I know all about today's meeting and. . . ." She paused, eyes teasing. ". . . I know all about you from Kirstin. She told me about the boat you sank, and how you did it. I think she is very fond of you. I would not know all this, would I, if she hadn't told me herself? Her report was factual, but only a person to person would disclose the emotions involved. Well?"

"I'm flattered," Gallagher said. He got into the Saab.

"I envy her," Kamapova said boldly as she took her place behind the wheel. "She spoke about you so much, I felt I had to see for myself."

"Why Miss Lundt," Gallagher said. "You'll make me blush."

They laughed as the Saab began to pull away.

"I take it you know where to go."

"Do not worry, Mr. Renwick. I know exactly what to do."

"Call me Paul, and I'll call you Ingrid, if that's alright."

"That is fine . . . Paul." She gave him another quick smile. "How do you think she has done?" Kamapova went on. "Was she competent?"

"She's a very brave young lady. She was frightened most of the time, but she handled that boat brilliantly."

"In time, we'll make a good operative out of her."

"You'll have to teach her how to shoot. She couldn't hit a house at two meters."

They laughed again.

"Speaking of guns," Gallagher went on, casually opening the glove compartment. The P226 was not there. "The SIG Sauer's missing. I had asked Kirstin to put it in, for the meeting . . . just in case."

She frowned. "I do not understand. She said nothing to me about it. I would have done it if she had said."

He thought he detected something rather more than regret in her voice. It was the annoyance of someone who felt she had been outsmarted. He glanced at her, saw a momentary snarl upon the beautiful mouth. It lasted fleetingly, as if it had never actually existed.

"I suppose you haven't got one either?"

"I'm sorry . . . Paul. No. I didn't think we would need one. If Kirstin had remembered to tell me. . . ."

"Oh never mind," he said unworriedly. "I don't like the things anyway."

His body was now finely tuned, fully on the alert. Kirstin would not have forgotten. He had drummed it into her. The P226 had been deliberately taken out of the car.

"I am so sorry," she repeated, sounding genuinely regretful.

"Don't worry about it. It was not your fault."

The Saab hurried toward the ice lake.

19

Kirstin had been sitting in the cabin of the motor cruiser, warily keeping an eye on Scipio. Despite original fears, he had made no move to molest her. Only the gun he kept unwaveringly trained upon her betrayed the potential danger to her life.

Scipio was a slim man of medium height with dark hair, dark eyes, and a twisting smile that pushed his lips slightly forward. He had sat at the far end of the cabin, near the exit, and had scarcely moved throughout the time she had been on board. She could hear life going on all around her as ferries came and went, as cars drove past, as people laughed and talked. They were all so close, yet if she tried to attract their attention she'd be killed, and no one would know about it until much too late. Scipio's gun was silenced.

Then she was staring at him disbelievingly. *He was putting the gun away and looking at his watch.*

"If you want to help your friend," he was saying to her astonishment, "we should be going."

She stared at him, dumbfounded.

He smiled. "Come on, young lady. There isn't much time."

"But . . ." It was all she could say. She tried again. "I don't understand."

"What matters is that I do. Shall we help him? Or do you want to sit here all day?"

Relief flooded through her, then she paused, suspicion returning.

"If I wanted to kill you," he began reasonably, "don't you think I would have done it by now? No one would have heard my gun." As if to encourage her he turned and went up on deck.

After a moment's hesitation, she followed. She breathed deeply. She never thought Aurland could look so beautiful.

"How is your shoulder?" he asked.

"It hurts, but I am alright."

"She enjoys giving pain," Scipio said emotionlessly. "I recognised that in her."

"You have worked with her before?"

"No. We need a car. She will have taken yours."

"If we go back to the house, I can call for the helicopter."

"Where is it?"

"I don't know, but. . . ."

"It will take too long. The fastest way is to get a car. Is there a hire company here?"

"A small garage. . . ."

"Let's find it."

They were able to get a Volvo, and she drove back to the house to pick up the Socimi and a good supply of ammunition.

He looked at the gun and said: "You intend to kill her?"

Kirstin said nothing as she took the maroon car up the mountain road.

The Saab slowed down as it approached the lake. Another car was parked up ahead over by the partially frozen water, and moving away up the slope was the gray-clad figure of the man Gallagher knew as Borodin.

Kamapova stopped behind the car. Gallagher zipped up his jacket against the expected drop in temperature.

He got out and said to her: "Wait here, Ingrid."

"Isn't there anything you want me to do?"

"Just wait. You're doing fine."

He crossed the road and began walking toward the waiting figure. The hard snow crunched beneath his feet, but the air was not as cold as he'd expected. Skoryatin was wearing a grey belted anorak over his safari suit. The lined hood was thrown back.

He turned as Gallagher approached. "You have brought a different girl."

"Kirstin's apparently had to go into hospital. Her shoulder's gone septic." Gallagher didn't trust Ingrid Lundt as far as he could throw her; but it was wait and see time.

"I am very sorry to hear that. Did you find my list?"

"No," Gallagher said.

In the Saab, Kamapova opened the glove compartment and stared at it before pushing it shut again. How could she have known about the gun?

"Bitch!" she snarled in Russian, thinking of Kirstin Størvaag. After this was over, she'd go back to the boat and finish the stupid little wretch herself. "How dare she think she can get the better of me!"

She took out her own weapon with its silencer and checked it. She glanced up the snowclad incline, at the two figures. Soon, it would be time and the new rank, with its attendant privileges, would be hers. She would be respected for the great service she was about to perform.

Skoryatin was smiling at Gallagher, who looked at him warily.

"You don't seem particularly worried," Gallagher began suspiciously, "considering the panic you were in when I last saw you. For a man supposedly in mortal fear of his life, why do you remind me of a cat that's got the cream?"

"They say a person who is near death becomes quite calm."

"Don't play games with me, Borodin, or whatever your name is. After what I've been through for your bloody list, I'm not in the mood."

Skoryatin looked at Gallagher for long moments, then turned to stare down the incline. They were directly above the lake.

"I'm afraid," Skoryatin began without looking round, "I owe you an apology."

"I know I'm not going to like this," Gallagher said tightly.

"There is no list." Skoryatin spoke quietly, still staring down the incline.

The silence that fell seemed to envelope the entire mountain range.

"You're joking," Gallagher said at last, in a voice that was almost a whisper. "You're fucking joking!" He thought of all that had happened since France; of how Rhiannon's life had been endangered; of Freddy Talheim getting shot; of the maniac lorry drivers, and the other maniac in the dark boat; of the car in the gorge, and felt the anger boil within him. In that moment, he hated Fowler and Borodin with equal passion.

"You bastards!" he shouted. "You conniving bastards! What the hell did I go through all that for? Why did you two decide to meddle in my life? What's so sodding important that you're prepared to risk the life of a woman who's very important to me; the life of a very good friend, *and* my own ... for what? For bloody what? So you can play silly fucking games?"

Skoryatin still did not look round. The mountains seemed to take Gallagher's words and toss them away.

"Do you have a gun on you?" Skoryatin asked.

"No, I don't bloody have a gun!"

"And if you did, you would probably want to shoot me." Before Gallagher could say anything, he went on: "In any event, there is already someone here who intends to do just that."

Despite himself, Gallagher said: *"What?* What are you talking about?"

"Your new driver...."

"Don't be ridiculous!"

"... is Captain Natalia Kamapova of, I regret to say, the GRU ... but working for the KGB.

"She's what?" Gallagher heard himself say in a stunned voice.

"Exactly the person I have just said she is."

"My God . . . Kirstin!" Gallagher said softly, his anger for the moment forgotten. He did not turn to look at the Saab. "I caught . . . your Captain out on something, on the way here; but I never imagined . . . I thought it was either you, or the devious sod back in London who had planned a nasty little surprise for me."

"You could not have imagined this one," Skoryatin said. "We can but hope the young lady is not already dead."

Gallagher felt sick. "A true innocent abroad," he said quietly, "but full of guts. They should never have put her on this. Jesus. You people. . . ."

"Please restrain your anger for a moment. Hear me out. There may not be much time. This has been a flushing-out operation. I am truly sorry that people close to you got caught in the crossfire. It was certainly not planned that way . . ."

"Is it ever?" Gallagher interrupted bitterly.

"Please. Grant me some time. Let us walk."

They walked slowly, above the lake.

"This operation began some months ago," Skoryatin continued. "Our dissident group does exist, as you know. It is not yet another smokescreen, devised by the machiavellian KGB and the GRU, to confuse the West; though I am certain such thoughts have exercised the minds of the people in your Department. . . ."

"It's not my bloody Department."

Skoryatin gave a brief smile. "My apologies. The reasons I have given you for the existence of the group are genuine. There are, as you can imagine, many who are inimical to our continuing survival. One of the most dangerous is my opposite number in the KGB. For some time now, he has been trying to identify the group members so as to eliminate them. He suspects me of being involved but is not certain. An accusation without basis would cost him dearly. He therefore tries to entrap me."

Skoryatin smiled again, as if at a private joke, before continuing: "We have had our little contest before. He lost quite spectacularly the last time and was demoted to an isolated outpost. But he has been rehabilitated and is now more determined than ever to not only even the score but to eliminate me totally. His first move was to infiltrate Kamapova. I spotted her, of course, but played along while I planned a counter-attack. For that, I needed help." Skoryatin paused. "From the West."

Gallagher retained a stony silence.

The ghost of a smile flitted across the features of the GRU man. "I remembered someone Irina had mentioned in her report; a man in the business, but one of sensitivity. If Irina thought so highly of you, then I felt I could take a chance. I let it be known that there was in existence a list of the dissidents that had been taken out to the West. I ensured this information found the right ears on our side of the Curtain; but I needed the West too, to give the tale credence. I let your ... er ... the Department who had sent Dalgleish out, know about it. I also requested a meeting, saying I would only speak to the man who had worked with Irina. I also let my adversaries catch a rumour that *I* was going to the West.

"I knew that would set the hounds running ... on both sides. The West would want the list as much as my own comrades. My adversaries would also want to kill me, since they would suspect me of defecting. The West, for its part, would also try to snatch me, if they thought they could get away with it. A bonus, you see. I devised a plan that would get me here, while the official records showed me to be on an inspection tour in the Far East...."

"My God," Gallagher said. "You played everybody along. You lured those killers, setting me as bait...."

"You acquitted yourself handsomely, as both myself and your ... sorry ... *the* Department expected you would."

"Do you know something?" Gallagher said with a faint touch of disgust. "I know another crocodile just like you."

"I do not see the connection."

"Don't bother."

"Obviously a secret joke," Skoryatin remarked, then carried on: "Any moment now, Kamapova will be coming up this slope. She is not sure whether we are armed and will want to come close to make certain of her kill. She probably already knows I've recognized her. She'll kill you too, of course. For all she knows, I may have been giving you information, which you have been recording. Are you going to allow yourself to be killed?"

"You brought me here. Besides, an old hand like you is bound to be armed."

Skoryatin gave another of his smiles. "How well you see through me."

"Not bloody well enough."

"The result of Kamapova's failure will have a devastating effect upon the career of my KGB opponent. It will also mean the bomber that went in off Greenland can remain there. He would have continued to press for its retrieval."

"I'm glad you think she's going to fail."

"Why don't we wait and see?"

"What a nice thing to say to a bloody target."

Then Skoryatin was saying in a hard voice: "She is leaving the car. Don't look round as yet. Let us stop here and look up the mountain. She is carrying her bag, so the weapon must be inside. Continue to pretend you do not know who she is."

They had again stopped directly above the widest part of the icy lake, and were perhaps 20 meters from its edge. Gallagher heard the crunching of Kamapova's footsteps, and felt his stomach tighten.

He waited for a few more long seconds, before turning. "Ingrid," he said in surprise. "I asked you to wait in the car. We're not yet finished." He moved down toward her, noting that his companion was also moving.

Kamapova, clearly believing Gallagher still thought her to be Ingrid Lundt, continued to climb, apparently making heavy weather of it.

Gallagher kept moving downward. "Ingrid," he said again. "We're not. . . ."

But she had stopped now, and her hand was digging into the bag.

Gallagher, now some way from Skoryatin, felt he was close enough to Kamapova and launched himself at her. He struck her just as the silenced pistol came out of the bag. He fell on top, slamming her onto the packed snow. The breath gasped out of her. The pistol coughed, and he felt something whizz past his left ear.

Then she was fighting him savagely, cursing him in Russian. They rolled down the slope, cracking the snow as they went. She held grimly on to the pistol. The water drew nearer.

Oh great, Gallagher thought. *All I need is an icy bath.*

He began to dig his heels in whenever he could. She was amazingly strong and fought him all the way, her dancer's body whipping at him. At last, they were stopped by a buried boulder; she was hanging feet-first toward the lake, while he continued to hold on to her gun hand. She was still trying to fire it.

Then a booted foot was placed on the arm. Skoryatin reached down to wrench the gun away. A massive Beretta 92F automatic was held in his other hand.

"You can let her go now," he said to Gallagher.

Gallagher released her and stood up. His breathing came quickly. "I must be out of bloody condition," he said.

Below him, Kamapova was getting unsteadily to her feet. Her chest was heaving. She stopped, looked up at them from two meters above the iced lake. Then her eyes fastened upon Skoryatin.

"Comrade..." she began.

The sudden bellow of the Beretta startled him, seeming to echo forever in the still mountain air. She took the 9mm bullet squarely in the chest, her eyes opening wide as she was flung off her perch and into the lake. The thin layer of ice upon the surface shattered into countless pieces that twinkled in the sunlight as she crashed through it. The cold water moved sluggishly as the body sank. There was no blood.

Gallagher stared, transfixed, expecting to see her come thrashing to the surface. But the water was already smoothing itself over her.

He turned to look at Skoryatin.

"You are shocked," Skoryatin said. "Do not be. She would have thrown you in there without regret." He threw her pistol in after her and put his own away. "But she has failed."

The sound of an engine at high revs made them look toward the road. It took a few minutes before the maroon Volvo came careering along the narrow strip. It screeched to a halt, nearly slamming into the car Skoryatin had driven. The doors were flung open, and Gallagher saw to his delight it was Kirstin who came out first, brandishing the Socimi.

"She can't hit a barn door with that thing," he said, grinning. "I don't know who's with her though."

"I am happy she is alive. The man with her is a member of our group."

Gallagher gave him a searching glance. "How many of your people were in place on this?"

"That would be telling too much." Skoryatin smiled.

Gallagher nodded slowly, knowingly. "Alright."

Kirstin had reached them. She stopped uncertainly, stared at Gallagher, then looked about her, clearly searching for someone.

"She's dead," he said.

She looked for the body.

He pointed to the lake. "In there."

"Who . . . ?" she began.

"I did," Skoryatin answered her. "It was fitting." To Gallagher, he said: "Now my KGB opponent will have to try and explain how my personal assistant, who everyone knows accompanied me on my rounds of inspection, came to be lying in a Norwegian mountain lake with a Western bullet in her. I believe he will have a very difficult time of it. Siberia will not be very warm this winter. He'd better get used to it."

Kirstin was silent for some moments. "I wanted to kill her," she said at last.

Gallagher looked at her in astonishment. *"You?* Why?"

She told them what had happened at the house. Gallagher listened grimly.

When she had finished, Skoryatin said to Gallagher: "Now, do you still regret what I have done?"

Gallagher stared at the lake, and shook his head slowly. He put an arm about Kirstin's waist. "Come on," he said. "Let's take you back."

Skoryatin followed them down the slope. They paused by the Volvo.

Scipio said: "We came to help you, but I see you didn't need it."

"He was too fast for her," Skoryatin said.

Scipio went round to the driver's side and got in. Skoryatin paused, gave Gallagher a quick embrace.

"I am glad to have worked with you," he said.

"Wait a hundred years or so, before the next time."

Skoryatin gave a tight little smile, nodding to himself as if coming to a conclusion about something. "I am truly glad," he said quietly, "you were the last for Irina. I meant every word in Laerdal."

He climbed into the Volvo, and Scipio turned it gingerly round. Gallagher and Kirstin watched as it made its way back to Aurland, bouncing a little on the uneven road.

"Let's give them some time to get away," he said. "He's got a long way to go." He was sure Borodin had a lot more up his sleeve; but that was Fowler's problem.

After a while, they got into the Saab and drove slowly back to Aurland, leaving Kamapova to her icy grave, with the car Skoryatin had driven standing vigil on the lonely road. When they got back, Kirstin saw that the motor cruiser had gone; but the helicopter had returned. Company was waiting at the house.

Gallagher recognized the two men from the Jaguar. They did not look at all happy.

"So where is he?" one asked bluntly. American.

"Where is who?" He must have left right under their noses.

"And what about the list?" This one was English.

"What list?"

"Don't push your luck," the American snapped in warning.

"And don't push yours," Gallagher told him harshly. "Talk to Fowler. He's got all the answers."

"Who the hell's Fowler?"

"Well, well, well," Gallagher said drily. "Winterbourne's been doing a little moonlighting."

They looked suddenly guilty. Seconds later, frustrated, they left.

"Who's Irina?" Kirstin asked.

EPILOGUE

When Gallagher eventually returned to London, he called Rhiannon from the airport. He had no intention of calling Fowler. He'd done enough.

Rhiannon was not at her flat.

He called again when he got home. There was still no reply. He played the tape to see if she'd left a message. She hadn't. He tried again later that evening, without success. There were phone calls, but none were from her. He had a terrible night.

In the morning, he called the gallery where she worked. A supercilious male voice answered.

"Rhiannon Jameson, please," Gallagher said.

"*Miss* Jameson is not here. May I ask who is calling?"

Gallagher knew he was going to have a hard time. "My name is Gallagher...."

"Yes, Mr. Gallagher. I'm afraid Miss Jameson is out of the country for the moment...."

"*Out* of the country? Where?"

"The United States," the voice said haughtily, as if doing a great favor. "She is there on business for the gallery."

Gallagher had a sinking feeling. "Can you give me a number. . . ."

"I am afraid it is not our policy. . . ."

"An address," Gallagher interrupted, trying not to sound desperate. "A date when she's due back. . . ."

"I'm afraid I cannot do that," the maddening voice said smoothly. "She left instructions not to."

Gallagher was stunned. He gripped the phone tightly, not wanting to believe it. The bastard was lying.

"You're enjoying yourself, aren't you?" he snarled into the receiver.

"I beg your pardon?"

"The Germans have a word for it."

"Oh yes?"

"*Schadenfreude*, you creeping bastard!" Gallagher slammed the phone down.

He couldn't remember how long he'd sat there, unmoving and hurting, simply looking at it. He ignored all the calls that subsequently came in, hearing, but not really listening to the messages people left. He couldn't believe she had gone.

At last, he went downstairs to the carport where the *quattro* waited, gleaming and silent. He stroked its roof.

"Looks like it's just the two of us again, Lauren," he said.

In the small office above the sleepy square, Fowler replaced the receiver on one of his telephones. Haslam was with him.

"He's clearly not answering his phone today," Fowler said.

"Can you blame him?"